UEEN ANNE. (*From an Old Engraving.*)

Presented to

Texarkana Public Library

~

By

Texas Loan Star Grant

2002

The SPIDER'S TOUCH

Also by Patricia Wynn

The Blue Satan Mystery Series:
The Birth of Blue Satan

The Parson's Pleasure

Sophie's Halloo

Lord Tom

Jack on the Box

Mistletoe and Mischief

The Bumblebroth

A Country Affair

The Christmas Spirit

A Pair of Rogues

Capturing Annie

The SPIDER'S TOUCH

by

PATRICIA WYNN

The Spider's Touch
2nd in the Blue Satan Mystery Series
Featuring Blue Satan and Mrs. Kean

First Edition
Cover design: kat&dog studios
Art: Anonymous, Interior View, La Fenice, Venice, Italy
By permission of Alinari/SEAT/Art Resource, NY

Publisher's Cataloging-in-Publication
(Provided by Quality Books, Inc.)

Wynn, Patricia
The spider's touch / by Patricia Wynn. -- 1st ed.
p. cm. -- (Blue Satan mystery series ; 2)
ISBN 0-9702727-4-X

1. Great Britain--History--George I, 1714-1727--Fiction. 2. Brigands and robbers--Fiction. 3. Historical fiction. 4. Adventure fiction. I. Title.

PS3573.Y6217S65 2002 813'.54
QBI33-603

This book is dedicated

to

Mabel Joubert Smith

Acknowledgements

A great many thanks to Laura Wallace of Sour Lake, Texas, without whom, among other things, I would never have discovered where the Duke of Ormonde lived in June, 1715. Thanks, too, to the other members of the 18th-19th Century List on Yahoo.groups, an amazing gathering of history enthusiasts in the best of 18th Century tradition.

These books could never have been written without the resources of the University of Texas Libraries in Austin, including the Harry Ransom Center with its priceless treasures.

I am also indebted to a number of sites on the World Wide Web for leads on antique road maps of Kent, Sussex, Middlesex, and Surrey, histories of St. James's Palace and Richmond, and the out-of-print books that have been so essential to this work.

And special thanks to Dean James, Rosemary Stevens, Barbara Peters, Leila Taylor, and Kathy Harig for their encouragement and support for this series.

The verses I have used in this novel are from Alexanader Pope's *Essay on Man,* which was dedicated to Pope's friend Henry St. John, Viscount Bolingbroke.

HISTORICAL BACKGROUND

From 1701 to 1713, a Grand Alliance of nations fought the War of the Spanish Succession against King Louis XIV of France. At issue for two members of the alliance, England and Holland, was the balance of power between Protestant and Catholic countries in Europe, which Louis had disturbed by placing his grandson Philip on the Spanish throne.

Known as the Sun King, Louis XIV was the longest-reigning and most powerful king in the history of Europe. His kingdom had ruled supreme through decades of war with its neighbors. Louis marshaled 450,000 soldiers for this new conflict, but in spite of the dysfunctional nature of the opposing alliance, his armies were beaten again and again by an English general, John Churchill—the first Duke of Marlborough and the greatest military genius of the 18th Century.

By 1706, France was beaten and sinking under enormous debts. When Louis made overtures of peace that year, and again in 1709, however, offering everything the alliance had demanded, he was refused. The allies' goal had become the total destruction of French power in Europe, with the added benefit of acquiring bits and pieces of French territory.

The English people were far from united on the issue, their opinions dividing strictly along party lines. The Whigs, who represented the trading interests, wanted to eliminate France as a competitor in their overseas markets. The Tories, whose strength lay among the country squires, were tired of manning and funding the war. Riding in on a wave of war exhaustion near the end of Queen Anne's reign, the Tory ministry led by Henry St. John, Viscount Bolingbroke, and Robert Harley (later Earl of Oxford) carried on secret talks with the French to end the war.

By this time, Marlborough had been dismissed from his command. His wife Sarah had long been Queen Anne's favourite attendant, the power behind the throne, but when she pushed the Queen too hard in favour of the Whigs, the best friends had a serious falling out. The Tory ministers used the rift to discredit the Duke, who, they believed, had become dangerously powerful. As the Duchess's star fell, so did the rest of her family's. In spite of his victories, the Duke was recalled, his reputation damaged. During the next few years, he stayed in Europe, courting the favour of the Elector of Hanover, who had been designated by the Act of Succession to inherit the throne of Great Britain and rule as George I.

Marlborough was replaced in his command by James Butler, the second Duke of Ormonde, a less brilliant, but also less arrogant gentleman. Ormonde was a Tory under the leadership of Lord Bolingbroke.

There is no question that the majority of the English wanted peace. With few respites, England had been at war on the Continent since 1687; however, these peace negotiations were carried on in secret, without the knowledge of England's partners in the Grand Alliance, who could not be persuaded to end the conflict. Under Bolingbroke's direction, Ormonde held back from battle with the French when his official orders from the Queen were to engage the enemy at every opportunity. It is not clear how much Queen Anne knew about the negotiations, but many documents were found to have been issued without the appropriate signatures and seals.

The war was not the only object of intrigue. Since the overthrow of James II in 1689, his son and legitimate heir, James Edward Francis Stuart, had lived with his mother and his court on the charity of Louis XIV at St. Germain-en-Laye near Paris, hoping to regain the thrones of England and Scotland. More than once, Louis had financed troops and ships for the Stuarts to retake England, but every attempt had failed.

Both Bolingbroke and Harley, along with many Tories, corresponded with James. They led him to believe that either Queen Anne, his half-sister, would be persuaded to designate him as her successor or that they would manage to get Parliament to change the Act of Succession in his favor. If James could have been persuaded to forsake his Roman Catholic faith, this might have happened, but he staunchly refused. This put his English sympathizers in a bind, for they knew how strongly their countrymen opposed the notion of a Catholic king. To protect themselves and their political careers, they, therefore, carried on a simultaneous correspondence with George. By 1711, the issue of peace seems to have become more compelling for them than a second Stuart restoration.

Parliament had declared James an outlaw and had put a price of £100,000 on his head. So, during the secret peace negotiations, the terms of which eventually would have to be brought to light in order to be ratified, James was sold down the river. As part of the agreement, Louis agreed to recognize the Protestant succession in England and not to assist James in any way in his quest for the throne. The Whigs would have demanded that Louis surrender James to them for execution. Instead, Louis was made to exile him from France. The trouble was that James was such a hot potato that nobody wanted him. Finally, with the use of secret-service funds, the Tories paid the impoverished Duke of Lorraine to offer James a haven at Bar-le-Duc. Queen Anne, who, though a Protestant, sincerely regretted her brother's plight, was party to this transaction at least.

Once the Tory ministers came to their secret peace with France, they approached their allies with a completed deal. Without England, the others knew that they would never succeed in unseating Philip from Spain and would have much less chance of gaining territory, so after two more years of negotiations, the long war was finally brought to an end.

The peace had no sooner been made and James sent to Bar, than Queen Anne died. George succeeded her to the throne when the Tories were in complete disarray. Caught in the midst of indecision, most Tories, including Bolingbroke, decided to throw in their lot with the elected king. During the years of the Tory ministry, however, the Whigs had been courting George. They convinced him that the Tories were all Jacobites—adherents of James—and as a result, when he arrived, he appointed only Whig ministers.

Infuriated by the secret peace negotiations, the Whigs immediately began an investigation of the Tory ministers, who were impeached for betraying the interest of their country.

Ironically, the Treaty of Utrecht, as it came to be known, was the most important treaty in English history. More than any other single event, it was responsible for the expansion of English mercantile power. Through it, England gained Newfoundland, Nova Scotia, the Hudson's Bay Territory, Gibralter and Minorca, and a thirty-year monopoly on the American slave trade, which would make her the richest trading nation in the world.

But in 1715, when this story opens, the trading interests in England were so intent on punishing their rivals that they did not foresee the benefits of the Peace of Utrecht.

The spider's touch, how exquisitely fine!
Feels at each thread, and lives along the line.

Alexander Pope
An Essay on Man in Four Epistles

To Henry St. John, Lord Bolingbroke,

Awake, my St. John! leave all meaner things
To low ambition, and the pride of Kings.
Let us (since Life can little more supply
Than just to look about us and to die)
Expatiate free o'er all this scene of Man;
A mighty maze! But not without a plan . . .

CHAPTER I

April, 1715

A pair of tiny overlapping circles embossed the baby's forehead, carving an edge like an embryo moon. Reddish brown, they marked her perfect skin like the scar from a branding.

The infant girl, sucking hungrily at her mother's breast, seemed completely unaware of this touch from God—if so it was.

Only yesterday, the news-sheets had reported the birth of a child with the sign of the eclipse upon her forehead, scarcely one week after the moon had cast its ominous shadow over the City of London. It was said that her mother had been frightened by the event too near her time. Whatever the cause, people of all walks had flocked to this tanner's house in Grace Church Street to see the curiosity, which, if nothing else, had provided a boon to the baby's parents, for no one had been admitted without an exchange of coins.

Harrowby, Lord Hawkhurst, riding high on his newly acquired wealth and title, had brought his beautiful, young wife, Isabella, and their little coterie to witness the miracle for themselves. Arriving in the late afternoon, he had been irked by the necessity of waiting below in the filthy street for the previous visitors to descend from the cramped room over the shop. Then, upstairs, being greeted by the unremarkable sight of a woman nursing her baby had done nothing to quell his annoyance.

Gathered with their party round the flimsy bed, Hester Kean, cousin and waiting woman to Isabella, pondered the significance of the mark. As she peered down at the baby, she wondered what the future could possibly hold for this tiny girl. Given the meanness of her parents' house, the number of mouths they had to feed, and the smallpox, which threatened rich and poor alike, she likely would not survive until the age of five, unless the *sign*, as people called it, truly was proof of favour from the Almighty.

Standing beside her, Sir Humphrey Cove, a short, plump gentleman with small, nervous movements, drew closer to the nursing pair. He lowered the handkerchief he'd been holding to his nose to block the stench from the tannery below and bent to examine the mark.

"Yes, I see it!" he whispered eagerly, his fingers fluttering against his chest. "It *is* a miracle, I am sure. A sign of something great about to dawn."

"If something were about to *dawn*, I should think there'd be a sun without the moon."

Delivered with his customary irony, Lord Lovett's comment brought a smile to Hester's lips. A dark, handsome gentleman with thick black brows and a satirical bent, Lord Lovett was vastly more entertaining than her cousin's other friends.

"But I assure you, my dear Adrian," Sir Humphrey went on excitedly. "Sun or moon—it truly does not matter. Why, my uncle's neck erupted with a carbuncle on the very eve of King James's departure!"

Lord Lovett gave a brief laugh. "What perfect rubbish you do spout, Cove!"

Turning to Isabella and taking her gently by the elbow, he asked, "What say you, my lady?" He addressed her with a great deal more courtesy than he had accorded his friend. "Does it indeed appear like the eclipse to you? I recollect no such shape. As I recall, all that occurred was that the sky grew dark and the light returned a few minutes later."

"I did not see it. I was not out of doors that day." Isabella stared at the baby's forehead from behind the half-mask she had worn to protect her face. "But Hester did!" With an ingenuous look, she turned to her cousin. "Remember, Hester? You came into my chamber, saying something about seeing the eclipse, but I hardly attended then. Does this mark look like it, indeed?"

Hester was so taken aback that she could not immediately respond. She did not see how Isabella could refer to that moment without the slightest hint of shame. She could not think of it herself without a tightening in her chest, for it was during the eclipse that Isabella and her mother had cheated the real Lord Hawkhurst out of his fortune.

Hester had come indoors after witnessing a violent death to find that Isabella and Mrs. Mayfield, Hester's aunt, had hidden the only piece of evidence that might have cleared Gideon Fitzsimmons, Viscount St. Mars, of his father's murder. But if the evidence had cleared him, then he, and not Isabella's foolish husband Harrowby, would be the Earl of Hawkhurst now.

Since St. Mars's arrest and his subsequent escape, Isabella and her mother had enjoyed the fruits of their deception without the slightest inkling of guilt. But surely to be a countess—or even the mother of a countess—was a glorious thing.

Looking down at the infant again, Hester saw that it had fallen asleep. "I believe," she finally said, in answer to her cousin's question, "the mark reflects the shape we *should* have seen if we had looked at the sun when the moon was covering it. But I did not look directly at it. It is dangerous to peer at the sun."

"Then, how can anyone know what it looked like?" Isabella asked.

"Humph!" Harrowby snorted. "No one does, I'll warrant. This whole thing reeks of a humbug to me. The notion that a tanner's brat would receive a mark from God passes all bounds. Why, I have a birthmark myself on the back of my knee, and no one's said that it's a sign! And if I haven't had a run of good luck lately, I don't know who has." He barked a laugh.

"Indeed, my lord," Lord Lovett agreed, with a wry curve of his lips. "I had much rather have visited your chamber at Hawkhurst House to see your mark than have come to this stinking hovel. What a pity you did not mention it before!"

"Pooh!" Isabella pouted. "I have already seen my lord's mark an hundred times."

"One hundred already? And you married but a few weeks! I must congratulate you, my lord, on a prodigious performance—unless I err in attributing these sightings to an activity I can only reflect upon with envy."

Isabella giggled, and Harrowby guffawed, neither the least displeased to have their marital exploits admired.

Hester would have smiled, too, for Lord Lovett had delivered this quip with his usual wryness, and she was not immune to his wit, had Isabella not immediately ruined the joke.

Casting a flirtatious glance at Lord Lovett, and lowering her voice to a sultry note, she said, "Shall Harry-kins tell you of the marks he's found on me?"

He raised a leering brow. "And spoil the fun of discovering them for myself? My lady, I beg you will not."

Harrowby laughed almost as heartily as Isabella at this piece of gallantry, for having a wife that a gentleman as fashionable as Lord Lovett desired could only add to his sense of importance. And, indeed, it seemed to Hester that Harrowby felt no jealousy of the gentlemen who paid court to Isabella at her levees. She even wondered if he had already grown tired of his marital duties and might welcome a rival to occupy his voracious wife.

Throughout this exchange, Sir Humphrey had not taken his eyes from the baby, and his eager whisper floated to Hester now, "Yes, yes! It must be a sign. This *must* be the moment."

No one else seemed to share his excitement. Isabella's disappointment in the mark was so complete that she had forgotten the eclipse entirely, and it would be useless for Hester to repeat the explanations she had read. A pamphlet had been published last week, describing the astronomers' observations, and Hester had ventured a few precious pennies to learn about the extraordinary event, for it was one that she would never forget.

"Shall we go, my lady?" Lord Lovett offered Isabella his arm to escort her down the narrow stairs, and they exited with no further glance at the mother or her child.

"Well, I confess, I do not see what all the fuss has been about."

Harrowby started to precede Sir Humphrey from the room, but Hester prompted him before he could escape.

"My lord . . . ."

"What?" Turning at the top of the stairs, Harrowby had to step aside for Sir Humphrey to pass.

Seeing Hester curtsy where she stood by the woman and her child, Harrowby grumbled, "Oh—deuce take it! . . . Very well." He reached into the pocket of his knee-length silk coat and extracted a silver coin. He did not toss it to the woman, as Hester half-expected he would, but instead dropped it into an earthenware cup, resting conspicuously on a stool near the door. "Here's something for you, then, Goody. Buy the brat a gewgaw with it, if you want. But I shouldn't set much store on that mark of hers, if I were you. Seems a stretch to my way of thinking. And it doesn't do to hoodwink peers, you know."

Then, with the woman's grateful farewells ringing in their ears, they followed the others downstairs.

At the door Hester picked up her long skirts before stepping out into the street. Even the pattens she had worn would not raise her high enough to prevent the deep mud from soiling her hem. In front of the shop, Lord Lovett, Sir Humphrey, and Isabella stood waiting for them beside Harrowby's coach and four, with its door open, ready to receive them.

Out here in Grace Church Street, the odour was even more unbearable, so Hester clutched her handkerchief to her nose. They had all worn masks to protect their faces in this neighbourhood, which was too near the Leadenhall market for leather not to be filled with the acrid stench of tanneries and the waste from slaughterhouses. Dressed in their laces and silks, with Harrowby's footmen garbed in brown and gold livery, and the ornate carriage emblazoned with the Hawkhurst arms, they made an entertaining spectacle for the residents in the street. Urchins had stopped to stare. Mothers stood in doorways with their babies on their hips. Others leaned from upstairs windows to gawk at the gentlemen and ladies in their finery.

There was nothing unusual about this attention, but, still, a mood of uneasiness seemed to fill the street. Lord Lovett must have sensed it, too, for his indolent features reflected an impatience that Hester had never seen in them before.

"We ought to make haste." He glanced at his timepiece. "We mustn't be late for the Princess's drawing room."

"No, indeed," Sir Humphrey agreed. "Gentlemen in our position cannot be too careful, can we, dear Lovett?"

Lord Lovett answered with a shade of annoyance, "I was referring to the possibility that we will find ourselves too late to be admitted, if the crowd proves large. But no, I should not wish to offend her Highness."

"Well, if you ask me, this whole outing has been a damned waste of time," Harrowby said.

"My lady?" Lord Lovett handed Isabella to one of the footmen, and one by one, the others climbed inside.

It had been a squeeze for five people to ride in one vehicle, but Isabella had insisted on Hester's coming, too. Her pleasure on any occasion seemed directly related to the number of people who accompanied her. She did not care for the intimacy of a quiet evening at home. Since becoming a countess, she had taken advantage of her position as a married lady of consequence to make sure that hardly a moment went by that was not filled with some delightful scheme.

It was she who had urged this expedition after Hester had read the announcement of the baby's mark. Isabella had immediately solicited the company of their two friends—Lord Lovett, who haunted her levees even more than he did the new earl's, and Sir Humphrey Cove, who had been Harrowby's boon companion since their days at Oxford, when they had discovered a common love of gossip and clothes. Since Isabella, with Mrs. Mayfield and Hester, had moved into Hawkhurst House, hardly a day had gone by that part, at least, was not spent in the company of these two gentlemen.

On the way to Cornhill, Hester had found herself crushed between them on the rear-facing seat. Sir Humphrey's perfume had nearly overwhelmed her, and she had not looked forward to breathing it on their return. But the waste used in tanning was so offensive that anything was preferable.

Soon it would be summer, and the stench would be even worse. Another month and the aristocracy would be impatient to leave, for the Court usually passed the summer in the country to avoid the unhealthy air of London. But this year, the first of George's reign, they would be forced to stay for the King's birthday at the end of May. The London shopkeepers could look forward to more trade, but many aristocrats were already grumbling about the inconvenience.

They were settled in the coach when Lord Lovett suggested that they go by way of Lombard Street. "I believe it will be faster. And we've tarried too long."

"Lombard Street?" Harrowby gave a snort. "When it is half the width? We should be stuck there for ages while my footmen cleared a path. Why, the last time I went that way, some fool of a carter was driving a waggon with six teams directly up the middle! Best leave it to my coachman to decide."

Lord Lovett subsided with his customary good grace, though his shoulders betrayed a certain tension. "As you will, of course, my lord."

It could not be easy, Hester reflected, to see a gentleman who was his inferior in every way—whose prospects had been worse than his own—suddenly elevated to such a high-ranking peerage, when he must now be deferred to in all things. Overnight their relative positions had changed, and Lord Lovett now found himself waiting on a gentleman he might otherwise not have bothered to notice. But his lordship's attendance on the new couple was more likely due to his desire for Isabella than to any need to court her husband.

If Hester's cousin, with her golden curls and carefree laugh, had attracted the gentlemen as an unmarried girl, she did so doubly now as a married lady with a fortune and an influential peer for a husband. Gentlemen flocked about her, competing for her notice, a chair at her levee, and the privilege of escorting her out in the evening. As she had happily predicted, she and Harrowby had become one of the most envied couples in town.

As the carriage rumbled around the corner into Cornhill, Isabella was the first to remove her mask. She made a great show of it, turning her back to Lord Lovett and asking him to untie the knot. Harrowby, seated next to her, could have done it more easily, but Lord Lovett obliged, leaning forward and sliding his arm about her waist to drop the mask into her lap. Isabella turned her head to thank him just as he moved forward, and her lips nearly brushed his cheek. She gave him a provocative smile and bit her lower lip. Lord Lovett seemed unsurprised, but with a warning lift of his brow, he shifted his gaze to Harrowby and moved back against his bench.

"It was a sign!" Sir Humphrey's eager interjection startled them all. "I tell you, Lovett, it must have been a sign."

Lord Lovett issued a heavy sigh, his face betraying a weary amusement. "Yes, yes, dear fellow. I am certain you must be right. The mark on that brat was surely a sign that an extraordinary catastrophe is about to befall us. But must we contemplate it today? We should be changing our habits this very minute for Court."

"No, no! You misunderstand me, my dear Lovett!" Sir Humphrey clasped his knees and leaned forward to speak to him around Hester. "I do not refer to a catastrophe at all, but to something glorious."

"Well, whatever it is, I wish you would—"

His lordship's irritable response was cut off. Shouts and screams began to come at them from somewhere up ahead. "What the—"

"Beware, my lord!" Their coachman's cry let out, as the horses came to a halt. Then, they backed, harness jingling as they tossed their heads about in distress.

Hester gripped her seat. A door was thrown open, and a stranger's face appeared. Isabella screamed. Behind the rough-looking fellow, a raucous crowd had filled the street in front of the Royal Exchange. Some of the rioters must have blocked their coach, while others were attacking pedestrians.

"Hey! There's gen'lemen and ladies in 'ere!" the ruffian who had opened their door called out to the mob. He reached inside and made a grab for Lord Lovett, who sat closest to the door.

Lord Lovett resisted gently, saying in a reasoning tone, "Here, my good man! You mustn't frighten the ladies. I shall have to ask you to let us pass."

"Ye can go—" the man's breath reeked terribly of gin— "just as soon as ye drink a toast to 'is Majesty."

"Blast you, fool!" Harrowby, who had remained cautiously silent until this point, expressed his outrage. "Where do you think we're going? If you do not let us pass this very instant, we will be late for his

Majesty's drawing room."

Lord Lovett added quickly, "Yes, I'm sure you mean very well, but we must be going. You can take our wishes for his Majesty for granted."

He had been trying to free himself from the ruffian's hold, but the man refused to release him. "It's not the Cuckold we're drinkin' to," he sneered. "It's to our darling—what's over the water."

From the other side of the carriage, Sir Humphrey gave a gasp. "Lovett! What have I—"

"Will you shut your mouth and let me handle this!"

Giving Sir Humphrey a vicious glance, Lord Lovett tried harder to free himself, while Harrowby sputtered, "Why, you—! I'll have you taken up for sedition! How dare you speak of his Majesty like that! Where are my footmen? Why don't they seize these ruffians?"

The footmen were nowhere in sight, but the sound of slaps and fists on flesh, and an occasional encouraging cry from their coachman, told Hester that the men were engaged in their defense.

Lord Lovett had got command of his temper again, and he cut through Harrowby's speech to say reasonably, "You see what the consequences could be? If I were you, I should run before the militia comes to take you up."

But the man was too drunk to listen. He took up the cries, coming from farther up the street. "High Church and Ormonde! No 'wee German lairdie' for us!"

"A Stuart! A restoration!"

Through the pane to her left, Hester saw the mob break the windows of a house. People in the street were being attacked. She winced, as a young man was beat over the head with a rake. Others were stripped of their coats, while riotous cries filled the streets. The mob cheered the Duke of Ormonde and King James, and cursed the Quakers, Whigs, and King George.

Today was the Duke of Ormonde's birthday, but never had there been a celebration like this. The popular general would have been honoured this morning by private visits to his house. But no birthday other than a royal's should ever be celebrated in the streets.

Some men from the militia tried to break up the crowd, but they were quickly surrounded and beaten, too. Whoever had the courage to support King George was running to take cover.

"Where are my footmen?" Harrowby shouted again. His voice cracked on the final word. "Here, you! Coachman! Give them a taste of your whip!"

"Yer not goin' anywhere, till ye drinks to the 'ealth o' King James. Let me hear ye! Ormonde! No King George! Give us King James III!"

Lord Lovett gave a desperate shove, freed one hand, and reached for his sword.

As the man dived again and nearly dragged him into the street, Sir Humphrey shrieked, "Ormonde! No King George! King James III!"

The rioter had nearly managed to pull Lord Lovett from the coach. Hester and Isabella grabbed his coattails and struggled to hang on.

"High Church and Ormonde!" Sir Humphrey bleated again.

At last the man heard him through his drunken fog. He released Lord Lovett so suddenly that he fell backwards, landing on top of Hester, who had been pulling harder than the rest.

"That's more like!" The man gave them a friendly grin. "Now let me 'ear ye all say it— No, wait! I'll get ye a tankard so ye can toast 'is Grace n' our rightful king."

He turned to stagger away, and in that moment, Lord Lovett recovered his footing. He quickly banged on the roof of the coach, slammed its door, and shouted, "Coachman, whip up the horses!"

As their driver complied, the coach gave a huge lurch forward. "High Church and Ormonde!" Lord Lovett called back out the window. Sir Humphrey, who had never ceased his cheering, stuck his round face out the opposite window and cheered even louder. Hester joined them, waving with friendliness to the mob as their coach was allowed through.

One horrible sight after another met their eyes. One man who was brave enough—or foolish enough—to huzzah King George was dragged from his carriage box and soundly beaten. All the stockjobbers, who were presumed to be Whigs, had to run for their lives. The windows of any church or house not illuminated for the celebration were broken.

The Hawkhurst party had no notion of what had become of their footmen and dared not stop to see if they'd been hurt. No one in the coach spoke or even exchanged a glance until they had left the rioters far behind.

By the time they cleared St. Paul's, Sir Humphrey's breaths were coming in deep gasps and his eyes were wide.

He started to say something, but Lord Lovett cut him off. "It would seem—" he pinned Sir Humphrey with the earnestness of his gaze—"that I owe you an apology, Cove. You were right, and I was wrong. I must thank you for your quickness, which has saved me from a beating, if nothing worse."

Sir Humphrey looked as if he might reply, but he was too overcome with emotion. His eyes filled with tears, and he nodded, staying silent until they dropped him before his lodgings in Jermyn Street.

"Quick thinking, that," Harrowby agreed, once Sir Humphrey was gone. He was still holding onto Isabella, whether for his comfort or hers Hester could not tell. "I only hope his Majesty never gets wind of this."

"I doubt he will." Lord Lovett's amusement indicated that he had fully recovered from the frightening ordeal. Indeed, he seemed most admirably relaxed. "I doubt that anyone in that mob will be eager to report his participation in it, or even what was said. Our attempts at self-preservation are sure to go unremarked."

"The confound impudence of it!" Harrowby began to fume again. "How dare they hold up Ormonde so high? I have never heard them cheer his Grace of Marlborough in that scandalous way. Damned Jacobites! Ormonde had better be careful if he don't want trouble for himself. They shall see what comes of all this treasonous talk. Mark my words, but they will!"

Lord Lovett eased his body against the cushions. In shifting his position, he met Hester's gaze, where he must have spied a sign of his own reflections, for he gave her a secretive smile. "I am certain you will soon have them quaking in their boots, my lord."

Hester tried not to laugh, but after all the shock and the excitement, she found it nearly impossible to contain a smile.

Thomas Barnes, groom, valet and general man of business, had started to fret at the absence of his lord. If truth be told, he'd been anxious from the moment his master, the Viscount St. Mars, had decided to take himself off to France. They had quarreled mightily about St. Mars's going alone, Tom refusing to be parted from him, and his master insisting that Tom stay behind.

"I will not have you getting caught sneaking out of the country with me," St. Mars had said. "They would be sure to hang you. Is that what you want?" Then, with a hint of his former impudence, he added, "Besides, I thought you did not care for the French."

Ignoring an obvious attempt to distract him, Tom retorted, "And I thought you said you wouldn't be in any danger, my lord."

St. Mars sighed. "Travelling alone, I do not expect to be, but I can hardly escape unnoticed with an army at my heels."

"I ain't no army, my lord."

"A retinue, then. Have we not established that you are my gang of one? I am counting on you to keep up the pretence with Lade. I want him to think that I have a gang of cutthroats at my beck and call."

Lade, their landlord at the Fox and Goose, deep in the Weald of Kent, was a Newgate gaolbird, who harboured highwaymen and dealt in smuggled goods. Not the trustworthy sort, he had to be kept in his place. Neither St. Mars nor Tom had been able to discover whether Lade knew the identity of the mysterious Mr. Brown and his servant who had appeared over a month ago to take up residence at his inn. Clearly, he suspected St. Mars of something, but not, perhaps, of being the viscount charged with murdering his own father. At least, he had not "squeaked beef," as he would have said, to get the reward of three hundred pounds that had been placed on St. Mars's head. Instead, he eagerly pocketed the money St. Mars doled out to rent the Fox and Goose and its servants for his private use. And St. Mars had given Lade to understand that if he ever called down the law on his wealthy guest, then he would feel free to mention his host's connections with smugglers and highwaymen.

"I need you here, Tom," St. Mars continued. "I need you to keep an eye on my belongings, and to take care of Penny—" his beloved horse— "*and* to let me know at once of any reason that I should come back."

"You *do* mean to come back, don't you, sir? Before too long?"

Tom had not liked the way St. Mars had hesitated over his reply. The despair that sometimes showed through his careful demeanour had briefly betrayed itself . "I shall return when I cannot bear to stay away any longer, or when I am needed. For the last, I count on you to let me know. You should open any letter that comes for me. Is that understood?"

"Yes, my lord, but—" Tom had found it difficult to shape the question he had wanted to ask, so he had ended with, "You won't leave me here too long?"

"If you find it too long, you must write to tell me. Address your letters to my steward, Monsieur Lavalle, at St. Mars. He will see that I get them."

And Tom had had to be content with that.

Now nearly a month had passed since St. Mars's departure, and nary a word from him had come. Tom had thrown himself into improving his master's quarters in this flea-ridden inn they now called home. With a few discreet repairs—nothing too grand, which might draw the attention of the authorities to the house—some furniture ordered from tradesmen in Maidstone, and the hiring of a cook and laundress, he had made the place ready for St. Mars's return. These lodgings were not so bad for a man like Tom who had slept most of his life over a stable, but they were a degradation to the heir of Rotherham Abbey and Hawkhurst House, two of the six important properties St. Mars should have inherited upon his father's death.

If there was one thing Tom had learned in his short time as groom to an outlaw, however, it was the need for secrecy. It was secrecy that kept him close to the inn with virtually nothing to do all day. He exercised Penny and Beau—the horse he had taken for himself from Lord Hawkhurst's stables—along the footpaths and drovers' trails throughout the Weald, memorizing their turns and twists, in case he and his master had to flee the King's Messengers, and learning to think—if he only knew it—something like the highwayman's accomplice he had become. But no two horses could occupy an experienced groom all of any day, and he found himself with far too much time to think about things that he would rather ignore.

As he was doing this evening, while he brushed Penny down after a long, sweating ride. He caught himself ruminating about the woman who kept house for the innkeeper, Lade. A pretty woman, turned harlot after going to gaol for being gulled by a thief. A warm, cheerful sort of female, skilled with a needle, who had spent hours happily working over the silks and satins they had bought for St. Mars.

Katy still had to serve Lade's customers in the taproom, where Tom took his meals now that St. Mars was gone. Tom had rejected her friendly advances. He didn't truck with whores. But he had noticed that, even though she still put on a smile for the men who came into the taproom, she never asked for their attention. If anything, since begging for the job of caring for St. Mars's clothes, and getting it, she had become adept at fending them off. She managed Lade's customer's with cheerful goodwill—to avoid angering Lade, Tom suspected.

These observations had been a torment to Tom. He did not want to admire Katy. Staying away from her would be so much easier if he could only find fault. He wanted nothing at all to do with a whore, former or otherwise. His father had died of the pox, and Tom knew that there was no greater torture on earth—maybe not even in hell.

If only St. Mars had not left him here alone!

He was putting away his brushes, about to face the daily ordeal of watching her serve his dinner, when he heard the rare sound of hoof beats in the yard and a man's voice calling for service.

Avis, the stableboy, dropped his pitchfork and ran running to take charge of the man's horse. Tom stayed out of sight. He tried to get a glimpse of the rider, but the man disappeared into the inn with hardly a word to the boy.

The Fox and Goose was a ramshackle inn in a hamlet known as Pigden, which had nothing to recommend it but a few hedgerow alehouses. Deep in the Weald, it did not lie on any important road. Nor did it receive the custom of men on horseback, unless they, like St. Mars, had something to hide.

As soon as Avis returned, leading the visitor's horse, Tom accosted him, asking, "Who's the stranger?"

Avis answered cheerfully, "Oh, Mr. Menzies ain't no stranger. He stops every now and then. And he tips me a George, if I'm quick enough."

"What kind of rogue is he?"

"You mean, is he a *banditti*?" Avis scratched one ear, then shrugged, unconcerned. "I don't think he is. But *if* he is, then he'd be one of the gen'lemen for sure."

Tom did not like the thought of any stranger staying at the Fox and Goose. The locals and drovers who came to drink posed enough of a threat to St. Mars, but someone who traveled through on other business might inform the authorities in London about the mysterious Mr. Brown who resided in a house where no respectable person should ever lodge.

Walking into the taproom, Tom caught a look at the man, standing with Lade. He was dressed in a gentleman's riding wig, tall leather boots, and fashionable traveling clothes. An arrogant face and bearing, combined with an insolent manner, did nothing to make him more appealing. Lade, however, greeted him like a welcome guest, and Katy obviously had seen him before. No curiosity showed in her eyes, as she bustled to serve him with a deference that no other customer received.

Tom seated himself at a table near the cage where the dog was turning the spit. As the animal trod its wheel, Tom was only able to observe the stranger a few more seconds before Lade conducted him into the private parlour. The parlour that was leased to St. Mars, who had paid for its use.

Katy made three trips into the room, taking trays of food, and once, she carried in a bottle of Lade's smuggled French wine. Each time she returned, her pretty, brown eyes looked a little more clouded. And on one of these occasions, she threw Tom a glance, filled with a mixture of hurt and resentment. Tom couldn't imagine what reason she had to be angry with him, but after a few minutes of wondering, he decided it was time he discovered what was going on.

He rose from his bench and sauntered across the tight, mean corridor to Lade's private parlour. Emboldened beyond his usual state, he did not knock before opening the door.

"What the—!"

He was greatly taken aback, when the gentleman seated with Lade leapt to his feet, scraping his bench against the floor, and drew out his sword. Tom retreated a step, while Lade, who was slow to react, stood between them and said, "Everything's *bene*, sir! That's Tom, what works for the gentry-cove I was tellin' ye about."

Tom was far from pleased to hear that Lade had been wagging his tongue about St. Mars. Taking matters into his own hands, he asked, "Why's this gen'leman using Mr. Brown's parlour, Lade? It's been let for the time."

Menzies sneered. "I am not accustomed to having my comfort challenged—least of all by a servant."

"There's no need to make 'im brush." Lade's tone was wheedling, which meant that he was in the wrong. "Mr. Menzies 'ere's one of us. He's a rum 'un, 'e is."

"And you mean to charge him for a room that you've already been paid for. I know how your mind works, Lade."

Lade scowled. "Now that's where yer wrong, ye chub! I haven't asked 'im fer a grig. Ain't that right, Mr. Menzies? I would never try to nip one of 'is Majesty's men, now would I?"

The stranger ignored him. Sitting down again, he leaned back on the bench, the better to examine Tom. His glance raked Tom from head to toe, with so much insolence that an angry pulse started in Tom's ears.

"I should like to meet this master of yours," Menzies finally said. "Lade has told me some curious things about him."

"Has he?" Tom feigned an indifference he could not feel. Every hair on his back had stood up in warning. He would have something to say to Lade as soon as this gentleman was gone. "My master would be happy to meet you, too, if only to find out why you and Lade here are so chatty about another gentleman's business."

Menzies responded with an angry gleam. "Oh, you mustn't blame Lade. He has been in my service these past two years. This parlour, which your master has taken, *according to you,* has always been placed at my disposal. I find myself wondering why a man, such as Lade describes your master to be, would bother to stop in such an out-of-the-way place?"

Tom had learned a thing or two these past few months. He countered immediately, "I was wonderin' the same about you, Mr. Menzies. What business do you have in these parts?"

Lade gave a guffaw. "Why, the same business we *all* have, chub! Do y'think I don't know yer Mr. Brown is gone to France? Now what sort of business would 'e get up to over there?"

Menzies regarded Tom closely, as if searching for a sign that he understood. "Indeed, I am very sorry to miss him. I'll look forward to seeing him on my way back through, but for now—" he turned to Lade— "I would be glad to retire to my room. Is it the same as usual, or has Mr. Brown taken it, too?"

Turning scarlet, Lade rubbed a hand across the back of his neck and squirmed. "Now ye knows I don't like to disoblige ye, but that room is sort of took. I can turn Katy out of hers for ye, though."

Menzies grimaced. "I shall want the sheets aired, but you can tell the wench to join me as soon as I'm settled."

A knot started forming in the pit of Tom's stomach. Katy had been made to entertain Lade's guests in the past. But that was all supposed to be over—wasn't it? She had not been used that way since St. Mars and he had come to the Fox and Goose. St. Mars had hired her to tend his clothes, for there was no man in Pigden with the skills to do it. It had never occurred to Tom that Katy would be asked to whore again.

He heard himself say belligerently, "Katy works for my master now. She's not Lade's servant any more."

Lade threw him a glare, but Tom drew himself up, daring either man to contradict him.

Fortunately, Menzies looked only mildly annoyed as he turned to say to Lade, "If this is the sort of welcome I am to receive in this house, you will be very fortunate if I ever stop here again. But—" he glanced at Tom, with a less than friendly look— "perhaps your Mr. Brown will no longer be here when I return. Either that, or he will find a way to satisfy me for the inconvenience."

He picked up his tricorn and riding cloak and, with a sneer for Tom, strode past him and up the stairs.

"Now why did ye go and do that?" Lade asked, as soon as he was gone. "As if yer master had ever lain wif my wench. 'E don't even fancy 'er to my way o' thinkin'."

Tom hedged, unable to explain. "The less that gen'leman stops here the better."

"Well, ye'd better get used to 'im. He rides from Lunnon to the coast and back. Two or three times a year at least. And whenever 'e's been, ye always hears of somethin'. There must be somethin' brewin' up in Lunnon fer sure or 'e wouldn't be comin' through now."

Tom, who was shaking queerly in the wake of his confrontation over Katy, didn't bother to attend. He took himself upstairs to his own chamber, where, after musing for a moment, he started to tidy his things.

Later that night, when he heard Katy's light footfall on the floor of the gallery, he went out to meet her. Her look of surprise made his innards go topsy-turvy.

"You're to sleep in my room tonight," he said roughly. "That fellow Menzies has taken yours. The master won't mind if I use his room this once." Tom would sleep on the floor, but she didn't need to know that.

"I wouldn't want to turn you out—"

He stopped her with a glare. "You'll do as you're told! Mr. Brown told me to watch over all his belongings, and that means you, too."

Her eyes grew round, before they assumed a wary, but friendly stare.

Tom could not be sure, but he thought he saw a hint of relief in her gaze.

He knew he should say something cutting—something like he wouldn't have her wagging her tongue about Mr. Brown to every man who stopped at the inn. He couldn't let her think he cared if she slept with Mr. Menzies or anyone else. But he couldn't bring himself to say it, not when it just wasn't fair.

St. Mars had given no sign that he regarded her as his property. But, Tom reasoned, she had always belonged to somebody or other. Better St. Mars than anyone else he could think of.

She was still staring up at him, as if wondering what had brought on his anger when he had always been careful to take as little notice of her as possible.

Tom felt a hoarseness in his throat. "I just don't like this Mr. Menzies, is all."

The smile Katy gave him was rather sad. "Neither do I. So I'm glad if Mr. Brown doesn't want me to please him."

"I'm sure he don't. Not him or anyone else. You've got enough to do, and you couldn't do a proper job if—well, if—" His tongue was tied.

"I understand, Mr. Barnes." She gave a lift to her shoulders. "Thank you very much for giving up your room."

Vexed by the lies he had just made up, Tom lowered his head and mumbled a goodnight.

He did not breathe again until the door to St. Mars's chamber was closed behind him and locked with a key.

Fools! who from hence into the notion fall,
That Vice or Virtue there is none at all.
If white and black blend, soften and unite
A thousand ways, is there no black or white?
Ask your own heart, and nothing is so plain;
'Tis to mistake them, costs the time and pain.

CHAPTER II

His opponent was swift and keen, with a wrist so astonishingly supple that Gideon had been forced more than once to leap sideways to avoid the point of his blade. The two men padded about the empty room, silent except for the sound of their breathing—each breath coming faster now—Gideon's light and quick, his opponent's deeper, like the huffing of a bull.

Gideon would not make the same error he had made the last time the two had fought. He had learned not to mistake the master's wheezing for a sign that he had tired. His carelessness on that earlier occasion had almost cost him an eye. In a moment of recklessness he had pressed an advantage that had existed only in his mind. It was a feeling that had no place either in a master's classroom or on the dueling field.

"*Attention*! *Parez . . . riposte!*"

He steadied himself for the moves. A sudden lunge. His parry *en tierce*. The master's riposte and his parry again.

With a quickness that surprised even him, he followed his parry with a lunge. But a start from his opponent made him check himself, even as Monsieur Andolini drew away. At the safe distance of a few paces, the Frenchman touched the point of his small-sword to the floor and regarded his pupil with a cold eye.

"*Monsieur le vicomte* grows tired of Andolini, *oui?* He wishes to dispatch him to *l'enfer?*"

"No, of course not. Forgive me. I would never be so careless. When I see an opening, though, I find myself eager to take it."

"If *monsieur* had taken that particular opening, I am not certain that Andolini would have parried it in time. In that case, *monsieur* would have found himself accused of murder in France as well as England."

This last was said so wryly that Gideon knew no offence had been meant. Still, he found it hard to laugh, even at a sympathetic jest, about his situation. Perhaps in time he would be able to find a certain irony in it, but not so recently after his father's death. It had only been two weeks since he had come to the Chateau of St. Mars, his French estate, hoping to find some manner of relief—here, where he was not an outlaw and had the freedom to go anywhere he pleased.

But the relief he had prayed for had not come. Certainly he had welcomed that first day when he could ride out in the sunlight without the fear of being caught. He had been able to breathe with all the freedom of the innocent man he was. But soon, his malaise had returned—not from any fear of being captured, but from a combination of guilt and loneliness that refused to go away. Guilt, because even though he had not murdered his father, he knew that his own foolishness had made it easier for his father's murderer to kill.

And loneliness, because, no matter how welcome he was here on his own estate, his heart belonged to his home in Kent.

"I have offended my lord." Andolini bowed, with the serenity of a man who knew the superiority of his fighting skills.

"It is nothing." Gideon shook off his gloom. "You must not regard my ill-humours. They come upon me with no warning, but they have nothing to do with you."

Andolini's face betrayed a concern that surprised Gideon, for they were not of long acquaintance. Scarcely more than a week ago, Gideon had stumbled upon the master on the road to Chateaubriant, where Andolini had just given lessons to its lord. Restless and eager for distraction—though not for the company he had found at Versailles—

Gideon invited Andolini to instruct him at St. Mars before returning to Paris. Their sessions, numbering two per day and each lasting for an hour or two, restored the strength Gideon had lost when the wound from a sword had festered, rendering him as weak as a posset with no ale.

Gideon had taken to the Frenchman, who offered him this counsel now, "*Monsieur* must always resist the temptation to make the lunge, especially when dueling with a poor student of the art. It is the unexpected that gets one killed. The *épée* is not the English back-sword, my lord. It is not even the French rapier."

"That is understood. At least—" Gideon laughed— "I say I understand, but it is not in my nature to think before I act. My impulsiveness has landed me in trouble on more than one occasion."

"Then it is good that monsieur has the grace of a cat. For only a cat will always land on its feet."

"I cannot always do that, *Maître* Andolini."

The master's expression—which usually reflected the pedagogue —underwent a significant change. He spoke with genuine sympathy. "*Mais non, bien sûr.* There is no one who can always land on his feet, *monsieur.* But you have the grace *and the heart* to endure more misfortune than your enemies." His briskness returned. "Your quickness can be your ally. But you must not let it lead you. You must be the master of it. There is no place for carelessness in the duello. It will only lead to a *contretemps*, which is not a good thing."

"I shall try to keep that in mind, *monsieur.*"

They put their swords away and walked to the centre of the house. At the top of the marble stairs they parted, Andolini to his room to collect his belongings, Gideon to his chamber to dress for a solitary meal.

Today's lesson had been their last. Gideon was sorry to see the master go. They had enjoyed conversation over their meals, and the lessons had been invaluable. During their sessions, too, Gideon had come close to rejoicing in the use of his body and in the challenge of meeting someone whose skills were superior to his own. But caution, which had to be used in a classroom in which two men were armed with *épées,* with no protection from their sharp points, had kept the exercise from quieting his restless soul. He needed to do something unrestrained to purge him of his unhappy thoughts. He wanted something to make him burn, a sense of purpose, a quest, or a goal. But everything he truly cared about had been torn from his reach.

Andolini's sympathy was the first he had received since his last meeting with Hester Kean. Perhaps that was the reason—while the master was speaking—that an image of her had entered Gideon's head. He had pictured her the way he had seen her last, standing in her bedchamber with the neck of her bodice untied. He did not know why that particular memory should have come to him then, though he had visited it many a time. Andolini certainly looked nothing like Mrs. Kean.

Mrs. Kean, in fact, had not looked very much like herself at that moment, when he had startled her in her room. He had waited too long to inform her of his presence, to warn her before she removed the modest piece of cloth at her breast. But it was the very curve of her neck that had made him hesitate. The graceful sight of it in the glow of her candle had formed a huskiness in his throat—which he had been forced to clear before speaking.

Then, when she turned, her look of delight startled him. Her face was lit with so much warmth. Shock, he had expected—even fear—for how could she know for certain that he would never hurt her? They were completely alone, with the thickness of the Abbey walls between them and anyone else. But she was certain of her safety, and her pleasure in seeing him warmed him in the most unsettling way.

She completely forgot the opening at her throat, until he reminded her of it himself. And then she showed such a pretty confusion, the sort of girlish emotion that he had never expected to see on her face, for Mrs. Kean had always seemed such an imperturbable girl. She had never flinched when he had abducted her, had not shrunk when he had asked for her help in a murder involving treason, and had not screamed when she had watched him put a sword through a villain. That a little thing like an opening in her gown could throw her out of countenance brought a smile to Gideon's lips every time he recalled it. He had actually tried *not* to recall it, for the pleasure it brought him was inevitably followed by the lowering realization that he might never see Mrs. Kean again.

Shaking off this depressing thought, Gideon dressed himself in a fresh linen shirt with a long, ruffled *jabot.* He completed his costume in the *style négligé*, leaving the neck of his shirt open, the collar loosely turned down, and his waistcoat unbuttoned. He had lost his valet Philippe along with everything else, but he was not of a mind to replace him yet. He could not think of taking on a personal servant until he knew what his next course should be.

On top of his dressing table lay a paper that he had found waiting for him the moment he had arrived at St. Mars. It had been sent with no message attached. Gideon picked it up and stood musing over it for, perhaps, the hundredth time.

It was a document that he had read last year, along with everyone else, when many gentlemen had received copies in the London post. It was a declaration from the Pretender, James Stuart, which had arrived in England a few months after his sister Queen Anne's death. Dated the 29th of August, 1714, and written from Plombières, where James had gone to take the waters after being rebuffed by his Majesty of France, it was the desperate plea of a prince who believed he had been betrayed by his friends.

The first time Gideon had read it—in England, in English, and in possession of his life—he had not given it the degree of attention he did now. This copy had been printed in French, but the message was the same.

James declared that he had been led by his supporters in England to expect that his sister would name him her successor or, failing this, that his loyal British friends would change the Act of Succession in his favour. Believing all they told him, and expecting to be restored to his throne, he had waited, leaving the management of his concerns to "his trusty and well-beloved Cousins and Counsellors, then encompassing the Throne" who, he said, from time to time sent him intelligence and encouragement. He went on to say that these counselors, "whose names, till known," would be concealed, either falsely or foolishly did lose the opportunity of bringing him home. And to his further mortification and disappointment, when he gave notice of his intention to cross the water, he was prevented by some of his best friends.

The news-sheets in England had reported that, on hearing of his sister's death, James had set out from Bar-le-Duc in Lorraine, his current place of exile, for Versailles, where he had expected to receive the French king's help. But notified of his departure by England's spies, Louis XIV had dispatched the Marquis de Torcy to intercept him and send him back. In the peace with England, France had agreed not to harbour the Pretender, which the marquis had reminded him. James had only been allowed to travel to Chaillot to see his mother before seeking comfort from his woes in taking the waters at Plombières.

As recently as last autumn, all that had concerned Gideon in the declaration was James's refusal to forsake his Catholic religion. Unlike Charles II, James was unabashedly a papist and unwilling to pretend a conversion to the Protestant faith, though he promised that he would allow his subjects to worship as they pleased. Gideon had not known whether to admire James or blame him for his honesty, because it had certainly cost him the throne. With the former ministry in chaos—many of them professed Jacobites, according to James's declaration—Gideon had privately concluded that the cause was lost.

But that was before his own misfortunes made him an exile, too. Gideon could now feel James's bitterness and disappointment as keenly as his own.

When he arrived at St. Mars, he opened the declaration and read it again.

It carried the Great Seal of England, which had been smuggled by James's father, the deposed James II, to France. In it, he made several promises that he termed his Royal Will and Testament. Gideon's eyes were immediately drawn to the phrases that the anonymous messenger had marked for him by hand.

"And for quieting the Minds of all our Loving Subjects from Fears," James had written, "for offences committed against us, and our Pretences in times past, we do farther promise and declare under our Great Seal, that (as soon as Counsel can draw the same after the said Exchange) we will cause a general Indemnity (as good as any Act of Oblivion) to pass under the said Great Seal, for pardoning all Traitors, Murderers, Felons and Fugitives, and Felons of themselves, Forefaulters, Fore-stallers, Fidlers, Fortune-Tellers, Prize-Fighters, Flesh-Eaters in Lent without License, and all other Offenders whatsoever, who have any ways acted contrary to Law."

Whoever had sent Gideon the declaration had known exactly how to attract his attention. James's supporters were experts at offering people whatever would tempt them to his cause. And in Gideon's case, this was not a title or a place at court. James had promised peerages to so many men, it was questionable whether he would be able to make good on his pledges, even if he did ascend the throne. But could he regain it, he would be able to grant Gideon's greatest wish with merely a stroke of his pen.

Night after night, Gideon tried to think of a way to clear himself through the courts of justice, but could not find any means. If he did nothing, his estates would never be restored to him, but he still did not know what he was willing to do to get them back. Make war on his countrymen? Force a king on them against their will? Take the chance that James would prove to be a tyrant and impose his Catholic religion on England?

On his tour of the Continent Gideon had met James and had liked him. It was impossible not to like a prince with the Stuart charm. James's followers, though, had not inspired him with their leadership or their disinterest. Gideon had turned his back on the Stuart cause two years ago. He still could not bring himself to join them unless his path became clear.

For nearly the hundredth time, he put James's declaration back on his dressing table. Then he left his chamber in search of his dinner.

Harrowby's footmen returned to Hawkhurst House in Piccadilly with blackened eyes and bruised lips. Then, later, the family learned that the riot had been repeated in other towns, especially in those, like Oxford, where the Stuarts had always held sway. Clearly the Tories' fall from power had exacerbated the people's feelings, and King George, by appointing only Whigs to the ministry, had convinced some that their duty was to fight.

Now, Isabella and her mother had to take more servants with them on their shopping expeditions, for throughout the month of May, the Jacobites seized every pretext to riot. The anniversary of every Stuart triumph brought them out, from the Pretender's birthday to Queen Anne's coronation day. The populace even revived the celebration of the Restoration—not observed these past twenty years—to riot against King George.

When visitors now came to Hawkhurst House or the family attended another hostess's drawing room, the conversation turned as often to the latest political pamphlet as it did to fashion or the plays. Mrs. Mayfield declared that she never wanted to hear another word from the Tories or the Whigs, and that as far as she was concerned, they could paper the city with their accusations and justifications, but *she* would never lower herself to read them. If they choked on all those nasty papers, it would only serve them right.

She refused to let the turmoil interfere with her own plans. Her mind was ever employed on the many ways that her daughter's brilliant marriage to an earl could benefit the Mayfield fortunes. With summer approaching soon, when the Court would leave town, she had very little time to waste.

She cornered Hester one morning before Isabella was awake and drew her into the small withdrawing room, which was equipped with an escritoire for the countess's use.

"I want you to write a letter to Mayfield for me," she said. Mrs. Mayfield never referred to her eldest son by his first name, Dudley, for she thought it beneath his dignity. It was she, and not her husband, who had framed the Mayfield genealogy and had it hung in the hall of his house. "I want him to come immediately, so Hawkhurst can get him a place at Court."

"You want *me* to write to your son?"

Mrs. Mayfield bristled. "I hope you are not too good to do a service for your aunt, now that you are waiting woman to a countess! I wonder where you would be if I had not taken you into my house?"

"I meant no ingratitude, Aunt. I was simply wondering why you would not choose to write to him yourself?"

"I *shall* be writing it, Dame Prig. The letter is to be from me, but Mayfield insists that he cannot read my writing, and I must have him understand. This is too important. So, sit and write what I tell you to."

Hester sat at the small bureau and took out paper and ink. She checked the quill, but, as usual in this well-governed household, it had already been sharpened. As she put her pen to paper and began with her aunt's salutation, she braced herself for a blatant piece of self-serving foolishness.

Mrs. Mayfield's letter was just that. She exhorted her son to abandon his siblings and his land to travel to Hawkhurst House as soon as was possible. She told him that his new brother-in-law, her dear Lord Hawkhurst, was anxious to see to his advancement and would welcome him with open arms. Though Hester knew this to be a fabrication, she did not remonstrate, for she also knew that nothing would divert her aunt from a course designed for her own aggrandisement.

She thought she had hidden her reaction to these lies fairly well, until her aunt said, "And you needn't sigh like that, Goody Kean! I know very well what I'm doing. There is no reason why Mayfield shouldn't get a share of my lord's influence, when every Tom, Dick and Harry is asking for the same."

Mrs. Mayfield gave a little shake to her shoulders, like a hen settling down to roost. "Besides," she said virtuously, "I have quite another reason for bringing Mayfield here. And if I tell him what it is, he will keep on shooting and riding with his friends and refuse to come."

"*Another* reason?"

"Yes, Sir Humphrey Cove's sister, Mrs. Jamison, is quite the matchmaker, I'm told. She is a widow, but her husband was a merchant in the City, so she has an abundance of relations with persons of that sort. I want her to find Mayfield a splendid match. They say she found Lord Lunley's son an heiress, and if she can do that for a coxcomb with nothing to recommend him but a squint and a pair of spindly legs, she can very well do it for my son."

Since Hester knew that the success of any matchmaking on Dudley's behalf would depend entirely on Mrs. Mayfield's ability to extract money from her son-in-law for a settlement, she could not doubt that this statement was true.

Before Dudley could receive the letter, Mrs. Mayfield paid a visit to Mrs. Jamison and engaged her interest. Mrs. Jamison promised to make a list of possible brides. Then, there was nothing for Mrs. Mayfield to do except wait for the unwitting bridegroom to arrive, but she was afforded an opportunity to review the list when Sir Humphrey brought his sister to a drawing-room at Hawkhurst House.

Isabella preferred to go out in the evenings, but even she was aware that a lady must sometimes be at home to welcome her friends. A steady stream of visitors had passed through her drawing-room since eight o'clock. Most had not lingered, but had moved on to other houses where, Hester suspected, they would find the conversation more enlightening. The ones who remained were Harrowby's usual cronies, who made themselves comfortable on the satin and velvet cushions.

Lord Lovett had brought a friend, Colonel Potter of the Foot-Guards. He was a tall, lean gentleman with a military bearing. Neither a brown full-bottomed periwig nor a sandy moustache could conceal his decidedly ruddy complexion. Every inch of his face and hands was covered in large, reddish freckles, and his features were set in sullen lines.

His career had not taught him the necessary skills for a lady's drawing-room, for he paid Isabella only scant courtesy and ignored every other woman present, to fix his attention exclusively on Harrowby. Even from where she sat in her corner, Hester could see that the Colonel's conversation was far too sober for Harrowby's taste. Lord Lovett occasionally tried to lighten it by throwing in a sally, but even though the Colonel attempted to respond in kind, his humour was much too dour to be amusing.

Lord Lovett gave up on the gentlemen and went to join Isabella on the sofa, only seconds before Sir Humphrey and his sister burst breathlessly into the room. Their shortness of breath turned out not to have been caused merely by a hurried climb up the stairs, for before they could even be greeted, Sir Humphrey called from the door, "It's good I've found you here, Potter! You are sure to be needed in the park! There's been the most frightful to-do."

Colonel Potter frowned. He threw a glance at Lord Lovett, and an invisible intelligence passed between them. Lord Lovett made no response except to raise an eyebrow in Sir Humphrey's direction, before asking, "Whatever is the trouble now?"

"I'm sure it can wait," the Colonel said. "I was speaking to his lordship."

"I beg my lord's pardon, of course." With a brief bow in Harrowby's direction, Sir Humphrey extracted a handkerchief from his pocket and wiped the perspiration from his face. "But there's trouble in the Foot-Guards. We were coming up from St. James's and saw a group of them waving and shouting outside the Palace. They were burning the shirts the King just gave them today—something about inferior cloth. They looked very unhappy, I assure you. I thought you might be needed to quiet them down."

The Colonel did not seem alarmed. Indeed, he looked rather grimly pleased, when he said, "Perhaps that will teach Marlborough not to cheat them."

Harrowby turned to him in shock. To criticize Marlborough, the hero of Blenheim and Malplaquet, now that the Whigs were in power, was blasphemy.

Lord Lovett leaned back against the cushions and languidly said, "Tut, tut! I wonder what our new monarch will have to say on the matter? Or, rather, his interpreters, of course, for he cannot address the troops, since very few of them speak German. It might be hard for him to sleep if his Foot-Guards are unhappy with their general. They might even think of holding his Majesty to blame, and then what?"

"They were building a bonfire in the middle of the street as we passed," said Sir Humphrey, waving his handkerchief in excitement, "and now that you mention it, Lovett, I believe I *did* hear his Majesty's name called aloud."

Colonel Potter twisted his lips into a sneer. "I shouldn't be surprised if you did."

Sir Humphrey's expression changed from concern to an almost eager speculation. "I had not thought of that at all. Now we *will* have something to consider!"

Hester was no expert on the army, but even she knew that it was no small thing for troops this close to the King to be angry with him. Not when it was their duty to protect him and to uphold his reign.

"Shouldn't you do something about it?" Harrowby said helplessly to Colonel Potter. "We regret the loss of your company—very amiable and all that, of course—but your duty to his Majesty will naturally come first. I am not a military man, thank God!—but that's what I should think. Needn't be concerned about offending us. An't that right, Little Woman?" he asked his wife.

Isabella was making sweet eyes at Lord Lovett and tapping his thigh with her fan, but she raised her eyes to her husband and agreed, "Whatever you say, my Lambikins."

Urged to leave by his hosts, the Colonel truly had no choice but to go. He hid his irritation with imperfect grace as he begged Harrowby to excuse him and promised to pay him another visit as soon as he could.

Once he quitted the room, Sir Humphrey recalled with a start that the rules of politeness had not been observed. He made Mrs. Jamison known to the few in the room who had not already met her. Isabella called to a footman to place a chair for their guest beside Mrs. Mayfield, and Sir Humphrey looked over his group of friends with pleasure.

"Well, here we are then, my dears," he began afresh, once his sister was settled. He folded his fingers over his paunch and beamed. "Very well met, indeed. I have not seen you since the day of our going to see the infant with the mark. I hope everyone is recovered from that incident. The ladies took no serious fright, I hope, for in truth there was nothing to fear."

This statement amused Hester, when she recollected how shrilly Sir Humphrey had shrieked, but they all assured him that they had come to no harm.

"No, of course, you did not," he agreed. "You were all perfectly safe as long as Lovett and I were with you. Were they not, my dear Lovett?"

Lord Lovett sighed and rolled his eyes. "Yes, Humphrey, perfectly safe. But, for my part, I should rather forget the episode. Being beholden to you for my deliverance has grown rather tedious, so I beg you will forgive me if I neglect to thank you again."

He ignored Sir Humphrey, who protested that that had not been his intention and would have appealed to Lord Lovett again for his assurances of the ladies' safety, if Mrs. Mayfield had not welcomed the opportunity to draw attention to herself. She regaled Mrs. Jamison with the palpitations she had suffered that evening on hearing of the danger in which her precious daughter, the countess, had found herself, and did it so loudly as to distract Sir Humphrey from his speech.

She was eager to hear of the candidates the go-between had found, however, so soon she changed the subject, and before too many minutes had passed, the ladies had their heads together over Mrs. Jamison's list.

Hester was sitting in her usual chair, where she could work with her needle by the light of a branched candlestick. The tapers in Hawkhurst House were made of such superior wax that they never spit, and Hester preferred spending her evening hours this way to participating in her family's trivial conversations.

She could not help overhearing the talk around her, however, and her mind wandered in and out of the various discourses. Mrs. Jamison had a tendency to repeat herself, for every young woman she mentioned was either "very amiable," "a polite sort of girl," or from "a very respectable family." They all had enormous fortunes, of course.

The name Mrs. Agnes Hobbes soon emerged. Her father was a master brewer who had made such an enormous fortune supplying the inhabitants of London with beer that he had recently purchased his family a tidy estate at Kingston-on-Thames. Mrs. Agnes was his only surviving child. Whoever married Sir William Hobbes's daughter would come into possession of her sizeable fortune and estate, with a strong possibility of getting a title, when the combination of name and wealth obliterated the source from which the fortune had come.

"From the point of view of prospects, fortune, and connections," Mrs. Jamison said, "no other candidate can approach Mrs. Agnes Hobbes. It is rumoured that her father will be elected Lord Mayor in next year's election."

While the potential brides were being ranked, sight unseen, Lord Lovett whispered bits of nonsense in Isabella's ear. She responded with rippling giggles and an occasional rap of her fan. Harrowby and Sir Humphrey came to sit in armchairs across from the sofa, and Harrowby, who'd been lost in his thoughts, cut into their flirting.

"Now why should that fellow want to blame Marlborough for those shirts, I wonder?"

Lord Lovett quickly took his gaze from Isabella, who pouted at having her amusement spoiled, and said, with an irony undoubtedly lost on Harrowby, "*Could* it be because the Duke is responsible for their pay? If I am not *misinformed*—" Hester had to smother a smile at the way he drawled this word— "the troops receive one new suit of clothing every year as a major part of their compensation. And if these shirts are truly inferior, perhaps they have cause to imagine that he's abused them."

Harrowby snorted, but could not find words to dispute this logic. "I am certain that his Majesty will put everything to rights, now that the matter has been called to his attention. But the soldiers would have been wiser to keep their mouths shut."

Though his back was turned towards her, Hester could almost see the amusement beneath Lord Lovett's reply. "If they *had* kept their mouths shut, I am certain that one of his Majesty's *German* gentlemen would have called the problem to his attention. They must surely be aware of his concern for his English subjects."

"Quite right," Harrowby said, feeling better now that they appeared to be in agreement. "I've never known a king to be so fond."

"Fond, indeed! And loyal, too! Or surely he would have found a way to leave those ugly mistresses behind in Hanover. King George's taste appears to be rather *catholic* in women, if not in religion. Instead of a fair English rose—" Lord Lovett inclined his head at Isabella beside him— "he binds himself to a Maypole with the one hand and an Elephant with the other. But perhaps this reflects some German taste, which we will never grasp."

The English had all been astounded by the unattractiveness of the King's favourites, when Charles II's many mistresses had been so very beautiful. The two ladies who had accompanied George from Hanover were Madame Schulenberg, so skinny as to have been dubbed "the Maypole," and Madame Kielmansegg, whose profusion of chins had earned her the nickname "the Elephant."

Isabella had misunderstood Lord Lovett's nod, which was a compliment to her English fairness and not a recommendation. "I wouldn't want the King to choose me," she said, making a face. "I shouldn't know what to say to him in bed. But I did hear that the Countess of Platen begged him to take her, and he was good enough to oblige."

"I do not doubt his eagerness to *oblige,* my lady. Indeed, the whole clan seems ready to share itself prodigiously. It is his lack of fastidiousness that puzzles me."

Harrowby lowered his voice, though there was no one in the room who did not hear him."I have it on good authority that Madame Kielmansegg is his half-sister,"

Hester was shocked.

Lord Lovett replied, "My point precisely, my lord. A curious taste, indeed. But who are *we* to question the habits of royalty?"

His speech was so heavy with irony that Hester could not doubt his disapproval. But she was dismayed to hear her own relations break out in boisterous laughter. Harrowby tried to smother his guffaw, and Isabella hid her tickled gasp with her fan.

Mrs. Jamison looked as shocked as Hester felt, and Sir Humphrey said, "Well, if she *is* his sister, why don't he acknowledge her? I never heard such scandalous goings-on. Not even with Charles II!"

Indeed, the Stuarts had acknowledged their bastards, given them titles and wealth, and married them to princes and peers, in the way Louis XIV took care of his. It was accepted that every king would have his mistresses.

Why shouldn't George's father have acknowledged his daughter, or George his sister, if that was what she was? The fact that George did not seemed to confirm the charge of incest. There were secrets about this King that made even Hester uncomfortable.

Harrowby and Isabella could laugh at the suggestion of incest, for they were titillated by every notion of sex.

But, if the English people got a whiff of this worst of sins inside the Palace, then many of them would believe that something should be done to bring it to a halt.

Man cares for all: to birds he gives his woods,
To beasts his pastures, and to fish his floods;
For some his Interest prompts him to provide,
For more his pleasure, yet for more his pride:
All feed on one vain Patron, and enjoy
Th' extensive blessing of his luxury.
That very life his learned hunger craves,
He saves from famine, from the savage saves;
Nay, feasts the animal he dooms his feast,
And, till he ends the being, makes it blest;
Which sees no more the stroke, or feels the pain,
Than favoured Man by touch ethereal slain.
The creature had his feast of life before;
Thou too must perish, when thy feast is o'er!

CHAPTER III

Before the fortnight was out, Dudley Mayfield arrived and was immediately shown into a chamber where he could change out of his riding costume into something more appropriate for dinner in town. Then a footman ushered him into the withdrawing room where the family were taking their meal.

Hester and the others put down their forks to greet Isabella's brother, a short, beefy, young gentleman with a large head and his sister's vacant blue eyes. Dudley wore a light brown wig of inferior quality, tied at the nape of his neck, a coat with very few pleats, and a pair of breeches that looked as if they had never been pressed.

After Mrs. Mayfield presented her son, Harrowby seemed happy to welcome his new brother. Since he and Isabella had been married in a clandestine ceremony, foregoing the irritation—and the expense—of a public marriage, he had not had the pleasure of meeting his brothers and sisters-in-law. Hester made no doubt that he would meet them all, as Mrs. Mayfield foisted her progeny upon his purse one by one. Since Dudley was the first, however, Harrowby could welcome him to Hawkhurst House with the expansiveness of a man who had usurped another gentleman's fortune.

In truth, Harrowby had not tired of the attention he received as the Earl of Hawkhurst. Daily requests for preferment and loans from men he scarcely knew had not yet spoiled his appetite for notice, when they were always accompanied by flattery and fawning. He was not offended by the connection between his popularity and his new-found wealth, not when as recently as two months ago, he had been one of the supplicants attending peers' levees.

With a generous wave of his hand, he invited Dudley to join them. While another cover was being brought, Isabella greeted her brother with a kiss and declared herself vastly surprised and happy to see him. His mother offered a cool, painted cheek for his salute. Harrowby recalled his cousin Hester to him and presented the only other person at table, James Henry, receiver-general for the Hawkhurst estates.

Mr. Henry had just returned from inspecting his lordship's property in Norfolk and had stopped in to make his report before going on to Rotherham Abbey. As he stood to make his bow, he cast a cool, assessing gaze over the new arrival, making Hester wonder what he thought of her cousin Dudley. Of the people seated around the table, Hester alone knew that James Henry was the bastard son of the former Lord Hawkhurst, half-brother to St. Mars, and, therefore, Harrowby's cousin.

Watching him from across the table, Hester was reminded of his kinship to St. Mars by his hawk-like features, his admirable sense, and his overall grace. She could not see James Henry without remembering St. Mars and wishing for things that could not be.

The footman returned with a chair and looked to Mr. Henry for instructions. With a nearly imperceptible nod, the receiver-general directed him to set it next to Isabella, then waited for Dudley to be seated before sitting again himself.

As Dudley received his plate, Isabella looked her brother over and exclaimed, "Lud! But something will have to be done about your clothes, if you've a mind to go about with us. That costume looks as if you bought it off a rag-and-bone-man. You'll have to find a tailor immediately if you don't want to be taken for the veriest country bumpkin."

Harrowby cast him a look of sympathy. "Afraid she's right, dear boy. The clothing you have on may be the very thing for the North. Fortunately, I couldn't say. But only the best will serve at Court, y'know.

I can give you the names of a dozen good tailors in London. They are very likely to be busy this time of year, what with the King's birthday upon us. But you mustn't let them fob you off. Just tell them that I'm your new brother-in-law, and your credit will be good until they can track you down at your lodgings."

James Henry discreetly cleared his throat. He leaned forward to add, with a grave courtesy, "What his lordship means to suggest is that, by using his name, you will get the credit you require until you have time to make the appropriate arrangements with your bankers."

"What?" Harrowby glanced up from the bite of eel on his fork. His innocent gaze met James Henry's, and something he saw there caused him to say with a touch of alarm, "Oh—yes. Just so. Can't have you running up too many debts now, can we? Word of that gets around, and you'll never be invited to sit in on a decent game of cards. Have to be good for your debts of honour, y' know. The play at Court is rather deep these days. Odds fish, but it is! You can't sit down to Hazard without two hundred guineas in your pocket at least."

"I'll be going to Court soon, shall I?" Dudley asked, delving eagerly into a lemon and chocolate cream. "How quick before I get a place?"

Four pairs of startled eyes turned his way. Even his mother stared—taken aback by the stupidity of his blunder. Hester, who relished most anything that embarrassed her aunt, hid her enjoyment with a touch of her napkin to her lips.

James Henry caught the movement out the corner of his eye and turned in time to catch her smile. He quirked her an eyebrow, conveying his comprehension to her, if to no one else. Hester fought a rush of shame, which she suffered whenever they shared a thought, for, afraid that he would betray St. Mars, she had lied to James Henry about the highwayman Blue Satan. And with that lie between them she could not be comfortable with his friendship.

Mrs. Mayfield broke into the silence with an embarrassed laugh. "A place at Court! Why, you silly boy, one would think that they grew on trees! They are not so easily come by, I assure you! Nobody comes by a place without they have a very influential person as patron."

"But you said—"

Dudley's mother cut him off before he could expose her further.

"You will see how it's done, Mayfield, after you've been at Court awhile. And you could not do better than to watch how your brother-in-law comports himself with the King. Why there is not a prettier-behaved gentleman at his Majesty's Court than my Lord Hawkhurst, and so I always say."

As Harrowby basked beneath her flattery, she continued, "Then, once you have got the lie of the land, so to speak, and you have got someone to take an interest in your advancement—a *relation*, perhaps, for it is always in a gentleman's best interest to see that his family and his wife's family get ahead—then, perhaps this *generous person* will see what his Majesty can do for you."

Throughout this speech, Mrs. Mayfield had kept one eye on Harrowby to see if her hints had found their mark. So far, they had produced nothing except a congenial expression, so she pushed on.

"Of course, this person would have to have the King's ear. He would have to be a peer with a great estate, else why would his Majesty care about pleasing him?"

As her hints grew even broader, Hester reminded herself that she must not let her aunt's vulgarity get under her skin. There was no one likely to notice it, except James Henry, who must already have seen Mrs. Mayfield for what she was. She avoided meeting his gaze again, however, for fear that he would see her discomposure.

Mrs. Mayfield had almost exhausted her circumlocutions before an idea brightened Harrowby's face.

"I'll tell you who's important enough to get you a place with his Majesty, Mayfield—me!"

"Oh, my lord!" Mrs. Mayfield erupted in raptures, though the energy she had spent getting through to him made them shorter than they otherwise would have been. "You must make your thanks to Lord Hawkhurst now, Mayfield. How fortunate you are to have such a generous brother-in-law!"

Prompted by his mother, Dudley thanked Harrowby, though he seemed confused by what had just transpired. If he had any guile, Hester decided, it was not as practised as his mother's.

"And what else do you think, my dear?" his happy mama added. "A particular friend of my lord's has presented me to his sister, and she has agreed to help you find a rich wife."

"A wife!" Dudley looked horrified. "I never said I wanted to marry!"

"Don't mean to get leg-shackled yet, hey?" Harrowby gave a sympathetic chuckle. "Not ready for the old ball and chain?"

"No!"

"Well, I'd advise you to take cover if that's the case! When it comes to marriage, your mother has more tricks up her sleeve than a comb has teeth. Zounds! But I ought to know!" Harrowby accompanied this witticism with such a loud shout of laughter as to make Hester jump.

At least, James Henry had as much reason to squirm for his relatives as she did, though since he did not know that she was aware of his connection to Harrowby, he could feel free of that embarrassment.

But Isabella seemed to find her husband's joke very merry indeed, and Mrs. Mayfield wagged her finger at him coyly.

"Fie, my lord! You know you was head-over-heels in love with my Isabella. And if it wouldn't make me blush as red as a cherry, I could tell a thing or two about your lordship's courtship of her. But you gentlemen all pretend that you never wish to wed!"

Harrowby winked grotesquely at his brother-in-law, and said, "Your sister is a saucy baggage, who never ceases to plague me o' nights. I haven't had a full night's sleep since I fell into parson's mousetrap."

Isabella and her mother laughed uproariously. None of this banter served to soothe Dudley's horror, though it did divert him long enough to plant the hope that this talk of his own upcoming nuptials was nothing but a bad jest. His expression wavered between terrified doubt and headstrong resentment.

Hester smothered the sigh that a more intimate acquaintance with her family inevitably provoked. Her impression of Dudley was no more favourable now than it had been on first meeting him, during her brief stay at Mayfield Park before traveling with her aunt and Isabella to London. He had been raised with no sense or taste, and she doubted he had the personal qualities to benefit from good instruction if he had received it. At home he thought only of his pleasure in riding and shooting with his cronies, who were no more intelligent or sensible than he. Like Isabella, he had a cheerful temperament provided that everything went his way. He only seemed to differ from her in his propensity to sulk whenever something did not. Although she could sympathize with his resentment over his mother's manœuvrings, she also knew that his main objection to marriage was likely to be the threat it posed to his pleasure.

She could only imagine what James Henry must feel on learning that a part of his father's estate was to be wasted on an undeserving oaf like Dudley Mayfield.

Harrowby was not immediately able to take Dudley under his wing, for the next day he had to attend the interment of the Earl of Halifax in Westminster Abbey. Without a day to lose, Mrs. Mayfield decided to take it upon herself to improve her son's appearance by taking him to visit the shops in the City. Dudley would rather have gone to see a public execution, but since the hangings for this term—six men and a woman—had already been carried out, he consented to accompany his mother after dinner.

Isabella was promised to Madame Schulenberg at four o'clock. Hester was to accompany her, for Isabella had refused to set foot in the Palace again without her cousin's support. Her last experience at a drawing-room given by the Princess of Wales had been a disaster. That evening the King had made one of his rare appearances and had addressed Isabella in French. Weak in any language but her own, she had become so tongue-tied as to embarrass both herself and the King. She had no more understood his German accent than she had been able to reply, so she still did not know if her panicked *"oui"* had been an appropriate response. The King had quickly recognized her dilemma, which was common to most of his courtiers, and with an inclination of his head had dismissed her. But Isabella had vowed never to be caught in the Palace without her own interpreter again.

Mrs. Mayfield was piqued at having to forego a visit with the King's mistress, but her ambitions for Dudley gave her no choice. After expressing her resentment that Lord Halifax had chosen that day to be buried, when Harrowby might have taken his brother into London, she set off, but not before drawing Hester out into the hall to speak to her alone.

With a talon-like grip on her niece's arm, she said, "Hester, see if you can discover how much it will take to win Madame Schulenberg's influence for Mayfield."

"I thought Lord Hawkhurst agreed to speak to the King for Dudley."

"Yes, he did. So you know his intent, and there is no cause for you to refuse me, Dame Right."

"I do not mean to be difficult. I only wonder if my lord would not wish to speak to Herr Bothmar or Herr Bernstorff instead."

Mrs. Mayfield dismissed this notion with a laugh that expressed her fondness for her son-in-law, and her total lack of faith in his abilities. "That will never work, and I shall tell you why. Dear Lord Hawkhurst is so congenial, he is likely to let Mr. Bothmar put him off. That gentleman is besieged night and day with requests for posts, and those are from people who are much more ruthless than Isabella's husband. A simple request will never do the trick, even from an earl, when so many others are paying dearly for the privilege. I have heard a clear three thousand may be required, either to La Schulenberg or to Madame Kielmansegg.

"Besides," she went on, "Hawkhurst will be much happier if we can tell him how it is to be done without he bestirs himself too much. So I want you to bring it up with her today."

Hester did not even try to hide her dismay. "Aunt, I fail to see how I, a mere dependent, can raise such a sensitive subject. Wouldn't it be more suitable for Isabella to introduce it?"

The expression on Mrs. Mayfield's face reflected a continuous battle that raged inside her. She could never bring herself to admit that her daughter did not have the brains to undertake the mission, yet she was determined to keep Hester in her place.

After a few moments' struggle, she finally said, "My daughter, the Countess, must never appear to doubt her husband's ability to pull it off. She must remain above such things.

"But *you,* Hester—you will be expected to contrive for the advancement of your family. Why, I am sure Mrs. Jamison will not help us to find a rich wife for Mayfield without we send her a good haunch of venison—if not the whole beast. Such manœuvrings must fall to the dependents of the great, else where would the money come from to keep us all?"

With that pointed reminder of the fate that might yet be Hester's if she failed to fulfill her duties, Mrs. Mayfield left her standing in the hall.

They would not leave to call on Madame Schulenberg until half past three, but Hester doubted she would have enough time to gather her wits for such an enterprise. How did one go about proposing a bribe?

In the hope that a quiet place would be more conducive to scheming, she left the hall with its marble staircase and headed to a comfortable closet on the first floor, where some of Lord Hawkhurst's books had been shelved. She had noticed that Harrowby never used them, and it was unlikely that any of her relations ever would. She could count on this room's being empty most days, which made it almost hers.

She still could not reconcile herself to her change in circumstances, which had been brought about by Isabella's marriage. In every direction she turned, she saw splendour—marble columns and floors, furniture in satin and gilt, great paintings by the masters, and ceilings on which the plaster had been carved by Gibbons himself. She was surrounded by beauty, clothed in gowns she had never dreamed of—even if they had once been Isabella's—and introduced to some of the most powerful people in England.

It all tasted bitter, though, because it rightfully belonged to St. Mars. And she did not even know where he was.

She was on the point of entering the smallish room when James Henry surprised her by coming out of it. Nearly colliding with her, he looked almost as disconcerted as she felt.

"Mrs. Kean, I was looking for you. May I beg a moment of your time?"

"Certainly, sir." She was taken aback to discover that he must have observed her habits, else he would never have known to look for her here.

He stood aside and let her pass, with that unconscious grace that reminded her of his brother.

"Is there something I can help you with?" she said, turning to face him. She was uncomfortably aware of being in a small space with him alone.

"Yes. I should like your opinion of a gentleman you may have met, a Colonel Potter."

Hester was puzzled by the request, but she answered, "I hardly know him at all. Merely that he is a friend of Lord Lovett's and Sir Humphrey Cove's." She remembered Colonel Potter from the night of Isabella's drawing-room, a man with a frowning disposition, which, in view of the frivolous nature of his hosts, he had tried to overcome. "Lord Lovett brought him once to this house. But I have never been in conversation with him. Why do you ask?"

Disappointment creased his brow. "Colonel Potter has asked his lordship to engage him as his secretary. Lord Lovett recommended him to my lord's notice, but that is all I know about him. I hoped you might have formed an opinion of his character. But you have never spoken to him? Never heard anything said about him?"

Hester shook her head. "The only time I saw him, he was very intent on speaking to my lord. But I did not overhear their conversation."

"You truly heard nothing?" he asked, searching her face. Then, realizing that he had as much as accused her of eavesdropping, he had the grace to laugh. "Pray forgive me. I did not mean that the way it sounded. I simply hoped you might have overheard something that could help."

She smiled. "No. But if it was employment he wanted, I doubt that his conversation was very revealing. Does his interest trouble you for any particular reason?"

He began a denial, but after seeing her skeptical gaze, he sighed, and said, "Yes, it does." He glanced back at the door, before turning to her again and asking quietly, "Did you hear of the trouble in the Foot-Guards?"

"Yes, Sir Humphrey brought us the news. He saw them burning their shirts when he was on his way here. And I read in the news-sheets that some of the soldiers threw their flaming shirts into the garden at the Palace and over the fence at Marlborough House."

James Henry threw another quick look over his shoulder, before saying, with a sober face, "Unfortunately, that was not all. The news-sheets did not report the worst, but it is known in the street. While they were rioting, those soldiers were shouting Jacobite slogans. They called for the Pretender and the Duke of Ormonde and would not disperse until Ormonde appeared and promised them that the shirts would be replaced."

As Hester grasped the reason for his caution, a feeling of disquiet seized her. "Colonel Potter was here with us that evening. Sir Humphrey thought he would want to know about the riot, so he could help control the men. I cannot say that the Colonel showed any concern. In fact, he only left because my lord urged him to do it. Do you fear that he lacks good judgement, or a proper sense of responsibility?"

James Henry shook his head. "No, my concerns are much greater than that." He paused. "The Whigs are saying that the Foot-Guards are rife with Jacobites. They say the former ministry filled the Guards with the Pretender's adherents so that when the rising came, they would turn against King George. There is evidence that this true. At some of the riots this past month, members of the Life-Guards have been heard cheering for James Stuart."

He looked at Hester, his expression very serious. "Whether Colonel Potter is a Jacobite or not, I must protect this house from any hint of treason. Mr. Walpole is gathering evidence, some of which may be true, but some which is sure to be exaggerated. It is my duty to warn Lord Hawkhurst, for he must never be thought to harbour Jacobite sentiments."

Hester wondered if James Henry knew that his own father had been a Jacobite. He must have known something about the former Lord Hawkhurst's sympathies. But St. Mars had sacrificed his own good name to preserve his father from the taint of treason. And his older son would do no less to save the Hawkhurst estates from attainder.

She said, "I would not like to ruin anyone's chance at a livelihood, unless reasonably certain that he does not deserve it. But for the sake of this house, I will promise to discover what I can about Colonel Potter and his loyalties, however little that is likely to be."

He thanked her, and since he had no excuse to linger, he left her alone.

Hester found that her appetite for reading had vanished. She could not think of the welfare of this house without thinking of St. Mars.

She had not given up on the idea that Gideon Fitzsimmons would one day return as the Earl of Hawkhurst, as was his right. And until he was here to protect his estate, then she could do no better than to help James Henry preserve it for him.

At the Palace that evening, they were conducted to the private sitting room where, it was said, the King supped with his mistress every night. The guard passed them through the Tudor Gate, where a servant came to lead them through the courtyard to Madame Schulenberg's apartments on the ground floor, overlooking the garden. Since this was the first visit Isabella had paid to La Schulenberg, Hester did not know what kind of reception to expect from a lady who, many said, was the Queen of England in all but name. But neither she nor Isabella was prepared for the scene that greeted them inside the lady's sitting room.

Neither was the guard, who was accustomed to escorting visitors directly in, when the King's mistress expected them, else he might have asked them to wait outside. He opened the door to her apartment without knocking and halted in his tracks.

Madame Schulenberg was reclining on a sofa, surrounded by a handful of ladies, who were trying to stem her weeping. They moved about her like anxious bees, dabbing at her face with wet handkerchiefs and holding hartshorn beneath her nose. German issued from her mouth in wails. Hester did not need to understand the words to know that the King's mistress was very upset, indeed.

The opening of the door took her ladies by surprise. They turned as one body, but their alarm soon changed to relief. They must have been working over their mistress for many minutes with no success, for they even seemed grateful for the distraction.

Instead of shooing the visitors out, they eagerly beckoned them to come in, while urging their mistress in a cheerful mixture of German, French, and English to compose herself for their sakes.

The guard announced their names and made a hasty retreat. Hester and her cousin stood nervously in the center of the carpet, waiting to see if they would be invited to sit.

While the ladies fussed, their voices chimed in rallying tones.

"But see here, *madame,* my Lady Hawkhurst and her cousin are here to cheer you. You will not wish to miss their visit."

"Just think what his Majesty would say! You would not like him to see these tears!"

"Do not forget that you are here to support him. You must be very brave for his Majesty's sake!"

Reluctant to stare at their hostess, Hester stole a look around the room. This was her first visit to the Palace, and she found it ironically fitting that her introduction should involve a king's mistress. St. James's had not been built for a royal court, but by Henry VIII for his mistress Anne Boleyn, when his Court lay at Whitehall. Since then, it had been occupied by various members of the royal family and was the seat of the English Court under Charles I. Cromwell's men had looted it, leaving none of the famous treasures Charles had amassed, and the Roundheads had used it for years as a prison and barracks. Upon the Restoration, Charles II had ordered it renovated for the use of his mistress, Lady Castlemaine, and his brother, the Duke of York. It had only finally become the official court of England when the Palace of Whitehall had burned to the ground, taking with it all the valuables collected by Charles II, his brother James II, and William and Mary, who had barely escaped the fire with their lives.

The result of all this turmoil, people said, was that the English king was housed worse than any European monarch. Courtiers complained about the plainness of the ceilings and the small size of the rooms. They said it was a disgrace for the King of England to be lodged in such an old, dim edifice when Louis XIV of France lived at Versailles. Hester, who had never seen the Palace of Versailles and did not expect to, had to admit that the little she had seen of St. James's could not compare even with the splendour of Hawkhurst House. But whatever elegance was lacking in the Palace itself was more than made up by the richness of the furnishings in Madame Schulenberg's sitting room.

It was draped in silk tapestries, filled to overflowing with damasked chairs, gilt tables, and porcelain from China, and lit with expensive candles—all provided by the royal commissaries. The gossips said that no sooner had the King's mistresses heard of the Board of Green Cloth and the Great Wardrobe than they had raided them both, adorning not only their apartments but themselves with the glory of dead queens.

The gems that hung about Madame Schulenberg's skinny neck were worth a considerable fortune. Hester believed she had seen the emerald and diamond necklace in a portrait of Queen Anne.

Despite the opulence of her surroundings and the jewels, however, something clearly had occurred to offend the poor lady. The appearance of strangers eventually recalled her to herself. She was persuaded to sit up and take a piece of linen to cool her swollen eyes. As soon as she could speak, she invited Isabella and Hester to sit, while a servant brought them tea in exquisite China dishes. Then, as she regained a degree of composure, she dismissed her ladies, assuring them that she could be left to enjoy her visitors alone.

As La Schulenberg took a sip of tea, Hester saw that her hand was still trembling. Her eyes betrayed a vulnerability that put her age at sixty rather than the forty she allowed.

After that first sip, she hardly touched her tea, which made Hester, to whom tea was still a new and longed-for luxury, fret at the restraint imposed by polite manners.

With the opening courtesies barely observed, Madame Schulenberg reverted to the thoughts that had overset her and still occupied her mind. "I do not underschtand de Englisch," she wailed. "I begged his Majesty not to come to dis terrible country. I told him dat de English are a wiolent race who cut deir kings' heads auf! But he vas assuring me dat de peoples of dat persuasion vere all on *his* sides. He said he vould be perfectly safe! So vy do dese peoples shout at me so and trow deir fruits when I try to go aut? I do not underschtand!"

Isabella's eyes were as round as platters, her nerves too frozen to allow her to respond. So, Hester shook her head for both of them, making suitably sympathetic noises.

Madame Schulenberg continued, "Today, ven Madame Von Kielmansegg and I vere only taking a drive in de park—his Majesty's own park!—some of dese ruffians trew *stones* at my carriage! Vy do dey hate us so? I told dem dat I haf only come for deir goots!"

It took nearly a minute for Hester to realize that Madame

Schulenberg's last expression was an unfortunate peculiarity of her German accent. But before she understood, it had cost her an exercise of will not to cast a jaundiced eye over the goods in the room. If Madame Schulenberg had made the same linguistic error with the crowd, they would have understood her to mean their chattels, which would have confirmed them in their worst opinions of the King and his mistresses, both.

She tried to calm the lady, adding her voice to Isabella's, since her cousin had fortunately found hers.

"I am sure you have nothing to fear, *madame*. You must not forget how warmly you were greeted when you first arrived. And even if there is a disturbance or two, the army is near."

Too late, Hester recalled the recent incident with the Foot-Guards and hoped that Madame Schulenberg would not think she had spoken of the army just to frighten her more. She seemed firmly convinced that the English were about to rise, and that their intention would be to relieve both the King and herself of their heads.

"Jawohl!" Happily for Hester, Madame Schulenberg grasped at these words of comfort. "De King vill make wery sure of de army. He *knows* how to command. He iss a wery great general, and he vill never keep traitors about him. Dey vill see dat he iss not to be fooled."

The notion of the army and his Majesty's military expertise seemed to calm her, enough that she appeared conscious of having uttered an indiscretion. She gave them her most distant smile, and Hester sensed that the intimacy they had reached was at an end.

"I tell *you* dis," Madame Schulenberg said coyly, "because I know dat you luff his Majesty. Lord Hawkhurst and his Countess could only vish him vell. Und perhaps dere is a tiny favour you vould like to ask off him, yes?"

Isabella was about to deny any such motive. But, mindful of her aunt's instructions, Hester hastily exclaimed, "How very kind of you to ask, my lady! Perhaps, you have heard that Lady Hawkhurst's brother, Mr. Dudley Mayfield, has come into town. I know that he would be very glad for a place in his Majesty's household . . . if one could be found?"

Instantly Madame Schulenberg's manner underwent a subtle

change. Her smile took on a keener shape. "A place vit his Majesty? Vut talents does dis gentleman possess? If he is de broder of Madame Hawkhurst, I do not doubt he hass wery many."

Hester was completely unprepared to answer this question, not being aware that any talent was required for a royal sinecure, and not having the slightest notion of any that Dudley had.

It fell to Isabella to supply them, which she did ingenuously. "My brother is very fond of playing at cards, and he shoots and is good with a horse."

A delicate frown marred the Maypole's brow. "I do not tink his Majesty iss in need off any more gentlemen in his schtable. And ve vould haf to ask Herr Von Kielmansegg, who might vish to be disagreeable. But—" the cloud vanished— "perhaps von of de young princesses vill haf him. I shall be happy to inquire."

Hester was amazed at how simply the chore she had dreaded had been accomplished. She was grateful to Madame Schulenberg for offering her assistance, which had spared her from raising the awkward topic herself. Hester even felt ashamed for suspecting the lady of mercenary motives.

Until they began to take their leave—when their hostess mentioned that she had been longing for another lady to keep her company whenever the King was away. Her niece would be able to fill the post, if only she had the funds to employ her. Two thousand guineas would be required, but she did not dare ask his Majesty for the money. He had been more than generous to her already, and in view of the recent disturbances, she would not care to worry him for something the English people might not believe she deserved.

In the end, Hester was obliged to say that she would mention the matter of Madame Schulenberg's niece to Lord Hawkhurst, who, she was certain, would be honoured to fulfilled the wish of such a devoted friend to the King.

After all, why should he object, when he would be using St. Mars's fortune to do it?

Wits, just like Fools, at war about a name,
Have full as oft no meaning, or the same.
Self-love and Reason to one end aspire,
Pain their aversion, Pleasure their desire;
But greedy That, its object would devour,
This taste the honey, and not wound the flower:
Pleasure, or wrong or rightly understood,
Our greatest evil, or our greatest good.

CHAPTER IV

At the end of May—only one month after the Duke of Ormonde's birthday and a week after the incident with the Foot-Guards—Harrowby, Isabella, Mrs. Mayfield, and Hester rode to St. James's Palace in the gilded Hawkhurst coach with the family crest upon the doors. Four perfectly matched bays had been harnessed to pull the carriage through the gates of Hawkhurst House into the dust of Piccadilly. Harrowby would have preferred to have three teams, but the coachman had insisted that, in the expected crowd, six horses would be too many for safety. However, both he and the footmen, hanging onto the back, contributed to the overall splendour of Harrowby's equipage, since they were decked in new livery in the Hawkhurst colours of brown and gold.

The occasion was the first birthday King George would celebrate in his new kingdom of Great Britain. His Majesty's drawing-room was also to be Hester's first real appearance at Court. Mrs. Mayfield would have it that her daughter, the *Countess,* was conferring too great a privilege on her cousin—one that Hester simply did not deserve. More frightened than ever by the prospect of speaking to the King, however, Isabella had insisted that Hester come, and Harrowby, who did not speak French or German either, was perfectly happy to have an interpreter along.

An immediate boon for Hester had been a splendid new dress. This afternoon, as she climbed into the coach and took her place next to Mrs. Mayfield, nervous as she was about her presentation to the King, she wished that my Lord St. Mars could be there to see her new gown. She could not expect to make a dazzling impression on him—how could she, when Isabella would always outshine her? But in her pink, embroidered silk with a neckline scooped low enough to show that, after all, she did have a rather graceful neck, Hester knew that she had never looked so handsome in her life.

The distance from Hawkhurst House to the Palace was not far, but as soon as the carriage pulled into the road, their coachman had to fight the crowd of coaches and horsemen all trying to make the turn into St. James's Street. Then, as they reached the pavement, with the stone walls of houses bounding them on both sides, the clattering of hundreds of hooves, the shouts from angry drivers and chairmen forcing their way through, and the cheers of spectators lining the street were so deafening as nearly to overwhelm them.

Looking out the window, Hester spied banners and streamers waving from the roofs. Cavalry officers in colourful coats trotted by, while sedan chairs and single horses crowded just outside. Every coach had been freshly painted, some with gilt, and glimpses of their occupants revealed a rainbow of new silks and satins, full-bottomed periwigs—some powdered and some not—and well-rouged faces with patches artfully placed. Ladies and gentlemen fluttered their fragile chicken-skin fans, for the day was warm, while others languidly waved their handkerchiefs from fingers ringed in gold. Bishops, ambassadors, and judges nodded gravely from their seats. Feathered hats, lace ruffles, and clouded canes stood in relief against a satin tableau.

As the Hawkhurst carriage inched forward, Isabella and her mother exclaimed at the jewels adorning the ladies in the other coaches. Isabella wore a close-fitting necklace of diamonds set in gold with matching pendant earrings, which had belonged to St. Mars's mother. The buckles on Harrowby's shoes were encrusted with diamonds, rubies sparkled from his heels, and the sword hanging from his hip had a hilt that was jeweled and gilt.

Among the people who had gathered to watch the nobility arrive, Hester spied members of the Life-Guards and the Horse-Grenadiers. They had been stationed among the crowd in both Westminster and London to discourage rioting. Harrowby had learned that morning that constables and beadles were also to be posted at corners to preserve the peace.

Thus far, all seemed well. The watchers, crammed along both sides of the street between the buildings and carriages, cheered mightily for King George, but Hester had no doubt that demonstrations against him would occur in the counties at least. With so many guards on duty here, however, it would be foolhardy for the Jacobites to start a riot.

Eventually, amidst the clamour and the pageantry, their carriage pulled up at the Palace gate. Hester awaited her turn to descend before she was handed out by Will, her favourite footman. A fair, hulking lad, he had the impudence to grimace behind Mrs. Mayfield's back after catching sight of her startlingly dark hair. She had rinsed it with the famous Italian water, which was guaranteed to keep one's hair either brown or black, and while her hair was certainly *one* of those colours, it failed to resemble anything Nature had devised. As Hester gave Will a look of gentle reproof, he cocked a complimentary eyebrow at her new gown, and she found it impossible to remain out of charity with him.

In the very next instant, she had been bustled through the gate, and she forgot all about Will in her excitement. She was gently pushed along with the hundreds of courtiers making their way towards the stairs. The air was full of their perfume. Wafts of minced tobacco occasionally escaped from the gentlemen's snuffboxes, producing some sneezes from the courtiers behind them. As they entered the Great Staircase, nervous laughter echoed down its well, and Mrs. Mayfield called to her daughter to guard her skirt from the gentlemen's swords.

Hester had not expected to be intoxicated by the light flickering from the sconces or the rustling of silk skirts, but she could not deny her pleasure even to herself. Today a greater company than usual had come to Court, attracted not only by the promise of a ball and illuminations this evening, but by the certainty that a failure to appear at Court on the King's birthday would be taken as a serious insult. This was true for any monarch in any year, but particularly now and for this king, for the number of riots protesting George's reign had increased all month, and he was sure to take note of those who had chosen to absent themselves.

As Hester raised her foot to the first step, she heard the palace clock strike one. The immediate boom of guns nearby made everyone jump. An eruption of titters and gasps filled the stairwell as the courtiers recalled the scheduled salute to the King in Hyde Park, but they had hardly settled down by the last of the three volleys.

Nervousness seemed to have affected them all, but soon they resumed the murmurs and laughter that were the usual tenor of the Court.

The King's drawing-room had been scheduled for one o'clock, but the crowds and the traffic had made it impossible for the Hawkhurst party to arrive on time. They could only inch up the Great Staircase—which was truly not so great, Hester thought, as to have merited the name. The marble staircase at Hawkhurst House, with its pillared and arched entryway by Inigo Jones, was far more impressive. Hester began to see why so many courtiers complained that the English kings were not well-housed, but Parliament was highly unlikely to vote money to build a new one to rival the Sun King's any time soon.

At the top of the cramped staircase she found herself in a chamber, which was paneled from ceiling to floor, with hundreds of weapons hung in circles and other patterns on the walls. A few large windows provided the only light by which the Yeomen of the Guard had to examine every visitor to ensure that he had dressed with sufficient grandeur to enter the royal presence.

Hester had no real fear of being refused—not in her splendid new gown, and accompanied by the Earl and Countess of Hawkhurst, even more magnificently garbed—but still she could not help experiencing a moment of unease. She doubted that the King would consider a waiting woman worthy of his notice, even if she was cousin to a countess. She could only hope that no mean-spirited person would inform his Majesty of the post she held in her cousin's house.

They waited impatiently while a few people were turned away. It was expected that everyone purchase new clothes for the King's birthday, and some, either through ignorance or insolence, had appeared in old clothes. A group of gentlemen was admitted, despite the fact that all three were dressed in mourning. It would be impossible for the guard to know if someone truly mourned or if he had dressed in black to protest the Hanoverian succession. Today, the Court was supposed to put off its mourning for Queen Anne, but this week the gossips had reported that the Jacobites planned to dress in black.

A yeoman finally waved the Hawkhurst party through, so they passed through the cramped presence chamber, then the privy chamber—neither larger nor more ornate than the previous room—before turning to enter the drawing-room itself. And there, on a throne beneath a great canopy, guarded by Beefeaters, with the Princess of Wales at his side, sat his Majesty King George.

A hush had already fallen on the gentlemen and ladies in waiting and the guests standing along the edges of the room. The Hawkhurst party was too late to observe the King's entrance, but it must have taken place only moments before, because the poet laureate had not yet delivered his birthday ode. Hester and her family found a little space along one wall and took their places just as the reading began, accompanied by music from the orchestra.

From where Hester stood, she could see the throne. The look of ennui on his Majesty's face made her guess that he found the ode at least as tedious as she did. It was no more fulsome than the prologues read before a play to thank the author's patron for his support, but its blatant flattery naturally robbed it of anything worthwhile. Whether the King understood his laureate's words or not, however, his counselors had insisted on all the forms being observed.

As soon as the recitation was over, Isabella grabbed Hester by the arm. "Come, Hester. Let's get our curtsies over. Once we've paid our respects to his Majesty, we can find our friends."

"And mind you do it properly," Mrs. Mayfield said, giving Hester a vicious poke between the shoulder blades, as she bustled behind her through the crowd.

A low murmur resumed in the room. Until her moment with the King was behind her, Hester hesitated to look around, but she was tempted by the curious sights. His Majesty's "young Turk" as everyone called him, a dwarf by the name of Ulrich, was seated on a perch very near the King's chair, dressed in clothes so fine that they rivaled any lord's. One of Ulrich's many servants, provided by the King, hovered behind his chair.

Isabella's wish for haste could not rid them of the need to wait for their turn. His Majesty's chair was surrounded not only by aristocrats who had come to pay their respects, but by members of his German household. His Turks, Mehemet and Mustapha—who some said were slaves, and others insisted were not—stood behind him dressed in their turbans and exotic robes. They both had been made Grooms of the Chamber, an honour with a handsome salary, which many of George's English subjects would have been glad to have for themselves. Just as some of England's ladies would have wished to be his mistress, if he had not brought his old ones along.

Hester saw Madame Schulenburg standing with her cluster of ladies. She thought the lady standing near the throne and fanning herself from the heat, with chins like stair steps down her throat, must be the King's other mistress Madame Kielmansegg, the *Elephant,* as the scurrilous pamphlets had named her. Hester tried to find a family resemblance between this lady and the King, and to her consternation found one. But, she told herself, there was still no reason to believe the rumour of incest. Not yet, at least. Perhaps it would have been more credible if the lady had been beautiful, but then, Hester did not find the King very alluring, himself.

At the age of fifty-seven, he was past that time of life when every prince would be called handsome. His figure had spread a great deal more than his portraitists allowed, but in painting him slimmer than he was, they had exercised no more discretion than Queen Anne's painters who had trimmed her enormous girth by several percent.

George sat, acknowledging his birthday greetings with about as much pleasure as a rock on a riverbank, as courtier after courtier bowed or curtsied before him. Beside him, Caroline, Princess of Wales, more courteous than he, made introductions and translated painful exchanges between the English subjects and their king.

Before long, it was Isabella's turn to make her obeisance. Harrowby, who had paid his respects that morning along with the officers of state, foreign ministers, and grand nobility, made the King another bow. His mother-in-law followed. Then Isabella drew Hester forward and in torturous French made it known that she would like to present her cousin, Mrs. Hester Kean. The King gave a nod, his boredom most painfully clear. Then, Hester, who had been told by Harrowby precisely what to say, thanked King George in her serviceable French, going on to convey the birthday wishes of all her cousin's family for his long and happy reign.

At the sound of intelligible words, the King visibly perked up. "*Ah, vous parlez français, mademoiselle. C'est excellent.*" He went on to say that he was astonished at the number of his new subjects who did not, and he asked her if she had lived abroad.

Thrown momentarily by his German accent, Hester finally grasped his meaning and replied in kind, "No, your Majesty, I have never left England, but I have applied myself to learning the tongue. I am happy to find it useful."

"French is useful, yes. Better dan dat poetical nonsense ve just heard. But you should ask my daughter-in-law vat she tinks of poetry and so forth."

"Your Majesty does not care for poetry?"

The King turned to Caroline, who had been listening with one ear while engaged in a conversation of her own. Summoned now, she gave Hester a look that assessed her even as she welcomed her with a smile.

"Tell dis lady, *Mademoiselle—*"

"—Kean," the Princess supplied, bestowing an even more gracious smile.

"—vat I tink of dese poets and painters of yours."

His tone was scathing. Hester had the impression that she had walked into the middle of a family argument.

Caroline's smile turned stiff. "I fear the King is not a great admirer of either art."

"Your Majesty does not care for painters?" Hester asked, unable to help herself.

"I hate dem. De only ting vorse iss a poet." He gestured disgustedly at the poor poet laureate. "Gentlemen should find someting vorty to do—like musick—und not try to force deir scribblings on me. Do you tell me you care for dese tings, mademoiselle?"

Hester did not know the proper response to make. She was trying to decide if the King was jesting, when Mrs. Mayfield, who was fidgeting due to her exclusion from the conversation, gave Hester another hard jab in the ribs.

"Make him our wishes, Hester, and don't rattle on so," she hissed.

"I have already paid him your compliments, Aunt, and am now answering his Majesty's question about art."

Princess Caroline intervened in English. "You must pardon your niece, Mrs. Mayfield, but his Majesty is always charmed to meet a young lady who can converse with him with such ease. You must bring Mrs. Kean to see him again."

Hester was forced to hide her smile, as her aunt nearly choked on the protest that sprang to her lips. This was one occasion on which she could not disparage Hester in favour of her daughter.

"Yes, your Highness." Mrs. Mayfield curtsied. "As your Highness wishes, of course."

The Princess gave no sign of having noticed her resentment. She gestured for Hester to bend close, then kissed her on both cheeks. "You are welcome at our Court, Mrs. Kean. Both you and your beautiful cousin.

"But I do not see her." Searching for Isabella, the Princess looked around, and her tone underwent a subtle change. "Oh, yes, there she is—speaking to his Royal Highness, who is charmed with her, of course. You must both of you come to play at cards one evening."

With a half-turn of her head and a graceful flick of her wrist, she summoned one of her ladies standing behind her chair, a tall, fair woman with a tranquil expression. "What do *you* think, Mrs. Holland, my dear?"

The Princess directed the lady's gaze to where her husband stood chatting with Isabella. "I was saying that Mrs. Kean should bring her cousin, the lovely Countess of Hawkhurst, to play with us one evening. Do you not agree?"

The Prince, indeed, seemed to be more than a little enchanted with Isabella. As Hester watched, he chucked her cousin under the chin and whispered something in her ear. Isabella giggled at what surely had been a prime piece of gallantry.

Harrowby was beaming to see his wife so admired by a prince, but Hester thought her cousin would do well not to encourage his Highness overmuch.

No such worry seemed to disturb the Princess of Wales, who regarded Isabella the way a mother might inspect a potential playmate for her son. As she looked for Mrs. Holland's reaction, though, a touch of malice seemed to taint her smile.

Nothing disturbed the tranquility of that lady's face, however, as she agreed with her royal mistress and asked her if she would like her to extend a particular invitation to Lady Hawkhurst.

But the subject was exhausted. The King had lost interest the moment they had switched into English, and noticing his ennui, the Princess waved Hester and her party on. As they retreated from the King's presence, he roused himself to advise Hester to learn German, too. She curtsied and thanked him for his condescension.

Not to like paintings! Hester was still amazed as she and her aunt followed Isabella through the standing ministers and gentlemen ushers to the other side of the room. She had the sinking notion that a great many of the things that had been said about King George might be true. How one could live surrounded by beautiful objects and not admire the artistry that had created them was beyond her imagination. She considered that he might have shown some interest in learning English, instead of resenting his English subjects for not speaking French. Since last autumn, when George had been crowned, the news-sheets had carried advertisements for books that could teach one German, but she vowed to ignore them. She wasn't certain that she wanted to learn it, if it would mean that she would be called upon to entertain the King.

She tried to hide her disappointment with the King, as ladies and gentlemen parted for the Earl and Countess of Hawkhurst and their retinue. Hester had not got used to sharing this glory—though the number of gentlemen who came daily to pay their respects to Harrowby, attended both Harrowby's and Isabella's levees, and haunted Hawkhurst

House in the evenings had begun to accustom her to her cousin's importance. Even here at St. James's where nearly every peer was in attendance, their attention was still solicited, for Harrowby was rich, and many would hope that by flattery or persuasion, either Isabella or he could help them get a place at Court. They would have to wait, however, for Dudley to get his first.

After their visit with Madame Schulenberg, Mrs. Mayfield had passed along that lady's message about the money that would be required to support her niece. With skillful manipulation, Mrs. Mayfield had managed to make it sound as if the King's mistress had asked for it before any mention of Dudley had been made. And Harrowby, as gullible as ever, had come away with the impression that La Schulenberg had requested the favour of him because she knew she could depend on his loyalty. The sum was not small, but Harrowby had swallowed his protest and had ordered James Henry to see that it was paid. Hester was glad she had not been around to witness James Henry's reaction.

With so few days between his arrival and the Birthday, Dudley had not been able to arrange for suitable clothes to be made in time. All the tailors had been rushing to complete orders they had already received, for not only were the courtiers to be dressed, but their servants in new livery as well. Dudley might have resented missing today at Court if he had not heard of the public ball at Lambeth tonight. With that area's reputation, Hester could not imagine the level of rowdiness and lewdness that he was likely to encounter. She preferred *not* to imagine it, but the prospect had not appeared to daunt her cousin at all.

They had progressed only a little way down the room before they met Lord Lovett. He was with Colonel Potter, who looked as dour as before. The two made a space for them, Lord Lovett taking a place behind Isabella where he could whisper into her ear, and Colonel Potter pinning Harrowby to himself.

Hester wondered what Colonel Potter had done after leaving them on the night of the riot. She recalled her promise to James Henry to try to discover his political leanings, but here, the opportunities for overhearing would not be great. They had to stand while others were received and to keep their voices low since the occasion was strictly ceremonial.

She was standing next to Isabella, so she overheard most of Lord Lovett's attempts to entertain her. Though he had not acknowledged Hester's presence, she was very aware of him. He had dressed with his usual magnificence, choosing not to powder his black, shoulder-length peruke. He had the good taste to know that black became him, with his heavy, dark brows with their cynical arch, his striking white skin, and thickly lashed eyes that were as deep a blue as violets. Tonight he had set these off very well with a habit of black satin embroidered with silk and jet beads. The glistening threads traced a pattern of birds and leaves over his waistcoat and coat.

He seemed unaware of his own handsomeness as he whispered compliments to Isabella, provoking outbursts of laughter, which she had to suppress.

"I trust you have paid your respects to his German Majesty?" he inquired, on a sardonic note.

The change in his tone made Hester glance nervously around her, but no one had heard him except Isabella and herself.

"Yes." Isabella pouted at the disagreeable thought. Then she lifted a hand to send her softly spoken words back to him. "At least, Hester did. Lud, but I'm glad she speaks French! I don't know what I should say to him otherwise."

"Mrs. Hester speaks French?"

Hester could not prevent herself. She ventured to peek at him over her shoulder.

Lord Lovett was staring at her, obviously startled by the news. A sweeping gaze took her in thoroughly for the first time that day, and he seemed to remark the changes in her hair and clothes. With a bow, and a quirk of his eyebrows, he signaled his appreciation of both her appearance and her achievement, which provoked an unexpected flush.

She turned back to face the throne as he said, in his lowest voice, "I shall have to keep her French in mind, then—shall I not?—in case the admiration I feel for my Lady Hawkhurst inspires me to utter indiscreet words of love."

Isabella gave a delighted gasp, before smothering it.

After a few moments Lord Lovett resumed talking, and now Hester had the feeling that he was speaking to her as well as her cousin. "It will not be easy having a monarch who cannot speak our native tongue. Let us hope that his Majesty's tutors will soon correct the problem.

"Did the King *converse* with you, Mrs. Kean, or did he simply wave you on as he does the more provincial among us?"

Hester did not know whether Lord Lovett numbered himself in that group, but she answered softly back to him, "He did speak to me . . . of his regret that not more of his subjects spoke French, and of his dislike for poetry."

"Alas . . ." Lord Lovett's sigh made her struggle to hide a smile ". . . it's no wonder, then, that poor Mr. Gay has been cooling his heels on the Backstairs for so many weeks, in spite of a truly admirable ode to the Princess. And here he imagined it was because she had requested it in Hanover and he had taken too long to write it. But, in all justice to Mr. Gay, a poet must be inspired."

Leaning closer to Hester, he asked, "What else did his Majesty say?"

"That he is not fond of paintings either."

Still facing the Court, she could only imagine the humourous twist on his lips, when he hissed, "Hélas, indeed!—as I am persuaded King George would say, if he could share the sentiment. Except in Hanover, of course, when one presumes he speaks German and not French. Are we to go without paintings, too? I fear this *will* be a reverse."

Harrowby, who was standing to Hester's left, must have heard this remark for he shuffled uneasily. Hester glanced over at the Colonel's face and saw his sneering grin.

Harrowby sidled closer to address Lord Lovett. "Well, I'm sure that if his Majesty don't like 'em, then none of us should. Hey?" He gave a nervous laugh, which quickly turned into a cough.

Lord Lovett conceded this with a sober inclination of his head, but the arch of his brow belied the gesture. "Very reasonable, my lord, I am sure." He was whispering more loudly now. "We must none of us wish for anything his Majesty chooses to disapprove. Such loyal sentiments will serve us all in good stead." Then, under his breath he added, "And though some of us might wish him otherwise, we shall undoubtedly have to make do."

Hester felt a touch upon her hand, and when she turned, he was giving her a look of mock reproof. "I hope *you* did not presume to be disappointed, Mrs. Kean, to find that our new king does not have—what shall I call it—a taste for the arts?"

"I can hardly be disappointed, my lord," she answered quietly. "I do not have the means to acquire paintings, even if I had the walls on which to hang them. And I am so new to London and its riches that I may be content for a long while just seeing the paintings that have already been produced."

"A politic answer. But are the artists of our day supposed to starve?"

Hester hesitated before replying, "I believe they may find a friend in the Princess of Wales, sir."

Lord Lovett gave an enigmatic smile. Then, he turned to Isabella and seemed to forget Hester entirely. Still, she could not help feeling gratified by the attention he had shown her.

She heard him clearly when he asked Isabella, "Has my lady nothing to say on the subject? Should she not wish to have her portrait painted by an Italian master, attracted to our Court by a generous patron? Say . . . a portrait of my lady as Venus?" He accompanied this gallantry with a touch on her waist.

Isabella parted her lips and gave a sigh. "Oh, yes, if you would help me to choose the artist, Lovett."

"But did you not hear Mrs. Kean? The painters in the kingdom are all to be banished. Now, if I were brave, I could find it in me to *fault* his Majesty for an opinion that would rob us of the pleasure of having my lady immortalized." Lord Lovett drew closer to Isabella to whisper directly in her ear. "I could wish he had never come. But how were we to know what a barbarian he would be?"

While he had been talking, Hester had grown increasingly restless. The tenor of his remarks had gradually changed, escalating in rancour, and now they had left the realm of humour to cross into what might be considered sedition. She could only pray that no one but herself had overheard his last comment. She thought she was the only other person near enough to hear. His words had been uttered in the low, seductive tones of a lover. At least—they had seemed like a lover's to

Hester, who had never had one herself. She could appreciate Lord Lovett's seductive skills, however, for what woman would be able to resist a gallant with the courage to express seditious sentiments on her behalf? Alone herself, and merely an eavesdropper, she had not been able to suppress a thrill at the sound of his voice.

She could not even blame Isabella for wanting to flirt with him.

That evening at the ball, the etiquette was more relaxed, but Hester felt exhausted long before it started. She had never stood for so many hours on end, and there would be no respite until the ball was over. The only promise of relief was that it was supposed to end at ten o'clock, since the next day was a Sunday, and everyone must arrive at home by midnight to avoid offending the Sunday ban on travel.

She would not be offered the chance to change her position, for she could not dance. There were too many ladies present, and the couples were formed by rank. She understood that at many Court balls there were not enough gentlemen to go around, so those who did attend had to dance several minuets until the ladies had each had a turn. But tonight there were gentlemen in abundance, so that would not be the case.

With such a crowd, and the orchestra squeezed at one end of the room, the available floor space was small, so only a few couples could dance at once. Isabella's and Harrowby's friends had gathered around them to gossip while they watched the dancers perform. Isabella had already danced her turn, and Hester could see that she was bored now and impatient to leave, but they were trapped until the King chose to end the celebration.

The Princess loved to dance and did it very gracefully. Those who had not seen her dance before were astonished to find that she wore slippers instead of heeled shoes, and their surprise circled the room with the speed of an ignited fuse. When it reached Hester, in the form of a shocked exclamation from her aunt, she was at pains to conceal her amusement at their interest in such a triviality. She did not know her reaction had been observed until Lord Lovett spoke at her elbow.

"You do not find the Princess's shoes to be as riveting a subject as the rest of us do, Mrs. Kean?"

She jumped at his low voice, then turned to see his arched brow questioning her. She felt warmth stealing up her neck, but she could not honestly say that she was displeased to have his company.

"I *have* noted that there is more concern in this room for what everyone else is wearing than there is for—" She had been about to say *the strength of the realm,* but she realized in time that the phrase would not be suitable to the occasion.

He seemed to divine the blunder she had narrowly avoided, for a corner of his mouth turned up. "I see you have their character precisely. What was it Dean Swift used to say about the Court? I have lost his exact expression, but something to the effect of what infants they all are. Always grabbing and biting their friends and fighting over cakes. He never ceased to complain of the inanity of their conversation until he was banished to Dublin, but I understand that he would give his soul to be back among us, nonetheless."

With a nod, he guided her attention across the floor, where the Duke of Marlborough was holding a court of his own. "Even the powerful have been banished for a while, but as you perceive, they always return. What do you say about Marlborough's chances now? Do you think he will fall out of favour again?"

"Should he?"

The Duke had been blamed for the Foot-Guards' inferior shirts, but he had explained the error by which they had been made and had sworn to replace them with all possible speed.

"You think he is loyal?" Lord Lovett sounded amused. "But he has been known to correspond with the Pretender, too. I wonder which side he will choose if James appears. Indeed, which side would any of them choose, and yet . . . *here* they all are."

The King's officers *were* all here. His standard had been displayed throughout the day, and his troops had carried out the formalities due on his birthday. His Grace of Marlborough had come more splendidly dressed than the King. He was also better housed than the King, if reports on the building of his manor were true. After his victories over Louis XIV at Blenheim and Malplaquet, a grateful Parliament had awarded him a fortune, in addition to a grant of royal land from Queen Anne. It was said that he was constructing a house as grand as Versailles to stand as a reminder that it was *his* might and *his* talent that had beaten the Sun King. Sarah, his duchess, never ceased to complain about the architect Vanbrugh and the slowness of his work, but it was a different complaint of hers that came into Hester's mind now.

Lord Lovett's questions about the Duke reminded her that, according to the Duchess, the promise of funds had never been fulfilled. She had repeatedly appealed to Parliament, but no matter how grateful the people had been after the Battle of Blenheim, Marlborough was no longer their favourite, so her complaints had fallen on deaf ears.

The peers surrounding him now were Whigs, where once they had been Tories. But that was before the Tory Party had pushed for a peace with France, which the Whigs had opposed.

The peace had brought its own troubles, of course, with soldiers flocking home only to find themselves without pension or pay. But they had a new champion now in the Duke of Ormonde. He, also, had been a general in the war with France and had always been popular with the troops. Handsome and dignified, he had an amiability that could easily undermine the appeal of any couple as arrogant as the Duke and Duchess of Marlborough.

Here, surrounded by his supporters, though, Marlborough could feel secure in the King's estimation. Not so, his Tory rival. Ormonde had come this evening, yes. Hester had spotted him in a shadowy corner near the entrance, deep in conversation with a lady. But a pamphlet had circulated since the riots, criticizing him for allowing the mob to use his name. Everyone said that Mr. Defoe had written it as a friendly warning to Ormonde to renounce his Jacobite friends, the men behind the riots, if he did not want to lose his good name and anger the King. To Hester's best knowledge, Ormonde had ignored the plea, keeping silent about the riots. She wondered if he simply relished the evidence of his popularity. But it was true that the more crimes the public committed in his name, the greater the risk that he would be blamed. King George had already removed him from his command. And Ormonde was certainly not loved by the current ministers, or by that ambitious gentleman from Norfolk, Mr. Robert Walpole.

Hester became aware that Lord Lovett was waiting for her response.

"You asked if his Grace ever need fear banishment again. He does not appear to have that worry now," was her safe reply.

His look upbraided her for a cowardly response. Then, changing directions, he brought them back onto safer ground.

"We have yet to establish the extent of your affection for the Court, Mrs. Kean. Would you care to be banished?"

Slanting a look at him, she tried to assess the seriousness of his query, but his sardonic expression confounded her.

"Are you asking if I could give up the Court, now that I have experienced it?" she said.

When he only shrugged, she thought of a dream she had often indulged herself with and sighed. "I can imagine a situation in which I could remove myself from the Court and from London without the slightest hesitation or regret, but since that particular situation is never likely to arise, I admit, I should hate to trade all this activity for a quiet life somewhere else."

"Do you not fear being banished for your impudence?"

She knew that he was teasing her, and took pleasure in the notion, but recalling his earlier comments, she thought she should give a prudent answer.

"It would be unwise for a woman in my place to complain of anything here, my lord. Or to laugh at anything either."

"Oh, you mustn't worry that I shall betray you, Mrs. Hester. It is a pleasure to find a woman with good sense. Shall I confess that, until very recently, I was unaware of the cleverness concealed behind those placid, grey eyes of yours?"

Hester tried to hide her gratification, but she felt a smile digging mercilessly into her cheeks.

Fortunately, Harrowby and Colonel Potter chose that moment to stroll up, and since they were in the middle of a discussion about the horse Harrowby planned to enter in the horse matches next week, Lord Lovett joined them before she had to respond. His final look was so provoking, however, that Hester's heart quickened its pace.

With the gentlemen standing next to her, she could finally listen to Colonel Potter's conversation. He seemed amazingly well-informed about Lord Hawkhurst's business. The questions he asked had the air of being rehearsed. Clearly, he was doing his best to impress Harrowby with the talents he could bring to the post of secretary.

Lord Lovett had introduced the Colonel into their house, however, and the things his lordship had said today made Hester wonder where his own loyalties lay. In the past two weeks, he had grown much freer with his jokes about the King, but so had many others as the ridicule in the streets had spread into the houses. Even Harrowby had been known to giggle at the King's expense.

Was Lord Lovett, with his clever tongue, simply indulging himself and his friends with a bit of harmless truth? Or was there something more serious behind his jests?

She did not know anything of his circumstances, merely that he held a barony in Scotland, which was hardly likely to support him very well in town. He often dined at his friends' expense, as gentlemen with minor fortunes frequently did. With his clever mind, she would rather have seen him engaged in worthier employment, but the sound of Isabella's unrestrained laughter reminded her that very few peers or their wives ever turned their attention from pleasure to endeavour. There would always be people so wrapped up in their own entertainment as to be impervious even to the tensions that could erupt around them and ruin their lives.

Isabella was certainly one of these. And Sir Humphrey appeared to be, too, as he joined them with his busy gestures and his usual breathless excitement.

He knew everyone, of course, and greeted them with affection. He seemed not to notice the frown with which Colonel Potter acknowledged him.

He had not been with them a minute before a tall, elegant lady came up behind him and touched him on the sleeve. In a heavy French accent, she said, "Ah, Sir Humphrey, here you are, my dear. How charming to see you! Will you present me to your friends?"

A French accent was not entirely surprising at Court, with so many foreigners about. Sir Humphrey greeted her cheerfully, declaring that he had been meaning to seek her out, but she refused to let him forget the introduction she had requested.

He presented Lady Oglethorpe, first to Harrowby and Isabella, then to Mrs. Mayfield and Hester. "You already know Lovett and Potter, of course."

The two gentlemen made their bows. There was a stiffness in Colonel Potter's, however, which Hester was at pains to comprehend. In the very carelessness of his introduction Sir Humphrey had implied that they knew Lady Oglethorpe well, that in fact they were friends and not merely acquaintainces. Yet her proximity seemed to make Colonel Potter nervous, as if he would rather have had the power of denying her. Hester might have questioned her instinct or taken herself to task for a fanciful imagination, if the Colonel, who had stuck stubbornly close to Harrowby all evening, had not soon excused himself.

He took Lord Lovett with him, and they disappeared into the crowd.

If Lady Oglethorpe was in any way offended by their departure, she did not let on as she latched on to Isabella. "I was fortunate to find Sir Humphrey with you, for I have been wishing very much to meet the enchanting Lady Hawkhurst I have heard so much about. And now that we have met, you must promise to visit me. My house is in the Palace Yard. You must come to take tea with me and my daughters—or better—come in the evening to one of my drawing-rooms."

Isabella made a polite reply, though it was clear to Hester, who knew her cousin well, that she would rather have kept her former companions over this one who, despite all her cordiality, was only a female.

Noting the direction of Isabella's gaze, Lady Oglethorpe added, "You are certain to meet your friends at my house. Lord Lovett and the Colonel are often there."

Isabella's interest was engaged at once, and she listened more attentively, as Lady Oglethorpe asked, "Do you follow the King to Hampton Court?"

"We plan to go. My lord is riding with his Majesty to Guilford to see the horse matches on the seventh. He says we shall have to spend some of the summer at Rotherham Abbey, because it will be expected, but we don't wish to leave the Court for very long."

Hester found herself wincing at her cousin's comment about

Rotherham Abbey, since Isabella made it sound like a burden instead of the undeserved privilege it was. And Hester was kept from forgetting the blunder by the sight of Lady Oglethorpe's knowing smile. "Of course you will not wish to distance yourself. The Court is vastly more diverting than the country. And, besides, you would not wish to lose any influence you might have with the King. Have you asked the Princess of Wales for a place?"

"No." Isabella could barely hide a shudder, so it was fortunate that none of the Princess's ladies were near enough to see her. "I shouldn't like to be in waiting—having to stand all the time would be horrible."

"But, *ma chère,* you must think of the power you could wield! The Princess does not know our country yet, and it is certain that her ladies have already helped their families with their influence—not to mention the places they have already got. Why, Lady Cowper has just secured her brother-in-law a post worth three hundred pounds a year! You should really try to get a place in the Palace, my dear, though I know how difficult it can be. My daughter Molly was refused a place, and she would have entertained his Majesty much better than Lady Cowper does, for all her virtuous airs. *Or* that spoiled little creature, Lady Mary Montagu, who boasts of her intelligence to all who will hear. But Molly *would* involve herself with the Marquis of Wharton and his rakish friends—which was a very grave error, and so she has learned.

"One can never be too careful in the choice of one's friends, *madame*. But with your husband well established in his Majesty's affections, I am certain he could get you a place with the Princess, even if she took a violent disliking to you. The Prince has foisted his favourite mistress upon her, and she could not refuse *you*, if the King willed it."

Mrs. Mayfield had pushed near them to hear. She had listened to her ladyship's advice with avid attention, particularly to the part concerning the influence Isabella could use to her family's advantage. But Mrs. Mayfield would never allow the slightest disparagement of her daughter, even unintentional, to go unchallenged, and so she huffed, "As if her Highness would not adore my little girl, like everyone does! Why, what can your ladyship be saying? My Isabella is loved wherever she goes."

"*Mais naturellement!*" Lady Oglethorpe was taken aback by this unexpected assault. "I did not mean to suggest otherwise, *madame.* You misunderstand me. I meant only to suggest that it is expedient to use the influence one has, while one still has it, *n'est-ce pas?* One cannot know how long a king will reign, or how long one can hold onto his affections. Your daughter and son-in-law would do well to take advantage of the chance they have been given."

Mrs. Mayfield inclined her head in a manner that would have been regal, had there not been too much offence behind it. "I am sure my daughter will appreciate your ladyship's advice, should she ever need it. But she is so well-placed with our dear Lord Hawkhurst for a husband that I doubt she will ever be in need of anyone's help."

Lady Oglethorpe's look conveyed both scorn and incredulity. "I do not believe the former Lord Hawkhurst ever doubted his security, *madame,* and yet he was banned the Court. A powerful name is no shield against treachery. But—" she peered past them— "I see someone I must speak to now. *Madame la comtesse—*" she offered her cheek for Isabella to kiss and included Harrowby in her smile— "I hope you will come to see me, for I should love it above all things."

In the next moment she had left, and it was only then that Hester noticed how many people had watched this exchange. Indeed, she had the impression that the Whigs in the room had found the sight of Lady Oglethorpe's being kissed by the Countess of Hawkhurst more than a little disturbing. She could not be certain of the reason, but she wondered if it had anything to do with the fact that Lady Oglethorpe was the lady she had seen in the shadows, conversing with the Duke of Ormonde.

Let Earth unbalanced from her orbit fly,
Planets and Suns run lawless through the sky;
Let ruling Angels from their spheres be hurled,
Being on Being wrecked, and world on world;
Heaven's whole foundations to their centre nod,
And Nature tremble to the throne of God.
All this dread Order break—for whom? for thee?
Vile worm!—Oh, Madness! Pride! Impiety!

What if the foot, ordained the dust to tread,
Or hand, to toil, aspired to be the head?

CHAPTER V

Throughout the month of May, Gideon had kept himself occupied with improvements to his estate. Whenever these failed to fill his loneliness, he tried to combat it in other ways, throwing his energy into the chase and taking comfort from the horses, dogs, and birds of prey that hunted with him.

At this time of year, the French nobility would be found at Versailles, but he had no wish to join them. He had paid the obligatory visit to Louis XIV immediately upon his arrival in France and had left for St. Mars as soon he could without giving offence. It was not that he had found Louis's court unsympathetic. On the contrary, the aristocracy of France had embraced him and petted him for his losses. But he knew how fickle they could be, and he would not stay until their favour turned to jealousy. Nor did he want to partake in the petty joustings for power either at Versailles or at the Stuart court at St. Germain.

It was near the end of that month that the people he had been avoiding came to St. Mars.

He had spent the morning in the mews and out in the fields, training a young hawk to hand. The brown of its feathers, glinting gold in the sun, reminded him painfully of home. These were the colours chosen by the first earl of Hawkhurst to honour his house, a manor built from the ruins of an abbey, which stood on a high piece of Wealden ground where the Saxons had observed hawks in flight. Since that first earl had been rewarded by James I, every Lord Hawkhurst had hunted with hawks.

Keeping birds of prey was no longer a fashionable pursuit. Gentlemen would rather cavort in London than spend the time in the country that it took to train a bird. Patience was required, but Gideon, who had never been known for his patience, had been robbed of his other distractions.

Returning to the chateau in the early afternoon, he once again applied himself to the ceremony of dressing for dinner alone. He was shrugging himself into a blue *justaucorps*, when a lackey came to inform him that two visitors had arrived.

"*C'est le Marquis et la Marquise de Mézières,*" the boy announced, breathless from his run.

Gideon paused, with his fingers still gripping the collar of his coat. Then, with a queer beat of his heart, he resumed, straightening his sleeves and giving a tug to the lace at his wrists. Noting the sudden pallor of his cheeks in the looking glass, he took a deep, steadying breath and said, "You may tell them that I shall be with them directly. I trust you have made them comfortable."

"*Oui, monsieur le vicomte.*" New to his duties, the young lackey appeared worried. He had been hired from the village when Gideon first appeared, and was clearly unaccustomed to tending to the needs of such illustrious company.

In spite of the knot in his stomach, Gideon managed an encouraging smile. "I am certain you did. Now, tell the *maître d'hôtel* to lay two more covers."

He returned to his dressing table to don a full-length peruke, which he would have left off, if eating alone, and pondered the meaning of this visit. The names of his visitors surprised him. Yet in a sense they were inevitable, too, for ever since reaching St. Mars, Gideon realized, he had been dreading this very meeting. Unconsciously, he must have been expecting it, but for weeks he had only been willing to face the present, not to recall the recent hurtful past or to consider how his father's death might dictate his future. Now, there was no way to avoid them. Nor should he be surprised, given the position his father had held in the Pretender's schemes.

The Marquise de Mézières, née Eleanor Oglethorpe, came from one of the most prominent Jacobite families in all of England. Her parents were so well known for supporting the Stuarts that many believed that James himself was their child. As the myth went, he had been smuggled into St. James's Palace in a warming pan to provide James II and his Queen with a Catholic heir when the king's own baby died of convulsive fits. One reason for the story, undoubtedly, had been the birth of an Oglethorpe baby—a son, also named James—only a year before the royal prince's birth. This Oglethorpe, therefore, was nearly the same age as the Pretender—the same age as Gideon, in fact, who had known him briefly at Corpus Christi College where many Jacobites sent their sons.

So, no. No Oglethorpe had posed as a Stuart to aspire to the English crown, no matter how hard James's enemies tried to keep the myth alive. But neither was there anyone more devoted to the Stuarts than Lady Oglethorpe, so it had not been too far to imagine that she would give her own child to the last Stuart king.

In Gideon's opinion, she had done the equivalent by seeing to it that all her daughters had been raised to devote themselves entirely to the Stuart cause. The two oldest, Anne and Eleanor, had been raised as Catholics at James's court. Another—Fanny—had been sent to live with Eleanor just two years ago to be instructed in the rites of Catholicism by a priest close to James, who was heavily engaged in Jacobite intrigue. Meanwhile, their mother, known as "Old Fury," remained in England, going to Court and conniving for the advancement of her brood, even as she schemed to overturn the throne.

And now her second daughter had come to see him. The moment had come when he would have to decide what his role in James's cause would be. He only wished that his head and his heart were as undivided as his father's.

He found the marquis and his elegant wife awaiting him in the salon. Tall, slender and, clearly, more French than English, Eleanor stood with her husband to greet him. In spite of his caution, Gideon could not suppress a spark of admiration for Eleanor's beauty, which at thirty was still striking. She had been blessed with the same noble features as her brother—etched lips, an aquiline nose, high cheekbones, and large, wide eyes.

Her husband could not have been more the opposite. Short and thickset, with very rounded shoulders, he had a yellowish face with soft prominent features, which gave him a mien like a frog's. He seemed entirely unconscious of his ugliness, however, and bowed with the air of a man who believed himself very attractive indeed.

It was his wife who, after an apology for coming unannounced, a polite inquiry after his health, and brief condolences on the death of his father, first broached the subject of their visit. She did it while sitting on the edge of a chair, her skirt spread in a wide, smooth circle about her ankles in the manner of a queen on a throne.

"His Majesty requested us to be his messenger in conveying his sympathy and sorrow on the loss of his faithful subject, Lord Hawkhurst."

In Jacobite circles, the title *Majesty* was given to James Stuart, even if in England to call him thus was a treasonable offence. In England he was politely referred to as the Chevalier de St. George, a title which had been conferred upon him by the King of France.

"You may tell his Majesty that I am grateful for his attentions, as I know my father would have been."

"Your father served him most generously. His Majesty knows that, and—"

"Does he also know that my father died in his cause?" Gideon had tried to keep the resentment out of his voice, but both his tone and his question disconcerted his visitors. Eleanor was quick to conceal her surprise. She had, after all, been raised from birth to conceal.

"The facts about your father's death are not *generally* known. Nevertheless, his Majesty and his most faithful servants are aware of circumstances which the present government of England has chosen to ignore."

"Are you saying the government knew I was falsely accused and did nothing to prevent the injustice?"

"We have reason to believe they suspected it, but have no wish to pursue a matter which has resulted in such an advantageous result for them."

"I presume you refer to the awarding of my father's title to my cousin Harrowby—because he is a Whig?"

Eleanor inclined her head. On anyone else the gesture would have been a simple assent, but she filled it with insinuation.

She struck Gideon as a woman without humour, but with a purpose both dangerous and indefatigable. He had the feeling that he faced a formidable will. Whether he could trust her, he was not at all sure.

"His Majesty regrets the losses you have suffered. And he pledges to restore your properties to you when he regains his throne."

"Please inform him of my gratitude," Gideon said, returning nod for gracious nod.

His visitors had clearly expected a more demonstrative response. Eleanor was too poised to reveal her disappointment, but the marquis glanced at his wife, as if seeking her lead.

She responded by asking Gideon if he was aware of his countrymen's feelings with respect to their new monarch. He told her that a servant was forwarding the news-sheets to him, but that he had not been in a frame of mind to give them much of his attention.

"Then you may not be aware of the current situation. Eugène-Marie—" she turned to her husband with an outstretched hand—"Let *monsieur le vicomte* read the latest news from London."

The marquis reached into a deep coat pocket and brought out several folded news-sheets, which he and his wife held out for Gideon to see.

The sections they showed him related news of riots throughout the months of April and May, in Oxford and in London. The most recent one in London had taken place over a period of two days in Cheapside, before the Royal Exchange, and at Smithfield, mimicking the one that had occurred a week before, on the anniversary of Queen Anne's coronation. The disturbances seemed both greater and more frequent than in previous months—with one important difference.

"So it is Ormonde they love now." In last year's riots, it was a non-juring priest by the name of Sacheverell, stripped of his pulpit for delivering a sermon against the Hanoverian succession, who had won the people's sympathy.

"That should not surprise you," Eleanor said. "His Grace of Ormonde is a loyal servant to his Majesty King James." When she continued, her manner demanded a response. "The people are ready for their deliverance from the German usurper, *monsieur.*"

"Perhaps, *madame*, but why do you come to tell *me?"* Gideon knew what her answer would be, but he wanted her to stop playing at cat and mouse.

"We have come to tell you that, if you mean to exert yourself in the cause of our rightful king, then the moment has come. At this very hour, his generals are planning to retake his kingdom. We must not discard this chance! Too many opportunities have already been lost. We still have the generous support of his Most Catholic Majesty Louis XIV, but he cannot live much longer. When Louis is gone, it is not at all clear that a regent will give the same support to our cause."

"I am not a Roman Catholic. Nor do most of my countrymen wish to be."

Eleanor gave an irritated shrug. "That does not matter in the slightest, *monsieur*. His Majesty will respect the wishes of his people. He only desires their welfare. But naturally he expects the right to adhere to his own faith, which is strong."

"He will not insist on bringing Great Britain under the authority of Rome?" In James's declaration, he had promised to seek bulls of absolution from the Court of Rome for anyone who would have to perjure himself to come to his aid. The bulls were promised to be executed "in due Form of Priestcraft" at "only reasonable fees." Gideon wondered how the Pretender could imagine that those phrases would fail to offend his Protestant subjects.

"You have his Majesty's word. What more could you wish?"

Gideon could have replied that he wished for much, much more. For proof that the quest she wanted to engage him on would succeed. But he was not fool enough to believe that any such venture would come with a guarantee.

"What does his Majesty want of me? I am an outlaw in England. I cannot move around the country freely in his or in anyone's service."

"And, yet, you managed to conceal yourself very effectively there, and to leave without being captured, *n'est-ce pas?* He asks only that you will bear a message for him, and perhaps visit some of his faithful subjects to alert them when the plan is ripe. They *must* be ready when the time comes. The whole country must rise as one, yet we do not know when that moment will be.

"The Duke of Ormonde is the person who must decide, and he has not called for the rising. Nor has he informed his Majesty when he should make for the coast. You could be of great use to his Grace in spreading the word. His Majesty would like you to put yourself at the Duke's disposal and to report back to him about the Duke's intentions."

When Gideon did not respond immediately, Eleanor turned to her husband again. A private look passed between them, and the marquis pulled out another sheet of parchment. He handed it silently to Gideon, who recognized the Pretender's declaration, the one he had read every day since arriving at St. Mars.

The Marquis de Mézières pointed his short, broad finger at the paragraph that had kept Gideon staring up at his ceiling night after night.

A full pardon could be his. Indemnification from the charge of murdering his father. A crime he had never committed, which had robbed him not only of the father he loved, but of everything else.

A chance to return to England. To reclaim his home.

For the hundredth time, Gideon asked himself how else he would ever regain it and heard only silence for a response.

Eleanor spoke with all the passion she had barely managed to hide, "His Majesty sends us with the message that he is perfectly convinced of your innocence, and that, should you agree to help restore him to the throne that is rightfully his, he shall return all that is yours to you."

Gideon's heart swelled with a gratitude he could not deny. How could he help but warm to a prince who believed in his innocence? Who knew what it was to have his patrimony stolen out from under him? The similarity between his situation and James's was so strong that it had to provoke his deepest sympathy.

But Eleanor had not finished speaking and her next words chilled him.

"And, in addition," she said, "he promises that in return for your help he will make you a duke."

So. James did *not* understand. No more than he had understood Gideon's father's loyalty. Which reminded Gideon that if he engaged himself upon a task for the Chevalier, it would be entirely at his own risk. That was what his father had done, and it had led to his death. Gideon had no value to James beyond what he could achieve in fulfilling James's own goals. He would promise anything to anybody—and had repeatedly—to regain his crown. His adherents were mere pawns in this game.

And, yet, there were other feelings Gideon had not been able to ignore. One in particular, which would always cloud his choices. Guilt—because he had refused to embrace the cause for which his father had died.

With a sense of fate, he raised his eyes. "You may tell . . . his Majesty . . . that I will do what he has asked. I will carry his messages, as long as his cause remains feasible. I do not engage myself to die in his service—not yet at least—but I shall go to England to gauge the progress of his cause and report it to him. You may assure him that his secrets will be safe with me and that I shall never betray either him or his agents."

Eleanor had started to glow with the success of her mission and began impulsively, "You will not regret the decision you have made, *monsieur*. There is no more generous master than our sovereign James III. Why—"

Gideon raised his hand in a gesture that was firm but polite. "Forgive me, *madame*, but my message is incomplete."

He saw a flash of anger in her eyes. Eleanor was not the person to accept anything less than full compliance with her designs.

Gideon continued, "You must make it clear to his Majesty that I shall not enter upon any activity that puts our countrymen at needless risk, nor will I continue with his missions if I believe his cause has become hopeless."

She bridled. "Then how do we know you are to be trusted?"

The marquis laid a restraining hand on her wrist. She feigned to ignore it, but Gideon could see that her husband's reminder had had its effect.

"I have given his Majesty my word, as my father did before me. If James—and you—" he said, with emphasis— "truly believe in my innocence, you should have no doubt of its worth. The conditions I've put forth are the same that my father's were."

When she did not unbend, he added in a soothing voice, "I have no affection for Hanover George, *madame*. I doubt that any of my countrymen do. Some pretend it undoubtedly to raise their family's status—some things will never change. But I am attached to the welfare of my countrymen and I will not do anything to bring a scourge upon them."

"You insult our king, *monsieur!*"

"*War* is the scourge I mean—not James. If the throne cannot be easily won—if our countrymen's hearts are not firmly with James—then I will not wage war against them. James said in his declaration that he wanted no blood shed on his account. He called for a peaceful uprising. Do you understand me, *madame*?"

Gideon was not particularly surprised to find that she did not, but she tried not to show it. His answer had to satisfy her for the moment, for she was not a person to waste even the slightest opportunity. Her sense of diplomacy, which must have been learned at a Stuart's knee, soon reasserted itself.

"I am certain we shall soon understand each other very well, *monsieur*. Now, may I inform you of the steps his Majesty wishes you to take?"

So—James had been reasonably certain of obtaining his services. But that was not surprising. What might have astonished him was Gideon's reluctance to act when he had so much to gain. James undoubtedly would have put it down to cowardice, instead of to its real motive—uncertainty about what was right and just.

"I shall be only too happy to hear them, *monsieur et madame*. But, first—" Gideon abandoned all notion of his solitary meal— "If you will do me the honour . . ."

Once Gideon had decided to go, it took him only one day to prepare for his journey. After riding to the coast of Brittany, he left his horse with his groom to be returned to St. Mars, and took ship for Boulogne, where bales of smuggled English wool lined the docks. There, following the instructions given to him by Madame de Mézières, he transferred immediately onto a French sloop, captained by a man by the name of Larouche.

The whimsical channel was eerily calm, so they managed to sail with that day's tide. The small sloop was hardly bigger than his own yacht, which was moored beyond his reach at Deal. Once they were underway, Gideon resigned himself to enforced idleness for the duration of the voyage. He wrapped a heavy woolen cloak about him and gazed over the bow at the pale grey water, inhaling the chill, salty spray as he pondered the task the Pretender had given him.

On his person he carried two notes, one curled and inserted into the stem of a pipe, the other folded and sewn into one of his buttons. His mission was to speak to the Duke of Ormonde and discover when he planned to start the uprising. Jacobite agents had been busy recruiting men from London to the Highlands of Scotland and priming them to be ready when the signal was given. Rabble rousers had been at work, inciting the mob. The Pretender needed to know when and where he should land. Exiled as he was at Bar-le-Duc in Lorraine and dependent on his half-brother, the Duke of Berwick, for news—when Berwick was always away from Paris in the service of his sovereign Louis XIV—James was desperate for direct communication with his subjects in England. He knew that he could not ask men to risk their lives in his cause unless he was prepared to lead them himself. But with a price of one hundred thousand pounds on his head, he could not afford to land when he might fall into the hands of his enemies.

Gideon could understand James's frustration. His own property had been taken from him unjustly and bestowed on another man. Whatever he had felt about his inheritance before—whether he had taken it for granted—no longer mattered. He had discovered his unwillingness to abandon what was his. And so, like many of the Pretender's followers, he had decided to put ambition before safety in the hope of gain. But he had refused to pledge unconditional aid. He would have to see for himself first what the mood of the people was, and this could not be got from the news-sheets, no matter how many riots were reported.

The captain of the sloop steered a course for a spot well south of Dover, where the castle's huge cannons protected the coast. The little vessel was swift. The French could design them to out-race any larger ship that might set out in pursuit. In a matter of just a few hours they came to anchor in a bay off Kent, far enough from shore not to be seen, to wait for dark before meeting the smugglers from the English side.

This close to home, Gideon found his impatience very hard to contain. The hours that remained seemed interminable. At the same time, they would be insufficient to decide his course. He had given his word to James Stuart to assist him if his cause was right. What might constitute *right* would not be easy to judge. Whether a king's right to his throne was something no mortal could take away, as his father had believed, or whether it could only be bestowed by the people he ruled, was too great a matter for any one man to determine alone. And, yet, there were principles that Gideon was sure he would always uphold, things that in his mind would always supersede the divine right of kings—compassion for his people being the highest amongst these.

Too many times in the century just past, wars had been fought over kings' rights and men's beliefs. In the end, had any of them been worth the misery they had caused?

He wished he could simply cherish a quest for its own sake and not constantly question its worth. But he would not be able to commit himself unselfishly to any cause until his own problems were solved. Until then, his desire to clear his name and to regain his freedom would surely be paramount.

Seeking relief from his quandary, Gideon turned from the gunwale just as the Captain walked over for a chat. Larouche was puffing on a pipe and, as if noticing Gideon's impatience, offered him another from his pocket.

"Here, *monsieur*. If you smoke one of these, the wait becomes more tolerable."

Gideon declined. He had never taken the habit of smoking or snuff. Another reason why Isabella Mayfield had not found him attractive, he supposed, since carrying a snuffbox was so very fashionable. But the smell of smoke had never appealed to him, and he did not care for the way the oily snuff soiled his fingers and clothes. Besides, he distrusted anything that was reputed to dull the senses.

With a shrug of indifference, the captain looked up at the moon. He muttered a curse. The moon was much too large and shone too brightly for their purpose tonight.

Aware of the man's discontent, Gideon asked, "If your business causes you such worry, then why do you do it?"

The captain darted a hostile glance his way. "We are not all allowed to choose our walk in life, *monsieur*. Most of us follow the paths our fathers have laid down."

Startled by this simple truth, Gideon wondered if that was all he was doing—following the path his father had laid. If that was the case, it would only lead to his death.

He was about to ask Captain Larouche about the need to follow a predetermined path if it might lead to dishonour or death, but in that instant, a light flashed from shore.

Larouche quickly smothered his pipe. "We must ready ourselves for visitors, *Monsieur* Brown. The men will unload before they take you aboard." He gave Gideon one last glance. "If you have not entered your country this way before, you will find that they work with their faces blackened. You should darken yours, too."

As the captain left him to prepare to receive the boats that would be coming out, Gideon pulled his black half-mask from his pocket. His tricorn and the voluminous collar of his cloak would hide the pale yellow of his hair.

It was still another half-hour before a cry came floating up out of the dark, in a carrying whisper from off the starboard bow. Captain Larouche's crew scrambled to catch the ropes that started to thump on the deck, as they were cast from the little fleet of boats below.

Then, strong, sinewy arms heaved bale after bale of raw English wool onto the sloop until every hole was filled and every surface covered. Smaller packages of finer goods were passed back down. Gideon spied what he supposed to be bundles of silk and lace. Crates of tea and barrels of brandy joined them over the side. When the exchange had been made, all but one of the boats set off for shore while one of the smugglers climbed aboard.

He was dressed in a shepherd's smock that reached to his knees. His hair was covered by a snug woolen cap, and his rough country face had been blackened with coal. He and the captain settled their accounts by the light of a lantern held cautiously below the level of the sloop's side. The lantern was of a style Gideon had never seen, its flame sheltered by a curved piece of metal. It must have been built especially for smuggling, since viewed from the shore any light it threw would seem too soft to have come from a lamp.

"Well, that does it," the smuggler finally said, raising himself to go.

As he pocketed his papers and his money, Captain Larouche gestured for Gideon to come forward. "I have one more piece of cargo for you. This gentleman needs passage ashore."

Now that he'd moved nearer, Gideon could see that the smuggler's face had been severely marked by the smallpox. He measured Gideon with a shrewd look. "One of his Majesty's men, eh? Well, yer welcome, though I warn ye, I charge the same for cargo whether it be quick or dead."

At Gideon's prompting, he named an exorbitant price which Gideon disputed, even in his trapped circumstances.

"Take it or leave it," the man said. "I would hate to disoblige his Majesty, God bless 'im, but I'm not in it fer him, ye see. And you gen'lemen are a risky cargo I can't sell. What I will do is this," he said, after a moment's reflection, seeing the negotiations might cost him the tide, "if ye want to stick with us as far as Cranbrook and help us unload, I can take ye for less."

Gideon knew he could not risk being seen in Cranbrook, which was too close to Hawkhurst. He might easily be recognized by the smuggler's customers, and, besides, he needed to make his way farther north. Captain Larouche had told him that these men were part of the Mayfield gang, and Mayfield was in Sussex, far from his route. They would be creeping ashore in the marshes near Lydd, then packing their contraband inland as fast they could ride. Gideon would need to part from them almost immediately to head into his part of the Weald.

He had been tempted to enter England without Tom's knowledge.

He did not want to draw him into any treasonable activities. But Gideon knew that Tom would fret so much at his long absence that he might even decide to head for France. When he didn't find his master where he expected, Tom would be frantic, and Gideon hadn't been able to reconcile his conscience to that prospect.

He shook his head at the smuggler's offer and, with no further discussion, handed over the amount the man had originally asked. "I shall need a horse."

The smuggler agreed to take him somewhere he could hire one, so Gideon wasted no more time before climbing over the side into the waiting boat below. A few seconds later, the smuggler joined him, and before the boat had stopped rocking, they were underway.

His crew plied their oars expertly and quietly. Orders given even this far from shore had to be issued in soft whispers. Hearing the soft slap of the waves against the side of the boat, Gideon reflected on how different his escape from England had been.

Gideon had boarded a merchant vessel in London on a day so heavy with fog that he had barely been able to see his hand in front of his face. The ship was carrying a load that had not been entered at the Customs House, and the captain had formed the intention of slipping past the sentinel at Gravesend. Under cover of the thick, grey air, and hiding behind the scores of larger ships that crowded the Thames, they had escaped the sentinel's notice until drawing even with the block-house, at which point he should have been firing his second warning shot across their bow. Then, catching a strong ebb tide under full sail, they had quickly flown past the cannons both there and at Tilbury-fort, where the warning had been heard too late.

Gideon had relished the speed of that escape. Its mad rush for freedom had been like racing his horse across a wide, open field with the wind raking his scalp. But silence had been the order on that journey, too.

This night-time row into unseen danger was much too slow and too quiet for his liking. How could the smugglers tell what awaited them on shore? The government had recently assigned excise men and dragoons to ride these coasts. On this moonlit night, how could they know that they had not already been spotted? And, if they had been seen, where was there to run? They could do nothing, but keep rowing towards the narrow beacon of light that guided them towards home.

As the sea gave way to marsh, the owlers, as smugglers were called, went over the sides to wade in the cold, brackish water up to their waists. As they went in, they even managed to splash quietly. They pulled the boats forward with ropes until the bottoms scraped against sand. That was when Gideon first spied the pack horses waiting, hidden between the dunes.

No orders were issued aloud now. Every command came as a hand signal, though few were needed as the men went rapidly about their work, transferring bundles, kegs, and wooden crates to the backs of the waiting animals. They bustled Gideon ashore, too, signaling him to keep his hat pulled down and his head bent low. Unaccustomed to standing about while others were active, he waited awkwardly for them to finish. As he leaned into the sandy shelter of a dune, he noticed that all the smugglers were dressed alike, from the length of their smocks to the tiny barrel of spirits each wore on a rope about his neck.

If a man was caught with his face blackened this near to shore, he was assumed to be a smuggler and would be taken with no questions asked. That was the law.

The same would be true for Gideon, if he was caught. He was entering his country as a traitor, when before he had only been suspected of treason. To some there would be little distinction, but the difference to him was vast. He only prayed to be able to realize when his actions were causing more harm than good.

In hardly more than a trice, the horses were loaded, and the fleet of boats put out to sea. They would lie on the beach at Lydd, right under the noses of the officials, until needed again.

Gideon was pointed to one of the pack horses. He counted himself lucky that more goods had been smuggled out than in, leaving a beast for him to ride.

The caravan started its trek westward across the marsh, the local animals sure-footed in both water and sand. Then they turned inland, following the great ditch that divided Kent from Sussex. The shelter of its walls should hide them, unless a Riding Officer divined their route, but there was too much coastline and too few men assigned to the task of patrolling it for that to be likely. The owlers rode in single file, their sturdy horses keeping a regular pace. They had to hurry to reach cover before the sun lightened the sky.

They followed the ditch for only a few miles before climbing out to head north over low-lying ground. The only reason Gideon could imagine for this risky move was that they had a delivery to make. He did not like feeling exposed, and had just pulled the corner of his hat farther down on his face, when a shot rang out from the left.

There was cry. One of the smugglers fell off his horse.

Another one shouted, "After him, lads!"

In a split-second, three men took off at a gallop in the direction of the shot. They dropped the leads to their packhorses, and other men hurried to grab them up before the frightened animals could bolt.

Gideon's first instinct was to ride after the men. Not only was it in his nature to act, but he feared that the smugglers might kill the man who had fired. It was most likely a Riding Officer or one of the dragoons, and neither deserved to be murdered for doing his job.

But the horse he'd been given to ride was a pack animal, not a saddle horse, and he soon realized how futile pursuit would be. He looked about for something he could do and saw that, in the haste and confusion, the owler who had been shot lay untended upon the ground.

He urged his horse in that direction, dismounted, and, holding fast to his reins, helped the wounded man, who was struggling to rise.

In the dark, and with the man's face blackened, he could not make out his features, but he helped him to sit. Then, when the smuggler spoke, Gideon realized it was the leader he had met on board the sloop.

"Did they catch him?" he said, in a terse voice.

"I don't know. But I haven't heard a second shot."

He felt the man relax. "They'll catch him, then. He didn't have but one of his pistols loaded, else he would have let off another. No sign of Dragoons?"

"No."

At Gideon's short syllable, the man looked up, as if only then aware of the person who had come to his aid. "And you didn't take off when you could have neither. Well . . . I'll have to buy ye a drink for that. Come on, then. Get me up on my horse."

He did not seem to be badly wounded. The bullet must only have grazed him, for he used both arms with no sign of difficulty. It was too dark for Gideon to see any blood. Gideon helped him into the saddle, then remounted and followed the remaining group of smugglers as they rode back in the direction from which they had come.

After less than a mile they were rejoined by the three who had ridden off in pursuit. They were pulling a Riding Officer behind them, tied on his horse. He had been gagged and blindfolded, but from what Gideon could see, he had not been harmed.

"Shall we leave 'im tied up somewheres?" one of the men asked.

"No, just point his horse shoreward and turn him loose. We'll be far away before anybody finds him."

Gideon had kept his face well-hidden during this exchange, but his hand had moved to the handle of his loaded pistol, ready to prevent a murder. Relieved that he was not dealing with a group of cutthroats, he released his hold on his gun.

As the Riding Officer lurched to the east, hurried on his way by a slap on his horse's rump, Gideon felt a touch of pity for the man. If there was a thankless task, it was the Customs job. No one respected the work they did, neither commoner nor peer. The men he was riding with tonight were likely farmers who only wanted decent pay for their wool, but they were thwarted by the Customs laws.

As soon as the government man was out of sight, the smugglers reversed their course again. Gideon wondered if their dialogue had been designed to deceive the Riding Officer about their destination. His suspicion was confirmed when the gang rode to a nearby inn, with the sign of the Woolpack, just above Romney Marsh and turned their horses into the yard. They quickly unpacked their goods into a cellar with an outside door.

"Don't you worry that the Dragoons might search this place?" he asked, as he and the leader dismounted. Gideon saw that the smuggler favoured one leg, so he offered him his arm.

As the innkeeper opened his door, the smuggler answered, "They'll be too busy looking for us south o' here. And by the time they get 'round to searching—when they've lost our trail—all them things ye saw 'll be packed under the church down the road. We'll come back and move 'em inland later, when things settle down a bit."

The two men left Gideon in the half-filled taproom while the innkeeper ministered to the smuggler's wound upstairs. He had taken a grazing shot to his thigh. His horse had reared, he claimed, else he never would have taken a fall. Gideon ordered a glass of French brandy, which was brought to him without the slightest hesitation. Then, his companion rejoined him, and they sat near the fire to sip the fruits of a previous night's work.

After a few appreciative swallows, the smuggler introduced himself as Gabriel Tomkins, bricklayer by trade.

"I won't ask for *yer* name," he said, with a shrewd look. "I doubt ye would part with yer real one, not in the sort o' game yer in. His Majesty's men are usually that close. But 'round here, except for that fellow who took a shot at me, I don't have any need to worry. These honest folk are glad for the goods I bring 'em. But I would hate to be tooken up for yer line o' work. So we'll just leave it at that."

"And, yet, on the sloop you seemed sympathetic to King James."

"Well, he's our king, an't he? And he's better'n this lot we've got on the throne right now." Gabriel raised his glass in a salute. "Here's to his Majesty King James III." He tossed the wine back. Gideon noted that Tomkins didn't bother to lower his voice, and yet no one in the taproom took exception to his toast.

"Are the people hereabouts for James, then?"

"Oh, not all of us, I reckon, but nobody loves the Turnip neither. Now if there was a magistrate in here, I wouldn't be so free and easy with my toasts. Most of 'em are Whigs now."

"If James were to come to reclaim his crown, how many people in this parish would rise to fight with him?"

Gabriel's grimace was revealing. "Well . . . I don't know as any of 'em would. Unless he had a great, big, hulking French army at his back."

Gideon questioned him with a look.

"I mean, they'd sort of have to then, wouldn't they?" Gabriel spoke without the slightest trace of irony. "If he had an army behind 'im, it would be better to join 'im than to be against 'im, which they're not. They just want to be left to mind their own business, which is what every man needs to do if he wants to put grub on his table, and don't want to be strung up with his arms thrown over here and his legs t'other way and his head up on London Bridge. No—" he shook his head— "I don't know as anybody's fool enough to risk that unless he had an army behind 'im—or better—out in front." He gave a chuckle. Then as he raised his glass again, he seemed to remember Gideon's connection with James's cause, for he cocked him a sideways glance and a rueful grin. "But I'll raise my glass to yer king, and no offence meant, so I hope none taken."

A mightier Power the strong direction sends,
And several Men impels to several ends:
Like varying winds, by other Passions tost,
This drives them constant to a certain coast.
Let power or knowledge, gold or glory, please,
Or (oft more strong than all) the love of ease;
Through life 'tis followed, even at life's expense;
The merchant's toil, the sage's indolence,
The monk's humility, the hero's pride,
All, all alike, find Reason on their side.

CHAPTER VI

After hiring a horse from the innkeeper, Gideon rode to Pigden, arriving at the Fox and Goose so early in the morning that the dew still coated the grass. On his way, he was treated to the bright green leaves of spring and the pink and white blossoms of cherry, hawthorn, and crab-apple. Even with the many doubts that plagued him, he could not help feeling happy to be back in Kent.

Avis, the tow-headed stable boy, greeted him with his usual cheer, but he cast a disparaging eye at Gideon's mount. "Y' should see the one that Mr. Barnes bought ye. He's a right sharp prancer, he is. Not like that bone-shaker yer on."

"I'm relieved to hear that Tom has been keeping himself busy," Gideon said, handing Avis his reins. "But you needn't worry that I mean to foist this beast on you. I wouldn't stand his gait for another minute if he were the last horse on earth. But I will ask you to return him to the Woolpack at Lydd for me. Where's Tom?"

Avis had no need to answer, for at that moment Tom came hurtling down the stairs into the yard. The extreme relief on his face changed quickly into a scowl, which made Gideon laugh.

"So, there you are," Tom grumbled, before adding a belated, "sir. I was afeared you'd been swallowed up in that Channel. You might have let me know you'd be coming so I could make things ready for you."

"And miss one of your scoldings? When they are one of the few pleasures remaining in my life? Now, why should I want to do that?" Gideon crossed the yard to clap Tom on the shoulder. He was happier to see Tom than he wanted to admit. "Come and help me off with these boots. We have a few things to discuss."

Upstairs in his bedchamber he found ample evidence of the work Tom had done. And Katy, too, Gideon realized. He would have to compliment the girl on her skill, for surely Tom had never managed to arrange all this finery on his own.

His new feather bed had been hung with velvet curtains. A wash-hand stand with a ewer and basin, a dressing table with a damask-covered stool, and a console with pewter candlesticks had been added since he left. He crossed the room to open the armoire and found its shelves filled with coats, shirts, undergarments, and periwigs, all waiting as if he had left them there himself.

With a sense of wonder, he realized that he felt as if this place were his home. Unsettled by the thought, he did not know whether to shudder or laugh.

He returned to the bed and stretched out so Tom could pull off his boots. Then, before he could break the news that he meant to leave again, Tom told him about the stranger who had visited the inn.

"So Lade offers shelter to Jacobites," Gideon mused. He turned on his side and propped himself on one elbow. "I shouldn't be surprised to hear it, knowing how violent his reactions are whenever the Pretender is mentioned. You say this gentleman questioned you about me?"

"Aye . . . and he seemed awful eager to meet you, too. I didn't like it one bit."

"Hmm . . . . Still, I don't think there's anything to worry about. He would hardly want to draw attention to himself. And if he were to discover who I am by chance, I could easily report *him* as a traitor. That might even earn me a reprieve." He thought aloud, "I wonder what his mission was."

"Seems like he comes through two or three times a year. Lade says that whenever he's around, there's sure to be trouble up in London. And the worst of it is that he acts like he owns the place." Tom gave an indignant snort.

"Well, I imagine he was the only gentleman stopping before we moved in, so he was used to having all of Lade's attention."

"But that blackguard wanted to put him in your room! I told him it was taken for the year, and that everything in it was yours. And I told him that he had no call to order the servants about for they're yours now, too."

"He ordered *you* to wait on him?"

Tom eyes became strangely evasive. When he finally gave an answer, he nearly choked. "No, it was Katy—the wench. He asked for her to be sent up. *But you put me in charge* and I won't have such goings on in a gen'leman's house! It's not seemly!"

Gideon raised a brow. There seemed to be more to this story than Tom was willing to tell. When his groom returned him a glowering look, though, he merely smiled. "Unseemly? Well, I'm sure you're right. I shouldn't like Lade to turn my chamber into a bordello while I'm away. Besides, he would attract more strangers with an inducement like that."

His answer helped to soothe Tom's embarrassment. Then, to change the subject, and because he needed to get back on the road as soon as possible, he asked Tom if he'd heard anything about the disturbances in London or anywhere else around the country—whether, for instance, he had seen any sign of unrest when making trips into Maidstone.

"No." Tom's blunt response reflected his astonishment on being asked. "I haven't seen nothing like that, my lord."

Gideon knitted his brow. "According to some very influential people, a goodly part of the country is ready to rise for King James."

"You're not going to mix yourself up with any of that, are you, my lord?" Tom's eyes filled with horror.

The only answer Gideon could make him was, "I'm afraid I must go to London, Tom." He rose reluctantly from the comfortable bed, ignoring both his desire for sleep and Tom's stammered protests. "I have to find someone and speak to him—without being recognized, of course. I shall have to wear a disguise."

"I don't like the sound of this, Master Gideon. Not one bit. What if we're spotted?"

Now, he had to meet Tom's gaze. "I shall not be taking you with me." Gideon went quickly on to stem the argument that was sure to follow. "I know you want to go, and I shall send for you if I decide to stay. But chances are, I shall be riding straight back to France. And two men are more noticeable than one."

"Except when that one has a price on his head! Aye, and speaks like a gen'leman, who wouldn't travel without he took his servants with him!"

"That can't be helped. You have my word that I shall send for you if I decide to remain for any considerable time. And, if I do, then I am certain to want you. Now—let's see what sort of clothes Katy has made me."

Searching through his garments, he found a sober coat and breeches that looked precisely the sort of thing a Mr. Brown would wear. It required no more than a few finishing stitches from Katy to make it fit, while Tom looked on with a sullen eye. A short, bobbed wig, in a style a viscount would rather die than be seen in, would complete Gideon's costume, along with an application of powder to his face and ashes rubbed into his eyebrows to make them a charcoal grey. Dressed like this, he knew that no gentleman or lady of his acquaintance would waste a moment's glance on the common figure he would present.

As Katy packed up a few shirts, some plain cloth cravats, drawers, and stockings, he went to examine the new horse Tom had found for him. It was a strong gelding of over fifteen hands with a gentle temperament, but Tom assured him that the horse could go.

"Just you put him through his paces, sir, and you'll see. Don't let him fool you, neither. He's not as meek as he looks. He's got a spot of mischief in him, which I'm sure you'll like."

Tom refused to elaborate, so Gideon put himself on guard to be ready for the horse's tricks.

Before leaving, he did not forget to pay a visit to Penny, his mare, sired by Mr. Darley's Arabian. She stomped and whickered angrily when she saw him.

"Still irked with me, my love?" Gideon asked. "But I thought we were agreed that you are much too pretty not to be noticed. Are you giving her enough exercise, Tom?"

"I don't go risking my neck over ditches with her, if that's what you mean. But I let her have a good run every time I take her out."

"Poor beauty," Gideon said, as she dropped her head affectionately into his hands. He rubbed her soft velvet nose and whispered in her ear, "I'll come back soon, and then we'll have a good jump or two. I promise." Like most grooms, Tom disapproved of jumping a horse and saw no use in the exercise, but the danger in it could not fail to appeal to Gideon, and surprisingly, Penny agreed. But, perfect as she was, he could not risk being spotted on her.

Two months ago, her beautiful copper coat had been recognized when Gideon had stopped his cousin's coach disguised as a highwayman. This event had given rise to the name Blue Satan, a result of the blue satin cape he had worn. Fortunately, Mrs. Kean and his old coachman had covered his tracks, claiming that the highwayman's horse was a bay, but Gideon could not risk being seen on such an easily spotted animal. It sometimes seemed that even the few things he had managed to bring away from his home would be taken from him, or at least the pleasure of using them. He tried to keep it foremost in his mind that James had promised to restore him fully to his place.

He left that evening, giving Tom a purse of gold and silver coins with which to manage Lade, and promising to send news of his whereabouts. His last glimpse of his faithful groom showed a man who had nothing to do but fret.

It was not Gideon's intention to drive Tom away, but he could not help believing that it would be best if Tom grew tired of waiting for his master to be settled and tried to find another life. Particularly now, when Gideon had to worry what might become of his faithful servant if he were ever caught acting on the Pretender's behalf.

Over the next day and a half, as he rode towards London, he was pleased with his new horse's endurance. Preferring not to stop at too many places on the road, and satisfied that his mount could stand the distance, Gideon ended by riding it all the way. He entertained himself by trying to think up a name for the horse, but for a while nothing seemed right. Then, on the second day, when Gideon stopped to eat at an inn, his horse shied at the sight of a pig, wallowing in its pen.

When the horse followed this with an attempt to bite the pig through the fence, Gideon called him a *great looby*, so Looby he became.

They traveled on to London, where Gideon's first risk would come in crossing London Bridge. Moving up its narrow street, he would be thrown amongst nearly every man, woman and child coming out of or going into the City. Gideon found it hard to keep his gaze straight ahead, concerned that he might be spotted by someone he knew.

It was not until he spied the two stone towers guarding the bridge, that he was struck by the thought that, if he were ever discovered carrying James's note, his head would be stuck on a pike and left up there to rot. Looby checked in response to his involuntary motion, and Gideon tried not to blanch as he urged the horse forward.

As the jumble of ancient buildings clustered at the Bridge-foot came into view, the traffic on horse and foot increased. Passing under a set of timbers that had been nailed to keep a pair of the houses from coming down, he fell into conversation with a man beside him. As soon as he ascertained that his companion was a vintner, he immediately declared himself a wool merchant, and he crossed the bridge, discoursing on the evils of Customs as they affected the sale of wool abroad. Then, before too many minutes had passed, the outlawed Viscount St. Mars, with a price on his head, rode into the City of London with no one the wiser.

He stabled his horse at one end of Cow Cross and took a room at the White Horse, which was far enough away from the sheep pens at Smithfield to avoid the worst of their stench. He might have stayed closer to his destination, but the streets about Smithfield offered a particular convenience for outlaws, with their twists and turns to aid in escape.

Gideon ate his dinner at a local cookshop and purchased a few news-sheets to see what news he had missed. Apparently there had been quite a fuss about the Foot-Guards' new uniforms, for the Duke of Marlborough and the factor who had undertaken to provide them had each taken the trouble to publish a vindication of his role in the scandal. Gideon was aware that the Foot-Guards contained a number of Jacobites, but he failed to see how these complaints could benefit James.

Then, something far more important caught his eye. An advertisement for a pamphlet on *The Conduct of his Grace the Duke of Ormonde, in the Campaign of 1712*, which could only be an attack on him by the Whigs. He read further down that the Tories had responded with *A Vindication of the late Queen Anne, of glorious Memory; of his Grace the Duke of Ormonde, and of the late Ministry.* But the fact that the Whigs had turned the same attention on the Duke that they had on Lord Bolingbroke, a former Tory minister, before his impeachment, was an ominous sign.

Ormonde was in danger. Gideon did not know if the government would manage to try the popular general, but that was clearly their intent. He wondered if James had any notion that the man who was to lead his army might soon be thrown into the Tower.

Gideon had no time to waste if he was going to speak to Ormonde.

The sun was setting, so he started the walk to Ormonde House, along Holborne, crossing the bridge over the Fleet, and cutting through Lincoln's Inn Fields. As he walked past the Fields, he was thrown off stride by the sight of Lord Cowper, the Lord Chancellor, in the company of Herr Bernstorff, one of King George's Hanoverians emerging from a house. As they descended the steps, Gideon was forced to walk on past them.

Either gentleman could have recognized him with one close look, but as Gideon had hoped, except for a quick glance to make sure that he was no threat, neither man spared an apparent merchant a second thought.

The incident rattled him, however. If the men had been closer acquaintances, could something about his physique have given him away? He decided to alter his gait and posture. A wool merchant, intent upon business, would neither stride with the arrogance of an aristocrat nor hide his face like a felon. Gideon hoped he could achieve a semblance of the modesty and purpose appropriate to the honest merchant he wanted to appear.

Drawing near Piccadilly, he felt the endless pull of Hawkhurst House. But he did not dare pass that way, for he would court not only the certain risk of being recognized, but also a longing he would find too hard to fight.

In the end, no matter how much he would have liked to stretch his legs after a two-day ride, he took a chair the rest of the way to St. James's Square, feeling the need of a curtain to shield his face from his acquaintances who might be coming out of the theatre at this hour.

Arriving in St. James's Square, Gideon told the chairmen to set him down on the south side of the piazza, at the back of the houses facing Pall Mall Street. This was the opposite side from Ormonde House, but he had been warned that government spies might be keeping an eye on the Duke's house. Reaching into his pocket to pay the chairmen, he stole a furtive look about, but saw no one who seemed to fill the role of spy.

St. James's Square was the most fashionable address in town. It had been developed by the Earl of St. Albans, who perceived a need for elegant housing for aristocrats who wished to spend more of their time at Court. The earl had sold his own house to the first Duke of Ormonde, and since his death, it had been occupied by the family of his grandson and heir, James Butler, second duke and military hero. Spanning the width of three houses, Ormonde House was by far the largest dwelling facing the piazza. It dominated the rest, but every house on the square lodged a peer.

Gideon was glad that his ancestors had built their home on a different site, for this piazza had become a convenient place for the parish to dump refuse. The glittering salons in which the Norfolks, Ormondes, Kents, and Pembrokes gave balls and banquets all looked out onto heaps of ashes, dung, and animal carcasses. There was even a shed that someone had built on the square to collect and sell rubbish. The remains of the fireworks that had been set off for the King's birthday still littered the square. The odour coming from the filthy combination should have been enough to chase off even the meanest of spies.

It was so distracting, in fact, that it took Gideon a moment to realize his error in choosing such a sociable hour. The plays had just ended, and groups of ladies and gentlemen were making their way to their evening's entertainment. Lights from some of the mansions, the occasional opening and closing of a door, and visitors descending from chairs announced that more than one supper or card party was taking place in the square tonight.

Luckily, the onset of darkness was on his side. The oil lamps were just being lit. Nevertheless, he could make out the identity of some of the arrivals by the sound of their voices. He wished he had padded his coat to disguise his young man's physique, but decided that a crooked back and stiffer gait would conceal him as he crossed to the other side of the piazza.

The Duke's house was scarcely lit when Gideon pulled on the bell to the porter's lodge and waited for the servant to answer.

A faint sound of footsteps came through the heavy portal, heralding the servant's arrival. Gideon gave him a false name and asked to see the Duke.

But Ormonde was out. The rustic porter, an Irishman from the Ormonde estate, could not be brought to say where his master had gone or even to guess the hour of his return. He asked Gideon to state his business, and Gideon gave the answer Madame de Mézières had told him to use.

"I have important news for his Grace concerning his cousin Jonathan."

The man became instantly alert, though he volunteered no more information than before. Whether or not he knew the Jacobite's code for James, he did appear to think that Gideon's visit would be important to his master, for he asked if Gideon wished to leave a message.

Rather than try to catch the Duke at home again, when he would have to dodge his acquaintances in the street, Gideon decided to leave a note. The porter invited him in, and they walked through the massive hall, which was lined with dozens of leather buckets bearing the Ormonde crest and coronet, to an antechamber, furnished with nothing more than a table and two simple chairs. The porter fetched him a piece of paper and an inkstand and stood at the door, while Gideon wrote.

He had just finished scribbling a note, in which he begged the Duke to appoint a time for him to deliver the news about his cousin Jonathan, giving his address at the White Horse in Smithfield and signing his name as Brown, when he heard a lady calling out for the porter.

The man gave a start. "That'll be the masther's daughter," he said, as light footsteps came hurrying through the hall. "I'll have to see what her ladyship wants. Just you stay here."

As soon as he stepped through the door, Gideon flattened himself behind it. He could hear the porter's answer to his mistress, followed again by the lady's voice.

He recognized the voice as belonging to the Lady Elizabeth, the Duke's eldest daughter, an unmarried lady of Gideon's age. They had met as children and had danced together at Court, paired by rank in the minuet.

She asked the porter who had rung the bell, in an anxious tone that hardly seemed warranted, given the number of people who habitually visited this house. It was unusual for a lady to concern herself with the identity of an evening visitor, particularly the Lady Elizabeth, who with her wit and charm had always attracted friends. Even the hard-to-please Dean of Dublin Cathedral, Jonathan Swift, had confessed to being one of her admirers.

Gideon was torn by the desire to set an old friend at ease and uncertainty as to how he would be received. The porter assured her that it was no one she knew—only a tradesman come on business. Gideon heard her doubt, and he longed to reassure her that she had nothing to fear. But the moment's delay had made his position clear.

The Duke would not want his daughter dragged into a conspiracy. Neither would he wish her to converse with a man who had been charged with murder, a person he might believe guilty.

In another moment, the porter had convinced her that the visitor was not worthy of her notice, and she retreated upstairs. After waiting to be sure that she would not reverse her steps, Gideon handed the note to the porter in the hall and headed out, careful to make no noise. He left Ormonde House behind and started to walk with no particular destination in mind.

The inability to divulge his presence to a friend had bothered him more than he cared to admit. It wasn't long before disappointment spurred his anger, and he strode from the Square, careless of his gait. Fortunately, night had fallen now. It would hide him again.

He wandered blindly, made heedless by his temper, until he found himself perilously close to Hawkhurst House. He had automatically turned his steps up Duke Street towards home. Burlington House, with its tall gates and its imposing courtyard, loomed just ahead. Only one more turn to the right and he would be able to see the walls of his house.

A feeling like a clamp threatened to squeeze the breath right out of him. It took all his fortitude not to give in to the desire to see his home. At the moment, he could not think of one house in this whole parish that he could enter and be safe.

That left him with the choice of retiring to the White Horse, to a flea-ridden bed, or finding a coffee house in the east end of London where few aristocrats ever went.

He was about to settle for the latter, when he thought of the one place in the City of Westminster where he might be welcomed. With a slight easing of the clamp, he turned and directed his steps to the Palace Yard.

❧

Earlier that week, Harrowby had returned from the House of Lords to relate, with a touch of unease, that Mr. Walpole had announced that the Committee of Secrecy would soon be ready to make its report.

"He had the Tories quaking in their boots, I can tell you," he said, to the ladies and Dudley, who had gathered in the salon before going for a stroll in the park. "'Pon my honour! But the man seems out for blood! He said there would be charges of treason laid—against Harley, I'm sure, but it seems there will be arrests. He even said, 'Heads will roll.'"

Harrowby gave a shudder, while nervously playing with his fob.

"But why should Lord Oxford or anyone else get his head cut off?" Isabella was playing with a ribbon on her bodice and asked this in a tone suggesting that her mind was really on something else.

Harrowby's gaze was unfocused, too, but he answered, "They will say that he schemed with Louis to end the war and did it secretly, behind our allies' backs."

"Then maybe he deserves to die." Mrs. Mayfield folded her arms with a righteous huff. "I don't hold with creatures who connive behind their friends' backs, and I'm sure his Majesty don't either."

No one would have dared to challenge the accuracy of this statement, but Harrowby was not even listening.

"There was some talk of papers," he mumbled, musing aloud. Then, a sudden fright leapt into his eyes. "I must speak to James Henry." He started to bolt from the room, tossing over his shoulder, "You will forgive me, Isabella, if I do not come with you?"

"James Henry left for Rotherham Abby yesterday," Hester said, before he could reach the door.

"Plague take him! You're right!" Harrowby turned, and his face went pale. "We must send for him immediately. I don't even know what sort of papers my cousin kept, but they must be burned right now!"

"St. Mars's papers?" Isabella was confused.

Hester glanced at her aunt and saw that she had tensed.

"No—well, perhaps his, too! But I was speaking of his father's, y'know. The old gentleman was a terrible Tory. I don't know what he might have written down." Another thought struck him and his eyes grew wide. "What if the government took his papers after he died? They took Bolingbroke's about then."

"But wouldn't someone have told you?" Hester asked. "I cannot believe that James Henry would neglect to mention something that important."

Her calm sense finally penetrated his panic. A desperate relief lit his face. "That must be so! You are sure to be right, Mrs. Kean. What a treasure you are, to be sure! Now, you must write to James Henry at Rotherham Abby and tell him to burn all my cousin's papers. Then, there will be nothing to worry about."

"I still don't see what Lord Hawkhurst's papers have to do with Lord Oxford's head," Isabella complained.

"Nothing, my dear!" Harrowby's mood had turned ebullient, now that Hester had quieted his fears. "There is very likely nothing in them at all. But, with Walpole's blood up the way it is, I assure you, we cannot be too prudent." He reached over the back of her chair to pinch her cheek. "And you wouldn't like to lose your pretty coronet, just because of some bit of twaddle the old man jotted down, now would you?" He sobered slightly. "But, now that I think of it, I don't want any of you writing letters or keeping diaries, or whatnot."

"That won't be hard," Dudley said, with a laugh. "I never write letters unless I have to."

"I hate the very thought of writing," Mrs. Mayfield agreed.

"Good for you!"

"Hester does all my writing for me," Isabella said, with more honesty than her mother.

Harrowby turned to face Hester again, but he seemed reluctant to be as strict with her as he was with the others.

"Well, I suppose *some* kinds of letters will have to be written. But you must be careful, Mrs. Kean! Nothing must be said about the King or the government, or especially about any person or anything over the water! In fact, if I was you, I should never employ the word *water* in any of my letters."

Hester managed to smother a smile, long enough to assure him in a serious tone that the word *water* had never figured largely in her prose.

He accepted her reassurances with gravity. "Well, you can thank me for alerting you to the danger of using it. I doubt you would have suspected it on your own."

Hester agreed, and as he had just given her the task of writing a letter to James Henry, she excused herself from their walk. She saw them off before seeking pen and paper in Isabella's escritoire.

The message would have to be carried down by one of the grooms, for she dared not entrust it to the post. If government agents were reading letters, as everyone believed, their ears were sure to perk up at the news that a peer's papers were being destroyed. And whether there were any papers remaining at Rotherham Abby that could implicate the former earl, Hester knew that there once had been.

That was not the largest problem facing her, however, for she would have to ask James Henry to burn the remnants of his dead father's thoughts without revealing that she knew what their relationship had been.

A few days later, Harrowby and Dudley left for Guilford with a great many other gentlemen to watch the horse matches with the King. Their conversation over chocolate that morning had consisted of excited speculations as to which horse was likely to win the Fifty-Pound Plate. Harrowby had not decided whether to put his money on the Duke of Somerset's bay, Star, or the Lord Great Chamberlain's grey horse, Governor. Dudley was certain it would be a mistake to underestimate Mr. Broderick's Hermitage. But Harrowby cautioned him not for any fortune in the world to bet on Sir William Windham's gelding, Smiling-Tom.

"Why not?" Dudley asked. "Have you seen the horse?"

Harrowby pursed his lips and arched his brows, as if he could tell his brother-in-law a thing or two, but all he said was, "There have been whispers. And it wouldn't be wise to be seen to support Sir William right now, or even his horse."

That seemed to put him in mind of the fright he had taken earlier in the week. His parting orders for his wife were to be careful who she was seen with. The Committee had not yet delivered its report, but would after the King's return.

He was no sooner gone than Isabella announced her intention of going out in the evening, and of taking Hester with her. It was the privilege of a married lady to go wherever she liked, unescorted by either mother or husband, but tonight would be the first that Isabella exercised her new rights.

Since they would not be venturing into the City, a pair of footmen was all the protection they needed as, later, they wandered from one friend's tea table to another's drawing-room. But, finding nothing to hold her interest at the first house, where the company discussed the latest play, or at the second, where Mr. Pope was roundly criticized for taking on the translation of Homer, Isabella said that they would drop by Lady Oglethorpe's.

In vain, Hester reminded her that Harrowby wanted her to exercise exceptional prudence in her choice of companions. Lady Oglethorpe's invitation had promised the sort of entertainment that Isabella particularly liked. And she shrugged off her husband's concern with the argument that several of their most intimate friends knew and visited Lady Oglethorpe. Hester suspected that she was thinking of

Lord Lovett in particular, for they had not seen him that week. Another reason for her uneasiness was that Harrowby's absence might give Isabella a chance to advance her flirtation with that gentleman, whose handsome ways many ladies would find hard to resist.

But to try to dissuade Isabella from indulging her desires was fruitless, and Hester soon found herself being handed down from the Hawkhurst carriage in the Palace Yard.

Their hostess greeted them eagerly. In her withdrawing room, they found some of the friends Isabella had alluded to, Sir Humphrey and Colonel Potter among them. Lord Lovett, however, was not in attendance. Sir Humphrey whispered that he had been called away to Kensington to conduct some business for a relative, but that he had promised to see them at Isabella's card party that week. Isabella would have pouted and left, if Lady Oglethorpe had not presented another gentleman, dressed in exceptional finery and sporting a very fine periwig.

Despite a rather unprepossessing name, Mr. Blackwell had the decided manner of a courtier. A quantity of lace at his throat, a coat and vest embroidered with flowers and birds in the palest of shades, and a slightly foreign air suggested that he had just arrived from the Continent. His luxurious blond peruke had to have come from France. He had large, rather flattened features, and hazel eyes that held no warmth. His interest in Isabella increased the moment that Lady Oglethorpe informed him of her name.

"And Lord Hawkhurst?" he inquired, as he bent to kiss her hand. "He is with you this evening?"

"No, my husband has gone to Guilford with the King. To see the horse matches."

"And left his pretty, young wife all alone? One hopes that he will not learn to regret such a serious neglect." The compliment was delivered with the appropriate smile. Nevertheless, Hester got the feeling that the gentleman's keenness had waned as soon as he had learned of Harrowby's whereabouts. She doubted she would ever have reason to worry that this gentleman would try to lead Isabella astray, but she wondered what his interest in Harrowby was. Most likely he was searching for a patron like everyone else.

Colonel Potter, who was still waiting to hear whether Harrowby would engage him as his secretary, came over to join them. Since asking for the position, he had not missed a single one of Harrowby's levees.

"I trust his lordship will not deprive us of his company for long?"

Before Isabella could answer, Sir Humphrey piped up, "I hope not, too. Lovett and I have taken a box for the opera this Saturday, and we are counting on all of you to come. We've taken a box on the stage—though I've read that none of the audience will be permitted to set foot upon it, what with all the moving scenery and machines. It sounds quite the spectacle. You must join us, Potter. Lady Oglethorpe has had to refuse me, Blackwell, but you would be very welcome to come in her place."

Sir Humphrey issued this last invitation with his customary genial spirit.

Both gentlemen accepted, though Hester noticed a hesitation on Mr. Blackwell's part. A pointed look from Lady Oglethorpe appeared to decide him. Her gaze moved commandingly from Isabella back to him, before he said, with scarcely concealed annoyance, "I should not waste so imminent a chance of meeting my Lord Hawkhurst, I suppose." He flashed Lady Oglethorpe a venomous smile. "If he is *not* to be met with here, where one might have hoped to have seen him, then a greater effort will obviously be called for."

He made no further attempt to charm Isabella, other than a feeble endeavour to conceal his immense boredom. This failed, however, where both Isabella and her cousin were concerned. Isabella required more flirting in her entertainment, and Hester could only ponder the motive of a gentleman who expressed a wish to know another, when that wish was obviously not his. She was certain that Lady Oglethorpe had forced Mr. Blackwell's hand, else he would not have accepted Sir Humphrey's invitation.

Colonel Potter took advantage of Isabella's presence to press his suit. He told her of the services he had performed for his superior officers in the Foot-Guards.

Hester said, "I read that the King is to review your regiment next week in Hyde Park. You must be quite busy with the preparations."

As soon as the words left her mouth, she knew that she had said something wrong. Colonel Potter recoiled, like a horse resisting its halter.

"He's not that busy now," Sir Humphrey dropped into the uneasy silence. "Poor Potter's been dismissed. He was replaced along with a number of our friends. Just got his letter this week."

Colonel Potter could not hide his annoyance at this interference. He nearly rounded on Sir Humphrey, but was stopped when Isabella exclaimed, "Poor Colonel! Well, you *must* come to work for my husband, then. A handsome gentleman will always be welcome at Hawkhurst House."

Colonel Potter had to restrain his temper to bow in her direction. "My lady is very generous, but I hope that Lord Hawkhurst can be brought to make a decision in my favour soon. I am not a man to be idle. I must have employment."

Isabella assured him of Harrowby's complete willingness to accede to her wishes, making it clear what those would be. Hester decided to use the moment to ask Sir Humphrey if he knew the reason the Colonel had lost his commission. James Henry would want to know if Harrowby was about to engage a man under disgrace.

It was easy to turn Sir Humphrey aside for a private word. He was a gentleman easily led, and he seldom, if ever, appeared to have a fixed object in mind. His temper was congenial to a fault, for he seemed completely unaware that his friend's confidence had been breached.

"Why were Colonel Potter and the other officers you spoke of dismissed?"

The baronet assumed a knowing expression. "They are *Tories*, don't y' know. The King sees what is coming. He thinks if he makes all his officers Whigs, then he won't have anything to worry about. But he's wrong, of course." This last, and most treasonous of statements, was said in an offhand tone.

Amazed that Sir Humphrey could speak so casually of rebellion, Hester threw a nervous look over her shoulder and found that not only was Colonel Potter frowning at them, but that Mr. Blackwell, too, had tilted an ear in their direction. His expression was more difficult to read than the Colonel's, but it gave Hester a sudden chill.

Lady Oglethorpe glided over to take Sir Humphrey by the arm.

"My dear, you must tell me what you know about this opera of Mr. Handel's. The news-sheets say that Nicolino will play Amadis, but who will sing Oriana's part if Mrs. Robinson is ill?"

She had deftly turned the conversation into safer channels. Hester allowed her to draw Sir Humphrey away, and soon most of the guests had seated themselves for cards. With no money to wager, Hester did not play, so she could do nothing but watch Isabella lose more of St. Mars's fortune, saying a prayer on every turn of the cards.

Bring then these blessings to a strict account;
Make fair deductions; see to what they mount:
How much of other each is sure to cost;
How each for other oft is wholly lost;
How inconsistent greater goods with these;
How sometimes life is risked, and always ease:
Think, and if still the things thy envy call,
Say, wouldst thou be the Man to whom they fall?

CHAPTER VII

Outside, Gideon stepped back into the shadows, still reeling from the shock of seeing Mrs. Kean and Isabella enter the home of a notorious Jacobite. He had arrived in the Palace Yard in time to see the Hawkhurst carriage, with his coachman driving and his footmen hanging on the back, pull up in front of Lady Oglethorpe's house. Gideon had halted in his tracks and watched, while first Isabella and then Mrs. Kean were handed out, then had turned to hide his face until they disappeared inside.

Even disguised, he could not be certain that his former servants would not know him, so he turned his back to the coach and headed out of the Palace Yard.

He wondered if either lady understood the risk she incurred by visiting that house. Harrowby had obviously not come with them. It would have surprised Gideon even more to see his cousin visiting a Tory house, especially when the fact that Gideon's father had been an ardent Tory could give the present government reason enough to doubt Harrowby's loyalty. Harrowby had been very eager to please King George and his Whig ministers, and since his party allegiance had no foundation in principle, he had been happy to change from Tory to Whig as soon as it had seemed expedient.

But it was not Harrowby's politics or his behaviour that concerned Gideon—or his countess's. He was worried about Mrs. Kean. He knew her intelligence was far above the ordinary, but her position as Isabella's dependent might have dragged her into a piece of foolishness she could do nothing to prevent. Lady Oglethorpe's sympathies were so well-known that it was a risk for anyone to befriend her.

Disturbed, Gideon forgot about the loneliness that had directed his steps to Lady Oglethorpe's house. As his feet carried him towards Charing Cross, he spared no attention for the people he passed, so lost was he in thought.

He had resolved, for Mrs. Kean's safety, never to seek her out unless his name was cleared and his friendship could do her no harm. But his resolve had just been shattered, broken into a thousand tiny pieces by the danger she might be in from an association with Jacobites. He would have to find out the purpose of her visit to Lady Fury's house. And he would have to keep her from going there again.

Gideon had walked the better part of a mile before he realized that, contrary to common sense or good intentions, he couldn't help being excited at the prospect of talking to Mrs. Kean again.

Late on the following morning, Hester was in her aunt's bedchamber, taking orders from Mrs. Mayfield, who was sipping chocolate in bed, when she was startled by the entrance of a footman who said that a messenger had asked to see her.

"What messenger?" Mrs. Mayfield demanded to know. "Who would send a message to my niece? You had better admit this person, so I can see him for myself."

Hester did not know whom the message was from, but a fluttering in her stomach told her that it might be from St. Mars. Then, annoyed by such a foolish thought, she tried to convince herself that St. Mars was still in France. And even if not, he would have no reason to see her. She even allowed the footman to leave the room to fetch the boy, but the thought of what might happen if the message *were* from St. Mars and her aunt discovered it brought her quickly to her feet.

"I've remembered what this will be about, Aunt Mayfield. There is no reason for you to trouble yourself with it. Isabella asked me to find her a monkey, and I told a man who keeps a shop of wild animals to send me word as soon as he found her one. This is certain to be him."

As she expected, Mrs. Mayfield uttered a grunt of disgust. "Well, if *that's* who it is, I have no wish to see him. Not if he's been anywhere near those filthy creatures! A monkey, indeed! I cannot understand why Isabella would even want to touch one."

"They *are* very fashionable, Aunt," Hester couldn't resist tossing over her shoulder on her way out.

A choking sound behind her told her how very much it troubled Mrs. Mayfield to hold any opinion that was opposed to fashion.

Hurrying in the footman's wake, Hester was able to stop him and the messenger, too, before they started back up the stairs.

"It is quite all right, Will," she said to the strapping, young footman. "My aunt has given me permission to speak to the boy down here. You needn't show him up."

"That's all right, then, ma'am." Will gave her an impudent wink, as if to say that the old hen should have kept her nose out of her niece's business from the start.

Not for the first time, Hester was grateful for the difference between the servants Mrs. Mayfield had employed in her former house and those at Hawkhurst House. The Mayfields' butler, whom Mrs. Mayfield had dismissed on the elevation of her daughter to the rank of countess, would have sneered at the notion that Hester had any right to privacy.

But she did not dare waste time appreciating the contrast now, not when her aunt might chafe at her absence and demand to see the messenger again, so Hester instructed the boy to follow her into an anteroom near the front door where visitors were asked to wait.

On the mornings of Harrowby's levees, this space was crowded with gentlemen who wished to pay their respects to the earl. With few exceptions, these were men who hoped the new Lord Hawkhurst would be able to help them with a problem they were having with the government, with their aspirations to a Court or government post, or with a loan of money. The exceptions, who were invited up before the others, were Harrowby's friends, who simply enjoyed visiting while the earl dressed. They would compare his lordship's new garments to their own and offer his valet advice, which undoubtedly drove Philippe to distraction, since he had decided opinions of his own, as well as a great appreciation of his own talent.

The boy standing before Hester now was a far cry from the room's usual visitors. His clothes were dirty, he smelled of the street, and the widening of his eyes as he gazed about the room told her that he had never been inside a house of quality. Despite these obvious disadvantages, though, he did not let the room intimidate him. When she asked to hear what he had to say, he drew back to regard her through narrowed eyes.

"I were told to giv'it to a bird by the name o' Mrs. Kean and nobody else."

"I am Mrs. Kean. You may deliver your message to me."

He frowned. "Now, 'ow am I surposed t'know if yer be tellin' the truth? Yer might be 'avin' me on."

Hester could see that this was no mere stubbornness on the boy's part. He had obiously had it impressed upon him that he must not relay his message to just anyone. Her pulse, which she had tried to stifle, began to dance. Who else would require such secrecy, but St. Mars?

"I do not know how to convince you of my identity. But you asked the footman to see Mrs. Kean, and he released you to me. Does that help?"

"It wouldn't," the boy said, "but the codger 'oo sent me told me somethin' about what ye look like." He examined her more closely. "'E made yer sound a bit better lookin', though."

Hester would have pleased to hear this, if his description of the sender had not thrown her. "The . . . codger? An elderly person sent you?"

The boy did not look certain. He reflected aloud, "Well,'is 'air an' 'is brows is gray and 'is back is all crook'd-like. But 'e don't *seem* wery old, if yer knows what I mean."

Hester's excitement had all but evaporated, until she realized that St. Mars would have to disguise himself. He could cover up his hair and make his brows look gray, but he would find it much harder to conceal the energy that characterized a younger man.

"Were his eyes very blue? And does he have long, slender fingers?"

The boy nodded quickly to her first suggestion and even more vigorously to the second, which made her hope return.

"Then I think I know the gentleman," she said. "And I'll warrant that he offered you a generous payment if you brought his message to me."

Beneath the dirt on his forehead, the boy's eyes gleamed. "'E sure did that! Which is why I don't want to bungle it, yer see."

"Well, if you don't deliver it, you will never be paid. I appreciate your efforts to obey his orders, but I can assure you that you have found the right woman, even if your employer's description of her is somewhat flattering." Hester's temperature increased in belated reaction to this piece of news. She had to bite her tongue not to ask the boy precisely which words the gentleman had used.

"Oh, yer all right." He must have read her thoughts. "'E just made yer sound a lil' more. . . I dunno, *special*, I s'pose."

Hester decided she could be perfectly content with that description, even as her wiser self said that anyone who had helped St. Mars to solve his father's murder would necessarily be a special friend.

At last, the boy seemed satisfied that she was, indeed, the person she pretended to be, so with visible relief he finally divulged the message he had been withholding.

"This ol' codger, see, at the White 'Orse—the one wif the rum glaziers—the blue ones like yer said—well, 'e says 'e'll giv me a slat if I takes this message to a Mrs. Kean what lives in a swell house in Piccadilly. So I makes 'im show me the slat, see, 'cause I weren't born yesterd'y. And 'e *'ad* it, so I tells 'im I'll go, but if 'e tries to picque without payin' me, I'll tell the bluffer 'e's a prig."

The boy's choice of words left Hester with a very poor understanding. "Yes, that is all very well. But what did the gentleman wish you to say to me?" They had wasted a considerable amount of time in getting this far, and her aunt would be calling her soon.

The boy proceeded to recite his message, as if he had been made to repeat it several times. "'E says, I'm to say that Mr. Brown is come up to town, an' if it wouldn't be too much of a pother, 'e'd like to speak to yer as soon as 'e can. 'E says I'm to wait for a reply and that the lady—

meanin' *you*—should tell 'im where and when to meet yer."

On hearing St. Mars's alias, Hester's heart gave a joyful leap. *"Of course,* I will meet him," she said. Then, she furiously searched her memory for a place where they could speak without being observed. As eager as she was, and anxious to discover why he wished to see her, she might not be at liberty to leave Hawkhurst House at any particular hour of the day. She could invent an errand, but either Isabella or her mother might require her at that moment or decide to send her somewhere else. And she couldn't be certain that St. Mars could risk walking the streets during the day.

Tonight would be out of the question, for they were promised to Mrs. Jamison, and tomorrow they were expecting guests. As much as Hester hated to postpone their rendezvous, she could think of only one place to suggest. And its name implied intrigue of an entirely different sort.

"Pray, tell the gentleman that I shall be going with a party to Spring Gardens on Friday night at ten o'clock. I should be able to step away from my friends for a few moments. Those are the gardens at Vauxhall—not the old ones at Charing Cross," she added. "You must be certain to give him the right location."

The boy was not shocked by her suggestion. No doubt he had seen much more scandalous behaviour in his short life than Hester would ever see.

"Ten o'clock, Friday night at Fox Hall gardens," he repeated. "Is that it?"

She would have liked to send word of how happy she was to know that his lordship was safe, but the sound of her aunt's voice coming from upstairs, decided her that anything else could wait.

"Yes, that's all." With an excitement akin to panic, she turned him by his shoulders and sent him on his way. "You had better go. And do not repeat our messages to anyone, even if you are questioned going out of this house. Just say that you came from the wild animal vendor to tell me he doesn't have any monkeys right now. And do not forget, *Friday, at Vauxhall.* Tell my—tell him, he will recognize the members of my party. And thank you," she whispered loudly to the boy's retreating back.

Her heart was beating so fast that she had to linger downstairs before returning to her aunt. *To see St. Mars! And this Friday night!* Hester had told herself again and again that it might be months—even years before she saw him. She had thanked providence for every distraction that Isabella and her new situation had provided, so she would not be forced to dwell on how long it might be. The days, filled with entertainments, had passed more quickly than she would ever have believed possible, but now the prospect of three more seemed to stretch before her like a dreary road. All she could do was pray that nothing would occur to stop St. Mars from finding her in the Spring Gardens after dark.

Gideon received Mrs. Kean's message to meet her on Friday night. He would have been intolerably frustrated by the delay, had he not also received instructions to return to Ormonde House at eleven o'clock that evening.

Arriving on the stroke of the hour, he found the porter looking out for him and was whisked inside without a minute's wait.

As he followed a liveried footman through the hall, Gideon could not help being anxious about the Duke's reaction when he learned the identity of his visitor. As far as the public knew, Gideon was a murderer who had escaped arrest. The Pretender's supporters in France were apparently convinced of his innocence, but he had no way of knowing if the Jacobites on this side of the Channel believed him innocent, too.

Another source of worry was the pamphlets he had read. If the government was making a case against the Duke, he would have to call for the rising before they pounced. With this uppermost in his mind, Gideon had prepared himself to ride for France as soon as he had warned Mrs. Kean. Clearly, it was time for Ormonde to act or to tell the Pretender that his chances were not great enough to risk men's lives.

The footman, Irish like the porter, led him up the grand staircase. Their footsteps echoed in the vastness of the house. Faces of heroic proportions gazed down from the painted ceiling over their heads.

Huge French tapestries lined the walls. Once on the drawing-room floor, they passed some rooms with open doors. Gideon wondered if the Duchess and her daughter were at home. The open doors revealed parlours that were furnished with hardly more than a few chairs each. The grandeur of the house, so impressive on the outside, seemed to extend only to a small portion of the interior, but the Butlers had not been in possession of their dukedom for long.

The Duke of Ormonde received him in his private drawing room, where velvet in white, green, and gold relieved the almost Spartan starkness of the rest of the house. Tall, broad-shouldered, and handsome, with a courtier's grace, the Duke faced Gideon gravely across an ebony table inlaid with gilt.

Ormonde did not know him at first. But when Gideon made his bow and began to speak, a look of recognition came over the Duke's face and his eyebrows snapped together in a frown.

"Is that you, St. Mars? Good Lord! How do you come to be in England?"

"The Pretender sent me. He knows I am innocent of my father's death, and has asked me to be his messenger."

The Duke did not contest either of these statements. Rather, he treated them almost perfunctorily, saying, "Yes, a tragic business, that. Sad about your father. But you are still in danger here, you know."

Gideon bristled at the casualness with which the Duke could dismiss the events that had caused him so much pain.

His Grace seemed to sense his blunder, though he mistook the reason for Gideon's displeasure. Waving him into a chair, he said, "I know what you're thinking, St. Mars. You are wondering why none of us came to your defence. But it happened so fast—at a time when the Whigs were threatening every one of us. You saw what happened to Bolingbroke! We were so busy defending our backs that we didn't have time to take on your troubles, too.

"Then you were gone—no one knew where—so naturally we assumed that you had fled to his Majesty's side." Ormonde gave him an avuncular smile. "And so you have, it appears. Welcome to the cause."

Gideon did not tell him that the Pretender had found him instead.

He was involved now, so what difference would it make?

"You are his messenger then," Ormonde went on. "What does his Majesty desire?"

His manner was curiously detached. Nothing about it suggested a man who was planning an imminent rebellion. Gideon had to wonder if Ormonde was trying to conceal something from him.

He took the pipe out of his pocket, extracted the Pretender's curled up note, and handed it to the Duke.

"I have been asked to discover when the rising will take place. James is growing very anxious. The Duke of Berwick has advised him to remain in Lorraine until he gives the signal to move. But it has been a very long time, and still James receives no word."

Gideon stopped, because Ormonde was reading the note. When he had finished, he nodded indulgently. "I know his Majesty must be impatient, and I honour him for it. The lad has courage. It will be a glorious day when he is restored to his throne."

"He's begun to doubt that his brother has his interests at heart. Berwick is ever engaged on Louis's business, and Louis keeps them far apart."

Still nodding, Ormonde gave Gideon a look of sympathy. "It must be hard on his poor Majesty. I assure you, my heart aches for him. But you must tell him that Berwick is surely to be trusted. The time is simply not quite right."

Gideon was nonplussed. This was not the reaction he had expected, particularly after reading the pamphlet against Ormonde.

"But the season—" Gideon had to restrain himself before he insulted Ormonde's superior knowledge of military affairs. Who should be better suited than a general to know the risk of a winter campaign? James could never win without a man of Ormonde's experience, so Gideon had to be careful not to offend him in the Pretender's name.

"So you plan to wait another year? If the country is not ready—" He tried very politely to frame his questions. *Are our people for James or are they not? And, if they are, why not strike now?* James was far away in Lorraine. He would need weeks of warning simply to journey to the coast. Even two more months would push the rebellion into the stormy season, making it hard for his boats to cross the Channel. And winter would be much worse. It would be impossible to raise men to fight in winter. Even ignorant as he was of armies, Gideon knew that much.

"Oh, the country is ready," Ormonde heartily assured him. "You may tell his Majesty that each and every day brings him more and more adherents. How could they not with that turnip farmer on the throne? Tell him that his countrymen will be overjoyed to see him. But we must not be too hasty, you know. It never does to plunge into a thing without the arms to pull it off, and we're still short there, from what I've been told."

"How long will it be before you have enough?"

Ormonde chuckled as affably as a country squire discoursing on the subject of his favourite pig. "One can never have enough. But you can reassure his Majesty that when the time comes, we will win with whatever we've got."

Vague statements like these were not what James would want to hear. Gideon could well comprehend his frustration, if this was the sort of report he always got. Gideon was so bemused by Ormonde's attitude that he had to wonder if the Duke was lying because he did not trust him. But a hint of indecisiveness in the man's features somehow brought to mind the unfurnished rooms of his house.

Gideon asked about the pamphlet he had seen advertised in the news-sheets.

His question brought a momentary cloud to Ormonde's brow.

"That's the Whigs' doing. And it galls me—I'll not deny it. But they make a mistake if they think they can discredit me. I've got the army's and the people's confidence. You do not see them celebrating Marlborough's birthday in the streets, as if he were a king.

"They attacked my wife's coach last night—did you know? Three men on horseback. My coachman, who's a sensible fellow, said that they were too well armed and well mounted to be highwaymen, but that's how they were disguised. They asked if I was in the coach, and when they saw that I wasn't, they let her go. She was on her way here from our lodge at Richmond."

"I hope her Grace was not harmed!"

Ormonde shook his head, but his mind was clearly on something else. "For the past two weeks, they've had men posted on that road. They're hoping to kill me."

At Gideon's anxious exclamation, he made a negligent gesture.

"I've nothing to fear from them," he said. "I've dodged more bullets than they can even imagine. And I doubt there's a military man among them, while all my servants have killed their man in battle.

"*And*, if they think that Marlborough will stop King James from coming and save their hides, they're even bigger fools than he. As soon as Marlborough realizes he's backed the losing side, he'll be begging James to forgive him. There's never been a man with an eye for the main chance like the Duke of Marlborough."

Gideon tried to turn Ormonde's thoughts away from his rival, pressing for answers that he never received. If anything, the Duke grew more equivocal, citing the poor store of arms in the West Country, where the rebellion was planned to start. He also referred to the advice he'd received from other Jacobites, which apparently had made him cautious, when what the Pretender wanted was action—and soon.

Gideon tried to get some notion of a date that he could take back to James, but in the end he left with nothing, merely the same platitudes that James had been receiving for years.

In a dearth of spirits, Gideon wondered how he could face the Stuart prince in Lorraine and tell him that he could still do nothing but wait.

The evening that Hester and her family spent with Mrs. Jamison passed tediously, since it was devoted entirely to convincing Dudley of the advantages he would enjoy in the married state. The next day was June 9, and Isabella had invited Sir William and Lady Hobbes with their daughter, Mrs. Agnes Hobbes, to see if the young lady—or her purse, at least—could capture Dudley's heart. Isabella had provided for her own amusement by including Lord Lovett and Sir Humphrey on her list of guests.

The hour appointed for their guests' arrival had almost struck, when Harrowby came home from the House of Lords in a terrible state. As he tottered into the salon, his pallor was so alarming that Isabella rushed to help him to a sofa. Her mother produced a smelling-bottle from the pocket of her gown, and while she waved it beneath his nose, Hester went to the door and told a footman to bring his lordship a glass of Canary wine.

By the time he returned with a bottle, Harrowby was ready to tell them about the fright he'd had. But he waited to begin until the footman had closed the door.

"What's happened, Lambikin?" Isabella asked.

"The Committee of Secrecy delivered its report," Harrowby gasped. "Walpole ordered the lobby cleared of strangers. Then, he gave orders for the back door to be locked so none of us could escape or run to warn the others. He even posted a sergeant at the door." Harrowby paused to take a deep breath. "Mathew Prior and Thomas Harley have been arrested."

His ladies stared open-mouthed, as he went on, "His Grace of Ormonde is accused of acting in concert with the French. Even Shrewsbury is implicated."

"What about Lord Oxford?" Hester asked.

"Oh, they haven't finished with Oxford yet. Walpole read his report until six o'clock before he would let us go. Tomorrow we'll take up with Oxford and some of the others. It was a blood-bath, I tell you!

"Mrs. Kean—" Harrowby sat up suddenly and grasped her wrist— "Did you send that letter to James Henry?"

"Yes. I had one of the grooms ride down with it. He should have received it by now."

Harrowby fell back onto the cushions in relief. "Thank God! But I must have him here. I shan't know what to say if they question me about the old gentleman's papers. You must send someone to fetch James Henry immediately."

Hester promised that she would that very evening, but first she wanted to hear more about what had occurred in Parliament that day.

By posing careful questions, she was able to learn that the accusations all involved the negotiations for peace with France. Lords Oxford and Bolingbroke were charged with misrepresenting the former Queen's wishes. Many of her letters had not been countersigned. The Great Seal had not even been affixed. This gave the appearance that the former ministers were trying to protect themselves by neglecting to put their names to anything in case their actions were ever examined.

The Whigs complained that the treaty should have forced the French to hand the Pretender over to the English. Instead, they were fairly certain that the ministers—with the Queen's consent—had bribed the Duke of Lorraine to take her brother into his care, had obtained a passport for him from the Emperor of Austria, and had paid a large sum of money for his keep.

The Duke of Ormonde acknowledged that, while acting as general in the field, he had received orders from Bolingbroke not to engage in any siege or battle against the French. He had been instructed not to divulge this order to anyone else and to hinder its being suspected. This, while he was still under orders from the Queen to wage war in concert with the other members of the Great Alliance, who were kept completely in the dark.

That was all that Hester was able to wring from Harrowby, before Isabella and her mother recalled the imminent arrival of their guests. Harrowby was sufficiently soothed by this time to be handed to his valet and made ready for the evening's engagement.

Hester went to send another groom to Rotherham Abbey, telling him to fetch Mr. Henry as soon as possible.

Harrowby's revelations and the manner in which he had delivered them had awakened her concern. If St. Mars had not heard of today's events—and she did not see how he could have—she would have much to tell him tomorrow night.

Isabella and her mother easily dismissed the day's events in the pursuit of their own ends, but Hester wondered what impression the report might have made on the gentlemen. Sir Humphrey was not a member of Parliament, but Lord Lovett had presumably attended the House of Peers, and Sir William, for all she knew, might occupy a seat in the Commons.

When their guests arrived, though, nothing was said about the day's events, which made her suspect that none of them had heard the news. Harrowby was grateful for the change in conversation, and the evening began in a normal way.

Mrs. Mayfield had warned Dudley to be on his best behaviour, if he wanted to achieve the best bargain in his marriage contract. Unfortunately, the young lady's beauty was far from equal to the attractions of her fortune, since her complexion had been sadly disfigured by the smallpox. When Dudley pulled a face behind Mrs. Agnes's back, Mrs. Mayfield whispered angrily that her complexion was nothing for him to care about. And, when he showed signs of disputing this assertion, she pinched him viciously on the arm, telling him to put his mind to business or she would tell Lord Hawkhurst to send him packing home.

Dudley complied, but with a sour expression quite unlike his usual cheer, and Mrs. Mayfield had to spend the first many minutes of the evening making up for his lack of manners by speaking with forced gaiety to Sir William and Lady Hobbes.

Isabella divided the party among three tables, with herself, Lord Lovett, Sir William, and Mrs. Jamison at one, Lady Hobbes, Harrowby, and Mrs. Mayfield at another, and Sir Humphrey, Dudley, and Mrs. Agnes at the third. Hester was never expected to play when piquet was the game of choice, since it could be played as easily with three as four, and she had no money to wager. Being excluded from the tables never bothered her since she preferred to sit in a corner and read a book from Lord Hawkhurst's library.

But tonight, as the company was settling into their chairs, Mrs. Mayfield pulled her aside and, in an anxious whisper, ordered her to stay near Dudley and make certain that he did not drink too much.

"For I shall be too busy to keep my eye on him," she said. "I mean to try my luck with Lady Hobbes. If her husband is as they say he is, she can afford to lose, so you will have to watch Dudley in my stead."

Hester listened in some confusion. "But how can I stop Dudley from drinking if he wants to?"

"I did not say you had to stop him, foolish girl! A strange thing it would be, indeed, if you stopped your mistress's brother from enjoying himself! I only want you to sit near, so you can—" And, here, Mrs. Mayfield broke off, gazing away as if unable, or unwilling, to explain precisely what she wanted. She left her with these unhelpful words, "Just keep your wits about you. I shall know who to blame if anything goes wrong."

Better for Us, perhaps, it might appear,
Were there all harmony, all virtue here;
That never air or ocean felt the wind;
That never passion discomposed the mind.
But ALL subsists by elemental strife;
And Passions are the elements of Life.
The general ORDER, since the whole began,
Is kept in Nature, and is kept in Man.

CHAPTER VIII

Three long hours later, Hester was finding it hard to stay awake. She had placed her chair beside Dudley's, as if for the pleasure of watching him play. Feigning any degree of amusement had been difficult, since her appetite for cards had never been great enough to make another person's hand a matter of fascination to her. The players' conversation, too, had lacked wit. Sir Humphrey and Dudley had discussed their common passion for shooting in all its aspects, from the extraordinary talents of their dogs and horses to anecdotes of particular hunts. They had become so friendly over this topic—and a considerable quantity of wine—that each had extended the other an invitation to visit his country estate in order to sample the regional sport.

Hester now understood her aunt's concern, as this was not the sort of conversation likely to entertain a girl who had been born and bred in the heart of London. Clearly the quantity of spirits both gentlemen had imbibed had made them forget their manners. But Hester could not have prevented them from getting into this state. The footmen, who had orders to keep every decanter full, had liberally supplied them both, and the two gentlemen had become so friendly that it would have seemed churlish for Hester to interfere.

From shooting, Dudley moved on to describe the race match just run at Merrow Downes, the various horses, and the winner of the biggest plate. Recalling the money he had lost on his wager put a sudden halt to Dudley's cheer and drew Sir Humphrey's symptathy. Again, poor Mrs. Hobbes was excluded, and her pock-marked face grew rigid with offence. Hester hoped that soon the girl would look back on this evening and be grateful that she had been warned from accepting Dudley in time. Now it was unlikely that she would be drawn in by Mrs. Mayfield's machinations, not if this was an example of what life with Dudley would be like.

Hester felt sorry for the girl, who had a look of intelligence behind her shyness. She would have made an attempt to draw her out—and she was certain her aunt would blame her for not doing so when the match was refused—if she had not been placed on the other side of the table from her. She couldn't address any comments to Mrs. Hobbes without cutting across the gentlemen's conversation.

For a moment, she thought a change of subject might give her the chance she'd been hoping for. Sir Humphrey suddenly looked up at her and said, "I remember now. The rest of us were at Lady Oglethorpe's the night of the first race. That is the reason I missed it, for I usually attend. Wouldn't have missed the twelve-stone race for the world if the Queen were still with us. And neither would she, God bless her! How her Majesty did love a good match! But with the Queen not there, we went to Lady O's instead."

Then, a thought furrowed his brow, and he continued, as if working his way through a fog, "But we weren't all at my lady's that night. My Lord Hawkhurst went to see the matches. I believe he rode with the King. And you, Adrian—" he turned to speak to Lord Lovett, seated at the table behind him—" you were supposed to go to Kensington on business." Sir Humphrey's round eyes clouded, as if the wine he had drunk had confused him. "But you did not go to Kensington, did you? I saw you later in Arlington Street."

Lord Lovett paused in dealing the cards. The glance he threw at Sir Humphrey conveyed a rare degree of irritation—as well it might, given the reproachful pout Isabella was directing his way. She had been flirting shamelessly with him all evening and was not very pleased to discover that he had been somewhere else that night.

Lord Lovett appeared to find this evidence of her jealousy rewarding, for his irritation vanished as quickly as it had come. He gave Isabella a tantalizing smile. "I was sorry to miss seeing you, of course, but it was not at all certain that you would be visiting Lady Oglethorpe that night. And, *sadly,*" he drawled most shamelessly, "there are times when a gentleman is forced to seek his entertainment in places where he is more likely to find it. Clearly the loss was mine." He inclined his head in compliment to Isabella.

She was not appeased, since everything he said, and the manner in which he delivered it, implied either a dalliance with another woman or a visit to one of the many bawdy houses in the neighbourhood of St. James's. She betrayed no embarrassment at the suggestion, however, merely pique.

The embarrassment fell to Hester, who found it hard to hide. She was praying that Mrs. Hobbes was too naive to understand the drift of his talk, when Dudley's voice cut in.

"Why the devil are you waiting? It's your turn to play."

Sir Humphrey, still looking confused, had just been about to ask Lord Lovett something else. But the peremptory note in Dudley's voice made him jump, and he jerked his attention back to the table.

"Odso! So it is!" he said, and studied his cards.

Lord Lovett cast a considering look at his friend. His thoughts were unreadable, but Hester imagined they would contain a degree of exasperation. If he truly had a conquest of Isabella in mind, then he could not have appreciated Sir Humphrey's indiscretion.

She was hardly aware of having stared. But, as he turned back to resume his play, his eyes met hers and lingered. Reading assessment in his gaze, Hester felt herself growing warm. She quickly glanced away, but not before seeing a speculative smile curve his lips.

She did her best not to be flustered by the brief exchange, shifting her attention to the game at Dudley's table. The interruption had not afforded her the chance she had needed to draw Mrs. Hobbes into their talk. Thinking about her again, and how Mrs. Mayfield would scold when Dudley's proposal was turned down, Hester did not attend to the gentlemen's conversation, until a sudden change in Dudley's tone brought her instantly alert.

"You blackguard! I saw you play that card before!"

The accusation—for it *was* an accusation and not the jest she had thought—had been uttered in a furious voice. As Hester turned her eyes to her cousin's face, he fixed a belligerent glare on Sir Humphrey, whose soft, round mouth fell open in stunned surprise.

With alarm, Hester saw that her cousin's mien, normally cheerful, had taken on a vicious cast. The alteration was so sudden and extreme as to leave her speechless.

She struggled to recall something that might account for the change. Then she realized that, as distracted as she had been, first by Lord Lovett, and then by her concern for Mrs. Hobbes, the unoccupied portion of her mind had still recorded things she should not have ignored. While Sir Humphrey had been speaking, Dudley had poured himself two more glasses from the decanter at his side. He had drained them without offering wine to anyone else. His eyelids had begun to droop. His gaze had lost focus. And his expression had changed from amused to morose.

"Ods fish!" Sir Humphrey blustered, once he had found his voice. "What the devil do you mean, sir?"

"You *know*. And you'll not ge' away with it." In spite of a drunken slur, there was no mistaking the menace in Dudley's tone.

Mrs. Hobbes gave a gasp. She looked nervously to the other tables, but no one else had overheard the exchange. They were still intent on their cards, except for Lord Lovett, who was busy trying to coax a smile from Isabella.

Hester knew she should do something, but she did not know what. She had not recovered from her astonishment. Dudley's fury seemed to have arisen with no provocation at all.

She reached out a hand. "Cousin—"

The fingers beneath her hand balled into a fist. She jerked her hand away, eyes going wide, as he slammed his fist into the table, overturning two glasses and sending his cards fluttering to the floor.

"You think you're so clev'r! But you won' make a fool out o' me! I won' let you get away with it!" He struggled to rise, fortunately hampered by dizziness. His chair fell backwards with a crash.

Now, everyone turned. Their eyes flew to Hester's table, and a range of emotions played across their faces.

Mrs. Mayfield, who had been studying her cards with the avidity of a confirmed gamester, gave a cry of alarm mixed with annoyance, making Hester aware that her aunt had witnessed such drunken scenes before. She stared daggers at her son, before turning a venomous gaze on Hester. Seated farthest from them, she had not noticed Dudley's descent into moodiness. It was too late to pretend that his outburst was somehow Hester's fault, though Hester made no doubt her aunt would try, if it became even remotely possible.

"What *are* you going on about, Mayfield? Have you lost your senses?" Harrowby's outrage betrayed his embarrassment. He had not been an earl long enough to be indifferent to others' opinions. But when Dudley swerved to face him, Harrowby's bug-like eyes grew round in fear. "Ye gods! Dear me—!" He strove for authority. "My dear—dear Mayfield! I fear I shall have to ask you to sit down—my dear, dear fellow!" he ended in a quiver.

Dudley's turn had thrown him off balance. He staggered two or three steps to one side before recovering his equilibrium. Then, he swore, gazing blearily down at the floor, as if forgetting why he had stood.

Sir William jumped to his feet, uncertain if his family was in danger or if his host had staged some sort of tasteless theatrical performance. A conclusion quickly reached, he narrowed his shrewd, tradesman's eyes and shifted them from Dudley to Mrs. Jamison, Dudley's mother, and finally to Harrowby, before addressing the last.

"So that's your game, is it, my lord? To foist a madman onto me. Well, I'll have you know, I wasn't born yesterday. I've never been taken for a fool, and I won't be taken for one now. You'll have to find someone else to take this young gentleman off your hands. I'll not have a lunatic's blood mingling with mine. You can keep your fancy titles—I'll not sell my daughter or my name for tainted blood."

"Sir William, please! I knew nothing about this." Mrs. Jamison's cry broke the ominous silence.

He ignored her. As he stepped around his table to collect his wife and daughter—both plainly eager to depart—Mrs. Mayfield let out a screech that drowned Harrowby's feebler protests.

"Lunatic! How dare you call my son a lunatic? Why the Mayfields' family tree goes back to Edward I—which you would see, if you was ever to go to Mayfield Park! Not that an upstart like you would ever be admitted to Mayfield's house! How dare you insult a family so superior to your own?"

She turned to Harrowby. "Make Sir William apologize to me and to Mayfield right this instant!"

But Dudley had recalled the object of his ire and was lurching towards a frightened Sir Humphrey, ignoring the tables and chairs in his way. Until Hester saw him throw the furniture aside like so many twigs, she did not realize how strong her cousin was.

She was not big enough to stop him, unless she could find something with which to subdue him. She glanced about for a hard object, but quicker than she, Lord Lovett darted in front of Sir Humphrey, to place himself directly in Dudley's path.

Dudley swung.

Hester let out a cry. Isabella did, too—but neither was needed, as Lord Lovett gracefully ducked the blow before returning a well-placed punch to Dudley's jaw. Hester saw her cousin's head snap back. He wavered for a moment, then crumbled unconscious to the floor.

The silence was tense, as they all held their breaths to see if Dudley would rise. Then, as it became apparent that Lord Lovett's blow had done its work, everyone stirred at once.

"My dear, dear Adrian!" Sir Humphrey clapped his saviour on the back with breathless relief. "That was very well done! I am in your debt, my very dear fellow. I cannot imagine what came over the lad!"

Confusion dimmed his baby features, as he stared down at Dudley, who had started to snore. "But a minute ago, he seemed as merry as you or me. An't that right, Mrs. Kean? Mrs. Hobbes?" Unaware that the second young woman he addressed was being bustled out the door to the stairs, he went on, "The very next moment, he had turned so nasty that I was too startled to defend myself. I tell you—" Sir Humphrey's relief overwhelmed his tongue.

"Think nothing of it." Lord Lovett straightened the deep red cuffs to his blue silk coat. "If my memory serves me, you performed a similar act for me, not so very long ago. We shall call ourselves even."

For a moment the reference escaped Sir Humphrey, who looked even more puzzled. Then, with a flush of pleasure, he recalled, "You are talking about that day in the carriage. But indeed, dear Lovett, I was not—"

"Please, do not be modest, or I shall accuse you of fishing for greater praise. I suggest we take our leave and give our hosts some peace, so they can recover from the evening's excitement. Don't you?"

Mrs. Mayfield had not been noticeably upset to see her son knocked to the floor, but had immediately turned on Harrowby to share her injured feelings. Now, as their guests made ready to leave, her voice carried to them all. "I fail to see what right they have to be offended when a gentleman gets a bit too deep in his cups! And to call my son a lunatic—!"

Isabella, who had been holding back, with expressions ranging from pique to dismay—but neither surprise nor shock—spoke impatiently to her mother. "How can you say that, Mama, when you've always known what Dudley's temper is! He should never be allowed to drink, when he is likely to spoil our fun."

Even Harrowby, whose wits were not the sharpest, understood by this speech that Dudley had behaved in a similar manner before. With a look of betrayal, he started to berate Isabella and her mother for involving him with such a troublesome young man, even to the point of extracting an exorbitant sum to pay for a position at Court.

He had not got very far into his spleen when Lord Lovett, with his customary sangfroid, managed to stem the bitter flow without appearing to have interrupted. "I trust you have no concerns on our account, my lord," he said, including Sir Humphrey in his remark. "There was no real harm done. You have none but friends here now, and nothing Sir William says will spread very far where it counts."

Ignoring the offence on Mrs. Jamison's face, he took Isabella's hand and, raising it to his lips, said with a secretive smile, "Shall we say goodbye, then, until tomorrow? We have an engagement at Vauxhall, I believe."

"Lovett is quite right, my lord." Magnanimous, now that he was feeling safe, Sir Humphrey said, "There was no harm done at all."

Dudley made a noise in his sleep, and Sir Humphrey jumped.

With a new wave of fury, Mrs. Mayfield rounded on Hester, and said, "What can you mean by standing there, when your cousin is clearly ill! Go fetch the footmen to carry him to his room."

Hester would have left the drawing room gratefully, if she had not heard the two gentlemen and Mrs. Jamison taking their leave behind her, which meant that they would follow her down the stairs. She was feeling weak in the knees, and was afraid that a reaction to Dudley's violence was about to overtake her.

She did her best to hold herself up as she walked down, but she was obliged to hold tightly to the banister. The guests had nearly caught up with her, when dizziness dimmed her vision and her legs gave way.

A pair of long, strong arms prevented her fall. Ashamed to find herself in a gentleman's embrace, she struggled to find her legs. She murmured an apology, but Lord Lovett, who had caught her, refused to let her go. He held her closely by the waist, making her blood heat for an entirely different reason.

In a cool voice, he said to Sir Humphrey. "You had best attend to your sister, Cove. Ladies are unaccustomed to violence. It can be too much for their nerves. See that Mrs. Jamison is settled, and I shall look after Mrs. Kean."

Wakened from their posts by the sound of voices, two sleepy footmen started to climb the stairs. Lord Lovett ordered them to attend the family in the drawing room, before he half-led, half-carried Hester down to the small antechamber, where he forced her to sit on a satin-covered chair.

"Pray, do not disturb yourself on my account, my lord." Distressed by this unaccustomed attention, Hester tried to convince him that she was perfectly all right. "I am fully recovered. Indeed, I do not feel the slightest bit faint. It was just that my knees failed me, when I was fine only moments' before."

Looking down at her, Lord Lovett nodded, with an amused but sympathetic smile. "Shock, I should imagine. You have undoubtedly never seen a gentleman turn violent before."

On the contrary, Hester thought. She had once witnessed a duel to the death, and with someone much dearer to her at stake. But that was a secret, so she lowered her lashes and gave her head a little shake. "I suppose it was. I do not know my cousin Dudley very well, but he has always seemed perfectly amiable until now." Disquiet over what Sir William had said made her raise her eyes to Lord Lovett's handsome face. "You do not think—?" She caught herself before saying something she ought not to voice.

But he had read her mind. "Do I think he's mad?" He gave his lips a rueful twist. "Not unless one gentleman in twenty is. He is not the first man I have known to lose his temper in his cups." Then, he sobered. "That does not mean that his tendency will not pose problems for his family, or that he might not do something he will live to regret. I take it you were unaware of his propensity for violence?"

Hester could not miss the implication. She felt a rush of discomfort for Mrs. Mayfield and Isabella, who had obviously been aware of Dudley's tendency. She looked down at her hands. "As I said, I am only recently acquainted with him."

To her astonishment, Lord Lovett cupped her chin and forced it up until she met his gaze. The warmth she saw there made her gulp. "You must not feel responsible for the faults of your family. Do you think I have not noticed how superior you are to every one of them?"

He released her jaw, and Hester's mouth fell open. She could not have spoken for the life of her, so it was lucky that he did not wait for a response. He stepped back, gave her his most respectful bow, then left, before she could recover enough to wonder if she had heard him aright.

She had been aware of Lord Lovett's intelligence ever since meeting him and had formed a favourable impression of him because of his wit. His attentions to Isabella both in front of her husband and in his absence had bothered Hester, even as she had excused him for courting their influence. Her own attraction to him could no longer be denied, not when her pulse had raced at his touch, but that he should have noticed *her*—

Afraid that someone might find her in this incoherent state—unable to sort through her feelings—she gathered herself and started up the stairs. As she passed the door to the withdrawing room, she heard raised voices, telling her that Dudley's performance would be the first source of friction between the new earl and his bride, with Mrs. Mayfield providing the tinder for a fire.

Hester had no wish to become a party to their squabble. She had enough on her mind to be grateful for the cover it afforded her, though, for they had obviously forgotten her in their fury. She took herself off to bed where she spent a good many hours contemplating what Lord Lovett's attentions could mean. They so confounded her that they almost took her mind off her coming meeting with St. Mars.

On Friday evening, Harrowby brought home the news that Parliament had voted to impeach Robert Harley, Lord Oxford, and Henry St. John, Lord Bolingbroke, of treason. None of the Tories had dared to protest the charges against Bolingbroke, who had already fled to France, but Mr. Jekyll and Mr. Foley, Lord Oxford's brother-in-law, did try to defend him. It would, perhaps, have been wise for Lord Oxford to seek safety in France, too, but he was indisposed with the Gravel and too ill to flee. He would be given a chance to defend himself in the House of Lords on Saturday. Their lordships had not yet issued any charges against the Duke of Ormonde.

By that night, Harrowby had been comforted by the fact that no one on the Committee of Secrecy had mentioned the former Earl of Hawkhurst. Exhausted by two strenuous days of sitting in fear, while the Lords debated charges of treason against some of their own, he was primed for a bit of rowdiness.

Their party for Vauxhall contained very few of the friends they had entertained the previous night, neither the Hobbeses nor Mrs. Jamison to be sure. After last night's exhibition, it was doubtful that Sir Humphrey's sister would risk her reputation as a matchmaker on Dudley, for despite what Lord Lovett had said, Sir William was quite capable of informing the other candidates' families that she was conspiring to unload a madman on one of them.

Dudley had not been invited to join them either. Harrowby was not yet ready to forgive him, and it would have been too soon to expect Sir Humphrey to feel at ease with his attacker along.

Nor did Mrs. Mayfield accompany them, for she found strolling in the gardens tedious. She had accepted an invitation to play at cards.

Now that she was presumed to have access to the Hawkhurst fortune, she was invited to card parties with what Hester could only consider an alarming frequency.

Before St. Mars had sent the message to Hester, she had even tried to persuade her aunt to join them in their exercise to divert her from losing his money. But the only result had been that Mrs. Mayfield had questioned her daughter on the need to have Hester accompany her and her friends.

"For you spoil her, Isabella," she had said. Mrs. Mayfield never felt any compunction about discussing her niece in this manner, and had not evinced any discomfort when the subject had come up over the tea table a few days ago. "I do not know why you persist in treating her so well. Hester is lucky enough to be a servant in this house. And so I remind her, whenever she gets ideas above her station.

"But when you constantly allow her to accompany you on all your diversions, you run the risk of giving her and others an elevated notion of what her situation is. Why, next—" she gave a snort of laughter—"you will find some poor, ignorant gentleman paying court to her! And you cannot tell me that you would ask Lord Hawkhurst to fund a dowry for her."

"Why not?" Isabella said, with wide open eyes. "Why shouldn't Hester have a husband?"

Before she was married, she never would have challenged her mother's statements, but being a countess had given her the right to her own opinions. Not that these were ever very profound—in fact, they were often quite silly—but on more than one occasion Hester had been grateful to Isabella for standing up for her.

Required to explain herself, Mrs. Mayfield was struck speechless. Before she could rally to reply, Isabella turned to Hester with an excited look in her eye. "What do you say to that, Hester? Should you like me to find you a wealthy husband? I think I can do it if he does not have to be very handsome. I'm sure I could talk Harrowby into giving you a dowry of some sort. He has so much money, we could never run through it all."

Before Hester could respond politely, but negatively, to this, Mrs. Mayfield sputtered, "No!" Her colour threatened apoplexy at the very least. “You must never plague your husband for anything so foolish! You mustn’t wear out his generosity!”

“But haven’t you asked him to help with Dudley’s settlement?” Isabella asked, in perfect innocence. She had never seen through her mother’s schemes.

“Dudley is your brother, which makes it right for your husband to do something for him. But you cannot be expecting him to throw his fortune away on every relation you have.”

“Not every relation, just Hester. Come,” She turned to Hester eagerly. “Don’t you think it would be fun? And as Mama says, you can amuse yourself with whoever you want after you are married.”

Hester had judged it the proper time to put an end to their argument. “You are very good to me, Bella. Very kind and generous. But your mother is right. You should not trouble yourself with a husband for me.” She had not added that Isabella’s notion of a good husband would never be the same as hers, or that she would not appreciate having to fend off Isabella’s candidates.

But her answer had appeased her aunt and for once had gained her a grudging compliment. Mrs. Mayfield had called her a good girl who knew what was due to her family, and she had left off her complaints about Hester’s attending the outing to Vauxhall.

So tonight Hester was relieved that Mrs. Mayfield was not to accompany them. Her aunt would have been sure to notice the care Hester had taken with her dress and grown suspicious, and she would not have been likely to let her out of her sight. Hester had chosen one of Isabella’s tossed-off gowns, in a becoming shade of greenish blue with pale yellow embroidery on both the bodice and skirt, with three-quarter bell sleeves. She did not think St. Mars would recognize the dress, for the chemise lace had been removed from the sleeves to be used on another of her cousin’s gowns. Besides, Isabella had filled the garment in an entirely different way. For Hester, the bodice had had to be taken in and a modesty piece attached.

Isabella’s motive for including her cousin was not entirely unselfish, Hester learned, as she helped Isabella prepare to descend the stairs. She straightened Isabella’s new satin cloak over the back of her skirt and took up the old one for herself. Then, as they went down, Isabella turned and said, in an urgent whisper, "I need you to keep Harrowby and Sir Humphrey busy, should Lovett and me wish to go off by ourselves. Can you to do that, Hester?"

Hester's heart sank. How was she to keep the two gentlemen occupied and still slip away to speak to St. Mars?

She could not object to any request Isabella made on her own account, but the protest she finally did make was sincere. "Do you think that wise, Isabella? What if your husband begins to suspect you of something . . . not quite *comme il faut?*"

"Oh, he won't mind overmuch. He might even think it's rather diverting! All the fashionable ladies have *affaires.* Look at the number of mistresses the Prince of Wales has! And if their husbands don't care, why should Harrowby? It's not as if he can't amuse himself without me."

A familiar ache began to grow in Hester's breast. She could not deny that the morals of the new king's court left much to be desired. Queen Anne had tried to improve the conduct of her subjects, but if King George ever were to suggest better standards than he set for himself and his family, he would be justifiably ignored. As far as Hester had been able to tell, nothing was farther from his mind. But her concern was not for all of George's subjects. Just for Isabella who, in spite of her flaws, was still dear.

She could see that her reluctance would harm the confidence with which Isabella treated her, however, and she had no right to dictate to her cousin. What had waiting-women been used for always if not to ease their mistresses' *affaires?* It was not a duty Hester relished, but neither did she have a choice.

"I shall do what I can to see that they are occupied," she finally said.

Radiant with anticipation, Isabella led the way down to the antechamber where Harrowby, Sir Humphrey, and Lord Lovett waited for them. Recalling the manner in which Lord Lovett had parted from her on the previous evening, Hester could not help wondering if he would betray any sign of a friendship between them.

Her own feelings about the way he had acted had undergone a series of changes. At first, as soon as the initial shock had worn off, she had felt gratified. In the loneliness with which she faced every day, being in perfect harmony with no one around her, unable to share either her opinions or her innermost secrets, she could not help welcoming the friendship of an intelligent and attractive man. Uneasiness had soon stolen away this feeling, though, for both Lord Lovett's manner and his words that evening had suggested that he was offering something a degree beyond friendship. Hester was not at all certain how she felt about the prospect of his admiration. And, if he had meant to imply that he found her preferable in some way, why was he always flirting with Isabella?

She quickly discovered that she would not have to worry about a transfer of his attention from Isabella to herself. Lord Lovett betrayed not the slightest recollection of their conversation the night before. His gaze might have lingered on her face a second more than usual, but, as always, he turned the full force of his charm on her cousin and there it remained.

He and Sir Humphrey had secured the use of a hackney coach to bring them this way. They chose not to disturb the arrangement, so the three from Hawkhurst House followed in a second carriage to Whitehall Stairs, where Lord Hawkhurst's private barge was docked.

The bargemen had been alerted to their coming and stood ready to help them board in their livery of brown broadcloth, trimmed in golden baize. Hester had never ridden in a private barge and could not help being excited as she was handed in. She would have infinitely preferred to receive the privilege from St. Mars, to whom the barge belonged in justice, if not in law. But since she was on her way to see him, she could almost persuade herself that the treat was truly his.

A reflection of the moon lit the water. Ripples glistened behind them as the bargemen expertly plied their oars. A late spring breeze blew refreshing air off the cooler Thames. Dozens of wherries, tilt-boats, and barges made their way up and down the river, crossing one another's paths. It was hard for Hester to imagine a more beautiful evening.

In the distance they could see the dark outline of the City of London with its many steeples and the new dome of St. Paul's. A celebration seemed to be going on. The faint ringing of bells came from a far-away church, and the glare of bonfires showed in some of the streets.

Hester was about to ask what the occasion was, when a man called out from one of the shadowy boats, "Long live King James!"

He was booed and hissed by some of the other boats, but a Jacobite ditty was taken up in others.

"Damn fools!" Harrowby growled. "They'll be celebrating the Pretender's birthday today. Well, we'll see how happy they are when the lot of them are packed off to gaol!"

No one else in their barge made a comment, but the incident seemed to cast a pall.

The bargemen rowed them up the river and deposited them on the opposite side at Vauxhall Stairs. Lord Lovett leapt out first and gave his hand to the rest. When her turn came, Hester was startled to feel his other arm come around her waist. He drew her near enough to feel his breath in her hair, before letting her go.

Her heart start beating in her throat. She did not know what game he was playing. And she was not certain she wanted any part of it. How could she trust a man who played court to two women, under both their noses?

As Harrowby and Isabella led the way up the bank amidst a throng of debarking ladies and gentlemen, many of whom were masked, Hester fell back with Sir Humphrey and was surprised when Lord Lovett did the same. He made no attempt to engage her in conversation, however, as they made the short walk up the lane to the gate of Spring Gardens.

Once inside, Isabella turned to appropriate Lord Lovett for herself. He gave her his arm, and they continued up the main promenade, surrounded by arrivals on all sides.

It was far too soon to draw the gentlemen away, but Hester wanted to be ready for the best opportunity. Her only hope was to engage them both in the sort of conversation from which gentlemen were accustomed to excluding their female companions, before dropping back and out of sight. Only now did she realize how foolish her suggestion of a meeting place had been, for she had not appointed a specific place within the gardens. Even should she be able to escape her companions, she could do nothing but wander the dark lanes alone and pray that St. Mars found her before someone else did.

Harrowby raised his perspective glass to one eye to ogle the women who passed, some of whose gowns had been cut very loosely at the neck. On those who were masked, a glimpse of pink nipple above the neckline was not at all rare. An occasional shriek as a gentleman availed himself of this invitation could be heard up and down every lane. Giggles, oaths, and grunts came to them from behind the shrubbery. Hester saw that Isabella had chosen the perfect place to deceive her husband, if Lord Lovett had a mind to the same.

He seemed in no hurry to lead her away from the rest of their party, however, but kept turning to include Sir Humphrey and Harrowby in their talk. Hester wondered how late it would be before she could lose them. She studied the face of every bewigged gentleman, young and old, thin and fat, hoping to recognize St. Mars behind a disguise, but all she saw were strangers. And she quickly learned that it was dangerous to show too great an interest in any gentleman's face, if she did not wish to attract their impudent remarks.

Tall trees with their fresh springtime growth widened overhead as they slowly made their way to the center of the gardens. Attracted by the sweet notes of the wandering musicians, Lord Lovett led them to a box where they could sit and eat. Waiters brought them slices of hung beef, with glasses of Burton Ale for the gentlemen and mead for the ladies.

Sitting, trapped, Hester felt as nervous as a bee bumping into a pane of glass. She would never find St. Mars if she had to stay at the table. The only good thing about her situation was that Isabella could not expect her to distract the other two gentlemen when Lord Lovett had led them here himself. Hester could do nothing but bide her time and hope for a change in her circumstances before it was time to leave.

Pleasures are ever in our hands or eyes;
And when, in act, they cease, in prospect, rise:
Present to grasp, and future still to find,
The whole employ of body and of mind.
All spread their charms, but charm not all alike;
On different senses different objects strike;
Hence different Passions more or less inflame,
As strong or weak, the organs of the frame;
And hence one MASTER PASSION *in the breast,*
Like Aaron's serpent, swallows up the rest.

CHAPTER IX

Two hours later, she had to wonder if any of the gentlemen would be able to make it back to the boat on their own two feet. Lord Lovett had appointed himself their host and had kept the waiters filling their glasses to the brim. It had taken very little encouragement for either Sir Humphrey or Harrowby to drink beyond their capacity. Both had been in queer spirits before setting out—Sir Humphrey, low in mind for a gentleman who was usually cheerful in his friends' company, and Harrowby, garrulous and loud, as if relief from his fears had turned him hysterical.

Seated beside Lord Lovett, Sir Humphrey was faring the worst. After several glasses of ale, he had started to bemoan the fates of Lord Oxford and the others. Using every form of persuasion from cajolery to rebuke, Lord Lovett and Harrowby had advised him to hold his tongue, and his mumblings had quickly subsided. Occasionally a morose comment still escaped him, but it had been many minutes since his sentences had made any sense.

Under the influence of mead, Isabella's eyes had grown brighter, and her intentions even more blatant, though she had spared an occasional provocative glance for her husband as well. These seemed to satisfy Harrowby's *amour propre.* In any case, he took no exception to the flirting between his wife and their host. On the contrary, it was not long before he began showing a keener interest in the masked ladies, who threw out lures to him as they passed. Some of their language was so coarse as to leave Hester in no doubt as to their trade. In deference to the presence of his wife, she supposed, Harrowby made no response other than to laugh at their invitations. But as the night wore on, his laughter diminished, and, after one very large and buxom woman strutted past him, promising him greater delights than he had ever experienced in his life, he waited a mere twenty seconds before excusing himself for a piss and stumbling after her.

That was the chance that Isabella had been waiting for.

"I should like to take stroll amongst the shrubbery before we go. Will you escort me?" she said to Lord Lovett, with a look that left nothing in doubt.

Hester fought a rush of mortification from her toes on up. Even forewarned, she found it difficult to accept adultery in someone she loved, and she could not help but love her cousin. Isabella was heedless, often selfish, ignorant, and foolish. But she had a heart that could be generous in spite of the rapaciousness with which she had been raised. She was happiest when everyone around her was merry, and she even found it in her occasionally to be distressed by someone else's suffering.

Harrowby, though, had just evinced his own lack of fealty to the vows they had spoken, so Hester doubted that he took them seriously either. To her a vow was all the reason required to keep faith.

These painful thoughts took only a few seconds to race through her mind, but they must have shown on her face, for Lord Lovett seemed to notice her embarrassment.

"I would rather not leave Mrs. Kean alone," he said, giving her a look of understanding that brought a lump to her throat. "I'm afraid our dear friend Humphrey has drunk far too much to be a companion. Isn't that right, Cove?"

Thus applied to, Sir Humphrey made an effort to see who had spoken. His blurred eyes located Lord Lovett's face, where they rested before closing in a peaceful sleep. Lord Lovett caught him as he fell forward and eased his head down onto the table.

"Hester won't mind staying here," Isabella said, peering over Lord

Lovett's shoulder. "Will you, Hester? Harrowby is sure to come back soon, and she should stay here to tell him where we've gone."

"Unless she had rather stroll with us?"

Lord Lovett's invitation surprised them both. Hester wondered if his flirting had been nothing more than that. She even felt some hope that Isabella could return home without the stain of adultery on her soul.

She had no thought of playing chaperone, though. Not when her opportunity to steal away had finally come.

"Thank you, sir," she said, smiling openly at him for perhaps the first time in their acquaintance. "But my cousin is correct. I shall be perfectly happy listening to the musicians play, and if my lord were to return and find us missing, he might regard it as an inconvenience at least."

He inclined his head, but his manner indicated that he would have preferred for her to join them.

Hester waited until they had disappeared down one of the shorter alleys of trees before she quitted her chair. Terribly afraid that Harrowby would come back before she could get away, she started in a third direction, glancing nervously over her shoulder to keep a watch for his arrival.

With her gaze diverted, she did not perceive the gentleman who stepped in front of her until she stumbled into his chest. Letting out a cry, she tried to retreat, but he took her by the arms and would not release her until she looked up.

Blue eyes greeted her from behind a black mask. A teasing smile softened the harsh set of features she remembered, filling her with joy and relief. "St. Mars!" she whispered, a smile bubbling up from inside her, too.

He stared down, holding her in his grasp a moment more. "I thought you would never be rid of them. Come, let's get away, before any of them return."

He released her, then took one of her arms to urge her away from the box towards a towering row of trees. Within moments, he had drawn her hand into the crook of his elbow, and they had joined the lines of promenaders, who strolled up and down, giggling and calling out to strangers and friends. At Vauxhall, it seemed, no distinction between lord and commoner was observed, for who could tell what face lay behind a mask?

After they had covered a reasonable distance, Hester stole a sideways glance at St. Mars. Tonight, he had not bothered to disguise his age. But a shorter wig than any fashionable gentleman would wear, a plain brown suit with no lace to distinguish it, Quakerish shoes, and the mask had altered him enough that she felt sure that no one would know him.

Her scrutiny did not escape him. "What do you think of my disguise?" he asked.

"It is admirable, sir. But do you not think the mask poses a slight inconsistency with your choice of costume?"

"Because I affect the Quaker?"

She nodded.

"But, surely, even a Quaker could be tempted to sin on an evening like this when the nightingales are singing. And if he were to sin, who would be more likely to wish for concealment?"

His teasing started a pulse deep inside her. The feel of his muscles beneath her palm was wonderfully warm and hard.

"Very logical, my lord. I see that you gave the matter adequate forethought before taking this risk. And may I apologize for not doing as well? Until this evening, I had not thought how difficult it would be for us to find each other here. I am very relieved to have encountered you so quickly."

"Did you think I would allow you to wander about in a crowd like this?" St. Mars had dropped his playful tone. "I've been watching you all evening. I followed you up from the riverbank and did not take my eyes off of your table once."

Hester was so overcome that she could only murmur a shy, "Thank you, my lord."

"Who is that gentleman who walked away with your cousin?"

Nothing could have punctured the cloud on which she'd been floating faster or more completely than a question about Isabella. For the past few moments, Hester had forgotten that the man beside her had been in love with Isabella, indeed, that he must be in love with her still.

"That gentleman is Lord Lovett. He is a friend of both Isabella's and Harrowby's." She hardly knew how to refer to Isabella's husband when speaking to St. Mars, for to call him Isabella's husband or Lord Hawkhurst would remind him of all he had lost, and to acknowledge him as his first cousin might not be something St. Mars still wished to do.

"His actions this evening scarcely fit those of a friend to Harrowby," he said significantly.

She felt a rush of shame.

Before she could think of a suitable response, he asked, "Is their marriage already so weak?" —then, with scarcely a pause— "No—do not answer that, Mrs. Kean. It is inappropriate for me to speak to you of such a matter. Tell me instead how everyone does at Hawkhurst House."

Relieved by the change of subject, but with her mood properly subdued, Hester gave him news of his servants—Will, who had won a race against five of the fastest footmen in town, Mrs. Dixon with her painful tooth extraction, and his former valet Philippe and his annoyance with Harrowby's morning callers.

He responded feelingly to the first two, and laughed at the third. "How I should love to witness one of Harrowby's levees! I make no doubt that he loves them. You have been charitable again, Mrs. Kean, in reminding me of something I cannot and do not regret. I do not possess the temperament for a levee."

"It turns out that Philippe does not either, when I believe he had anticipated liking them very much. He is not averse to an audience, as you undoubtedly know. But he cannot abide being told how he should perform his tasks."

"No, he wouldn't, which is what made him so amusing to me."

Hester wondered if she heard him sigh.

She had been so happy speaking to him, in a way she could with no one else, that she had allowed herself to forget that her absence must not last long. Reluctantly, she reminded him. "Is there anything particular you wished to speak to me about, my lord? Your message sounded rather urgent."

Now she did hear him sigh and wondered what had made him.

They were just about to reach the end of an alley of trees. St. Mars halted, gave a good look about, and turned to lead her back to a short path leading off of it. Rustlings and murmurings from behind the densest shrubbery, where no lamps shone, gave warning that they were not alone.

With a muffled oath St. Mars took her hand and led her farther down the path until they had passed the last of these sounds by thirty feet at least, before telling her to wait while he checked for listeners. Then he returned, and with a courtly gesture, invited her to join him behind the shrubbery.

It would have been foolish to demur, given the friendship they had shared, so Hester concealed a slight trepidation, which was accompanied by a definite thrill.

St. Mars came after her. He stood to face her, and said, "I came to warn you."

His words astonished her. She had not known what to expect, but certainly not this.

"I saw you going into Lady Oglethorpe's house with your cousin the other night, and I wondered if you knew how dangerous a friendship with that lady could be."

Hester's mind leapt quickly to the reason. "Because she is a Jacobite?"

"You knew? And still you went? Does Isabella have any idea of the risk she's exposed you to?"

Not noticing the way he had phrased his question, Hester offered an apology. "I did try to stop her, my lord. Truly. Harrowby—pardon me—*your cousin* had expressly told her to take care of the friendships she made, and I tried to remind her. But Isabella had hoped—that is, Lady Oglethorpe promised her the kind of entertainment that Isabella likes, and Bella cares nothing for politics. They hold no meaning for her. She merely wishes to enjoy herself."

"What sort of entertainment does your cousin like?" His tone was harsh, and Hester believed she knew why. "It must not be gaming, for she might find that anywhere."

"My lord . . ." She couldn't help the pleading note in her voice. "I had rather not discuss Isabella's faults with you. It would be disloyal of me." *And only give you more pain,* she thought, not saying this aloud. "Suffice it to say that she went hoping for a pleasure she did not find there. I doubt that she will want to go again. But if you wish, I can make sure she does not by telling her husband beforehand. I believe he would stop her."

"Whether he can or not, you must refuse to accompany her. Is that understood?"

His apparent shift disconcerted her. It seemed a puzzling tack. "I shall refuse if you wish me to, my lord." Though how her refusal would keep Isabella safe, she did not know, unless he believed that Bella would not go if she did not.

She could almost feel him relax. "That will do. I shall not worry then."

A curious point had risen in her mind. She was about to ask him what he had been doing in the Palace Yard on Tuesday night, when he said first, "I have learned to rely on your good judgement, Mrs. Kean. I hope you can give me the benefit of it again. But, before I ask you what I need to know, you must promise to trust me. I should not like you to doubt the goodness of my intentions."

"I have never doubted you, my lord." Amazement filled her voice. "I cannot believe I will begin to doubt you now."

By way of response, he took her hand and pressed it with a kiss. Then, he gave it a squeeze and let it go.

He started to pace, as he did when troubled, she had noticed. She thought he was on the point of speaking when a loud set of voices came from the other side of the hedge.

A coarse expression from one of the men with respect to a female physique made Hester flush with horror, then anger.

St. Mars moved quickly in front of her, as if to block the unpleasantness. "Try not to regard it," he said. "Some men are worse than beasts, but you should not let them distress you."

"Is it truly only *some* men, my lord?" Hester was immediately sorry for this speech, which was unfair. And for her bitter tone—the result, she supposed, of the conduct she had witnessed all evening.

St. Mars did not take offence. He did sound concerned, however, when he said, "I can assure you that not all men—not even all gentlemen, despite what you may have seen to the contrary—regard your sex with so little respect."

Feeling small, Hester could only gaze down at her hands and give a nod.

St. Mars took a finger and gently forced her chin up. "After that fine example of manliness, I am reluctant to draw nearer so that no one can overhear us. But I trust you will presently credit my need to do so."

Hester fought back a gasp, but St. Mars only possessed himself of her hands before bending to whisper in her ear, "I have been away for one month, but certain stories have reached me in France. Could you tell me . . . do you know the extent of the people's discontent with King George?"

Immediately, all Hester's previous concerns went flying from her mind, replaced by the fear that St. Mars was risking his life for treason. But she had promised not to judge him from his questions.

"I cannot tell you the extent of it," she replied, "but surely it is much greater than even a month ago. Or at least, the manifestation of it is bolder, for I have no way of knowing what was in the people's minds before."

Speaking in a rapid whisper, she told him about the Jacobite riot they had stumbled into, Madame Schulenberg's terror, and the King's dismissal of so many officers from the army, delivering it all in a low voice to match his. Throughout her speech, St. Mars listened intently, giving an occasional nod, and looking not at her, but at some troubling vision in his head. When she had finished relating the news from Parliament of the last two days, the arrests and impeachments, she waited for him to tell her the reason for his questions.

He did not offer one, but asked instead, "What have they said about the Duke of Ormonde?"

This, too, surprised her, but she answered him as best she could. "He has not been impeached—as yet, but there are charges leveled against him. But, my lord, you must understand that the only news I have to give you is the little bit your cousin has let drop these past two days, which was neither very much nor very clear. He was much more concerned—almost frantic, in fact—over the possibility that your father's name would be raised in connection with a conspiracy. It never was," she assured him, "but I'm afraid he ordered Mr. Henry to burn all your father's papers, just in case."

In the dark, Hester could not see well enough to read his thoughts. She braced herself for his reaction, but St. Mars said nothing. He simply stood still, holding her hands and absentmindedly rubbing them with his thumbs. The effect was so arousing as to make it hard for her to swallow. Even her knees grew shaky.

At last, feeling that any more of this would raise a fever in her at the very least, Hester gently pulled her hands from his grasp, saying simultaneously, "My lord . . . ?"

He took an inward breath, as if she had startled him out of a deep concentration. Taking her hands again, he kissed one hurriedly and then the other. "My humble pardon, my dear Mrs. Kean. I have used you most abominably, but you must accept my word that nothing but a very serious matter could have made me forget your presence, even for the briefest of moments. I have one more thing to ask, though. I read that Lord Peterborough left London some days ago for his country seat. Do you know if he has returned?"

She shook her head. "I have not heard, and surely the news-sheets would have mentioned it, if he had returned to town."

Lord Peterborough was a former military leader, another Tory who had been banned the Court. Hester hoped that St. Mars would now tell her the reason for his questions, but instead he began to worry about how long he had kept her.

"I must get you back to your party. You will not find it easy to explain this long an absence, I'm afraid."

Hester's excuse did not trouble her, for she had not come to their rendezvous unprepared. This would not be the first time she had to make up a story to explain the minutes she spent with St. Mars. And in this particular case, she thought it would be relatively easy.

"Do not worry yourself about me, my lord, although on no account must you be seen by any of them—even Lord Lovett, who would not recognize you—for he would be sure to report that I had met with an acquaintance, and Isabella would ask me who it was. My imagination does not extend to inventing friends I do not have."

"Any more association with me, and you will have to become a proficient liar." His tone was jesting, but she could hear the regret underneath.

"If that ever becomes the case, I shall be even *more* valued as a waiting-woman, for I assure you that prevarication is the skill most highly cherished in any domestic servant. So again, you have no need to worry about me, my lord."

He laughed genuinely then. Hester felt a great reward for turning his mood so easily.

And, still, they faced each other closely in a place where no light from a lantern or lamp could penetrate the darkness. She thought she heard his breathing change.

"If we were not in a very compromising situation, and I did not fear for the consequences to your honour, Mrs. Kean, I should be tempted to kiss you for that remark."

Her heart felt a thrill, but he had no sooner said those words than he added, "Come. I must restore you to your friends. Shield your face with your cloak."

As she followed him out from behind the bushes, she hardly knew where to look. She was afraid to meet his eye for fear that he would see her elation, when he had only been teasing her. He had not meant anything lover-like. But even the thought of a friendly kiss from him had thrown her into a foolish rapture. She needn't have worried about facing him, though, for his attention was focused on getting her past the other pedestrians without exposing her. Both knew that any witness to their emergence from the secluded spot would assume their activity to have been something quite different. He was masked, and she was not. If anyone who knew her were to see them, she was the one who would be compromised.

As they came closer to the table where she had left Sir Humphrey snoring, St. Mars inclined his head to whisper. "You must lead from here. I will follow you to make sure that no one bothers you, but it would be better if you were to appear alone."

This was to be goodbye, then. And with no word of farewell, or promise that she would see him again. Hester's elation evaporated in an instant, leaving her breast and her throat both sore.

She made a grasp for his hand. "You will be careful, will you not, my lord?" The nature of his questions had raised a presentiment of danger. "You will not take any more risks?"

She could tell by the hesitation in his manner that he understood her worry. But all he said, giving her hand a friendly squeeze before letting it go, was, "You can trust me not to be as foolish as I once was." And, with a firm, but gentle hand in the small of her back, St. Mars sent her on her way.

Hester knew that to peer back was to endanger him, so she walked quickly towards the table without turning around. Not surprisingly, she discovered that the others had returned and were looking around with expressions ranging from annoyance to concern. She did not have to manufacture a flustered appearance, for parting from St. Mars so suddenly had caused her real distress. Her eyes even managed to produce a few tears.

To Isabella's exclamations and questions, she only said that she had stepped away to find a place in which to relieve herself, had wandered farther than she intended, then taken a wrong turn and gone quite a way before realizing her error. Then the importunities of not one, but a number of strangers had forced her to take several detours before finding her way back.

Of them all, only Lord Lovett appeared to doubt her story, though he was far too polite to say. Hester simply had the feeling that he saw through her acting, so she tried to stay away from his more perceptive eyes as their company prepared to leave.

Sir Humphrey proved too drunk to rouse. Harrowby's attempts to wake him met only with indistinct mumblings, ineffectual attempts to open his eyes, and once an exclamation, when on opening them he looked at Lord Lovett and said, "Walpole?"

This surprising utterance caused Harrowby and Isabella, who were in the greatest of spirits after their evening frolics, to break into uncontrolled laughter.

"He's mistook you for Sir Robert, by gad! Well, if he's that deep in the soup, I don't suppose we'll ever get him up."

Lord Lovett, who seemed put out, said acidly, "Very astute, my lord. May I suggest we put him into a chair unless we wish to be here all night?"

Hester wondered what had put him so much out of humour, though she could not fault him for being fatigued with their attempts to get Sir Humphrey to stand.

Presently, they found two servants to bundle Sir Humphrey into a chair. Then, they followed the chairmen down to the river where he had to be lifted out and put into the barge. On the other side of the Thames, the Hawkhurst carriage waited, as well as several hackney coaches looking for fares. Lord Lovett hired one and promised to see Sir Humphrey home and into bed.

Exhausted by the stresses of the evening and the range of emotions she had experienced, Hester rode silently home, while Isabella and her husband prattled on about what an amusing evening they had enjoyed.

Gideon had much to think about after watching Mrs. Kean rejoin her companions, not the least of which was how hard it was to see her go.

He had done what he had come there to do. To warn her away from Lady Oglethorpe. But it had been much harder to stick to that purpose than he would ever have imagined. He reasoned that he deserved the Garter for the restraint and gallantry he had shown.

He would have liked so much to keep her with him longer. She had not been unhappy to see him either. The brilliance of her smile had told him that. But neither had she given him the opportunity to greet her properly, once they had got out of sight. He wondered why she had not greeted him as friends should after a long absence. It was normal—was it not?—for friends to kiss in a friendly way on seeing each other again. It was true that they had both been eager to get away before one of her companions returned and spotted him. Perhaps it was that haste that had driven the usual forms of courtesy from Mrs. Kean's mind, but the opportunity had been lost.

Then, of course, it would have been inadvisable to kiss her, once they had gained the privacy of the shrubbery. She had been brave enough to allow him to lead her there, and he would never have taken advantage of her trust. Still, having greeted each other once without the embrace of old friends, would they ever be able to amend the custom in future?

Mrs. Kean had looked . . . so uncommonly fine. So lovely, that he wondered how he had ever considered her the least bit plain. He could not regret his remark about wanting to kiss her, though—even if he had frightened her—for she had to be warned that she must never go into the shrubbery with any other gentleman. Mrs. Kean was so naive that she might not be aware that they would all of them want to kiss her—and do other things as well.

All of these feelings—for they were feelings more than thoughts—passed through Gideon's heart and mind in a flash. Then he pushed them aside to deal with the news Mrs. Kean had given him.

The government was plainly moving against the Jacobites. Troops had been stationed in Hyde Park and others sent to suppress the rioters in other towns. Both the King and Parliament seemed to be taking steps to ward off a rebellion. And, if that was the case and their information was good, it would not be long before they took Ormonde and the other conspirators into custody.

Surely now Ormonde would act. He would see that he was no longer safe, which would give him three choices. He could do nothing, like Oxford, and try to defend himself, or like Bolingbroke, he could run to France. The first would be prudent only if the government's information were bad, but from everything Gideon had heard, it did not appear that the Jacobites in England or in France had been particularly discreet. If the Duke chose the second option, James would have no leader for his troops in England. He was too far away to lead them himself, and there was no one else with Ormonde's experience to lead a rising.

That left the Duke with the third possible action, which was to call for the rising now.

Gideon knew that he would have to speak to Ormonde again, and soon, before the Duke could be impeached. He would surely have made his decision, and it might take Gideon two weeks or more to convey the news to James in Bar.

Gideon had been standing in the shelter of a tree, watching while the gentlemen in Mrs. Kean's party tried to rouse one of their friends to go home, but now he turned and strode out of the Spring Gardens ahead of them. He walked to the river as fast as he could without attracting attention, but most of the people leaving with him had imbibed so much that they were in no condition to notice another man's haste.

In another few minutes, he had flagged one of the watermen waiting along the bank, had climbed into the bark, and was being rowed across the Thames to Westminster Stairs.

This time, the Duke's porter answered the door after only one knock. He recognized Gideon immediately.

"I'll tell his Grace yer here," the Irishman offered, without bothering to ask Gideon to state his business. He left him standing briefly down in the hall, then brought a footman to lead him up. This servant had one arm missing, which meant that he was probably a former soldier. It was common amongst the Tories to employ wounded men from the army, and Ormonde was no exception.

The Duke was standing in the middle of his private drawing room, staring off into space, but he looked up immediately when Gideon entered the room. Until that moment, Gideon had not known what action to expect in the wake of the arrests, but certainly more than was evident. There was nothing on Ormonde's desk or in this room, no sign of anyone in the house, to make Gideon think that his Grace had decided to act.

Ormonde seemed a bit less relaxed than the last time he had received Gideon, but he did not betray any alarm. Gideon waited impatiently to speak, then said, "I came because I heard about Prior's arrest and the report from the Committee of Secrecy."

"Yes, it's a shame about Prior—and poor Thomas Harley, too. They were both good men." He sighed. "Walpole seems to have obtained a great deal of information."

"How much of it is true?"

Ormonde looked surprised. "I suppose it is all true in one way or the other, but that doesn't mean that what we did was wrong. The country had been at war too long. How many more battles did we have to fight to bring it to an end?"

Gideon knew that the Whigs believed that Marlborough had

defeated Louis's troops in so many battles that there was no need to negotiate at all. And, there was the matter of their allies, who had not been informed of the peace negotiations until they were done.

But he had not come to ask Ormonde to defend his actions as captain-general of the British army.

Preferring not to give offence, he merely nodded. "I came as soon as I heard, for it seemed to me that this attack will force you to hasten your plans. I wanted to know what message to carry to James."

"Why should it hasten our plans?"

Gideon tried to hide his astonishment, but the truth was that Ormonde seemed obtuse.

"Forgive me," he said, "but have you no fear that Parliament will bring charges against you? I hear that issues have been raised, concerning your orders in the field."

"I do not see why I should fear arrest. I merely followed the orders of my minister. If they have Bolingbroke's letters, which they say they have, then they will see that is correct."

"You think the letters will absolve you?"

"Whether they do or not, Mr. Walpole wouldn't dare to come after me. You spoke of the pamphlets you read, but did you see the one by Mr. Defoe? Even he said that nothing I did was illegal. They wouldn't dare to charge me, or the public would burn down every Quakers' meeting house between here and Scotland.

"No," Ormonde said, with a confidence that worried Gideon. "He'll never get a vote against me. I've got too many friends on both sides of the House. Why, even the Whig generals count me among their friends."

"But what about those who have been charged? Can you afford to lose more men?"

"They've only detained two. They might have persuaded themselves to impeach Oxford, but he has no real role in the rising. The man's too sick. And we must not be frightened into doing something rash. We've got to have everything in place. This will not be like a government action, you know. Nothing will be as clear, and the arms and support must be there."

"So none of your plans have changed?"

"No, nothing. Except that we can anticipate a great many more to join our cause when they see how mad these persecutions are. The Tory government was popular. The country wanted the war to end, and we ended it for them. They will not thank Walpole for trying to hang us for it.

"Mark my words," the Duke said. "If Walpole tries to go after me, he will find himself at the end of his own rope. There will be such an uproar that he will wish he never came down from Norfolk, and in a very short time, the name Walpole will be long forgotten."

Ormonde squared his shoulders and gave Gideon a meaningful look. "You should remember this, St. Mars, when you take your place in James's army. The public never forgets its military men. But gentlemen who spend their lives playing at politics will never capture the people's interest."

And except for reassurances like these, that was all that Gideon got out of Ormonde that evening.

Heaven from all creatures hides the book of Fate,
All but the page prescribed, their present state:
From brutes what men, from men what spirits know:
Or could suffer Being here below?
The lamb thy riot dooms to bleed today,
Had he thy Reason, would he skip and play?
Pleased to the last, he crops the flowery food,
And licks the hand just raised to shed his blood.

CHAPTER X

The next evening was the opera. After sleeping till noon, the members of the Vauxhall party were sufficiently recovered to face the prospect of another night out.

For Hester, who had no talent for music but enjoyed it, merely visiting the Italian Opera House was an immeasurable privilege.

Designed as the Queen's Theatre by Sir John Vanbrugh, the famous architect still at work on the Duke of Marlborough's mansion, the magnificent playhouse had caused quite a hubbub when first built. Rakes in the Kit-Kat Club had pooled their money for its construction, and the pious had complained that its columns and pilasters, gilt entablatures and particularly the dome—the like of which had never been seen in England—should more properly have been devoted to God than made a temple to vice. A silver plate laid over the foundation stone with Kit-Kat engraved on one side and Little Whig on the other permanently honoured the gentlemen for whose pleasure it had been built. But, by now, the public had embraced its beauty. Renamed the King's Theatre on George's accession, and modified a few years past when the building was discovered to mangle sound, it still had the power to overwhelm anyone new to its interior.

Sir Humphrey seemed no worse for wear as he welcomed them to his box on the stage. He assured his guests, as he had several times before and, indeed, as they had read in the advertisements, that there was no reason to fear the spectacle would be interrupted by members of the audience.

"For no one will be permitted to enter the stage," he said, handing Isabella into a chair. "The gallants are certain to be displeased, but according to the management, there's a considerable danger posed by the intricate machinery and the changes of scenery, which was why all the tickets, even in the pit, were only by subscription. Not even the most daring young spark is likely to halt the performance to embrace the dancers, which ought to serve our wishes if not theirs." Sir Humphrey's hands fluttered often in the direction of the stage as he issued this promise. He was clearly delighted to present his friends with such a treat.

He had purchased a large number of tickets, enough for Harrowby's entire family—even Dudley, since the invitation had been issued before the unfortunate card party—as well as Lord Lovett, Colonel Potter, and Mr. Blackwell, the Frenchified gentleman they had met at Lady Oglethorpe's drawing-room. Harrowby had not yet encountered Mr. Blackwell, but he was too impressed by the fashionable style of the gentleman's dress to question the wisdom of a connection made through that particular lady. Though, to be fair, Hester thought, there was nothing at all certain about Mr. Blackwell's politics, for Isabella and she might not have been the only guests at Lady Oglethorpe's who were not Jacobites.

Colonel Potter's presence made her and at least one other member of their party uncomfortable. Hester had told James Henry that the Colonel had been dismissed from the Guards. She did not want to be the cause of his or anyone's disappointment, but, with St. Mars's warning fresh in mind, she believed she had done right to protect his house in the current suspicious climate. She could do little to separate her cousin and her husband from the friends they chose, but she could help James Henry see that no one under suspicion of treasonous sentiments became a part of the Hawkhurst household.

Judging by the glower on the Colonel's face, he had been informed of Harrowby's—or, rather, James Henry's rejection. Harrowby had been told of it, however, and he had forgotten that the Colonel might be a member of their party this evening. He started to greet him with a nervous laugh, before remembering his privilege as an earl and snubbing him instead.

Colonel Potter turned away, gnawing angrily on the side of his mouth. As he took a chair on the other side of the box, he glared resentfully at their host, and Hester was reminded that a slip of Sir Humphrey's tongue had betrayed the loss of his commission. No doubt he blamed Sir Humphrey—and her— for costing him the position.

With this matter so recent, as well as Dudley's attack, a certain embarrassment attended the seating. Contrary to Harrowby's wish, Dudley had come. His mother had insisted that he must be seen to be on good terms with Sir Humphrey again. It would be necessary to squelch any rumour of his being a lunatic, she said.

For once, Hester had agreed with her, and she had helped persuade Harrowby, with much more tact, and in a far less strident tone, than his mother-in-law had used. In the end Harrowby had given his permission, either because he had seen the sense in her reflections on the need to uphold the reputation of his family or else because he could not stomach another minute of Mrs. Mayfield's voice.

He managed not to wince too visibly as she broached the awkward subject even before the first greetings had subsided. Urging her burly son forward with more bustle than grace, she pushed him to shake hands with their host.

"My dear Sir Humphrey, you must allow Mayfield to sit beside you. He's been so distressed over that little misunderstanding between you and he the other night. I've vowed and assured him that you are as eager to make it up as him. But the silly boy must have the words from your own two lips, or he'll never believe me. The two of you have so much in common. Lud! but you would be astonished to hear how fondly he speaks of you—several times a day, I vow! I'm sure you would not want a little tiff to spoil such a merry *amitié.*"

Confronted by one of his guests, and a determined one, as only Mrs. Mayfield could be, Sir Humphrey had no choice but to acquiesce. A momentary look of unease showed that he still harboured a fear that the young fellow might take it into his head very suddenly to buffet him with a chair. But Dudley had not been permitted any wine at dinner today—only the quart of beer he always took with his breakfast—and Mrs. Mayfield would be sitting close enough to supervise her son.

Having accepted Dudley's apology, Sir Humphrey soon resumed his cheerful humour, saying more than once what an auspicious evening it was, and promising that his guests would not go away disappointed. When he said this, he rubbed his hands together, as if he were a conjurer about to produce a golden guinea from behind someone's ear.

As the only servant in the party, Hester held back, waiting to be assigned a chair. In spite of her better judgement, she couldn't help feeling gratified when Lord Lovett beckoned her to the front row. As he held her chair for her, his gaze skimmed her approvingly, and a conspiratorial smile curved his lips. He left her immediately, however, to take his usual spot behind Isabella's chair.

Last night, Hester's head had been so filled with St. Mars that she had not bothered to wonder about the outcome of her cousin's tête-à-tête, but Lord Lovett's attention to *her* must raise the question now. Certainly, this evening, Isabella had not behaved like a woman scorned. Indeed, whenever she turned to Lord Lovett, which was often, a sultry smile always accompanied her gaze. Whether it was a *satisfied* smile, Hester did not have the experience to say, but it seemed that something, at least, had passed between them. With a feeling of unease, she wondered again what Lord Lovett's intentions could be.

Last night, St. Mars had told her that not every gentleman held her sex in contempt. But to Hester's untutored eye, most of them did. Women were denied most rights enjoyed by men, one result being that the streets were filled with prostitutes both day and night. From the bits and pieces she had heard, it seemed that some of these women were clever and talented in ways beyond the requirements of their profession. If they had been blessed with a different means to earn their fortune, the aim of most marriages, perhaps they could have taken a respectable place in society.

Gentlemen avoided marriage as long as they could, until their family required them to produce an heir, or their fortunes became so poor that they could not support their manner of living. If Lord Lovett had no need to wed, he would naturally seek diversion among ladies for whom marriage was not a reasonable goal—other men's wives or dependent females, perhaps, who could not expect a gentleman's attentions to be accompanied by a promise of matrimony.

Not for the first time, Hester cautioned herself against opening herself up to attentions of that kind, no matter how flattering they might seem.

For now, she was determined to put this all out of her mind, so she could enjoy the opera. It had been composed and was to be conducted by Mr. Handel, a German gentleman who had been appointed Kapellmeister at King George's court in Hanover before arriving in London a few years ago. The story went that he had obtained leave to travel to England, but after achieving a spectacular success here in the Haymarket with his Italian opera, *Rinaldo,* he had failed to return to his royal patron.

This had resulted in some awkwardness later when George acceded to the English throne. King George was not particularly known for his willingness to forgive, having punished his wife for one transgression by locking her away for life and refusing to let her see her children ever again. For months, Mr. Handel had not dared to appear at Court. But Baron Kielmansegg, who had always been the composer's advocate, had at last managed to obtain the royal pardon.

Tonight's performance was by command, but a glance across the stage at the royal box found it empty. The normal tumult floated up from the pit, vulgar shouts and laughter, with which the people in the boxes had to compete to be heard. A movement near the stage, followed by the arrival of the orchestra, seemed to indicate that the performance was about to start, when a flurry in one of the royal boxes caught everyone's eye. A relative hush fell upon the house, and the audience came to its feet to pay respect to the Prince and Princess of Wales.

The royal couple acknowledged the applause. Her Royal Highness smiled and the Prince waved genially. It was said that he had expressed great love for the English, but he seemed more in love with the flattery heaped on him than with the people who delivered it.

They had been accompanied by the lords and ladies who were in waiting this week. Mrs. Howard took a chair beside the Prince, instead of by her mistress, as might have been expected, but the Duchess of St. Albans, Lady Dorset, and Lady Essex Robartes surrounded the Princess's chair. Hester was glad to note that this last lady had survived her visit of obligation to Cornwall, for every time her ladyship faced the necessity of journeying to that wild, lawless place, she said, she dreaded for her life.

Of the King there was no sign, until Mr. Handel made a deep bow to one particular box. The audience hastened to their feet, craning their necks to see what he had seen.

The second royal box still stood empty. The one which had attracted all the notice was a private box, and there Hester saw the Baroness von Kielmansegg, sitting in all her bulk. In response to the bows, she inclined her head as graciously as her many chins would allow, exposing another broad figure behind her in the shadows.

Hester would not have known it was the King, if George had not been flanked by his grooms of the chamber, Mehemet and Mustafa, but there was no mistaking the exotic dress of the King's Turkish servants.

A monarch who preferred not to be noticed was something that no English audience could understand. It simply did not suit their image of a king. People murmured amidst their applause, and more than one face evinced a sullen dissatisfaction. Some with greater cheer waved their hats above their heads until George was obliged to acknowledge them with a wave. Then he retreated, giving no sign of pleasure at having been seen.

Mr. Handel waited for the royal nod before taking the director's place at the harpsichord.

Then the music began, and from the very first note, Hester forgot everything but the spectacle on the stage.

The story was a Spanish tale of chivalry, the romance of Amadis of Gaul, his beloved Oriana, and the attempts of Melissa, a jealous sorceress, to come between them. Hester was carried away by the magnificent scenery—which moved with hardly a squeak with the aid of pulleys and ropes—the dramatic story, and the virtuosity of the Cavaliero Nicolino Grimaldi, the famous castrato, who, as Amadis, raised his pure, angelic voice in alt.

But it was the character of Melissa, sung by the Signora Elizabetta Pilotti Schiavonetti, who captivated Hester from her very first aria.

Until the aria was sung, Melissa had seemed just a simple villainess, conceived for the sole purpose of throwing Oriana's goodness into bright relief, but suddenly, in song, Melissa's unrequited love for Amadis was revealed, pricking at a tender spot in Hester's heart.

By the light of the great chandelier hanging from the ceiling, she could read the words in the libretto, which Harrowby had bought for Isabella in the street. Without it, Hester would never have understood the anger with which Melissa began her song. But when her notes turned plaintive, with the aid of a solo hautboy, the painful emotions of the rejected lover required nothing else to make them felt.

"Ah! Spietato!" Oh, pitiless man, are you not moved by so constant a love, which makes me die for you? The notes of the music alone conveyed an inconsolable sadness. Her tenderness and longing ended in despair. To Hester, it was a major revelation to learn that music was a language, too, that the secrets of a woman's heart could be expressed with nothing more than a sequence of notes. Perhaps no other woman in the audience felt these emotions as keenly as she, but every sigh of Melissa's plucked at a chord in her breast, revealing feelings even she, in all her honesty, had not acknowledged.

True, she had done nothing purposely to separate her cousin from St. Mars. And Isabella had not returned the love he had nobly offered. But he had been in love with her cousin. He probably loved her still.

And, as Melissa's mood drifted between gentleness and misery, defiance and despair, Hester admitted to herself that she had experienced all of those feelings. She had merely pushed the ones she could not tolerate aside, so that even she was unaware of them.

Had the fact that she possessed them kept her from doing all she could to prove St. Mars's innocence? Had she feared to clear him, when, outlaw that he was, she could keep his friendship to herself? What had she done, or not done, to aid him? Could she be as selfish and deluded as Melissa?

For the remainder of the first act, she could not stop these guilty questions from rising, so by its end, her spirits were morbid. The *intermezzo* was announced, and her companions stood to stretch themselves. They chattered about the music, laughed and waved to friends, and smothered yawns—in Dudley's case—preparing to leave the box. Harrowby was the first to go, having as his object a neighbouring box. Colonel Potter exited with Dudley. Lord Lovett took Isabella on a stroll, making Hester's company unrequired, and Mrs. Mayfield found her escort in Sir Humphrey. Mr. Blackwell was the only guest besides Hester to remain in his chair.

Hester could not bring herself to join the crowd. Her conscience hurt. She would have preferred to have been left alone, so she could think without worrying that her thoughts might be written on her face. But Mr. Blackwell took no notice of her, and she might have forgotten his presence altogether, if half-way through the interval, he had not stood up to peer into the pit.

After a moment, he gave a backwards start, and moved into the shadow cast by the wall that separated their box from the next. It was as if he had glimpsed someone he did not wish to see. He abruptly turned, then, taking note of Hester, he tried to disguise his haste.

Making her the briefest of bows, he said, "Pray, madam, will you convey my apologies to our host? I have recalled a prior engagement and fear I shall not be able to stay for the rest of the entertainment."

Then he left with no further word, and Hester gained the privacy she had wanted.

The performance, with its revelations, had affected her more than she was willing to accept without an examination of her feelings by day. Unused to reveling in guilt, she was still familiar with the effects of night upon the emotions, and knew how the hours of dusk could magnify morbid thoughts. The power of the music had taken her unawares. She had not expected the composer to be able to express the mortification of unrequited affection, or certainly never so eloquently. What had shaken her more, though, was the suspicion of a selfish core she might possess, whose existence she would have denied. Nothing short of a complete examination of her actions from first meeting St. Mars to last night's rendezvous would resolve whether she had one or not.

She was so taken up with this soulful search that she hardly heard the others returning to the box. Smiling in absent-minded greeting, she was vaguely aware of the sorting and shuffling that often takes place during an interval. Harrowby, by some rare miracle, returned with his own wife upon his arm. Lord Lovett followed shortly with Colonel Potter on his heels. And Mrs. Mayfield arrived on the arm of an old admirer who wished to be presented to her children, the earl and countess.

This gentleman, if the title could be applied to one who gazed so lecherously on a former lover's daughter, seemed disinclined to leave. He kissed Isabella with the freedom of an old friend, queried Harrowby on the number of livings in his possession and offered to provide him with the names to fill them, flirted loudly with Hester's aunt, and kissed Isabella again, this last time risking injury to his back in attempting to squeeze her waist as she was seated. Isabella accepted his attentions good-humouredly and only laughed at his more outrageous attempts to embrace her.

An acquaintance like this was not one Hester wished to make, and she gladly kept her distance. Lord Lovett and Colonel Potter did the same. As sullen as ever, and with no reason left to conceal his opinions from Lord Hawkhurst, the Colonel made no effort to hide his disgust at the visitor's vulgarity. Lord Lovett chose to be amused instead, and even gave Hester a wink.

It was only a few minutes more before the musicians resumed their places, and only after the music started that Mrs. Mayfield's swain was persuaded to depart. At the door of the box, he bumped into Dudley, who was just returning. Hester felt a moment's disquiet when she saw the droop of her cousin's eyelids, a certain sign that he had been drinking. As he stumbled into his chair, the odor of wine wafted through the box. Mrs. Mayfield whispered to him sharply to behave himself, drawing a sneer from the Colonel, and a frown from Lord Lovett, who glanced at Hester again, this time with concern.

Then Hester noticed that their host had not reappeared. She experienced a stirring of alarm, but the feeling was quickly tempered by the fact that they had heard no commotion outside their box. If Dudley *had* lost his temper, surely someone in their party would have heard him, or at least another member of the audience would have thought to complain. No one could do anything about it now without calling attention to Dudley. So, by tacit agreement, she and Lord Lovett turned their attention to the stage.

In the second act, Melissa's aria was accompanied by a solo trumpet. As the sorceress threw off all tender emotions and gave herself entirely to revenge, her mood was defiant—even cheerful. And rather inappropriately so, Hester thought, still smarting from the wounds to her conscience. But she no longer felt a kinship with the villainess, so her burden began to lift.

A sound of scuffling behind her intruded on the music. Frowning, Hester tried to ignore it, but her companions, who were not engaged as deeply by the music as she, all turned around in their chairs.

Something was seriously wrong. To Hester's right, Isabella and her mother stared speechlessly at the entrance to the box. As Hester turned to see what had startled them, she saw that everyone else had frozen, too.

Sir Humphrey stood in the doorway with wide, staring eyes and a strange, unfocussed look upon his face. The sheen of perspiration gleamed on his forehead. An ashen pallor had covered his normally rosy cheeks. The hands that habitually fluttered near his belly were still, pressed against the framing for support.

"Humphrey? Dear fellow, what it is?" Lord Lovett was the first to break the silence. His colour, too, had gone white.

A man of action, Colonel Potter jumped to his feet just as Sir Humphrey fell forward. As the Colonel caught him, everyone gasped, except Mrs. Mayfield who made a huffing sound and spoke indignantly of people who would blame other gentlemen for their over-indulgence. Sir Humphrey's round, wild eyes stared up at them with a plea.

"'Pon my word!" Harrowby exclaimed. He was hushed by people in the neighbouring boxes, as Nicolino started to sing.

With a start Colonel Potter held up the hand he had used to lower Sir Humphrey to the floor, his fist clenched around a horrifying object.

"My God!" Lord Lovett said. "Is he . . . ?"

"Yes," Colonel Potter answered, staring amazedly at the bloody knife in his hand. "I'm afraid that Sir Humphrey has been murdered."

Virtuous and vicious every Man must be,
Few in the extreme, but all in the degree;
The rogue and fool by fits is fair and wise;
And even the best, by fits, what they despise.
'Tis but by parts we follow good or ill;
For, Vice or Virtue, Self directs it still;
Each individual seeks a several goal;
But HEAVEN'S great view is One, and that the Whole.
That counterworks each folly and caprice;
That disappoints th' effect of every vice;
That, happy frailties to all ranks applied;
Shame to the virgin, to the matron pride,
Fear to the statesman, rashness to the chief,
To kings presumption, and to crowds belief.

CHAPTER XI

Sir Humphrey Cove had been murdered with a knife from Hawkhurst House.

This became obvious in the chaos that followed his collapse. Isabella was the first to spy the Hawkhurst arms on the handle of the knife, which shocked her so forcibly as to prevent the screams she might otherwise have produced. She had no sooner pointed to the knife and blurted out its ownership than her mother fell into hysterical shrieks.

The audience booed and hushed, ignorant of the crime that had taken place. The trumpets, hautboys and harpsichord continued to produce their beautiful notes, while Nicolino's tragic voice soared eerily above them. Visibly distressed, Lord Lovett took charge, and, with no concession to rank, instructed Harrowby to remove his mother-in-law at once. He turned to Hester and, placing a hand on her shoulder, quietly requested her to escort Isabella and her mother home, his manner conveying implicit confidence that she, at least, would not lose her head.

Agreeing with his plan, Hester complied, but she was far from tranquil herself. To see Sir Humphrey, with his harmless cheer and innocent goodwill, so brutally cut down was more upsetting than anything she had ever witnessed. Her hands and knees trembled as she put her arms about Isabella and urged her past the corpse, whose blood lay pooling on the floor.

At first, Isabella refused to go. She clung to Lord Lovett, who, in addition to making order out of confusion, had to soothe her by promising to call at Hawkhurst House as soon as he had finished here. He helped Hester get her cousin out of the box, suggesting she lift Isabella's skirts so they would not be stained. With both of her hands engaged in supporting Isabella, Hester's own gown was not so fortunate. She cringed as her hem was dragged through the blood.

Busy as she was, and nearly overset, she did not realize the full importance of the knife until she, her aunt, and her cousin were seated in their coach, Isabella sat huddled in her arms, and the clop of the horses' hooves had broken the tense silence. Then, when she realized the truth, that someone who had been in Hawkhurst House must have committed the murder, she chastised herself for not observing everyone's reactions. Without seeing them, she could not even venture a guess as to who might be a killer.

Universal fear and shock were all that she could recollect, but whether those emotions had been shared by everyone was something she would never know. For now, she was too shaken to do more than regret the disturbance of her mind.

Mrs. Mayfield said suddenly, "Hester, you must say that you strolled about with Mayfield during the *intermezzo*."

For a moment Hester was too stunned to reply, but as soon as she found her voice, she protested firmly, "That would be perjury, Aunt, and I cannot believe you wish me to commit a crime."

"This is not an occasion for foolish scruples! Your family needs you, and that should be enough. After all I have done for you . . . ."

Seething, for there was nothing she could say to stem her aunt's angry flow, Hester remained silent while Mrs. Mayfield talked herself hoarse. There was no mistaking the hysteria beneath her words. She believed either that her son had murdered Sir Humphrey, or at the very least that he would be accused of it. The prospect was frightening even to Hester, who had no particular affection for her oafish cousin. If word of Dudley's earlier assault got out, who would not suspect him of attacking Sir Humphrey again? Hester was in no condition at the moment to conjecture whether Dudley had been drunk enough to turn violent. Certainly, he had returned to the box reeking of spirits.

But now Mrs. Mayfield had finished her speech and was demanding an answer.

Hester repeated her refusal to perjure herself, following quickly with this advice, "Even if I were willing to lie, nothing good could possibly come of it. Everyone must have noticed that I stayed behind in the box. And everyone was present when Dudley returned alone." She did not say, *returned drunk,* but ended, "It would look suspicious, indeed, were I to say otherwise. In all such cases, surely, telling the truth is best."

"But what if they won't believe the truth? Then, what?"

A cold, stony hardness formed in Hester's breast. Her aunt was asking this question now, when she had refused even to consider St. Mars's innocence. Faced with the truth, she had denied it in order to keep his wealth for her daughter and herself. Were Dudley guilty of murder, she would just as willingly deny the truth again.

Their arrival at Hawkhurst House spared Hester the need to respond. She handed Isabella to her maid and sought her own chamber in order to remove her gown. She asked one of the laundry maids to put the hem on to soak, hoping that the stain could be removed, though she wondered how soon, if ever, she would be willing to wear the gown again. After changing, she joined Isabella and Mrs. Mayfield in the withdrawing room, where they waited for the gentlemen to come home.

Harrowby and Dudley returned more than two hours later. Harrowby was weary and upset, his brother-in-law red-faced and sullen. As Dudley stormed into the room, it did not take long for the ladies to discover the reason for his rage.

"He thinks I killed him!" he announced, as soon as the door to the withdrawing room was closed behind them. "As if I would stab a fellow in the back like a damned coward!"

As one, his female relatives turned their gaze upon Harrowby, still standing just inside the door, while he spluttered, "For the Lord's sake, keep your voice down, Mayfield, unless you want the servants to carry the tale to every news-sheet in town!

"And I did not say I thought you had murdered poor Humphrey," he added. "I only said you had caused enough trouble as it was."

"Well, I am sure there is nothing in that," Mrs. Mayfield said. "Not when we've all been so upset. Lud! but I've never suffered such palpitations in my life! To think that anyone would harm our dear Sir Humphrey! What kind of monster would do that?"

Even Harrowby, who was not often aware of Mrs. Mayfield's ploys, seemed to feel that her speech savoured of something false. He threw her an offended look, and Hester found it in her heart to pity him, for in his own way, he had been very fond of his friend. The two had shared a childlike pleasure in simple distractions, as well as their gullibility.

Who could replace Sir Humphrey at Harrowby's levees?

"You will have to excuse me," he said coldly. "I am going to bed. The coroner will want to question us all soon enough." Harrowby opened the door and called to a waiting footman to have Philippe attend him in his chambers. Then, with a frosty bow, he retired.

Mrs. Mayfield lost no time in rounding on Dudley. "Now, see what you have landed us in—you, with your temper? If Lord Hawkhurst doesn't throw the lot of us out, it will not be because of you.

"Isabella—" she threw over her shoulder— "I want you to go to your husband's chamber and make him comfortable. We cannot have him angry with us now."

"But Lord Lovett promised . . ."

"Forget Lord Lovett! This is no time to behave like a harlot! You can see him all you want another day. But you'll never see him again if your husband sends us in disgrace to Rotherham Abbey and decides to keep you there."

"I don't think Harrowby is mad at *me*," Isabella said, pouting. At the look on her mother's face, however, she said, "Very well, I'll go see if there's anything Harrowby wants. But I doubt he'll want me right now. Not when Philippe is there to fuss over him."

As soon as she was gone, Mrs. Mayfield pressed Dudley to tell her what had happened after they had left. His feelings were so wounded that several minutes passed before she was able to pull the story out of him.

After taking charge, Lord Lovett had insisted that all the gentlemen remain, and only then did they notice that Mr. Blackwell had not returned to the box. His absence suggested the possibility of a second murder, but neither he nor his body was found. Lord Lovett sent a footman to alert the Watch—who came, but not until the opera was letting out, so they had to fight their way into the theatre against the crowd.

On regarding the body, the knife, and the illustrious personages involved, the Watch, which consisted of two decrepit old men, insisted on calling the Coroner. When the Coroner finally appeared, he proved to be scarcely fitter than the Watch, being not of that estate from which a subordinate magistrate should legally have been appointed. He principally wanted to know how a knife, bearing the Hawkhurst arms, had come to be at the opera house.

That was a question which no one could answer. No one except the murderer, of course, who naturally chose to remain silent. But the knife pointed a finger at someone in Sir Humphrey's own box, where Lord and Lady Hawkhurst, members of their family, friends who had dined at their table, and gentlemen who had attended Harrowby's levees had been the victim's guests. The Coroner had been distressingly unconcerned about Mr. Blackwell's departure, especially once it was established that the gentleman had never set foot in Hawkhurst House, but he did agree that Blackwell's testimony should be sought. But so should everyone's, he had emphasized. And to that end, he told them they would all be notified when the date of the inquest had been set and required to appear.

By the time Mrs. Mayfield had extracted this much from her son, even Dudley had sobered. No quicker than his sister, still he had managed to surmise that his recent attack on Sir Humphrey would make him a suspect in his death. Unfortunately—or so he insisted—he had absolutely no memory of the first incident, which unsettled him in the extreme.

"Well, I'm sure that nobody would accuse *you* of anything so horrible," his fond mother averred. "Not when your sister is a countess and her husband an earl! I hope this will teach you to be properly grateful to our dear Lord Hawkhurst, and to Isabella for catching him, too."

This was not precisely the expression of confidence Dudley had hoped for. That his mother based her conviction of his not being accused, not on his certain innocence, but on the reluctance of the legal authorities to prosecute an earl's brother-in-law, seemed to speak to her own doubts. The nervous manner with which she picked at her necklace failed to inspire him with any belief in her faith.

"You don't think I had anything to do with it, do you?" he inquired, on a rising note.

Mrs. Mayfield snapped, "What your mother thinks will mean nothing to a Grand Jury, I assure you! The justices will want to know why you came back so late to the box!"

Dudley's heavy face flushed. "I had to piss! There's no crime in pissing, is there?"

"Don't ask me to believe it took you that long to relieve yourself! You had no business drinking, or this never would have happened!"

He went pale. "You think I did it, don't you? You think your son's a fucking murderer."

Her slap rang against his face so fast that neither Dudley nor Hester had a moment's warning. "How dare you speak to your mama that way! I should have left you at home to run to waste! But it's too late now."

While Dudley cradled his scarlet cheek, her outrage changed into determined spite. "I will do what I can to get you out of this mess, but if I can't, do not think that your sister and I will suffer with you. I have already given you much more care than you deserve."

She turned on her heel and left the room, slamming the door behind her. Hester felt as if her body had been filled with a painful poison. She would have given anything not to have been present at that scene, but she doubted that her aunt would care either way.

Dudley sat staring after his mother with a mixture of fury and despair. He seemed unaware that his cousin had witnessed his disgrace and did not speak until Hester stirred. Then he started and scowled.

"I'll wager you think I did it, too, eh?"

Beneath his surliness, Hester detected a strong need for reassurance.

"Why don't you tell me what happened so I can form an opinion? I promise you, I haven't the slightest notion what to think."

Her offer of a fair hearing made him wary. Dudley had never paid her even the courtesy of his attention, but at the moment he was too desperate for friends to be very particular. After mulling over her statement, he smoothed his ruffled feathers a bit.

"Nobody has the nerve to accuse me aloud, but I could see it in their eyes. They think I stabbed the old fool!"

Hester bit back the words she wanted to say—that perhaps no one would suspect him, if he showed a proper respect for his family's dead friend. Instead, forgiving him for his obvious panic, she encouraged him to sit and drew him out by sharing the only information she possessed.

"I was in the box when Mr. Blackwell left it. He seemed to catch sight of someone in the pit he wished to avoid and took himself off very suddenly. I do not know where."

Dudley seized on this. "I know that blackguard did it! If the Watch did their job, they could have caught him straight away. Now, only God knows where he can have got to!"

Seeing he was about to fall into the dismals again, Hester quickly asked, "You did not see Sir Humphrey after you left the box?"

"No. Colonel Potter and I went for a drink, but we didn't drink that much."

"I will take your word, but, to be honest, you smelled very strongly of spirits when you returned. Everyone must have noticed."

His eyebrows snapped into an angry frown. "Some oaf jostled my glass of wine all over me. I would have had to pay for another if the Colonel hadn't treated me to it."

"He returned with Lord Lovett, several minutes before you did."

Dudley's suddenly hooded eyes made her wonder what he was trying to hide. "I didn't want him looking over my shoulder while I pissed, did I? I don't know why they can't build a bigger privy for that many gents. Had a devil of a time making my way into it."

Hester wanted to shake him for being so stubbornly foolish, but she could not force him to confide in her.

"Did you see where Colonel Potter went after you two parted?"

Dudley was thrown off balance by her change of direction. Eventually, though, he understood the purpose of her question. "You mean he could have done it, don't you? Why that—!"

Hester halted him with a raised hand before she could be subjected to more of his vulgarities. "We know nothing at all. But surely everyone must be considered a suspect at this point. I would imagine the magistrate in charge will want to know if any of us was ever alone."

"Not all of us." He gave a bitter grimace. "No woman could have driven that knife between Sir Humphrey's ribs. A female wouldn't have had the strength. Or, at least, that's what Lord Lovett said when I asked him why he let you and Bella and Mama go."

A rueful smile tugged at Hester's lips. There was certainly nothing heroic about Dudley, but still she felt obliged to help him. If he *was* innocent, as he claimed.

"There's no need for you to assume that you are the only suspect. If they had any evidence against you, either the Watch, the Coroner, or even one of the other gentlemen would have been within their rights to arrest you on the spot. Mere suspicions do not add up to a conviction. So, if I were you, I should not worry myself excessively over what others might think."

Dudley's face brightened. He cheered so quickly, in fact, that Hester felt compelled to add a few cautious words. "All the same, I should be very careful what you say about Sir Humphrey. It wouldn't hurt for you to express a little sorrow at his death. And I should consider limiting my consumption of spirits to thwart any unfavourable impressions others might have formed." She could have gone on, but decided that two pieces of advice were already more than Dudley was likely to accept.

She could tell this last was not to his liking, but in phrasing it as she had, she had removed most of its sting. Certainly he took it in greater part than he had his mother's cruel jabs.

Hester would have liked to ask him more about his movements during the interval, but they were interrupted by the sound of an arrival downstairs.

Still nervous, Dudley had no wish to encounter anyone. He instructed Hester to say that he was not at home and ducked out of the withdrawing room through the back door. In the next minute,

Hester was very much disconcerted to find herself greeting Lord Lovett alone.

She made her apologies for the rest of the family, saying that the evening's events had driven them all to their beds. In a hurry to leave the room, she offered to go in search of Isabella, who had particularly wished for him to come.

Lord Lovett stopped her with a gentle grasp of her wrist. "Please stay. I would not have you disturb either her or Lord Hawkhurst. I have just come from seeing Sir Humphrey's sister, and in all honesty I doubt that I am up to their *chatter* just yet."

A bitter tone accompanied these words, which Hester might have found unpardonable if not for the weariness she read in his face. She found his touch disturbing, though, if not downright improper, so she tactfully removed herself from his reach. She invited Lord Lovett to rest himself, then summoned a servant to have refreshments brought up for him. Then she seated herself in a chair safely across the carpet.

A flicker in his gaze revealed an awareness of her shyness, but it quickly vanished beneath the weight of the day's events. Hester thanked him for his efforts on behalf of the family. He had spared them not only the inconvenience of dealing with the authorities, but also the distress of seeing that Sir Humphrey's body was cared for.

He did not bother to deny it, which would only have called greater attention to his kindness, but instead moved straight to his concerns.

"I wonder—and you must forgive me for asking—what did Mayfield have to say when he came home?"

Hester was not surprised by his curiosity on this point, only that he wished to discuss it with her.

"He was concerned that there might be some suspicion that he had lost his temper with Sir Humphrey again. He insists there is nothing in it, however."

Lord Lovett leaned one elbow on the arm of his chair and rubbed his eyes. Hester had never seen anyone so spent. "I worried that that would be the case, but the story is bound to come out, you know. Once Cove's murder is generally announced, Sir William is certain to come forward with his evidence. Failing that, Mrs. Jamison may choose to make the accusation herself." He looked grimly at Hester. "I must ask you this, Mrs. Kean, though it pains me to do it. Do you believe your cousin could have killed my poor friend?"

Hester felt a lump in her throat. Lord Lovett was the first to express a genuine feeling about Sir Humphrey. The others had been shocked and upset, which was natural under the circumstances, but none of them had evinced a sincere feeling of pity.

She was spared an immediate answer by the arrival of their tray. She poured a glass of wine for Lord Lovett, and took a dish of tea for herself. As new as she was to drinking it, she found it amazingly restorative.

After the servant left them alone again, she said, "I am afraid I cannot answer that question, sir. I know you will think me biased, since Dudley is my first cousin. I should not have thought him capable of such an act, however, and I do believe him when he says he is innocent. But how can anyone be sure?"

He nodded and sighed. Then his ironic smile appeared. "You can see why I was not ready to speak to Lord and Lady Hawkhurst. Although there was more to it than that. You are an intelligent woman, Mrs. Kean, and I believe it would behoove us to put our heads together on this."

Hester felt a quiver of surprise. She could not be entirely comfortable with the manner of his compliment, but she was glad that it dealt with her mind, rather than with a physical attribute she knew she did not possess. She would never have believed any flattery about her appearance.

"Very well," she said. "Then I should like to ask you some questions if I might."

He seemed taken aback, but acquiesced with a rakish smile. "Ask whatever you like, as long as you leave out my romantic escapades."

Hester flushed. "I wanted to ask you about the other gentlemen in our party, sir."

"Ahhh . . . . Well, under the circumstances, I promise not to feel piqued. How can I help you?"

Ignoring this flirtatious statement, she said, "I was in the box when Mr. Blackwell departed. At first he seemed disinclined to take the air. And I would have wagered that he had no intention of leaving, until he saw someone down in the pit. It seemed as if he had spotted someone he did not wish to encounter, for he almost hid himself along the edge of the box. Then he could not leave quickly enough, and only remembered to make his excuses when he noticed I was there."

"Did you look down to see who might have caught his attention?"

"No." Hester squirmed when she recalled how she'd been occupied. "I was rather lost in thought."

"And he said nothing about where he might be going?"

"Only that he had forgotten a previous engagement—not that I believed him. It is the polite excuse that everyone gives when they want to be somewhere else."

"Hmm." Lord Lovett mused. "It is possible that he killed Humphrey, of course, but I wouldn't know why. Blackwell is a bit of a mystery."

"Have you known him long, my lord?"

He gave her quick look. "I?"

Then, as if making a difficult decision, he nodded. "You will hear this from someone else, if not from me, but yes, I have known him for a number of years, although never very well. We run into each other at Lady Oglethorpe's occasionally. Blackwell is . . . a man who is often out of the country."

His emphasis on the last few words as much as informed her that both of them were Jacobites, or, at least, that their sympathies lay that way. Hester could not help being flattered by his confidence. She was not so intensely political that someone else's party affiliation would come as an affront to her, but he could not have known that she would not report him. She was honoured by the risk he had taken.

"Sir Humphrey was often in Lady Oglethorpe's company, too, I understand."

He sighed again. "Yes, he was. Poor old Cove." He did not elaborate, but asked, "Was there anything else?"

"Yes. And please forgive me, for I know you are friends. But—Colonel Potter—I know he was angry that he did not get the position as Lord Hawkhurst's secretary. And I believe he thought he lost it because of something Sir Humphrey let slip. My lord would not wish to have a person under suspicion of disloyalty working in this house."

"You think that Potter could have killed Sir Humphrey out of revenge?" He seemed to take the notion seriously.

"I do not know what to believe. That is why I ask you if it is possible."

"My dear Mrs. Kean," he said, and she thought she saw moisture in his eyes. "Anything is possible now. I should not have said two weeks ago that Humphrey would be murdered. But now that it has happened . . . ." He did not finish, but looked dismally down at his hands.

Of a sudden he jerked, and his gaze flew to meet hers.

"What is it?" she said. Her eyes moved to the spot he was rubbing on the outside of his right palm. It looked very much like dried blood.

Hester felt the colour draining from her cheeks. Her pulse took great leaps. Lord Lovett had gone pale, too. He shuddered, before meeting her eyes.

"Yes, I'm afraid it is Sir Humphrey's. I thought I had washed it all off. I helped to lift him onto the litter, you see."

Now that his shock had worn off, his colour returned. Hester's was not so quickly restored, but she made an effort not to appear unsettled.

The blood made her think of something she had not considered.

"When Sir Humphrey was stabbed, would not some blood have stained his murderer's clothing?"

She blurted out the question so rapidly that Lord Lovett was taken aback. As soon as he saw the direction of her thoughts, however, he relaxed.

"There won't be anything to help us there, I'm afraid. After you left, we found what the murderer used to cover himself.

"One of the theatre servants spotted it. Humphrey left a trail of blood from the place where he was assaulted to the box. The murderer stabbed him through a curtain. From the amount of Humphrey's blood on it, it is certain that it was used to prevent any blood from spurting onto his clothes."

"Where was this curtain? In an empty box?"

"Not at all. It hung at the back of a box that was between ours and the stairs. In the same corridor in which everyone from the boxes had to walk."

Hester felt a chill when, with an angry smile, he said, "Whatever we can say about the man who murdered Sir Humphrey, it is certain that he does not lack audacity."

Heaven forming each on other to depend,
A master, or a servant, or a friend,
Bids each on other for assistance call,
Till one Man's weakness grows the strength of all.
Wants, frailties, passions, closer still ally
The common interest, or endear the tie.
To these we owe true friendship, love sincere,
Each home-felt joy that life inherits here.

CHAPTER XII

A full day after his meeting with the Duke of Ormonde, Gideon could not decide if he should wait longer or ride to Lorraine to deliver his news. To linger indefinitely in London, with nothing to do but exercise his horse, seemed to him the worst possible waste of time.

The rumblings in London made him believe that something would break soon, either another riot, which might spontaneously turn into a rebellion, or an even greater move against the Jacobites on the part of the government. Even the King was rattling his saber. He had planned another review of his Foot-Guards in Hyde Park for the morrow. But since Ormonde still seemed disinclined to act, there was really nothing worth reporting to James. Until something—at least *one* thing—changed, Gideon reckoned he should remain in London just a little while longer.

Sunday passed without any news. It was not in Gideon's nature to wait, yet being unresolved about the rightness of James's cause, he would not do anything himself to urge a rebellion. The Duke's indecisiveness, however, made him uneasy. If Ormonde thought his popularity with the mob would protect him from the Crown, he was wrong. If anything, the demonstrations of affection and support for him—many of them sparked by Jacobite agents in place, Gideon suspected—would make the government all the more eager to see him removed. If leading James's army had been left to Gideon, he would have struck before the unrest of the past few weeks could have a chance to settle down. And if there were truly no intention of fighting, the best thing to do would be to inform the Pretender that his hopes were groundless. It was cruelty of the meanest sort to encourage him to believe in, and every second of his existence anticipate, a fate that would never be his.

These thoughts circled through Gideon's mind through an idle day and still occupied him on Monday, when he paid a visit to his horse. He had Looby saddled and rode him across Smithfield, down Long Lane, past the Barbican, along Chiswell Street, and through upper Moor Fields, where the aspect was countryside. They walked, trotted, and galloped to the Essex Road and back, before Gideon returned him to his midday fodder.

Setting out to find his own dinner, he came across an oyster seller and nearly bought a barrel to eat. But on second thought he decided to find a place to sit down. Gulping down oysters in the street or back at the inn would not be conducive to the kind of thinking he had to do. Oysters were a particular favourite of his, but he could always find them when his mind was more settled.

He did not walk far before being tempted by the smells coming from a coffee house that also served meals. Gideon went in and took a bench by a window so he could watch the traffic as it passed. Within a few minutes, he received the ordinary, a heaping platter of mutton, which had been dried, cut in shivers, and boiled like Dutch beef.

Staying on at the White Horse with nothing to do and no acquaintance to speak to was the most daunting prospect Gideon faced. He had already begun to regret leaving Tom behind in Kent. The inn's morning fare was certainly good enough, and there was no shortage of cookshops in which to eat, but he hated dining alone. He had struck up conversations in some of the coffee houses, but inevitably found himself in a quandary when asked where he was from and what trade he was in. Londoners were only slightly less wary of strangers than their country counterparts. And he could not bamboozle a wool merchant into believing him one of his fraternity, which left him little to say. There were always men who had rather talk than listen, and he tried to attach himself to those. But no one could call a conversation of that ilk satisfactory, and he wondered how long he could tolerate this life without losing any sense of purpose he possessed. He also believed that his landlord would begin to think it odd that a merchant from the country stayed so long, particularly when he conducted no business at his lodgings, as was the custom. And when that happened, as it surely would, Gideon would be forced to move to another inn and wait again.

He wished he could see Lord Peterborough. The impetuous earl had been a friend of his father's, even though they had not always been on the same political side. Lord Peterborough was the sort of forthright gentleman who would tell him exactly what he thought of the Pretender's chances. As a former commander of the English troops in Spain, he should be able to explain Ormonde's indecision. But the earl had little reason to visit his house at Millbank since he had lost his commission and been banned the Court, too.

If Gideon had not had to wait for word from Ormonde, he might have gone to find the earl, but he knew he should not leave right now. Besides, the introduction he had used at Ormonde House would not work at Peterborough House since the earl had not committed himself to James's cause and would not know the cipher they used. Even if Gideon could gain entrance, he did not know if Peterborough could be brought to believe in his innocence. As impulsive as the earl was, he might attack before Gideon could explain.

Mulling over the dangers of presenting himself at the earl's country residence, Gideon slowly retraced his steps to the inn. As he crossed the threshold, the landlord hailed him with the news that a letter had come for him in the Penny Post. Gideon took the letter, which had been addressed to Mr. Brown in a woman's script. With a mixture of eagerness and worry, he unsealed the wafer and saw that it was from Mrs. Kean.

"Dear Sir," he read. *"At our last Meeting but one you extracted a Promise that if ever I should need Assistance, I should not hesitate to ask it of you. I find myself in such a Situation now. Rest assured that the Danger does not concern me, but one of my Relations, who might soon be placed*

in a Dilemma similar to yours.

"If you find you are able and willing to provide me with Information and Counsel, I shall be most earnestly grateful. If not, or if this Message never reaches you, which I shall assume if I do not receive a Response, then you may still be certain of my continued Friendship. Although I do now see the Foolishness in expressing the latter if you are not even there to receive it.

"May I suggest a Meeting at seven o'clock in the Morning in St. James's Park? The fashionable World will not be promenading yet at that Hour, so it is unlikely that you will encounter anyone you know. I shall be on an Errand to purchase Cream from one of the Milk Maids, and hope you will spot me with no particular Difficulty. I shall wear a Hood.."

She had signed it, *"Your Friend and Most Obedient Servant, Hester Kean."*

Gideon's reaction on reading her note was immediate and unequivocal. As soon as he realized that Mrs. Kean was not in any danger herself, he felt nothing but delight. It was difficult even to be sorry that she had cause to worry, when his relief at being offered an occupation was so intense. Her comment about her foolishness made him smile, and happiness at the promise of seeing her again bubbled inside him the rest of the day.

Early the following morning, Gideon dressed in his disguise and made his way towards St. James's Park, wishing that he did not have to wear a wig. Now that he no longer shaved his head, no peruke fit him comfortably. Since becoming an outlaw, he had not had his hair cut once, but had worn it tied at the nape of his neck. At Versailles, and here, he had no choice but to cover it, but the extra layer was itchy and hot. If he had not been on his way to see Mrs. Kean, he would have felt very irritable indeed.

St. James's was the oldest of the royal parks. It had been added to the royal demesne when Henry VIII acquired the land belonging to the leper hospital of St. James. He laid out a tilt-yard near his palace of Whitehall for bear-baiting and tournaments and introduced game for royal sport. After the Restoration Charles II transformed its rough pastures into formal gardens in the French style, complete with a canal supplied with gondolas from the Doge and Senate of Venice. He opened the park for public use, except on the rather frequent occasions when he feared that his life was in danger, when pedestrians would find the gates locked. Still theoretically only accessible to people with keys, the park was continually open by virtue of the number of keys that had been given out, so it had become the chief promenade for all walks of life.

Gideon had no difficulty passing through the gate to the brick fence and even strolled by the solitary guard without any fear of discovery. The sleepy man, lounging before his tiny guardhouse, would never have recognized the outlawed Viscount St. Mars even without his modest disguise, and, besides, it was not his business to examine his Majesty's subjects. Gideon made immediately for the Milk Fair, in the corner nearest to Covent Garden, where the cows were milked.

True to her word, Mrs. Kean was easily found, standing near a pretty, large-eyed cow, whose maid was bent over a pail. Her dark hood distinguished her from the maids in their simple cloth caps and the other women in their lace.

Stepping up behind her, Gideon said, "I hope you have not been reduced to fetching milk for my cousin, ma'am."

She whirled, with a smile every bit as welcoming as the one with which she had greeted him at Vauxhall. She quickly restrained it, however, and returned, in a primmer voice, "No, sir, you have a new clerk in your kitchen who attends to that perfectly well without my assistance. My errand is much less crucial. Isabella once expressed a curiosity about the effects of cream on her complexion, so I thought I would surprise her with a pint."

In spite of the lightness in her tone, Gideon thought he saw evidence of a sleepless night. She was paler than usual, and there was a sombreness in her eyes, no matter that she tried to hide it. He made simple conversation until the milkmaid had finished and had filled Hester's pot with cream. Then he gave the maid two shillings from his pocket, which she accepted with a blush of pleasure and several curtsies.

Mrs. Kean protested his generosity on the spot, but he diverted her with a request to seek a less open space for their talk.

They walked back across the field in the brisk morning air, with the dew coating their shoes. Mrs. Kean paused when they reached the trees and started her protest again, but Gideon took her firmly by the elbow and steered her onto Birdcage Walk.

"I know you have something more important to discuss this morning than a gift of two shillings," he said, annoyed. "So tell me what has driven the colour from your cheeks."

His annoyance unsettled her, and she stammered, "I did not mean to bother you with trivialities, my lord."

Gideon wanted to kick himself for adding to her distress. "The only thing that bothers me is seeing that something has upset you. And I can see that it has—what is it?"

She looked as taken aback by this as she had been by his irritation. She blinked, then hurried to speak, glancing down as if afraid to meet his gaze.

"I do not know if you have heard, but—" She looked up sharply then, as if a thought had struck her, and anxiously searched his face. "Have you ever been acquainted with Sir Humphrey Cove, my lord?"

"Cove?" Gideon did not know what he had expected, but the name on her lips had taken him unawares. "Yes, I have met him. Why?"

She seemed distressed to hear it. "Then I regret having to bring you this news, but Sir Humphrey was killed at the opera last night."

She watched him, as if wondering how much pain her news would inflict.

Gideon hastened to reassure her. "I am sorry to hear it—and astonished, for Sir Humphrey never seemed the kind of gentleman to have enemies. But he was never more than an acquaintance to me. My father knew him better, of course. But how do you come to be concerned with his death?"

Mrs. Kean's relief was followed by a rueful glance. "I was a guest in his box when he was murdered."

She told him about their evening at the opera, Dudley Mayfield's drunken assault, and the possibility that he might have killed Sir Humphrey in another fit of temper. Gideon listened as she described the other members of their party. He was particularly interested in the news that she had met Mr. Blackwell at Lady Oglethorpe's on the evening he had seen them enter her house. And he frowned when he heard that the knife that had been used to stab Sir Humphrey had been taken from Hawkhurst House.

His attention was so riveted by her story that he scarcely noticed their surroundings, until an early stroller was almost upon them. Startled by the gentleman's approach, he noticed that they were near Duck Island. He took Mrs. Kean's arm and turned her to face the birds in their hut.

King William had taken a particular interest in indigenous birds and had supplied this structure for the survivors of the Whitehall volary after the fire that had destroyed the palace. Other fowl had been added to his collection, and it was a popular distraction for the public to feed the ducks.

One lonely pelican stared moodily out of his cage at his neighbours, an aging stork, two cranes, and a rare milk-white raven.

As the stranger strode past them on the way to his own rendezvous, Gideon kept his face turned away. He had nearly forgotten the risk of being recognized this close to home.

While waiting for the gentleman to walk beyond earshot, Gideon recalled something Mrs. Kean had said in her letter, and a strange uneasiness made him ask, "So the relation you wrote of is Mr. Dudley Mayfield? It is *his* safety which concerns you?"

"Yes. Though why I should bother, I do not know. There is very little good to say about Dudley. He takes too much after his mother, my aunt, whom you will recall. But I cannot believe that he killed Sir Humphrey—not in that calculated way, at least. And, as I believe him to be innocent, I should find it hard to sit back and allow him to be arrested for something he did not do."

Gideon's discomfort vanished just as quickly as it had come, and he gave her his biggest grin. "Now, why does *that* not surprise me? If anyone knows your sense of justice, it is I. I believe you knew me much less when you decided to befriend me."

"Yes, but I assure you that there was always more merit in your case. I never doubted your innocence. With Dudley, it is quite a different matter. I know that he is capable of inflicting injury on an unarmed man, but there some aspects to this murder that just don't seem like Dudley or his temper."

She told him about the curtain the murderer had used to protect himself from any splatter of blood and explained that she could not imagine her cousin having that much foresight. "If Dudley were to attack someone, he would do it in a fit of drunken rage with no reasoning whatsoever. I cannot believe he would purposely take a knife from his sister's house—" but here she stumbled— "You must pardon me, my lord. I mean Hawkhurst House—that he would take a weapon with him to the opera and figure how to conceal a very messy crime in such a crowded place."

"It certainly shows a cleverness and audacity that your cousin—as you describe him—would not likely have." Gideon did not use the term "oaf," but he found it strangely comforting to think of Dudley Mayfield this way.

He asked her what her own suspicions were, and Hester told him about Colonel Potter and his dismissal from the Guards, just when he had applied to be Harrowby's secretary.

"I know that he resented Sir Humphrey for telling me about his dismissal, and in truth, it *was* due to Sir Humphrey's indiscretion that I informed Mr. Henry that his politics might cause trouble for the family. I hope I did nothing wrong, but I was persuaded you would not want anyone suspected of disloyalty to be taken into your house."

He readily gave her his assurances, in spite of his own involvement with the Jacobites.

"No, you did nothing you shouldn't. Until this business is sorted out, one can't be too careful. I'm convinced that the government is about to move against the Jacobites. If Harrowby is ever suspected, he could lose not only his head, but everything he holds that is mine for either of our descendants." *Not that I am likely to have any,* Gideon thought. Not in his current situation, but he pushed away that unwelcome thought for now.

"So you think Colonel Potter might have stabbed him over this disappointment? The timing would seem right, if, as you say, he had just learned of it. I wonder, though, why he would choose such a public place. It seems inconceivable that someone could commit murder in such a crowd."

He tried to picture it and received this help from Mrs. Kean.

"I suppose," she said slowly, as if working it out in her head, "that he could have followed Sir Humphrey through the crowd and taken advantage of a moment when Sir Humphrey was alone and was standing by the curtain to that box. If the opportunity had not presented itself then, he would have waited for another occasion. But Sir Humphrey did stand in a convenient spot, so the murderer stepped behind the curtain and stabbed him. Even if Sir Humphrey had cried out, the noise in the theatre was such that no one would be likely to notice. And in that press of people he could almost be certain of moving away before Sir Humphrey fell. And now, it appears that he did not fall, but stayed leaning against the wall until he marshaled the strength to stagger back to his box."

Mrs. Kean gave a visible shudder, then added, "I have even wondered if he ever knew he'd been stabbed."

Gideon had to restrain an urge to put his arm about her. But it would not do for Mrs. Kean to be seen in the park in a man's embrace—no matter how innocent the cause. He wished they had met at night again, but he understood her reluctance to wait.

She continued, "I imagine that he did not know. There was nothing behind him but a curtain, so perhaps he thought the sudden pain had come from his heart or an attack of the kidneys. He must have been too hurt to cry out and, over the course of many minutes, would have become both weaker and more confused. He bled a great deal, they say."

Gideon nodded, disturbed by the image she had drawn. Dudley Mayfield and his innocence aside, whoever had done this deserved to be caught and punished. Even if Mrs. Kean had not asked for his help, he would have felt a compulsion to do something after hearing her version of the event.

"What do you know of this Potter, and what can I do to help?"

Hester was so relieved by his offer of assistance that she gave him her most grateful smile. She had stayed up most of the night. Several memories had twisted through her brain—things she had not understood when they had occurred. But now she thought there must be a connection between them. She just did not know for certain what it was or how to establish it.

Before continuing, she cast a cautious look around, but there was no one to hear them except the ducks, who preened their feathers and napped along the edge of the pond. It would not be long, before the few members of the Court who rose early to take their exercise would begin to appear. It was a beautiful spring morning with just the right sort of breeze to make people who enjoyed a good walk want to leave their beds. The Princess of Wales herself was a great walker and often led her ladies from St. James's to Kensington Palace on foot.

Hester turned back to St. Mars and felt his support in the very directness of his gaze. It struck her that she had not seen him in daylight since before he himself had been arrested. All of their encounters had taken place in the dark, except for that one fateful meeting during an eclipse, when they both had been so intent on preventing a second murder that she had not taken the time to study him. And while those meetings had all been exciting, for her at least, still it was wonderful to see the blueness of his eyes as the sun came over the trees. She wished that it was his own fair hair, reflecting the sunlight, instead of this plain brown periwig.

She wanted to be completely honest with him, but not being certain of his politics, she was nervous of the ground she trod.

"When you last spoke to me," she began slowly, "it was to warn me against letting our cousins be seen too much in Lady Oglethorpe's company. We have not seen that lady since, but every gentleman that occupied our box *is* or *was* a particular friend of hers. It was through Sir Humphrey that we were presented to her at Court, and we met Mr. Blackwell that very evening at her house. Colonel Potter was there, also, and Lord Lovett was supposed to come, but he had made a different engagement in Arlington Street."

"What you're suggesting is that all these gentlemen are Jacobites. Is that it?"

Hester gave a quick nod, pleased that he had said it before she'd had to. In running through her memories, she had recalled the visit that she and Isabella's friends had made to see the baby with the sign of the eclipse on her brow, and especially Sir Humphrey's odd elation at the sight. Of all their party, only *he* had seen something prophetic in the mark, and he had likened it to a sign on the eve of King James's departure. Lord Lovett had been impatient with him—surely for being indiscreet about the Pretender, which Hester had realized after Lord Lovett had practically admitted their sympathies with James. What she did not know was how much St. Mars had involved himself with the cause, and whether any discovery of hers could place him in even greater danger.

"I am not political myself," she said. "And I cannot pretend to know the merits of one king over another. Nor do I know enough of the law to argue whose right it is to sit on the throne, not when even the legal authorities cannot agree. So, when I ask you about these people, my lord, I do it purely in the interest of uncovering the murderer."

She wanted so desperately to ask him what his involvement was, but could not bring herself to be that impertinent. The frown on his brow was enough to keep her silent, and so they remained that way for a full minute longer.

"I am not committed to James," he said finally. "And I will not be until I'm convinced that enough good would come from his victory to justify another civil war. I cannot deny, though, that my current plight makes me more sympathetic to his cause than I was. And I cannot forget that my father was willing to risk all he owned for the Stuarts, as you know."

He paused, and Hester could understand his desire to honour his father's loyalties. St. Mars did not dwell on this, but went on to discuss her statement about the gentlemen who had shared her box.

"You wonder if they are Jacobites? I suspect they are, though I do not know either the Colonel or this Blackwell you spoke of. I have glimpsed Lord Lovett at Court, but I did not know his name until you gave it to me the other night."

He asked her to describe the other two, so she did her best. Colonel Potter was the easiest with his freckled complexion, his straight military physique, and his sullen expression, which, it seemed, was a constant feature. Mr. Blackwell was harder to describe since what she mostly recalled about him was his clothes. St. Mars agreed, however, that it sounded as if he spent a significant time in France. There were other

Englishmen who dressed that elegantly, but there had been a touch of something foreign in his arrogance, too.

"The simplest thing for me to do would be to talk to Lady Oglethorpe and ask her about them," St. Mars said, startling Hester.

"But is that safe? I refuse to put you in more danger, my lord. I had rather Dudley hanged first."

"No, you wouldn't." His laughter teased her. "And you won't be putting me in danger. I was on my way to see Lady Fury myself, when I saw you entering and turned back. Next time, I'll make certain she's alone."

A sense of foreboding ran down Hester's spine, though she couldn't say why. Perhaps from a dislike for the lady, which she only now admitted to herself. Surely there was something untrustworthy about a person who nurtured rebellion while begging favours from the crowned King?

"Just please be careful," she begged St. Mars, with a growing belief that they could not know whom to trust.

They discussed the first steps they should take, and Gideon asked her to discover where the Colonel lodged.

After arranging to meet again, they parted.

Gideon left the park, feeling a surge of energy, which his meeting with the Duke had gravely sapped. Whatever faith he should keep with James and his agents would always be second to his duty to Mrs. Kean. And whether he liked it or not, she had become embroiled in an affair involving Jacobites, as well as a murder that he could only find appalling.

On his way back to the White Horse for breakfast, he tried to remember everything he could about Sir Humphrey Cove, but all he could recall was a harmless face and a pair of expressive hands. He found it hard to imagine any motive for putting such an innocent to death, but there was no question that Sir Humphrey had considered himself a Jacobite. How active he had been would be hard to say.

Regardless of the information he received from Lady Oglethorpe, Gideon knew that an investigation would take time. No murderer who was clever enough to get away with a crime in that hour and place would easily betray himself, which would mean that Gideon would be staying longer in town than he had originally planned. And given that, some things would be better changed.

❦

Tom had nearly lost all patience with his situation when his master's letter reached him near dark on the following day. It was not that Tom had been uncomfortable. In many ways he had never lived so well. His work was easy, his room was more commodious than any corner he'd inhabited over a stable, and Avis, the boy, did the messiest jobs, leaving Tom to exercise the horses as he liked. By any man's standards, he had begun to live a life of means, with excellent meals and beer, and his wash attended to by a cheerful, brown-eyed woman.

But she was the source of his misery, though he did worry about his master, too. He alternated between fearing for his lord and being furious with him for leaving him in such a tempting place, where idleness had led to feelings he did not wish to have.

Tom eagerly paid the messenger, who had been promised more money for making the journey in two days. He broke the seal of St. Mars's letter with hands made clumsy by anxiety. Scanning the paper rapidly, he felt an immense relief, for the message ordered him to London immediately, along with whatever of his master's belongings Tom thought best to bring for an indefinite stay. St. Mars told him to bring Penny, too, and to give Lade more money, so he would not be tempted to let Gideon's bedchamber or to sell his furnishings while they were in town. And St. Mars gave him the address where they would meet in three days time.

All of that was fine, but the postscript at the bottom of the letter gave Tom's heart a jolt, for St. Mars's had added as an afterthought, *"Bring Katy with you."*

The horror that filled Tom on reading these words was that of a man who knows that he is doomed, both in body and in his immortal soul. For if he could not resist Katy—and how would he, if she was continually placed before him?—then chances were in the end he would die of the pox that had ravaged his father.

Tom did not believe in fate; however, if there was a chapter in the

Bible he believed in without reservation, it was the *Book of Job.* And he had no doubt at that moment that his faith was being tested with every weapon the Almighty possessed.

When he told Katy that they were going to London, her eyes grew round and her pretty mouth gaped.

"To Lunnon—me?"

Tom nodded, feeling the darkness heavy on his brow. He growled, "If the master says you're to come, then you're to come, and that's all there is to it. I tried to tell him this wasn't no post for a woman. But you got it, so you'd better pack up his clothing this evening and be ready to leave before dawn."

She asked breathlessly, "But how will we get them there?"

Tom noticed that she had ignored his cruelty, which meant either that he had lost the power to hurt her feelings, or that she had simply grown used to his surly ways.

Neither possibility made him happy.

"I'm leaving now," he told her. "I've got to find us a post-chaise. You'll ride inside with the master's things, and I'll ride Penny and Beau by turns. We've only got two more days to get there, but we can make it with the good weather we've been having. You've just got to be ready, that's all."

"Me? Ride in a post-chaise?"

The idea seemed to stun her and tickle her all at once, and Tom could not restrain a grin. "Ay. You'd best get used to travellin' like the Quality now." He used this term, for Katy still didn't know that her employer was an aristocrat. And he would never be the one to tell her, Tom vowed, trying to resume his glower, but he found it impossible to frown in the face of her delight.

On him, their second Providence, they hung,
Their law his eye, their oracle his tongue.
He from the wondering furrow called the food,
Taught to command the fire, control the flood,
Draw forth the monsters of th' abyss profound,
Or fetch th' aerial eagle to the ground.
Till drooping, sickening, dying they began
Whom they revered as God to mourn as Man:
Then, looking up from sire to sire, explored
One great first father, and that first adored.
Or plain tradition that this All begun,
Conveyed unbroken faith from sire to son.

CHAPTER XIII

Gideon penned a message to Lady Oglethorpe, using the same words he had used in his note to Ormonde. He delivered it himself, feeling safer that way. None of Lady Fury's servants knew him, and he rather thought he had perfected the posture and shamble of an older man. His request to have a word in private concerning her Cousin Jonathan received the immediate reply that he should call on her after dark that very evening, when he would discover her and her daughter Anne alone. He was asked to enter the garden through the mews, where a servant would be waiting to let him through the gate.

He spent the rest of the day looking for better lodging for himself and his servants. He examined furnished rooms in the City of London, but found them all too small. There was no abundance of empty houses, for since the Great Fire, even constant building had not been able to catch up with the number that had been lost. Charles II had tried to regulate the style and materials used in the new buildings in order to avoid a future conflagration, but the displaced populace had not always had the patience to wait for shelter. Consequently, many houses in the City had been thrown up in the old haphazard way, with projecting second stories, in spite of the laws against them. Gideon doubted their soundness, for every now and then the news-sheets contained the tale of a house that had collapsed.

He combed the advertisements, and at last decided on purchasing a house. Only three had been listed, and one of those was in Covent Garden, much too near the people who could recognize him. The other two were across the river, one in Southwark and one near Vauxhall Wharf.

Gideon went first to see the property in Worcester Street in the Park, Southwark. It had a spacious brick house, with four rooms up and down, stables, and warehouses, and had been advertised as suitable for any number of trades—soap-making, brewing, vinegar-making, and sweet-baking among them. Its location had many advantages, in that it was not too far from the Kent Road, while still standing well away from any principal street. Plenty of inns, taverns, and eating establishments were also near.

He wondered, though, what the neighbours would eventually think of an owner who sold nothing from those warehouses.

The acre and a half in Vauxhall stood right on the Thames. A good, high wall surrounded it on the east, west, and south, while an iron palisade protected it from the river. The house on the property was smaller than the one in Southwark, but since he did not expect to entertain any guests, it should be large enough. With a bedroom and two other chambers upstairs for his personal use, and another three downstairs for Tom and Katy, not to mention a separate counting house, stables, and a long pile of buildings for any purpose he might choose, the property seemed more than sufficient for his needs.

There was something about the location, too, that felt just right. From Vauxhall Stairs, or even from his own dock, he could take a boat to anyplace in London. He would seldom, if ever, need to take his horses across the river, but if he did the horse ferry was near. And, though this house was not as close to the Kent Road as the other, on horseback he could take Kennington Lane, then ride cross-country until he joined up with the highway into Kent farther south.

There were, also, plenty of country roads nearby on which to exercise his horses.

He briefly debated the wisdom of living this near to Spring Gardens, where so many of his acquaintance would come to promenade, but the wall should shield him from their view.

Besides all the logical reasons, there was another that compelled him to take this property. From the bank of the river, on a clear day, as this one was, he could see across to Lord Peterborough's house. Beyond it were the streets of Westminster and St. James's, Hawkhurst House in Piccadilly, and all his old haunts. If he could not live where he had been raised, he would at least be able to see it and feel it when he gazed out of his windows.

Gideon quickly settled with the seller of the property and arranged to take possession on the following day.

❧

That night, on arriving at Lady Oglethorpe's back gate, he found the footman, as promised. The houses in the Palace Yard were closely clustered, and there was nothing to prevent the neighbours from seeing the visitors who paid a call on Lady Fury. Gideon was certain that many of her callers had the habit of arriving at strange hours. He was grateful, nonetheless, for even this much secrecy.

Lady Fury and her daughter, Mrs. Anne Oglethorpe, received him in the mother's bedchamber, neither giving him the slightest sign of recognition. They stood in front of the curtained bed, and made brief curtsies while the servant withdrew, shutting the door behind him. Then, as his footsteps faded, Lady Oglethorpe curtsied again, much more profoundly, and spoke in a clipped voice.

"My Lord St. Mars, I thought it would be you. What news from his Majesty?" Never a calm woman, in his remembrance, she seemed more than usually agitated now.

"I have no message from James. My errand to England is quite otherwise. I was asked to discover from Ormonde when he will give the signal for the rising."

"And have you? What has his Grace said?"

Her question astonished him. "Why, he's told me nothing at all! Surely you would be informed well before me?"

She turned to speak furiously to her daughter in French. "What did I tell you? I am beginning to doubt that Ormonde has the courage to lead. He will insist on listening to everyone who counsels him to wait."

She cursed in French then turned back to Gideon, and without excusing her rudeness, said tersely, "I had hoped that another gentleman would be able to rouse him, but you were unsuccessful, I comprehend." She railed, "If I had only been a man, that cuckold would already be hurrying back to Hanover with his horns between his legs!" When Lady Oglethorpe gave in to anger, her French took over.

Anne seemed every bit as distressed as her mother, the exception being that where her mother's primary emotion was anger, Anne's looked like fear. Other than that, she was very much like her mother and her sister Eleanor—tall and elegant, but with an intensity that would make every man within her sphere either gather near as if to a magnet, or make a run for the first hiding place.

Although Gideon found them both beautiful, he also found them lacking in the sort of gentleness that usually drew him to women. To him, a generous and accepting spirit was at the very core of womanhood. Not this grasping, self-centeredness, which one often saw in men, and which he despised in his own sex, too.

This latter thought led to a revelation—that the quality he was thinking of had nothing to do with a person's sex.

"It is not Ormonde I came to talk to you about." He noted that his hostess was too nervous even to invite him to sit down, though three chairs had been drawn up by the fire. That suited him well, since he had no wish to linger, but he wondered what had set Lady Fury off. "I have come to ask what you know about Sir Humphrey Cove's murder and the men who were in his box Saturday night."

At the mention of Sir Humphrey, her head shot up. *So that was it.* Cove's murder had rattled her.

"I know nothing about it," she exclaimed in a near-hysterical voice. "How could I know anything? Humphrey was nothing—a lamb. How can anyone have wanted to kill him?"

Lady Oglethorpe had started pacing back and forth. Gideon looked to Anne, in the hope of gathering more information.

Anne said, "It is true what *Maman* says. Sir Humphrey was no danger to anyone."

"But he was a Jacobite, wasn't he?"

Lady Oglethorpe made an impatient gesture. "Oh, he thought he was—*yes*—and it gave him great pleasure to think of himself as a conspirator, but he did it in the same way that he thought of himself as a hunter or a courtier. It was no more real to him than a hand of piquet. He *played* at being one of us. I cannot tell you the number of times he would write me from his home in the country and ask me how the rebellion was coming along—as if he were inquiring about the weather!"

Gideon frowned. "But wouldn't his letters have been opened by the government?"

"*Sûrement!* But I tell you, that is how naive he was! Do you think I ever answered his questions? Me? If I had, then we all should have been arrested. But even the government could not take Humphrey seriously. If I had risked responding, he would long since have forgotten his question anyway. To Humphrey our cause was something he inherited from his family—like his estate or his religion. It gave him something to talk to his friends about and nothing more."

Gideon did not like the easy way she dismissed her murdered friend. Lady Oglethorpe spoke of Sir Humphrey with something near contempt. He began to see how she had earned her nickname *Fury.* Nevertheless, he was certain that Sir Humphrey Cove had not been deep in the conspirators' confidence.

"I heard that you know all the gentlemen who were in his box that night."

She halted in her paces, staring furiously at him as if he had accused her. "I do not know *Mr. Dudley Mayfield*, nor could I be said to know your cousin Harrowby very well. Or do you prefer that I refer to him as Lord Hawkhurst?"

Gideon knew she had made that thrust to punish him for what she perceived to be an insult, if not an outright accusation.

He bowed low enough for an apology. "I'm afraid you have misunderstood me, my lady. I only wonder what you can tell me about the gentlemen, since none of them are known to me."

"What is your interest in this affaire, St. Mars? I thought you were here on his Majesty's business."

"There is no news I can carry to James right now. If there were, I would take it. Ormonde has instructed me to wait." He did not tell her that he would go only when he was sure that Mrs. Kean was satisfied that her cousin was not going to be charged with the murder.

Nor would he tell her what his real motive was, so he simply said, "As you have pointed out, there were also members of my family in Sir Humphrey's box. I may have lost my estates, *madame*, but I have not lost my responsibility to them."

A knowing glimmer came into her eyes, so Gideon could hardly be surprised when, with a sly look, she said, "And there is one member of this family that you are still very eager to protect. Eh?"

She was talking about Isabella, he realized, not Mrs. Kean, whom she would not regard as worthy of his notice. But he had not thought of Isabella at all. In fact, she was never in his thoughts now, and he wondered how he had ever become so obsessed with her.

But he would not discuss the change in his feelings with this woman, of all others, so he ignored her implications. "I do have a personal interest in bringing Sir Humphrey's murderer to justice, yes. I would be very grateful if you would tell me what you think of the gentlemen you know who were in that box. Colonel Potter, for one."

Lady Oglethorpe acted as if she considered this a great waste of her time, but she finally acquiesced with another impatient gesture. At Anne's suggestion, Gideon was finally invited to sit down. He did take a chair, but only in the hope that their sitting would encourage his hostess to be more forthcoming.

"Colonel Potter is a Jacobite, I'm assuming, which is why he was cashiered from the Guards?"

She nodded bitterly. "Yes—what do the Scots call him—the 'wee German lairdie' has been purging his army of James's men. There are still many more that he knows nothing about. I tell his Majesty, he will be gratified when he sees how many men in the army will rally to his cause."

He did not want to let her wander too far away from their subject. "But George did find out about Colonel Potter. Not enough to prosecute him, I suppose, or he would have been arrested?"

Anne answered him this time. "No, there is nothing the Colonel has done to warrant arrest. We do not know why the government has grown suspicious. But it would have been very useful to us to have him in the army. His role was to try to turn as many of his men as he could before the rising."

"He applied for a place in my cousin's household. He was refused because Sir Humphrey let it slip that Colonel Potter's loyalty was being questioned by the King."

Lady Oglethorpe gave Anne another furious look. "You see! It would have been better if we had never made friends with Sir Humphrey. He was much too open to be trusted."

Anne's eyes held even more fear now. She looked suspiciously near tears. "My poor Robin! Do you think Sir Humphrey could have told anyone about him?" She asked this of Gideon and her mother, both.

Gideon knew that Anne had been Lord Oxford's lover for many years. He was married, but Anne was his true love. She had sacrificed a chance for home and family to be his mistress, but with the upbringing her mother had given her, she was destined to lead a life of sacrifice to some man, whether it be her sovereign James or another.

Evidently the fear Anne felt was not for herself, but for her lover.

Gideon answered her question with one of his own. "Has Lord Oxford considered leaving for France?"

She shook her head. "He cannot leave. He is not well enough to travel. But when he went to the House of Lords to justify his conduct on Saturday, there was no one with the courage even to acknowledge him as a friend. Even Lord Poulet was shy of him, he said!

"If only Ormonde would act, there would be no reason for him to flee!"

Gideon nodded. He worried for them all, but tried not to show how troubled he was. If Ormonde did not act quickly, it would surely be too late for Anne's lover. And Gideon had come away from the Duke with no sense that he planned to move any time soon.

He tried to steer the conversation back to Sir Humphrey's murder. "It would seem that Sir Humphrey was a danger to someone at least, however unwittingly. If he had no discretion, as you say, then he often would have made free comments about his Jacobite friends."

He moved on. "Who is Mr. Blackwell?"

Lady Oglethorpe looked startled. Gideon could see her struggling over an answer.

She took the safest route. "I do not see what Mr. Blackwell can have to do with Humphrey's murder. He scarcely knew him."

Gideon sent her a look, meant to convey that he would not accept her evasions. "And yet, he was a guest in Sir Humphrey's box. He disappeared before the performance was over. During the *intermezzo*, which was when Sir Humphrey was killed."

"I fail to see why I should be questioned about my friends when you should be asking Mr. Mayfield why he killed him! Perhaps the lady who informed you about my friends had reason to leave out the news that he tried to murder Sir Humphrey over a simple game of a cards."

Again, she implied that Isabella was his informer.

"Not at all," he said, giving an amused smile. "I was told of that incident. I should like to know who informed you of it, though."

Lady Oglethorpe was a woman accustomed to hiding secrets. He could not tell if she was lying, as she smoothed her skirts and shrugged. "It is all over town. A story like that is certain to be repeated. I will not hide from you that Mr. Mayfield is strongly suspected of the murder. If you wish to be his friend, you should help *him* to leave the country before it is too late."

"I would hardly be the man to encourage that course, *madame*. Not unless there were no other choice.

"But you say this Blackwell is a friend of yours? He has been described to me, and it appears that he has spent a great deal of time in France."

"You English are all alike! You think that only villains can come from France!"

Gideon tried to stem her temper with a loud sigh. "You forget that my estates and my title come from your country, *madame.* That is not an accusation that can be made of me. I merely point out what is generally known about the gentleman. And if you wish to defend him, then the truth will be best.

"Besides, have you forgotten who sent me? I never should have been here at all, if not for your daughter Eleanor. I have come at her bidding, so I hope you will trust me."

For that was her reason for refusing to give him the information he sought, Gideon realized. His questions made her nervous. For all she knew, he could be an agent of the government trying to discover who was implicated with the Jacobites.

Lady Oglethorpe squared her shoulders. "I know who sent you. It was I who suggested it. I know that you did not kill your father. But since you did not seek to help his Majesty on your own, your loyalty to him must not run very deep, *monsieur,* surely not as deeply as your father's. And there must be other ways to regain your estates."

She had practically accused him of spying for the government. That did not bother him nearly as much as her comment about his father had pricked him. He tried to shove that hurt aside, so she would not see how effective her barbs had been.

"I told your daughter and your husband the truth, and I will tell it to you now. I am not convinced that another civil war is the best thing for England and Scotland, no matter how just James's claims are. I agreed to discover what his adherents' plans are and to report back to him. I did not promise to fight. But should I find the rebellion just and right, I shall fight for him and never for George."

She almost sneered at this. "Then you are no better than many of his so-called friends, who wait for someone else to incur the risks."

"That may be. I do not pretend to be a hero, *madame.*"

Irony lit her eyes. "But you should be," she said. "Was it not a Gideon who led the armies of God, *monsieur*? If you have not read the *Bible,* as you Protestants are reputed to do, I suggest you read that part and ask yourself why your father chose such a name for you."

She was trying to shame him. And doing a fairly decent job of it, he thought with a burning pang. Gideon did not trust her enough to let her sway him, though. He would never believe that God sent messengers in the form of Lady Oglethorpe, nor would he liken a Jacobite rebellion to the armies of God. He did not know why she had bound herself so tightly to the Stuart cause, but it seemed that her very nature demanded that she be a partisan. And, once committed, she would hold to that side until every resource at her command was exhausted.

He tried to calm his anger with the thought that whether his father had liked her or not, he would have honoured her for her devotion to the cause.

"I did not come here to talk about me, *madame.* I came for your help. If Sir Humphrey was indeed your friend, I fail to see why you would not want to help me catch his murderer. And if none of these gentlemen killed him, I will discover that, too.

"Who is Mr. Blackwell, and where do I find him?" he asked again.

It was Anne who finally volunteered the information. "Blackwell is not his real name. His name is George Menzies. He travels back and forth with messages and money to Boulogne. He takes the money that is raised in England to Lancelot Ord, his Majesty's almoner in France, who uses it to pay the Irish troops living along the coast."

The name Menzies stirred a memory. It was only a moment longer before Gideon recognized the name of the mysterious stranger who had stopped at Lade's and offended Tom. "I have heard something of this gentleman. Where do I find him?"

Anne looked at her mother, but Lady Oglethorpe shrugged. "I do not know where he stops when he is here. The name he uses here belongs to a printer in London, so you could ask this printer where to find Mr. Menzies. I know that this printer is very active in our cause. He raises money for the King." She shrugged again. "Menzies may lodge with him, for all I know."

"Do you know where Blackwell's shop is?"

She shook her head. "No, but it is certain to be near Stationers' Hall."

This was no particular lead, since many of the printers' shops stood in that quarter.

"I'm sure to find it. And you have no need to worry that you may have offended Menzies by telling me. As a matter of fact, I've heard that the gentleman has expressed a strong desire to meet me."

He thanked them, and after giving them his direction, bowed himself out, convinced that he would get no more from Lady Oglethorpe that night. It was good that he had sent for Tom, for false name or not, Tom would be able to recognize Menzies on sight.

The inquest into the cause of Sir Humphrey's death was held at the Court of King's Bench in Westminster Hall, and was presided over by the Lord Chief Justice himself. As the principal coroner in the kingdom, it was his prerogative to exercise his jurisdiction in any corner of the realm, and, given the illustriousness of the victim, not to mention the other personages involved, he had chosen to involve himself.

The Court took up only the southeastern corner of the ancient hall, where once coronation banquets and even tournaments of honour had been held beneath the vastness of its hammerbeam ceiling. The Court of Chancery stood in the opposite southern corner, with the Court of Common Pleas in the middle of the west wall. The remaining walls were lined with shops and booksellers' stalls, and the cavernous building resounded with muffled echoes from the shoppers' voices and the plaintiffs' pleas at the other courts.

It was neither the most comfortable nor the most convenient site for an inquest, since there were no chairs or benches on which to sit. The witnesses had to stand in front of the justices' bench, which had been built so high that the justices' faces loomed a good six to eight feet above them. They were intimidating in their robes and long periwigs, but Hester reckoned she would have been just as nervous anywhere else.

The formalities were soon got through. The sheriff led the jurors into an antechamber to view the body. They returned with sober faces, one man holding a handkerchief to his mouth.

The calling of the individual witnesses followed. One of the watchmen gave his version of how he had been called to the scene of the suspicious death. He reported the finding of the bloody curtain through which Sir Humphrey had surely been stabbed, and the evidence he had taken from the gentlemen who had sat in Sir Humphrey's box.

The Lord Chief Justice then moved on to hear that testimony himself. From the nature of his questions, Hester began to wonder if the Crown had other motives for employing its highest permanent judge in the case.

Lord Chief Justice Parker could not very well accuse the witnesses he called of being Jacobites, disloyal to the Crown—not without more evidence—but his suspicions were apparent to Hester from the start. He seemed particularly keen to know about Harrowby's relationship to the deceased, which would seem to have little bearing on the crime. Hester understood, even if her aunt and cousin did not, the danger of their association with Sir Humphrey and his friends, but Harrowby's answers seemed to convince his lordship that there had been nothing sinister in their friendship.

The Lord Chief Justice also took a great deal of interest in Mr. Blackwell, who had still not been found. The only evidence that Hester was required to give concerned this gentleman's departure from the box. When she was dismissed, she was relieved not to have been questioned about her cousin Dudley, for her willingness to help him still did not extend to perjuring herself.

Her aunt was eager enough to do that. When it was Mrs. Mayfield's turn to be questioned, she tried to distract the Lord Chief Justice from her son with an extreme show of grief. But after a few minutes of her tears, his sympathy became short-lived.

"I daresay this has been a terrible shock for you, Mrs. Mayfield, but if you cannot contain these emotions, I shall have to ask you to step aside."

Hester wondered if he could see her aunt's dry eyes from the bench, where he sat, looking down on the standing witnesses. Mrs. Mayfield had kept her features hidden in her handkerchief, and the only redness in her eyes was the result of vigourous rubbing. She peered up at his request, however, and promised to try to control her grief.

"It is the understanding of this court that you left Sir Humphrey's box on his arm at the start of the interval. Is this true?"

"Yes—but we was only together for a minute. Just a short, short while. I'm sure your lordship will be ready to spare my blushes if I tell you that I had a very private errand to attend to, so I parted from poor dear Sir Humphrey right outside the box. If I had known what was going to happen to the old dear, I never would have left him for an instant. But no lady would drag a gentleman with her on an errand like that, as I'm sure your lordship will allow."

If she had thought to captivate her listener with coyness, she was doomed to disappointment. Lord Chief Justice Parker scarcely managed to hide his grimace of distaste. The sudden change in the witness's demeanour led him to focus on what she might be trying to hide.

"Did you descend the stairs?"

"No, there was a servant in the corridor with a chamber pot. I gave him a penny to let me use it and was done."

"Did you see if Sir Humphrey stopped to talk to anyone?"

Mrs. Mayfield answered, "No."

"Did you see Sir Humphrey go downstairs?"

She responded to this so quickly as to make him prick up his ears. "No, he did not go down. I am certain of that."

"If you are certain, it must be because you never took your eyes off the deceased, in which case you should be able to give us some idea of the persons to whom he spoke."

"Well, I know he didn't go down, but no, I can't say who he spoke to. The crowd was something furious, you see. I really couldn't see him from where I was."

"Then how can you be sure that he did not descend the stairs?"

She stiffened, until an answer came to her. "I should have seen him if he did, because he would have walked right past me!"

Lord Chief Justice Parker gave an impatient frown. "My dear Mrs. Mayfield, are you not aware that there are two sets of stairs on that side of the theatre—one on each end of the corridor we've been speaking of?"

Hester's aunt refused to be daunted. "That may very well be, your lordship, but all I know is Sir Humphrey did not go down those stairs with my son, and so I swear."

Hester hid a wince. She had never known her aunt to be so clumsy with her lies, but his lordship acted as if this was not first time he had questioned a mother in fear for her son's life. He did nothing but sigh, and with an impatient look, thanked Mrs. Mayfield for her testimony. Then he asked the sheriff to call the next witness.

Both Isabella and Harrowby gave their evidence, including confirmation that the knife had come from Hawkhurst House. It was the knife that Isabella used to carve joints when she served their guests, but neither she nor her husband had the slightest idea how long it had been missing from their house, since they had not entertained guests to dinner for several days. Neither did they know how it had come to be at the opera in Sir Humphrey's back.

They were not questioned very long, for in the case of both, it soon became apparent that their attention had been on themselves and the friends they had gossiped with during the *intermezzo*, and neither had anything useful to say. Isabella had sought the same relief as her mother, so Lord Lovett, who had escorted her from the box, had left her to her privacy. When, on emerging from behind the curtain, she had not seen him, she had accepted another gentleman's escort back to the box, where she had stood talking until her husband had joined them. She had seen nothing of Sir Humphrey or any of the others, but as she ingenuously said, she had not really been looking for them either.

The Lord Chief Justice was rather harder on Colonel Potter, which was what made Hester believe that he had been instructed by the government to get to the bottom of the event. He asked the Colonel about his movements during the interval, and the Colonel responded much like the others, with the added information that he and Dudley had gone first for a drink. Colonel Potter said that he had left Dudley with the bottle, though, in order to speak to a fellow former officer of the Guards who had passed them.

When asked if he had seen Dudley after they parted, he paused for a second before saying no. Hester thought he might be lying, but could think of no reason he should.

Colonel Potter also said that he had seen neither Sir Humphrey nor anyone else in their party until he encountered Lord Lovett on his way back to the box.

"Did you know this other fellow, Blackwell?" Lord Chief Justice Parker asked. He glared at the Colonel from under his massive periwig.

Colonel Potter hesitated again, before saying, "I met him once—yes. Sir Humphrey presented him to me at some assembly or other. I cannot recollect where."

This falsehood startled Hester. She looked about her to see if anyone else had noticed it, and caught Lord Lovett's glance. He understood her quandary, for he raised one eyebrow as if to ask what she meant to do about it. Hester felt an answering flush. She could not accuse the Colonel of lying to the bench when she had no proof. She could remind him that she had seen him at Lady Oglethorpe's house with Mr. Blackwell, but that would only bring Lady Oglethorpe into the case, and she was loath to do anything concerning that lady without first consulting St. Mars. For her cousin's sake, too, she would rather not reveal the fact that they had visited the house of a well-known Jacobite.

She turned her attention back to the Colonel's testimony, feeling Lord Lovett's gaze on her profile. She did not know whether he studied her in amusement or approbation, but she was almost certain both feelings were mixed in his look.

The Lord Chief Justice was pressing harder with his questions about Mr. Blackwell. He asked the Colonel why Sir Humphrey had invited a relative stranger to share his box.

Colonel Potter steadfastly refused to admit that he knew anything about it. He said that Sir Humphrey might have known this Blackwell better than it had seemed, but that he had most likely invited him merely to be cordial.

"Sir Humphrey Cove was an amiable sort of gentleman," he said. From the way he said it, Hester could not be certain that he intended it as a compliment. He could just as well have been sneering at Sir Humphrey for his kindness. The Colonel's sullen manner often made it very hard to tell what his true feelings were.

The Lord Chief Justice again tried to ask about Mr. Blackwell, but the Colonel held fast to his story, and in the end, he was excused.

Lord Lovett was asked many of the same questions, but not in the same accusatory tone. He retraced his steps that evening for the jurors, telling them how, at the beginning of the interval, he left the box with Isabella and escorted her to the area that had been curtained off for the ladies. Then, how he went in and out of a neighbouring box to greet a pair of friends, before heading again into the corridor where he saw the Colonel returning to their box. Citing the number of people milling about in the tight space, he also answered no to the question of whether he had seen Sir Humphrey or any of his other guests during the interval. And he claimed to have no knowledge of Mr. Blackwell, or who or where he was.

Hester did not know what to make of this last statement. Lord Lovett certainly had some knowledge of Mr. Blackwell, for he had admitted that much to her. The way he had phrased his answer, however, might not be considered perjury for she did not know if his knowledge of the gentleman was significant enough to mention. She could hardly blame him for not saying that Mr. Blackwell was a Jacobite agent. Nonetheless, after the look he had directed her concerning Colonel Potter's lies, Hester felt entitled to question him again later on the matter.

The judge posed Dudley the very same questions. He had gone down the stairs at the rear of the theatre. When asked if he had seen anyone he knew, he flushed, darting a glance at his mother in a way that made Hester believe that he was hiding something. He told the Lord Chief Justice that he was relatively new to town and did not have a broad acquaintance. He answered truthfully that he had not seen Mr. Blackwell leave and that he had never seen him before that evening.

The Lord Chief Justice then asked Dudley about the reported quarrel between Sir Humphrey and himself. Dudley, who was well prepared for the question, and who had been instructed in his reply not only by his mother, but by his brother-in-law, too, said that he had foolishly lost his temper after drinking too much. He said that Sir Humphrey had graciously forgiven him for his bad manners.

This seemed to satisfy his lordship, who dismissed him with a warning to be careful how much he drank if he did not want to find himself held for breaking the King's peace. And Dudley retired, barely hiding a glower at being lectured about his drinking habits yet again.

To their surprise another witness came forward. Hester could almost feel the tension from her companions, when Mr. Henry Wise stepped to the front and, in a visible state of emotion, related how he had been stopped by Sir Humphrey near the very spot where the bloody curtain had been found. Mr. Wise, gardener to his Majesty as he had been to Queen Anne, had often advised Sir Humphrey on the planting of his fruit trees. They had stood and chatted for a good five minutes before Mr. Wise, believing that the performance would soon be resumed, had taken his leave, as he said, "turning his back on the poor gentleman."

As he was questioned further, it became fairly obvious that the murderer had taken advantage of their conversation to come up behind Sir Humphrey, but with the curtain concealing any approach from that side, Mr. Wise had not noticed anyone there. He could say, however, that Sir Humphrey had been standing very close to the curtain even before he had been hailed.

His was the last testimony, and it left them all sombre, even Isabella and Mrs. Mayfield, for it recalled the gruesomeness of what they had witnessed. They were all permitted to leave, for, except for the knife, there was no evidence linking the murder to anyone from Hawkhurst House or even to one of Sir Humphrey's guests, as the Lord Chief Justice was firm to instruct the jury.

Still, they could feel the accusations in the jurors' eyes, as they followed Dudley from the hall.

To Hester, by far the saddest aspect of the case was that Sir Humphrey had been killed in the midst of his friends.

Together let us beat this ample field,
Try what the open, what the covert yield . . .

CHAPTER XIV

The coroner's verdict was murder by person or persons unknown. Sir Humphrey's body was released, and the ladies from Hawkhurst House went to sit with his sister, Mrs. Jamison, in her house while his body was prepared for the journey to its burial place at his country estate in Bedfordshire.

Poor Mrs. Jamison had been sincerely fond of her brother, who had always taken pains for his widowed sister's comfort. As she tearfully told her visitors, sitting in her modest parlour with its old-fashioned, leather-covered chairs, no brother could ever have been kinder. He had always remembered to send her the very best cuts of the venison, beef, and pork he had brought down from his estates, not to mention the fruit from his trees, and dozens of other little kindnesses throughout the year. Although their uncle's grandson, who would inherit the baronetcy with the family estates, was not a bad sort, she feared his generosity towards her, a mere cousin, could never be expected to be the same as an older brother's.

Hester, whose only brother had left home long ago to seek his fortune and never returned, could readily appreciate the merit of a responsible brother. She expressed the hope that Sir Humphrey had left her with a pension of some sort.

Mrs. Jamison blew her nose, and said that, indeed, he had. "But it will not be the same as having him bring the gifts himself, as I'm sure you'll allow."

Hester's heart went out to the woman. Mrs. Jamison was not crying just because she had lost a benefactor.

"Of course, it will not," she said, patting the lady's hand. "We shall all miss such a kind-hearted gentleman."

Isabella's eyes began to fill. Slow at first to accept the fact of Sir Humphrey's demise, she had finally begun to grieve for him. And she had enough sympathy in her to be sorry for his sister.

Mrs. Mayfield broke in, "I know that Mayfield surely will. I vow he must feel the loss as much as anyone does, so much as he was looking forward to increasing his friendship with your brother."

Mrs. Jamison bristled. The look she gave Mrs. Mayfield was full of resentment. But she did not release the retort that hovered visibly on her lips, saying only, "My brother had a great many friends, madam, with friendships dating back quite a number of years. Your son was but a recent acquaintance."

Her comment reminded Hester of something. "Did he ever speak of a Mr. Blackwell as his friend?" she asked.

Mrs. Jamison turned towards her with a perplexed look. "I do not recall that he ever did, but you must remember that we did not inhabit the same house. Humphrey must have had many acquaintances of which I knew nothing. Gentlemen do, you know, what with their coffee houses and their clubs and all the business they do."

"I believe he was a very great friend of Lady Oglethorpe's."

"Yes—" Mrs. Jamison paused uncertainly, as if Hester's question had unsettled her. Then she stammered— "but he saw her much less than you might think. They simply had many friends in common. But as far as his activities were concerned, my brother was much too occupied with the management of his estates and amusements in town to be much in touch with her."

She seemed anxious to disassociate her brother from Lady Oglethorpe's political activities. Hester thought it unfair to press her at the moment, but she wished she could question Mrs. Jamison more about her brother's involvement in anything that might have put him in danger. With her aunt and cousin sitting with them, Hester knew it would be a great mistake to expose her curiosity. And, servant as she was, she would always have to be careful about putting herself forward.

For the moment Mrs. Mayfield was perfectly happy to let her guide the conversation, and, in fact, had brought her along to do just that. Although Hester's aunt would never admit it, she had no talent or taste for giving consolation, so that was one of the many "unpleasant" chores she preferred to bestow on her niece. That Hester did not find it unpleasant and, on the contrary, considered it important, her aunt missed entirely. So she was more in charity with her today than was usual.

Hester inquired about the arrangements that had been made for Sir Humphrey's funeral, and the result was a conversation in which Mrs. Mayfield and Isabella could both take part. Given the horrible cause of his death, which his cousin, the heir, seemed to think a blight on the family name, Sir Humphrey was to be interred within as short a time as was decently acceptable. Except for expressing a wish that he might have lain in state a trifle longer in London before being transported home, his sister seemed to accept the arrangement. She would not make the journey into Bedfordshire herself, of course, since it was only proper for men to attend a gentleman's funeral.

"His dearest friends will accompany him, of course. Lord Lovett and Colonel Potter have both promised to ride in the procession, and I do hope Lord Hawkhurst will find it in his heart to go."

They could readily assure her of Harrowby's intention, for he was feeling the loss of his friend very acutely at his morning levee. Sir Humphrey had fully shared Harrowby's taste for the trivial and had never importuned him for favours as most of Harrowby's early visitors did. After a few days without his cheerful presence, Harrowby had become very low in mind, indeed.

"We were grateful to Lord Lovett for taking charge after the events at the opera house," Hester said. "I believe he was sincerely attached to your brother. He was certainly quite distressed."

"Yes, he was. And he has been so kind—coming to tell me directly himself, and offering his services should I need them."

"I did not know that Colonel Potter was also a close friend."

"Oh, yes." Mrs. Jamison seemed certain. "The Colonel and Humphrey have been friends for the longest time. Our fathers knew each other, you see."

"No, I did not know."

Hester could see that her aunt and Isabella were beginning to grow impatient. They planned to go shopping right after this visit. Mrs. Mayfield was eager to try the famous Bavarian Red Liquor, which was supposed to give a delightful blush to the cheeks, and Isabella wanted to pick up a bottle of Dr. Stoughton's Cordial Elixir. She had awakened that morning feeling nauseous and did not want a slight indisposition of the stomach to spoil her plans to go to the theatre that evening.

Since Mrs. Jamison had put a halt to her matchmaking for Dudley, it seemed unlikely that they would be seeing her much in future. Hester thought she might be allowed to call on the lady herself with the excuse of taking her a few pieces of fruit from the Hawkhurst gardens, but she had hoped to discover as much from her as possible now.

They said their goodbyes and made their way downstairs to the street. Feeling in her pocket for her gloves, Hester got a sudden inspiration and called out to her companions that she believed she had left one of her gloves upstairs.

Her aunt was put out, and her more charitable feelings for her niece vanished at once.

"You should be more careful," she said. "I've a good mind to tell the coachman to drive off and leave you. It would serve you right for keeping the Countess waiting, and her not well."

"I will not be more than a second," Hester said, over her shoulder as she nimbly ran back up to Mrs. Jamison's withdrawing room. Chances were that she would be back down before the two ladies were settled in the coach, but that would not stop Hester's aunt from complaining that they had been inconvenienced in the extreme.

It was a price she was happy to pay, if she could only manage to extract something useful from Mrs. Jamison.

She found their hostess right where they had left her with the exception of the tray of sweetmeats now on her lap. She caught Mrs. Jamison weeping, and in the process of delivering not one, but three pieces simultaneously to her mouth.

She was startled by Hester's reappearance. She fumbled for her handkerchief, but did not seem to know whether she should first wipe her eyes or her mouth.

"Please do not allow me to disturb you," Hester said, with a smite upon her conscience. She knew how tempting sweetmeats could be when one was upset. "I simply forgot my glove, so I would like to look for it. But you must go on as if I were not here."

"No, I mustn't." The poor lady's face crumpled again. "And, besides, eating these treats is not going to bring Humphrey back."

Hester left off her pretense at searching and came around to sit close to Mrs. Jamison again. "You must not feel bad about eating them. Each of us must seek comfort where we find it. I know Sir Humphrey would not begrudge you the sweetmeats, not when he obviously enjoyed treating you himself."

Her hostess gave a trembling smile. "No, he wouldn't. Thank you, my dear. You are a kind young woman." She made a visible effort to be brave, then her face crumpled again and she wailed, "If only he had not been taken so suddenly! But I should have expected it, you see, for I had noticed there was something troubling him, and it was not like Humphrey to be troubled."

"What sort of thing?" Her statement was exactly what Hester had been hoping for. "What made you think he was troubled?"

"It was something in his demeanour. He seemed to be confused about something, and I think it made him unhappy at times—not always, mind you, or I would have been more worried. He was so happy to be treating his friends to the opera, for instance—oh!" As she recalled what had happened at the opera, Sir Humphrey's sister was nearly overcome again.

"Do you think that, whatever it was, it had been resolved by Saturday night?"

Mrs. Jamison shook her head. "I really couldn't say. My brother was easily distracted, you know. He had a very hard time being distressed about anything for long. He might simply have forgotten it for the while, but it might have been resolved. I saw him that day at dinner and he seemed very cheerful indeed."

"Do you remember when you first noticed that he was troubled?"

She tried to think, but it was soon clear that she could not be certain. "I know it was before we came to play cards at Hawkhurst House. I am sure of that. But how much longer before it, I couldn't say."

"And Sir Humphrey made no mention of anyone's name? He said nothing to give you the slightest hint of what was occupying his mind?"

"Oh, no. He wouldn't have wanted to tell his younger sister now, would he? Gentlemen do not place a great deal of confidence in their younger sisters."

"I am afraid I wouldn't know about that myself," Hester said, remembering how thoroughly the opposite her brother had been. Jeremy had talked about his complaints and concerns with her almost incessantly, it had seemed. But he was younger, not older.

By the time she did descend the stairs again, her aunt and cousin were well-ensconced in their carriage, and Mrs. Mayfield was fuming.

"I cannot imagine what took you so long, Hester," she scolded. "If your glove was that hard to find, then perhaps you should be wearing spectacles." Clearly she thought that this was the cruelest thing she could say to a female.

Hester apologized, but as she took her seat facing them, she did not trouble to make any excuses. And her aunt felt free to abuse her all the way to Mr. Paryn's Toyshop in St. Paul's Churchyard where the Bavarian Red Liquor was to be found.

❧

On the journey to London, Katy seemed happy, if overwhelmed. She still did not know why Mr. Brown had sent for her, and neither did Tom. It was something they discussed only tentatively on their trip up from Pigden, but all that Tom could tell her was that the master would never ask her to do anything that wasn't fair.

"Fair to who?" she asked. "Gen'lmens don't always think the same things are fair that women do. There's not a man in a thousand who would give tuppence to know how I felt about anything."

Tom was taken aback. "Well, his lordship would, and that's a fact."

"His lordship?" Katy's eyes grew round.

Tom bit his tongue and cursed himself for a gape-faced fool. He couldn't imagine how he had made a slip like that.

"I meant the master." Then he lied, "Before I worked for him, I used to work for a lord over by Hawkhurst, and sometimes I forget and call this one 'his lordship'."

"Oh." She seemed ready enough to believe him, though she tossed him a curious look.

And Tom did his best to hide his relief when she said nothing more about it.

They found their master at the White Horse after two days' drive. St. Mars gave them a short break to eat, before he led them across London Bridge to their new house.

The moment Tom saw it, he did not know whether to grumble or cheer. The house was in need of work, but it was decent enough. The problem was that its situation seemed much too dangerous. But tired of lodging at the Fox and Goose, where he had to fight with Lade nearly every day, Tom could hardly keep from relishing the idea of an establishment of their own.

Looking over the ground floor of their new home, he wondered how long they would stay in this spot. If the Fox and Goose had seemed small and isolated, even with Lade, Avis, and the men who came to drink in Lade's taproom, how much tighter and cosier would this one be, with only Katy and himself to keep house for St. Mars—sleeping downstairs, like an old married pair, and stranded together and alone, whenever the master decided to go out?

Tom thought of all this and immediately moved his belongings to the stables.

"I still don't see why you told me to bring the wench," he grumbled to St. Mars later that night, as he checked Looby's shoes and hooves. St. Mars had told him about the murder at the opera and why he had taken the house. He had also told Tom that the man named Menzies, the one who had angered him at the Fox and Goose, was a murder suspect, which had made Tom feel grimly pleased.

The two were alone in the stables. Katy was in the house, doing whatever a woman did to settle down for the night, which was something that Tom did not want to think about.

"I only thought of Katy at the last second," St. Mars admitted, "but she could be very useful to me as a messenger to Mrs. Kean. And, besides—" he gave a teasing grin— "something tells me that we shall both be more comfortable with her to keep house for us. You cannot deny that the Fox and Goose improved tremendously once I engaged her."

"But she don't know who you are! And if you bring her in, she's sure to find out."

"Do you think she'll betray us? I thought you decided we could trust her."

Tom grimaced and stifled a growl. He could not tell St. Mars why he minded her being there. He would never hear the end of it.

"No, I don't think that. She's happy as a lark to be making your lordship's clothes. And not to be working for Lade. You should've seen her face when I told 'er she were going to ride in a post-chaise. But—" he drove the thought of her joyous expression from his mind— "I just don't know—maybe we shouldn't drag her into it. What if we were caught? And women can talk, even when they don't mean to." These were none of his reasons, but he didn't want St. Mars to think he was worried about the danger to Katy or that he considered her at all.

"I don't mean to get caught. One thing I've learned is that I can move about London, certainly at night, with no fear of being recognized. With a change of wig, clothes, and gait, and a little paint if I need it, there's hardly a person here who would know me."

Tom was not so sure he liked the certainty in his master's voice. The young were often over-confident. "Well, I hope you don't go parading about, all the same. 'Hardly' a person ain't the same as nobody."

St. Mars reassured him of the care he was taking, then proceeded to give him his instructions. "Tomorrow, there's to be a sale of the Honourable William Russell's belongings at his house in Covent Garden. I want you to go to the auction and buy whatever we need to furnish this house for the three of us—beds, tables, chairs, a writing desk, linens—and have them delivered here. Don't worry about the cost. And don't stint yourself or Katy either. You are sacrificing enough for me already, and I shall be much happier to know that you are well housed."

Tom could hardly speak for the need to gulp. "Yes, my lord," he choked out. "And who should I say it's being bought for? Mr. Brown?"

St. Mars mused for a moment. "No, you should give the name of Mavors. I've developed a liking for it. And if anyone comes looking for Mr. Brown from Pigden, this will make him that much harder to find."

"Yes, my lord." Tom had not missed the sadness in St. Mars's eyes when he had spoken the name he had used only once. Mavors was a Latin form of Mars, Gideon had told him on that occasion. Tom could only imagine how hard it was for him never to use his true name—a name with so much pride behind it.

Tom hardly knew what to say to St. Mars's generosity, so he dismissed it for now, but he could only imagine what Katy would say when she found herself using a nobleman's furnishings. "Are you sure you don't want us to buy new things? You could sleep at the White Horse until we've got it ready for you."

St. Mars shook his head. "I don't have time to wait. We've too much else to do. And if that much furniture were seen to be carried here over a number of days, it might make the neighbours curious. If it arrives all together, they will think we moved from a former residence. I'll give you money in the morning. I brought plenty with me from France."

Tom nodded. He tried to imagine what it would be like to be bidding at an auction at a nobleman's house. He was glad he had spent a couple of weeks inside Hawkhurst House, helping Philippe nurse their master back to health. At least he would not be awed by the sight of the furnishings, for nothing could compare to the grandeur of Hawkhurst House.

Just two months ago, he would have been overwhelmed by his master's order, but in that time he had learned to manage quite a few things he had never been trained for.

"I should like to see the furniture here by tomorrow night so we all have something to sleep on besides straw. Do you think you and Katy can manage that, Tom?"

"That we can, my lord. Just you leave it to us."

Gideon stayed his last night at the White Horse and paid his reckoning in the morning, leaving instructions for any letters to be forwarded to him at the King's Head in Fore Street, Lambeth, a short ride from his new abode. That evening, while taking a look at the furniture that had been installed in the house, he got Tom to check the post and was rewarded by a brief note from Mrs. Kean. She informed him that Colonel Potter had his lodgings in Maiden Lane. She had managed to discover this quite easily, for he had been obliged to give his name and direction before giving evidence at the inquest. She told him what the jury's verdict had been, stating that her cousin seemed safe for the moment, though it had been obvious that the jury suspected him of the crime.

There was one more piece of news. Lord Oxford had been taken into custody. A plea from Lord Shrewsbury that he not be placed in the Tower had been approved because of his ill health, but he was to be confined at home in custody of the Black Rod.

This troubled Gideon, but he thought it was a positive sign that Oxford had been spared the Tower. It seemed to prove that the government was aware of the risk of imprisoning such a popular former minister.

That was all that Mrs. Kean's letter conveyed, except for a promise to meet him at the place they had agreed upon tomorrow afternoon and another request for him not to place himself in too much danger.

This last part made him smile.

Gideon could not decide which of his well-meaning friends had the greatest tendency to worry—or which one thought him the most incompetent—Tom or Mrs. Kean.

He decided to give Tom one night to settle in before asking for his aid in hunting Menzies. The best and most serviceable plan would be to investigate one man at a time. So an hour before dark, Gideon hired a waterman to ferry him all the way to Salisbury Stairs. From there it was a short walk to Maiden Lane, where a few questions helped him locate the house in which Colonel Potter lodged.

He had just achieved this, when three military-looking gentlemen emerged from that house and paused for a few seconds in front of it. Late as the hour was, on this June night the sun had just set, so Gideon could see all three men clearly enough. One of them had a complexion splotched with large freckles, so remembering Mrs. Kean's description of Colonel Potter, Gideon decided to follow them.

He did not have far to go. At the end of Maiden Lane, they turned left into Covent Garden, then right into Russell Street, where they were accosted by a few whores who tried to lure them into the buildings where they plied their trade.

A bawd from down the street called out they would find only "the purest girls, fresh from the country" in her house. A large group of fops sauntered by, throwing flirtatious looks over their fans at the three gentlemen, and giggling and whispering about them to their friends.

From the way the three men lingered with the whores, Gideon supposed they were out for a night of pleasure. Unwilling to wait for hours, only to discover that he had been mistaken in the man's identity, he took the opportunity to draw closer to the group to see if he could catch their names.

He strolled past them, gawking, as if amazed by the lewd conduct around him. He overheard a harlot addressing the ruddy gentleman as "Captain," which might have dissuaded him, if the title were not so commonly misused. He stepped over the legs of a beggar nursing her baby on the doorstep of a tavern, turned his back to the next wall, and tried to follow the rowdy banter between the freckled gentleman and his friends.

The men had already shared more than a few bottles among them, if their slurred diction was anything to judge by. They were fortunately too far gone to take any notice of him. The same could not be said for the whores and pickpockets, though, who believed they had found an easy mark. Gideon was quickly surrounded and had to strain to overhear the men's conversation.

"Hello, deary." One thin and aged whore, with spirits of juniper on her breath, planted herself in front of him, while two others claimed both sides. Gideon covered his pocket firmly with one hand and with the other lightly fingered the hilt of his sword. The whores' quick eyes did not fail to catch his gesture, and one of them waved her young accomplice—a filthy boy of indeterminable age—away with a sharp look of warning. The disappointment on all their faces was palpable, as they were forced to revise their opinion of his vulnerability.

He was not dressed in a manner to convince them that his purse was full, certainly not as fine as the aristocrats who patronized the street or the rich Jews who came from the City of London to seek their pleasure here. But none of them could afford to ignore a potential customer, no matter how meagre his funds might prove to be.

With both hands occupied in guarding his belongings, he could not do much to avoid being pawed, which the women would insist on doing in hopes of persuading him to choose one of them. But while they cooed over him in their vulgar way, he still was straining to hear what the other men said.

Finally, a scuffle broke out between two of the harlots competing for the gentlemen's business, and the freckled man became annoyed with the press of women around them. Giving two of them a rough shove, he said to his friends, "A pox on these whores! Not that they need it. Anybody can see that they are full of sores."

"There's no danger in a little feel," the second man sniggered.

"Perhaps not, but they're wasting my time. I told you, it's Mother Whyburn's or nowhere else."

"Who's wasting whose time?" One of the harlots he'd pushed was outraged. "If it's virgins ye want, then be off wif th' lot o' ye! And I wish ye joy of 'em, for all the pleasure ye'll get!"

The other women spat abuse at them, too, but three healthy officers armed with swords had no reason to fear. Still, as they strolled past Gideon, one of them complained, "I don't see why you had to provoke them, Potter. It's not as if you've anywhere to hurry to."

The freckled officer made a surly reply, while his other friend laughed at his expense.

Gideon had turned his face to the right, in case any of the three glanced his way. But trouble arose when the whore who met his gaze took his motion for a sign of encouragement. It was one thing to ignore a woman's ministrations when his attention was focused somewhere else—quite another when looking into her eyes.

This one was not so unappealing as the others. But as many weeks as it had been since Gideon had enjoyed a woman's caresses, he hardly thought that looks would matter. As soon as he caught sight of her face, she smiled and her gropings grew bolder. Inevitably, his body reacted, and her eyes widened first in surprise, then in admiration.

"Yer not as ancient as ye looks. Are ye, me naughty boy?"

Her remark snapped his mind back to business, even if his body was slower to settle down.

He pushed himself away from the wall, freeing himself of her grasp. Believing that he had already made his choice, the other whores besieging him had started to drift towards other men. He did not want a cry of outrage to attract attention, so he quickly reached into the depths of his pocket and handed the woman a coin.

It was more money than she would be paid for a job on the street, but Gideon reckoned that she had provided him with the cover he needed. Besides, she was clearly not a woman who would ever enjoy the luxuries of a highly placed courtesan. Working out in the street, she was probably already infected with the disease of her trade and would eventually need money for a physician's services.

He was sufficiently thanked, when the protest she had started to utter was stifled by surprise. She peered at his coin incredulously, then almost wildly, while doubt, suspicion, hope, and elation crossed her features in succession.

He said, "Thank you," and, not waiting to hear a response, strode quickly after the officers, catching sight of them just as they disappeared through the door of Mother Whyburn's bawdy house around the corner in Drury Lane.

It was a house that Gideon knew well enough, for it was the safest one for any gentleman wishing to avoid getting the clap. And Gideon, though too young to be prudent, had still been intelligent enough to eschew most risks he did not have to take. Mother Whyburn claimed to be able to cure the pox, but whether she could or not, it was certain that she paid for her girls to be treated, and that she prayed for them daily in her long devotions at St. Martin's Church. Gideon doubted that the Bible she kept on her hall table received much use from the harlots or their patrons either, but Mother Whyburn was too astute a businesswoman to ruin her reputation by infecting her customers if it could be avoided.

Her establishment was no longer a cure for his carnal desires, for she would recognize him instantly. She had approached him often enough to father an heir for one of her many female clients whose husbands could not produce one. Gideon had always refused her, but he knew that he could not stand outside her windows in case she herself came out to recruit "young stallions," as they were called.

The last thing he wanted to do was stand outside in Drury Lane where he would be importuned by every harlot and Molly in town, would have to be alert to every pickpocket's tricks, and might fall prey to the Mohocks who roamed the quarter. Not so long ago, Drury Lane had been home to dukes and duchesses, but now it was filled mostly with brothels, which catered to tastes of every kind.

It was nearly dark. He did not need his watch to tell him that it was near ten o'clock. Colonel Potter and his friends could stay for hours in the bawdy house, unless—on a sudden hunch Gideon grew more hopeful—unless they ran through their money and had to leave.

Now that he had a moment to reflect, he recalled that Mother Whyburn's was not the obvious choice for an officer who had been cashiered. Since she offered only the cream of harlotry, Mother Whyburn also charged the highest fees. As a gesture of her piety, she donated money to the Church, but Gideon could be fairly certain that her charity did not extend to her customers, not when famous courtesans like Sally Salisbury used her rooms.

A woman costumed in a Quaker's hood with a high-draggled petticoat spied him and started towards him, alerting him that he had stood too long. He ignored her cry, "Don't leave me, my charmer!" and fled back along Little Russell Street.

Luckily, the Mollies in the seedy taverns that filled Clare Market revealed no appetite for anyone disguised as an older man. But Gideon knew that no disguise would be sufficient to discourage their female counterparts, so he tried to find a place where he could sit and watch through a window for Colonel Potter's return. He saw the sign of the Postboy in Russell Street and headed towards it, until he recalled that Button's, the new coffee house which had opened beneath it, was said to be patronized by Joseph Addison and Richard Steele, both Whigs with Court appointments.

That left the older brick house behind him on the corner of Bow Street, which had for a long time been famous as Will's Coffee House. Will's had been a haunt for Addison and Steele, too, but its true fame had been as a gathering spot for poets. Dryden and Pope, among others, had both composed verses at its tables, but ever since Will's heirs had died off, its custom had dispersed.

The current tenant had not even bothered to remove the old sign. Gideon peered through the dirty windows and, seeing no one he knew, went inside. The house was almost empty, which did not bode well for the new owner's success, but it did suit Gideon's needs very well.

He took a seat at the end of one of the long oak benches facing Russell Street, ordered coffee, and settled in to wait.

So Man, who here seems principal alone,
Perhaps acts second to some sphere unknown,
Touches some wheel, or verges to some goal;
'Tis but a part we see, and not a whole.

CHAPTER XV

Gideon was lucky. After scarcely an hour, having sipped at several dishes of coffee and avoided the distractions that spilled in from the street, he spotted Colonel Potter and only one of his friends making their way back towards the piazza. Night had fallen completely, and he would not have seen them in the dark if they had not hired the services of a linkboy. Alerted to their approach by the torch, however, Gideon was easily able to recognize the man he sought.

He quickly paid his reckoning and caught up with them as they turned left towards Maiden Lane. He had hoped that Colonel Potter would part from his friend, and was making a plan for accosting two gentlemen, when the second officer bid the Colonel goodnight and moved off with the linkboy in the direction of the Strand.

Gideon's pulse beat rapidly as he paused at the corner of Maiden Lane, pulled off his wig, and stuffed it into a deep pocket of his coat. He hurriedly dusted the ashes from his brow, before pulling a black half-mask from his other pocket and tying it on.

The transformation took only a few seconds, before he was following his quarry again, but he had to stop the Colonel before he reached his lodgings and hope that no one interfered.

Striding so fast as to be nearly at a run up the deserted street, Gideon caught up with him just two houses shy of his door.

"A word with you, Colonel Potter!"

The man turned instantly, and with one look at Gideon's mask, waited only a split-second before drawing his sword.

His reaction came as no surprise to Gideon, who rapidly drew his own. He would rather have talked to Potter first, but when faced with a stranger in a mask, most men would fight—and pose their questions later.

Potter revealed even less hesitation than most. Almost before Gideon could be on his guard, Potter lunged—with an accuracy that reminded Gideon that he was facing off with an officer trained in his Majesty's Foot-Guards.

His quickness saved him as he leapt to one side. Potter lunged again, and then again, keeping him on the defensive, but after the first few moves, Gideon could read his opponent fairly well. He parried every subsequent attack, and before long had the satisfaction of seeing his opponent start to flag. Colonel Potter's breaths came louder. His face registered astonishment, and even a touch of concern, when he realized that the man who had accosted him was no footpad, but someone highly trained in the duello.

Keeping his focus on Potter's eyes, Gideon could almost divine the thoughts running through the man's head. The Colonel did not dare give in or he might become a victim of treachery. He had no choice but to fight to the death.

Growing shorter of breath, himself, Gideon got out, "I did not come here to kill you. I came to question you about Sir Humphrey's murder."

Surprise made the Colonel falter. Gideon was careful not to take advantage of the moment, knowing that he would get no answers from a corpse.

The moment passed so suddenly that he was grateful for the caution *Maître* Andolini had preached. In a fury, the Colonel lunged again. But this time his thrust was so wild, that with one fluid movement, Gideon was able to evade it, nick him on the sword hand, and grab him as the weapon clanged onto the pavement.

Gideon held on to the struggling officer by his neck. This was far from easy, since the man knew how to fight. But Colonel Potter's resources had been sapped, first by the spirits he had drunk and then, presumably, by his activity at Mother Whyburn's house. He was bigger than Gideon, but since Gideon could breathe and the Colonel could not, he eventually succumbed.

As soon as his captive started to go slack, Gideon lowered him to the pavement. Then, he stood over him, pressing the point of his épée to Potter's throat, while waiting for him to recover consciousness.

Gideon's own breathing was coming very hard. He could not recall ever being in such a hard fight. He was relieved that neither of them had been killed.

"Who are you?" was the first phrase that Colonel Potter managed to gasp out. He was holding his wounded hand to his throat, which made Gideon believe that he had already forgotten it, if the pain in his throat was worse.

"It doesn't matter. But I do have a few questions for you."

The Colonel cursed and struggled to sit, but the tip of Gideon's sword on his chest convinced him to stay down.

"I shall not harm you again, unless your answers fail to satisfy my curiosity."

Colonel Potter still refused to be reconciled. "What was Humphrey to you? Why should you care how he was killed?"

"I know *how* he was killed. It is the name of his murderer that interests me."

"Well, it wasn't me. You're wasting your time if you think it was."

"I will decide if my time is being wasted or not. I understand that you were angry with Sir Humphrey because he informed a member of the Hawkhurst household that you had been cashiered from the Foot-Guards."

Colonel Potter cursed again. He tried to catch Gideon's ankle to make him fall, but Gideon moved too quickly. He pinned the Colonel between his blade and the pavement.

"More of that," he said, through gritted teeth, "and I shall assume your guilt and save the hangman the trouble."

"I didn't do it! I was angry—yes! Who wouldn't be? Humphrey was an old fool! He couldn't keep anything to himself, even if he were locked alone in a closet. He told that interfering spinster—what's her name?—Mrs. Kean. And the next word I get from Lord Hawkhurst's agent is that he's *very sorry,* but his lordship has no need for my services."

His sarcasm had already started to grate on Gideon's ears, before he ended in disgust, "Meddling old busybodies—the two of them! What business was it of theirs?"

"So, you killed him," Gideon said. He tried to hide his annoyance at hearing Mrs. Kean referred to with so little respect, but he must not appear to know her. She would not be safe if Potter knew that it was she who had asked for his help. Her reputation would suffer, at the very least.

"No! I've already told you. I did not kill Cove! What would the sense have been in that? I hardly think it would have made Lord Hawkhurst change his mind."

His logic was sound. More importantly, he seemed to believe it. Gideon wondered if a person who would kill for a grudge or even revenge would be able to state the reason against it as clearly as Colonel Potter just had.

His doubt about the man's guilt disappointed him. He could not like Colonel Potter. Not as sullen and distempered a man as he was. He seemed the sort of person who was always quick to blame his ills on someone else.

Gideon gave a hasty look up and down the street. No one was coming, but he would have another few minutes at most.

He moved on. "Tell me what you know about Menzies."

The Colonel gave a huff of disgust, before he started. Then, after a loaded pause, he grumbled, "Tumbled onto his real name, have you?" He had evidently realized that it was too late to pretend ignorance of Blackwell's identity.

"Could Menzies have killed Sir Humphrey?"

"Maybe." His tone was indifferent. "He's an arrogant bastard. But I don't know why he would."

"He left before the opera was over. Why?"

"How should I know?" the Colonel said, angry again. "If you want to know, you'll have to ask him."

"I will as soon as I can find him. Would you happen to know

where he is?"

The Colonel shook his head, and Gideon could hear the weariness in his voice. "I don't know where he stops. I don't like him, I tell you! So why should I care where he lives?"

"Because he's a Jacobite agent, and so are you. I know what he does."

"There are more of us than you think."

"How many?"

Gideon held his breath for the answer, but the Colonel retreated. "Nobody knows," he grumbled. "But there are enough that I've no cause to live in Menzies's pocket, I assure you. I doubt that anyone on this side of the water likes him. He treats us English Jacobites like lazy bumpkins. He's always demanding more money, then cursing us when we can't come up with it.

"I'd like to see *him* come up with all we have! Or risk his life! He thinks it's easy! And he thinks he's better than we are because he's closer to his Majesty. Sometimes I wonder if they realize how dangerous it is for us. Look at what Walpole's doing now!"

"Is that why you wanted the position with Lord Hawkhurst? You were hoping to get more money for the cause?"

Potter made a motion that might have been a shrug. "Lovett's been trying to turn him. He thought that putting a Jacobite at his elbow might help to speed things up, fool that Hawkhurst is."

Ignoring the slight to his name, since this was a fairly good description of Harrowby, Gideon pondered the news grimly. He wondered if the strategy would have worked. Harrowby was certainly persuadable, but when it came to politics, his first consideration would always be his own safety, and there was nothing safe about supporting James. There was nothing quixotic about his cousin.

Something else was bothering Gideon, though. Mrs. Kean had said almost nothing about Lord Lovett.

"What about Lovett? Had he any animosity towards Sir Humphrey?"

Potter laughed. "Not he! They've been friends a long, long time."

"But surely if Cove could not keep a secret, he was a danger to all of you. Particularly now, when the government is making so many accusations of treason."

Colonel Potter shook his head again. "It wasn't Lovett. He's been too careful. And so have I. Humphrey could have spilled his guts in the Lords, and there would be nothing to back up his story. And who would bring a prosecution on the word of a man like him?

"Besides, they were friends, I tell you."

"Then, if neither you nor Lovett did it, who did?"

Colonel Potter barked a laugh, but there was a hint of guilt in the way he moved his head. "I hear the money's on Dudley Mayfield. Why don't you waylay him, if you want a confession?"

"Did you see him do it?"

Potter squirmed, and Gideon prodded him again.

"No!" After an inward struggle, he added, "But he's the only one that makes any sense. The fool can't hold his drink. He gets violent. He'd already attacked Humphrey once."

"You didn't see him. But I hear he left the box with you."

He felt as much as saw the Colonel go tense. "Who told you? Who hired you to prove I killed Humphrey?"

"No one's hired me." Gideon ignored his first question. "You left the box with Mr. Mayfield—then, what?"

It took a bit more prodding, but at last the reason for Potter's guilt came out.

"Yes, so I took young Mayfield to get a drink—what of it?" he admitted grudgingly. "That doesn't mean I wanted him to kill Humphrey. I'm not saying I would have minded if he had dealt him a good blow—not after Humphrey betrayed me like that! He deserved to be punished. But how could I have known that Mayfield was carrying a knife?"

His voice was as sullen as usual when he said, "I just thought it might be amusing to see the yokel go after him. But it wasn't my fault if he killed him."

"How much did he drink? I shouldn't have thought there was enough time for him to get very drunk."

"Oh, the boy can put them away. Still, no more than three or four, before he was off down the stairs after a harlot. She took his fancy, and he ran right after her."

"Did you see where they went?"

"Did I follow him, do you mean?" The Colonel scoffed. "That's not how I get my entertainment. And after spending ten minutes in his company, I was glad to see him to go. The fellow's a boor. I talked to a friend, drank another glass or two with him, then walked back to the box."

The light from a linkboy's torch appeared suddenly from the corner. Gideon recoiled instinctively, raising his sword from Potter's chest, and the Colonel jumped to his feet. He looked about him for his own weapon, but it was out of his reach.

He yelled instead, "Thief! Thief! After him!"

Gideon ran.

He fled in the other direction, towards Half Moon Street, turned left, and ran flat out. The Colonel's cries came fainter, but his accusations gained in strength. "Assassin!" was the last word Gideon heard as the street before him narrowed almost to an alley. He made a left into the Strand, then before the Colonel could round the corner, another quick left.

At the base of a dark and wretched court, he found a second outlet into an alley, which cut a path from the Strand back into Maiden Lane. Stopping in the shadows before entering it, he stripped off his mask and changed it for his sober wig. Then he doubled back towards Maiden Lane, walking past the paupers who lay huddled along the walls, trying to sleep. He used a limp to disguise himself, but he still hurried, keeping an obvious grip on his sword, in case a genuine thief decided to try his luck.

He ignored the commotion behind him, as voices were raised in a call for the Watch. The Watch-house was at least a quarter of a mile farther down the Strand, and there were several alleys off of it, any one of which he might have taken. Besides, even if he still answered the description of the man who had assaulted Colonel Potter, which he no longer did, Gideon knew he could easily outrun the Watch.

ℬ

The debate over the guilt of the former Tory ministers raged on in Parliament and the violence in the streets increased. Mrs. Mayfield and Isabella, who had been planning to spend part of the summer in Tunbridge Wells, gave over any thought of traveling until they could be certain of being safe. The King had not dismissed Parliament for the summer yet, and with more trials to come, none of the members dared leave town. People still rode out to Court and to the theatre, but the Hawkhurst ladies would not stir from the house without most of their footmen along for protection.

Hester was frustrated by how little she could help St. Mars with the investigation. As a woman, she could not easily spy upon the gentlemen who had made up their box. She could only hope to get information from her family, one of whom might have seen something significant.

She was reminded of the need to find the real killer, when she walked into her aunt's bedchamber to return a piece of mended linen and found her railing against Dudley. A family quarrel, even at the top of her lungs, was not something Mrs. Mayfield would bother to hide, especially not if she could bring someone else in on her side.

Hester moved discreetly to the wardrobe that held her aunt's clothes, replaced the linen, and was retracing her steps to go out, when she was stopped.

"You tell him, Hester!" Mrs. Mayfield said. "Tell him what his foolishness has cost me. Why, I hardly dare hold my head up when I go to the toy-shop. And I daren't set foot near the Exchange, for I'm sure my ears would burn with all the gossip."

Standing in the middle of the room, and hanging his head as if to avoid another blow, Dudley glowered at Hester, as if he dared her to add one word.

"I'm sure that Dudley never wished for any of this to happen, Aunt."

"Well, he might not have wished for it. But it did!" Mrs. Mayfield said, outraged. "I might have known that you would take his side. You have always been ungrateful! There's nothing to choose between the pair of you! If it weren't for the honour of the Mayfield name, I should say that you deserved each other."

The shock and horror on Dudley's face was as nothing compared to the revulsion Hester felt. With more experience at hiding her emotions from his mother, however, Hester concealed hers more politely.

It was, nevertheless, a moment before she could find breath with which to speak. "I know that you would never countenance such an inappropriate match for your son, so instead of quarreling, why do we not see if we can a find a way to mend his reputation?"

Mrs. Mayfield sat down on the stool to her dressing table and buried her face in a handkerchief. She was dressed in dishabille, the hair on the top of her head curled over pads. Her maid would soon be up to dress her for a visit to Madame Schulenberg. Hester was to be excused from their visit to the Palace today, for her aunt had insisted on accompanying Isabella herself. She wanted to see if the gossips had ruined Dudley's chances for a place in the young princesses' stables.

Mrs. Mayfield looked up, her eyes tired and swollen. "First, it was just a bit of temper. And now, it's murder!"

"I did not kill Sir Humphrey, Mama!"

"Well, you might as well have done it, for all anyone cares!" Her shriek bordered on hysteria.

Hester took a deep breath for patience, before endeavouring to calm her aunt. "But I am certain that you never give anyone the slightest reason to believe that you doubt your son's innocence. And that being the case, they will soon take their lead from you."

Mrs. Mayfield sent her a resentful glare. "Of course, I never let them see. But Dudley has got to act on his own behalf! I cannot always be saving him from every scandal he makes."

Hester wanted to ask her why she had summoned him to town if his behaviour was always this bad, but she knew the answer already. Mrs. Mayfield would never be satisfied until she had wrung every possible penny and honour for her children.

"It would help if we could discover who Sir Humphrey's murderer truly was," Hester pointed out. "If he were known, everyone would want to forget about the other incident. They would feel shamed for having suspected Dudley when he was innocent."

Both Dudley and his mother turned to stare at her, their expressions changing from surprise to something akin to hope, making Hester believe that they might even listen to reason.

Then, Mrs. Mayfield said, "You could be right." A glimmer of cunning shone in her eyes, when she said, "We shall say it was that Blackwell fellow!"

Hester's spirits sank, but she only had herself to blame for imagining that her aunt might use good sense.

"I believe we would be more effective, if we knew for certain who it was."

"And how do you propose to establish that, Mistress Prig, when it could have been anyone in the theatre?"

"Not anyone. We mustn't forget the knife. It had to have been someone with access to this house."

This reminder did nothing to soothe Mrs. Mayfield's feelings, since it would seem to implicate Harrowby, as well. Hester got the distinct impression that if her aunt had to sacrifice someone, she would sooner not have to choose between her son and her son-in-law, the earl.

"Sir Humphrey might have taken the knife himself," she exclaimed. "Then when he tried to stab the person he took it for, whoever that was might have managed to turn it against him."

"I find it hard to imagine Sir Humphrey's intending to stab anyone," Hester said. "And if he did want to kill someone, why would he have taken a weapon from this house?"

"To throw the blame on my son. That's why! I never believed he had forgiven Mayfield, and, if he had not even that much Christian charity in him, then it's no wonder he was a murderer."

Hester tried to stifle her exasperation. "But why point the finger at Sir Humphrey? Both Lord Lovett and Colonel Potter have come into this house. And, much as I would hate to think it, it is even remotely possible that one of the servants could have been bribed to steal the knife for Mr. Blackwell."

"I do not see why you insist on making this so difficult," Mrs. Mayfield said, on the edge of fury again. "Why not just leave it that Mr. Blackwell killed Sir Humphrey? He's not even a friend of ours, or of anyone else's that I can tell. No one will care if he takes the blame."

"Except for Mr. Blackwell, himself," Hester muttered to herself. But she had to confess that she hoped he was the murderer. He had done nothing to endear himself to any of their party.

She wished she had never broached the subject of an investigation with her aunt, and she spent the next few minutes trying to dissuade her from calling a magistrate in order to give false testimony. Finally, she convinced her against it by saying that if her charges could not be proven, they might draw even more suspicion on Dudley.

Dudley had remained silent throughout their argument, relieved to have Hester distract his mother's attention. But when his mother's maid came to dress her, he followed Hester out of the room.

"Wait, Cousin," he said, once he had closed the door behind them. "Do you really think you can discover who did Sir Humphrey in?"

Hester smiled at him weakly. "I do not know, but I think we should try."

He seemed more sensible than usual, so she thought she might get some better information from him today.

"It would help if we would all try to remember that evening. Any one of us might have seen something that in retrospect might be significant.

"When you were standing with Colonel Potter," she continued, "did he say anything about Sir Humphrey? Or did he behave strangely in any way?"

With a look of helplessness, Dudley shook his head. "I don't know the fellow, of course. But he seemed very genial to me. Wanted to buy me a glass of French Claret. Very amiable of him, I thought."

"It did not seem odd that he should be so friendly?"

Her question ruffled Dudley's feathers, and he frowned at her in disgust. "If that's your notion of friendship, then it's no wonder you haven't had any offers yet. I tell you, Hester, it's different with men. Gentlemen are much more generous than ladies. He would have bought me another glass, if I had not had to leave."

She did not bother to argue. But it had struck her as suspicious that the Colonel would go out of his way to be cordial to Dudley when he had just been turned down by his brother-in-law. It was more than suspicious. It might have been mischievous, for encouraging Dudley to drink had only drawn suspicion to him later.

"Why were you late returning to the box? Did you not see Sir Humphrey on your way back?"

His scowl made it clear that he did not want to tell her where he was. "I was detained," he said, frostily. "And I didn't see him, no. Came up the other set of stairs."

"When was your glass of wine spilled?"

"I've already told you. I was in something of hurry when I left the Colonel, and my glass was full. I was pushing my way through the crowd, when someone caught my elbow and tossed the whole thing onto my clothes." He spoke regretfully. "I doubt I had above three glasses of the Claret, which was too bad, because it was devilish good!"

It was the kind of accident that happened so frequently that Hester had no reason to assign it any particular significance. But, if Dudley was telling the truth, it had certainly been convenient for the murderer that Dudley returned reeking so strongly of wine.

❧

Hester's aunt had given her a list of purchases to make that day. Normally, Mrs. Mayfield would have wanted the pleasure of shopping for herself, but she had not exaggerated the treatment of the gossips. So, for the moment, she was avoiding as much contact with them as she could.

This, coupled with her aunt's visit to Madame Schulenberg, was the circumstance which had made this afternoon's assignation with St. Mars even possible. Hester completed her list of errands—for everything from a powder for cleaning the teeth to a smelling-bottle, which claimed to be the most volatile in the world—in Fleet Street, before moving on to their meeting, as if it were merely the next stop on her list. At every shop, she told Will, the footman, to wait outside for her, and brought him another parcel to carry, so he had no reason to be surprised when she left him outside the door of the warehouse where she planned to meet St. Mars.

Corticellli's warehouse was a vast building with row upon row of goods imported from the East. To Hester, its vacant corners had suggested the kind of seclusion where a serious conversation could take place.

She was a little taken aback by a group of rakish women who were giggling and picking through pieces of silk on a counter near the door. But she made her way past and thought no more about them, until arriving in the southern-most corner, Hester discovered that she was not the first young lady to choose this site for a tête-à-tête. A couple, who appeared to be secret lovers, started apart when she emerged from behind the last aisle of shelves. She halted, feeling more embarrassed by the encounter than they did, and was not comforted by the resentful looks they threw her way. Or by the knowledge that she had, once again, invited St. Mars to a site that was used for lovers' trysts.

She had no choice but to pretend the most minute interest in the bolts of chintzes, Geneva velvets, and brocades on the shelves, until the couple ceded their corner to her. Her heart had started beating in an agony of embarrassment, and it took considerable courage for her not to run away.

She was even more disconcerted, when a strange gentleman came from behind the next row and walked directly towards her. She had expected to see St. Mars in his Quakerish costume and his short, brown wig, but this gentleman was fashionably dressed. His long, chestnut peruke was clearly foppish. His face was painted white with two spots of bright colour on his cheeks. And he wore so many patches that she could hardly make out a single one of his features.

Hester's pulse began to pound in alarm. The last thing she had prepared herself for was the unsolicited attentions of a stranger, but the gentleman was aiming his footsteps purposely towards her. She could imagine what sort of female he thought she was, alone in a place like this.

She had started to flee in the opposite direction, when she heard a loud hiss behind her.

"Mrs. Hester! Don't leave. It's me!"

She whirled around, and a gurgle of laughter burst from her mouth. In the middle of that painted and patched face, two vivid blue eyes were grinning down at her.

St. Mars sauntered the rest of the distance between them, apparently highly gratified by the success of his deception. "You do not care for my disguise," he said, in a complaining voice. "And here I had dressed to please you."

"I strongly suspect that you dressed to frighten me, my lord," she said, unable to hide her amusement.

"That is not true at all. I was simply tired of having to hobble, and I thought you might appreciate a costume that was better suited to this place."

She paused to admire his coat, which was a startling garment of scarlet and gold, then said, "You are remarkably well-supplied for a fugitive, my lord. These are very fine clothes, indeed."

He took her teasing in such good part that she might have paid him the greatest of compliments. "I will not deny that I have become remarkably resourceful."

He told her about the house he had leased, about Katy and the clothes she had made, and his new direction for receiving messages.

Hester tried to conceal the dismay she felt on hearing that he had taken a woman for his valet. Some, she knew, were offended by the notion of any female domestic servant other than the usual laundry and dairy maids. She had never considered herself to be as prudish as that, but the idea of his having a female to dress him was so disquieting that she hastened to change the subject.

"Have you discovered anything yet?" she asked. "I hate to admit it, but I have very little to tell."

"Let's walk," St. Mars said, offering her his arm. He gave a look back over his shoulder before answering, "I questioned Colonel Potter last night."

Hester had fallen into step with him, but she froze before saying incredulously, "You spoke with him?"

St. Mars raised a startled brow. "Wasn't that what you wished me to do? I fail to see how else I could have got any information from him."

Hester tried to resume her normal breathing, but the effort was a strain. "I was expecting something *about* him rather than *from* him, but however you decided to get the information, I'm certain you went about it with perfect correctness, my lord." Hiding an absurd need to smile, she gravely apologized for the interruption.

In his narrative, which followed, she was certain he omitted the most interesting parts, such as how he had managed to stop and question a trained military officer in a dark street. But, since knowing how he had accomplished the task was not likely to make her feel any better about his safety, she refrained from inquiring about his methods.

As they talked, they strolled up and down the last two aisles, stopping to examine a piece of cloth whenever they encountered a person coming towards them. They kept their voices barely above a whisper, and, despite the occasional echo of a distant laugh or the bang of something falling, the room with all its goods seemed to enclose them in privacy.

"So, Colonel Potter admitted that he encouraged Dudley to drink in the hope that he would attack Sir Humphrey again," Hester said, once St. Mars had finished. "I had wondered why he was so friendly to Dudley, when it was plain to see that he harboured a grudge against our family."

"He insisted that he did not mean for Sir Humphrey to be killed—merely punished. He said he thought it would be amusing. And he claimed that he had no way of knowing that your cousin had a knife."

"All the same, it sounds as if he was pleased to throw the blame on Dudley. It has occurred to me that he might have encouraged Dudley to drink not so much to induce him to attack, but to make him drunk, so that the suspicion would fall on him."

St. Mars halted in mid-stride. Even beneath all the paint and patches he wore, she could see that his expression was rueful. "I confess, I never thought of that."

In a wry tone, Hester said, "I imagine you had other things on your mind—such as how to get *anything* from him. Once this mystery is resolved, my lord, I might get up the courage to ask you how you managed it. But for my part, I've had nothing to do but think."

Suddenly she heard a woman's voice singing in Italian. It seemed to be coming from somewhere above their heads.

Noting her surprise, St. Mars explained, "That will be Signora Checa. She lodges with Signora Corticelli. I have heard that she speaks no English.

As the high, operatic notes floated down, Hester was struck by the irony of her meeting here with St. Mars.

A group of ladies, who might actually have come to shop, seemed about to overtake them, so they started to stroll again. St. Mars called Hester's attention to a particularly fine piece of Mantua silk, and she gravely thanked him for giving her something new to covet.

As soon as the ladies drew out of earshot, she added, "I cannot remember everything I told you, but during the interval someone jostled Dudley before he went downstairs and made him spill a full glass of Claret on his coat. At least, that's what he said occurred to make him smell so strongly of wine when he returned to the box."

"He didn't see who did it?"

"No. And I know that a spill is too common an accident to be sure. But it does seem as if someone wanted to use Dudley's attack on Sir Humphrey against him."

He agreed, but remarked that they were never likely to know the truth about that event.

"I just wish he would be more honest and tell me where he went when he left Colonel Potter," Hester said.

She sensed a faltering in St. Mars's pace. The colour of his face was curiously red, when he said, "Colonel Potter gave me a likely explanation for that. He said that a woman of dubious virtue caught your cousin's eye, and he followed her down the stairs."

"Well, he must have stood talking to her an unconscionable length of time, because he was very late in coming back."

Beside her, St. Mars choked. "My dear Mrs. Kean, I doubt very much that they were talking."

So drives Self-love, through just and through unjust,
To one Man's power, ambition, lucre, lust:
The same Self-love, in all, becomes the cause
Of what restrains him, Government and Laws.
For, what one likes if others like as well,
What serves one will, when many wills rebel?
How shall he keep, what, sleeping or awake,
A weaker may surprise, a stronger take?
His safety must his liberty restrain:
All join to guard what each desires to gain.
Forced into virtue thus by Self-Defence,
Even Kings learned justice and benevolence.

CHAPTER XVI

Astonished by his possible meaning, Hester stopped and stared up into his eyes, but in spite of the laughter in his gaze, he seemed most convinced of Dudley's activity. Her doubt that anyone could be so lacking in—in plain *fastidiousness,* if nothing else—must have shown on her face, for he appeared to be extremely amused by what he saw. She turned forwards then, with her chin in the air, refusing to let him see how horrified she was.

It was not long, however, before disgust of her cousin overcame her, and she said, "What a perfectly awful specimen Dudley is! I wish my aunt had never summoned him to London. He almost deserves to be hanged."

Her remark quickly sobered St. Mars, who brought the subject back to Colonel Potter's revelations. In a careful voice, he told her that both the Colonel and Lord Lovett were Jacobites and that their plan had been to turn Harrowby in James's favour.

"James needs money," he went on. "It's not that he needs Harrowby for himself, but for the funds he might supply. I suppose they thought that, since my father was a Jacobite, his nephew might be more easily persuaded to the cause."

"That explains why—" Hester caught herself and stopped. She had been about to say that it explained why Lord Lovett's pursuit of Isabella had always seemed a bit insincere, but she was always reluctant to mention her cousin's name to St. Mars, particularly with regard to another gentleman. Lord Lovett must have reckoned that the way to Isabella's favour was through seduction. Hester would have been mortified by her cousin's weakness, if she had not already been forced to face it. And if so many ladies they knew were not just as corruptible.

What was the difference between Lord Lovett, who was using Isabella to get Harrowby's money, and the people who bribed the King's mistresses to win appointments from the King? In both cases, sex was exchanged for money, and money was won through sex. Assuming that Dudley had paid for the services he'd received, she saw little difference between the harlotry he indulged in and the Court's, except that Dudley's was more honest.

She became aware that St. Mars was waiting for her to finish.

"I have been wondering why Lord Lovett is so attentive," she said. "He has never struck me as the sort of gentleman who would choose either your cousin or mine for his constant companions, which they have been for weeks, without a more compelling reason than pleasure in their company."

"Could he have killed Sir Humphrey out of fear that he might give away his allegiance to James? From what the Colonel and Lady Oglethorpe have told me, Sir Humphrey was always indiscreet. You said so yourself."

Hester found that she did not want to think of Lord Lovett as a murder suspect. Of all the men involved, he was the only one she had any respect for, even if he had been using Isabella for his political purposes. Even were she his lover, Isabella's heart was not very likely to be involved.

"I don't believe he would have killed him for that reason. After Sir Humphrey was killed, Lord Lovett practically admitted to me that he, Sir Humphrey, and Colonel Potter were all Jacobites."

St. Mars looked startled. "He told you that he was a Jacobite?" The furrow in his brow demanded to know why a gentleman like Lord Lovett should have confided anything so dangerous to her.

She felt a little spark of satisfaction when she replied, "Not in those very words. But he told me they had all met Mr. Blackwell at Lady Oglethorpe's house, and that Mr. Blackwell often traveled to France. And I can assure you that he knew exactly what I made of that piece of information."

To say that St. Mars was annoyed would have been an exaggeration, but he was definitely uneasy. "I still don't see any reason for Lovett to have been so open."

"I asked him if he knew Mr. Blackwell, and he seemed to believe that I would hear the truth soon enough, even if he did not tell me himself. And I believe that he thought he could trust me."

Which was more than St. Mars was prepared to do, she thought. Hester knew that he had some involvement with the Jacobites, at least, else he would not have asked the questions he had asked. And he would not have found it so easy to visit Lady Oglethorpe. She knew she had no right to question his activities, but if another gentleman chose to confide in her, as he once had himself, then he had no business being surprised.

"What else did he say about Blackwell?"

"Nothing. That was all."

His brow was still drawn when he told her that Blackwell's real name was Menzies, and that he was a spy who carried cash from English Jacobites to James's followers in France.

With a chill, Hester whispered intently, "If Sir Humphrey revealed Menzies's identity or even if he knew what Menzies's mission was, he could have got him hanged and quartered. That seems a much stronger motive to me."

St. Mars could not argue with her. He told her about Tom's story of the gentleman named Menzies, who had stopped at the Fox and Goose, and of his subsequent discovery that this Menzies and Blackwell were the same.

"I have the name of a printer who might know where he is. And Tom can recognize him. Tomorrow, we'll begin our search."

A warning for him to be careful sprang to Hester's lips, but she refrained from giving it again. As much as she did not like it, St. Mars would decide what risks to take.

She remembered one last thing that she could tell him before they parted. "Sir Humphrey's sister, Mrs. Jamison, who was acting as go-between for Dudley, told me one thing that might be pertinent. She said that her brother seemed troubled the last few days of his life. I asked her if she questioned him about it, but she said that she did not.

"She wasn't certain, but she thought that his worry might have resolved itself by the evening of the opera. Either that, or he was simply so enthused with the pleasure of treating his friends that he put it out of his mind."

St. Mars gave a grimace. "Whatever Sir Humphrey had on his mind is another thing that we are never likely to know."

He promised to send her news as soon as he found Menzies, and between the two of them, they concocted a plan for delivering messages. St. Mars would send Katy to Hawkhurst House with strawberries to sell to the ladies for their complexions. In a matter such as that, Hester was certain to be the person sent down to see her.

❧

That morning Gideon had told Tom to discover the location of a printing shop owned by a man named Blackwell. As soon as he found it, he was to return, and together that evening they would watch Blackwell's shop with the hope of sighting Menzies.

Tom did discover it, almost in the shadow of Stationers' Hall. Then, on his way back to the house, he stopped by the King's Head and picked up a letter which had been forwarded for Mr. Brown from the inn at Smithfield.

Gideon was waiting to receive his news upstairs in his new sitting room. The auction had supplied it with a pair of chairs, a writing table, and a French divan, covered in a rich crimson brocade. Katy had directed the carriers to place it under the window that faced the Thames, and Gideon was sitting there, looking out over the water at the opposite bank, when he heard Tom arrive.

He opened the letter as soon as Tom brought it up.

The message was from Lady Oglethorpe. In obvious haste she informed him that Parliament had voted to impeach his Grace the Duke of Ormonde of high treason. Mathew Prior and Thomas Harley had been examined. Lord Oxford had gone to talk to them, but, afterwards, Prior had become so reserved in his answers that Walpole had moved to have him confined in close custody.

With Ormonde in trouble now, Lady Oglethorpe wrote, surely there was no more time to lose. She begged him to find Ormonde and persuade him to act.

Gideon was torn between his promise to James and his duty to Mrs. Kean. He was concerned that Menzies might already have left the country, in which case the murder of Sir Humphrey Cove might never be solved. On the other hand, if Ormonde was ever going to act, now was the time and James would need to know.

The fact that Tom could recognize Menzies, and Gideon could not, gave him, at least, a temporary solution to his dilemma.

"Bad news, my lord?"

Lost in thought, Gideon had forgotten that Tom was waiting, but he was glad to find him near at hand.

"It appears that I cannot go with you this evening. An important matter has been brought to my attention, and I must see to it tonight."

He could see that Tom wanted to know more. He was anxious for his master, as usual, but Gideon was not going to share the contents of his letter. His one consolation was that Tom's errand tonight would be neither dangerous nor illegal.

"I shouldn't be late," he said. "And I shall come back here before going anywhere else." He did not add that he might have to go to France—not yet. "If you see Menzies, follow him, find out where he lodges, and come to tell me. I'll decide what to do with him then."

Tom accepted this command without any argument. He had his own axe to grind with Menzies, but Gideon was confident that Tom would never exceed his orders unless the situation demanded it. Tom went downstairs to eat the dinner that Katy had prepared before leaving again for town. Unlike his master, he had no reason to fear being spotted, so he could come and go without waiting for night.

It was hard for Gideon to wait until dark. This late in June, there were so few hours of night that the days seemed to stretch into eternity. Before becoming an outlaw, Gideon had relished these long summer days. But now everything was different. He had to skulk and hide like a thief.

But now, more than ever, he had to avoid being seen with Ormonde. And, if the Duke called for the rising, Gideon would have to decide whether he would throw in his lot with James or accept the losses he had suffered.

With these disturbing thoughts occupying his mind, he forgot all about eating, until Katy came upstairs to look for him. At the sound of her footsteps, he looked up and was surprised to see her carrying a wooden tray, loaded with plate and China dishes full of food and drink.

She looked so proudly at the pretty dishes, he didn't have the heart to tell her that he wasn't hungry. He attempted a smile as she set the tray on his writing table.

"I hope yer hungry, Mr. Brown."

Her lack of formality, as well as her cheer, converted his smile into one more genuine. He thanked her, then noted the name she had used.

"Katy," he said, "I'm afraid you will have to address me by a different name. If anyone asks, you are to say that you work for Mr. Mavors."

She betrayed no surprise. "I guessed as much when Mr. Barnes gave the carriers that name. I just didn't know which one you'd want me to use. But I'll call you Mr. Mavors from now on."

"Did Tom tell you why I use one name here, and a different one in Kent?"

"No." She looked rather sad. "He doesn't talk to me . . . unless he has to. To get his work done, I mean."

"Not after living in the same house with you for three months?"

She shook her head. He saw a battle between shame and pride fought out in her features. "I don't think he wants nothing to do with a whore."

"But you're not a whore any longer, are you?"

She flushed, with an apparent mixture of joy and relief. "No, sir. Thanks to you, I'm not."

"Then Tom will come around. I don't know why he's such a prude." Then, seeing that she did not understand his fashionable expression, Gideon chuckled. He looked down at the meat on his plate and realized that he did have an appetite, after all. He picked up a knife and started cutting into a slice of ham.

"I'm certainly glad I asked Tom to bring you along," he said. "Where did you come by all this?"

She told him about the arrangements she had made to buy meat from a farmer a few miles down the Kennington Road, until they could raise their own pigs and chickens.

Gideon frowned. He had not realized how much work it would take to set up house, and now that he had, he saw that Katy looked as if she had not had much sleep. Tom could have helped her with some of her tasks, if Gideon hadn't sent him looking for Menzies. But only Tom could do that, and he had the horses to tend, too. It had taken them a day to unload the furniture, even with carriers doing the hardest work.

"I want you to get someone to help you," he said to Katy. "Find a girl or two as soon as you can. And if you need more than that, just tell me. Only be sure that you give my name as Mavors, and if they have any questions about me, you can tell them I'm a gentleman with a strange set of habits, but that I pay good wages and treat my servants well. If they ask you anything else, you can refer them to Tom."

"Yessir. Thank you, Mr. Mavors."

Katy left him then. She seemed cheered by the notion of help. Or, perhaps, he reflected, it was by the notion of company. For neither he nor Tom would be any company for her, and he could imagine how lonely she must feel.

He was grateful to her for distracting him from the thoughts that had killed his appetite.

It was just past dark when he arrived at Ormonde House, dressed once again in his Quaker's garb. It would not have served to put on a different disguise when the Duke's servants were in the habit of admitting him in this one.

The porter opened the door immediately, pulled him through, and, with a whispered, "Hurry, sir, in here!" closed it sharply on the back of Gideon's heels.

Inside, Gideon saw that the whole household had been roused. Footmen were running upstairs and down with boxes, trunks, and valises, clearly preparing for a journey. Following one of them upstairs and down the corridor, Gideon saw even more evidence that a trip was imminent. Maids hurried past him with ladies' gowns draped across their arms.

His first thought on seeing this activity was that his Grace had made up his mind to run to France. But, after reflection, he found it hard to believe that anyone would try to escape surrounded by so much fuss.

He found the Duke again inside his drawing room, staring down at a paper on his desk.

He looked up on Gideon's entrance, and said, "Leave us," to the footman, with a military peremptoriness that the servant seemed to expect.

This was the most decisive Gideon had ever seen Ormonde be. And he could understand now why men accepted his leadership, if he could be this firm.

Unfortunately, his air of command vanished the moment his footman closed the door.

"Did anyone see you?" he asked, in a disturbed manner, then barely waited to hear Gideon's denial, before coming to his feet to pace behind the ebony desk. "I was afraid you might come—"

While he walked, he rambled, wringing his hands. "I told my porter to be on the lookout for you. Had to tell you that you must never visit this house again."

Not bothering to look up, he went on, "I don't know what you have heard, but the whole affair has become more urgent. Walpole has taken after me. The Whigs in the Commons seem only too happy to back him, and we don't have enough members to overcome them. There will be a fight, but I can't be certain we will win."

Ormonde did peer up then, and Gideon saw a flicker of doubt in his eyes. "Walpole has a nasty way of getting what he wants. And he obviously can't abide me."

"Where are you going?" Gideon managed to ask.

"To Richmond—to the Lodge. I can work from there. It's time to count our forces. I have to be able to reach our men in the West—Landsdowne and the others—without our messengers being seen."

It was time. Gideon's throat went dry. In spite of having warned himself that this moment was inevitable, he still could not help feeling stunned. It would be up to him to notify James Stuart that the rising he had hoped and prayed for all his life was about to take place.

"I shall ride tomorrow to inform his Majesty of your decision."

"No, not yet!" The Duke's vehemence astonished him. "I am not at all certain that we are ready for his Majesty to risk himself."

In response to Gideon's look of confusion, he averted his gaze. "First, I must know the number of arms we have and how many men they've been able to raise. The plan is for James to land in the West Country, you see, and I must be absolutely certain that he will be safe."

"Then, what should I do? My instructions were to put myself in your service. I can carry messages for you, if you like."

Ormonde waved this offer away, in a manner that implied he had all the messengers he needed and would only be bothered by another. "It would be better for you to stay out of sight. I have your direction and will send word when it's time to send for his Majesty.

"And, now, I must ask you to leave. The horses will be ready soon, and I cannot afford to tarry."

Gideon had been dismissed. He left, feeling dumbfounded and uneasy. The reasons Ormonde had given for waiting tonight were the very same that he had given before. Only now he had more than enough reason to hurry. No matter how many members of Parliament would argue to save him, the government was sure to win in the end. And it was always wise to be on the government's side when charges of treason were made. Even the bravest peers and the Duke's closest friends would eventually see that.

How much longer would it take Ormonde to determine if James had the men and arms to mount a rebellion? Anything longer than a few more days, and Gideon feared that the Duke would not be at liberty to lead it. And even if he called for a rising tomorrow, it could be months before James could make it safely onto England's shores.

There was nothing Gideon could do tonight. But he pledged to himself that, if he had not heard from the Duke of Ormonde within a sennight, he would follow him down to Richmond Lodge and extract a decision from him, once and for all.

Tom had taken a boat to Puddle Dock Stairs, where he had to hurry past the Dung Wharf, before winding his way beyond St. Paul's Church to the narrow streets and cramped courts that surrounded Stationers' Hall. Having spent the greater portion of his life in the Weald of Kent, he could not fathom why anyone would live trapped in this dark, filthy corner, wedged between Newgate and the Fleet. With all the extraordinary tasks he had been called upon to carry out in the service of his master this past few months, he began to think that searching for a man in the City of the London could be the worst.

Since he had never lived in the City, it had taken him a while to locate Stationers' Hall. After that, finding a printer by the name of Blackwell had been easy. He would have avoided the Dung Wharf on this second trip if he had not worried that he might lose his way from another set of stairs. Having mucked out stables every day since he'd been old enough to swing a pitchfork, he would never have expected to be so repulsed by a pile of dung. But never had he seen so much heaped in one spot either.

Intent on finding his way, he failed to notice the unrest in the streets, until he arrived near the bottom of Ludgate Hill where a gathering of shouting artisans caught his attention. A group of carpenters, plaisterers, painters, and masons, working on the new construction that had been a constant feature of every London street since the Great Fire, had paused to argue outside St. Martin Ludgate Church. To his right, a fist-fight erupted at the bottom of Ave Mary Lane. It was only after Tom had been jostled by a boy running with his arms full of news-sheets that he began to suspect the source of their concern. He stopped the news-hawker, who was heading towards St. Paul's Churchyard to meet up with merchants from the Exchange, and paid him a half-penny for his news.

The news-sheet was not one he had heard of before, which probably meant that what it contained was illegal. Tom tried to make out what all the hubbub was about, before folding the paper and tucking it into his shirt to take to St. Mars, but what he had seen was enough to convince him that the Jacobites had been roused.

The few merchants who had ventured this side of St. Paul's seemed cautious as they rode past in their carriages. They must have been pleased to hear that the Whigs had charged the most prominent Tories with treason, but they would be wise not to let their elation show. With an unsettled feeling in his stomach, Tom wondered whether this was the news that had taken St. Mars on his mysterious errand, leaving him to search for Menzies alone.

He would not get an answer to this question now, so he crossed into a dark, cool maze which began in Cock Alley, zigzagged past the stationers' fine new livery hall—rebuilt after the Great Fire—and led him out into Amen Corner.

Here, where many of the printers were housed, he found himself hedged in by the hasty comings and goings from their shops. Whispered conferences in doorways and furtive glances, which had not been evident that morning, made him feel uncomfortably conspicuous. His plan, which had been to watch Blackwell's shop from a sheltered corner, was obviously not going to serve. Too many of the printers were on their guard. The Jacobites among them had no way of knowing whether a stranger in the street would prove to be a government spy, and Tom could tell by the suspicious looks he received that they had spotted him as a stranger.

He hesitated only the few seconds it took to arrive at this conclusion, before ambling off towards Paternaster Row, while he tried to think of a credible reason for lingering. Of all the areas of London, this had to be one of the worst for standing in the street. There were no inns or taverns, and only a few shops in which a man of his station could pretend an interest. Tom walked purposefully past the windows of booksellers' shops, where no groom would be expected to enter, and the printers' houses, where presses thumped away.

Finally, under the sign of the Three Black Lyons, he found a shop selling Turkey carpets and stopped to peer through the window. The proprietor spotted him and walked eagerly towards the door. Tom would have retreated in haste, even if the man had not got near enough to see his clothes, scowl, and wave to shoo him away.

There was nothing for it, but to return in the direction he had come.

He had not meant to stop here long in any case. Mr. Blackwell's establishment was almost in the shadow of Stationers' Hall, too far away to be seen from here. Tom had hoped for a few moments, though, in which to come up with a different plan, so he prayed that inspiration would come soon.

Inspiration did not, but good luck did. He had almost reached the corner of Stationers' Hall Court again, when two men, dressed in booksellers' garb, started a loud altercation in front of a shop and blocked the narrow footpath. Tom could easily have avoided them by stepping into the street, but what could have seemed more natural for an Englishman than to pause in the hope of seeing a fight?

He backed into a sheltered niche with a view of Blackwell's door. The bookshop on this side of it—the one in front of which the two men were shouting—bore a sign with the proprietor's name, Mr. J. Morphew. On Tom's first trip into this neighborhood, it had seemed odd that so many of the shops sported signs with words instead of pictures, but eventually he had reckoned that only people who could read would be visiting booksellers' and printers' shops.

The men's argument grew louder. Within seconds, a circle formed around them, with printers and their apprentices encouraging them each to take the first swing. The argument was certainly heated, but looking on, Tom doubted that the first fist would ever be swung. Aside from a few threatening gestures and puffed out chests, they almost seemed satisfied to wage their battle with words.

He was grateful for the excuse they had given him to dawdle, though. With everyone in the street intent on their fight, Tom could keep a watch on Blackwell's shop without fear of his interest being noted. Some of their argument did reach his ears. As far as he could tell, they were arguing over pamphlets that had been written about his Grace of Ormonde. One of the booksellers was defending his Grace, and the other was accusing him of treason. Since the Duke was a friend of the former Lord Hawkhurst and had always brought amiable servants to Rotherham Abbey, Tom almost wished that he could take on the job of shutting the Whig bookseller's mouth himself.

Too soon for him, the two men grew hoarse and their fight spluttered to an end. The man who had criticized the Duke of

Ormonde turned abruptly on his heels, went into his shop, and slammed the door. The other stamped past Tom and entered a house down the street.

The crowd that had gathered to watch them fight stayed on a little while longer to grumble at being denied the pleasure of a bout. Complaints about the men's lack of courage, and a tendency on the part of some to defend their friends, led to some more pushing and shoving, but a sombreness beneath their anger soon had even the spectators returning to their jobs. Before long, Tom was left standing alone in the street.

By this late hour, even the long June day had begun to fade over the roofs of the narrowly-spaced houses. The turmoil he had seen would be moving into the taverns with the onset of night. But for the moment, at least, Tom no longer felt conspicuous.

One thing he had noticed was that the door to Blackwell's shop had remained closed. No one had come out to watch the fight, which could mean either that nobody was there or that Blackwell had something to hide.

The thought that he might be watching an empty house made Tom restless. Irritably he wondered whether he could simply walk up to the shop and peer inside. He was seriously considering this option when another news-hawker came up behind him and asked if he would like to buy a postscript from *The Post Man*.

Tom was about to refuse, considering three half-pence an outrageous sum, when he recognized the boy's offer for the chance it was. So he handed over more of St. Mars's money for the opportunity to lean against a corner post and read his paper as long as the twilight would allow.

This was not very long, and he had begun to draw curious glances again, when the door to Blackwell's shop finally opened. A boy, who surely must have been an apprentice, emerged and, without pausing, came running straight towards Tom. He swerved past him with hardly a glance, before turning at the corner and vanishing from sight.

Well, at least one of his questions had been answered, Tom thought with more hope. Someone was in the shop. And, if he was not mistaken, that person had sent the boy on an errand.

He began to be concerned that the boy might take greater notice of the stranger lurking outside his master's shop when he passed him a second time. But he need not have worried. The lad came back nearly half an hour later, leading a saddled mount, and it was plain from the trouble he was having that he had never dealt much with horses. It was all he could do to get the horse to come, and he had no attention to spare for Tom, who had to dig his fingernails into his palms to stop himself from lending the boy a hand.

Clumsily, the boy eventually managed to tie the horse's reins to a hitching post in front of Blackwell's shop. He was about to rap on the door to announce his arrival, when the door swung open, and Menzies appeared.

Tom's pulse gave a leap when he saw that arrogant face. All his anger towards the man returned in a rush, so that it was a few moments before he noticed that Menzies carried a pack and wore a riding wig.

He took a glance around, giving Tom no chance to duck, before tossing his pack behind the saddle. Tom didn't think he'd been spotted. Night had almost come, and he was standing in the shadow of a wall. He watched Menzies buckle down his belongings and check the girth. Then, he told the boy to move out of his way, and leapt into the saddle.

St. Mars's had told Tom to follow Menzies to discover where he lodged. But, as Menzies headed east, Tom decided that he was making for London Bridge, which meant that he was probably on his way back to France.

There was not a moment to lose. Dropping the news-sheet in the street, Tom turned into the nearest alley and hurried as fast as he could trot down to the river. He hailed the only boat moored at Puddle Dock Stairs, jumped into it before it was untied, and offered the waterman twice his usual fee if he could row him to Vauxhall Wharf in record time.

❧

When, feeling dejected and restless, Gideon returned from Ormonde House, he found Tom waiting for him at the dock.

"My lord, you've got to come quick," he said. He shifted impatiently while Gideon climbed out of the boat and paid the waterman his fee.

"You've found him?"

"Ay, but he's left. I saw him ride for London Bridge, and I think he's heading back to France. You'll have to be quick if you want to catch him."

The urgency in Tom's voice spurred Gideon, filling him with an emotion strangely akin to joy. At last there was something he could do! No more of this infernal waiting.

Taking long, fast strides, he headed up the river bank towards the house, with Tom nearly running to keep up.

He would ride after Menzies, and the longer and faster the ride, the better he would feel.

"Have you got Penny ready?"

"Ay, my lord. And I've saddled Beau, too."

Beau would not be able to keep pace with Gideon's horse, but Tom would not be too far behind, and Gideon still needed him to identify Menzies.

Reaching the house, and taking the stairs two at a time, Gideon took a second to reflect that, for once, he had not been made to suffer an argument with his groom. Amused, but gratified, by his servant's planning, he wondered what exactly Menzies had done to earn Tom's enmity. But that story could wait.

In his bedchamber, he removed his Quakerish coat and bob wig and threw them on the floor. He grabbed a black ribbon from his dressing table and tied his hair into a queue, before reaching for his boots.

Gideon sat to pull them on, just as Tom appeared breathless in the door. "I took the liberty of packing your lordship's cloak and mask, in case you need them," he got out. "They're in the pack on your saddle."

"And my father's pistols?"

Tom blanched. "Do you think you'll be needing them, my lord?"

With his boots put on, Gideon sprang to his feet. "Strange things are going on," he said. "It would be better for us to be prepared."

"Yes, my lord."

"You carry them, though. I'd rather not be burdened with their weight. And that way, if you come along and discover me in trouble, you'll be armed."

"Yes, my lord."

Downstairs, Gideon found the horses, saddled and waiting in front of the house. He gave Penny a hasty greeting, before picking up her reins.

The noise they had made must have wakened Katy, for she appeared in the doorway wearing her nightdress and holding a candle in her hand.

"Is there anything wrong?" she asked.

Before Tom could tell her to mind her own business, Gideon said, "There's nothing at all. You'd best go back to sleep."

"Yes, Mr. Mavors," she said, and retreated back into the house.

When Tom bent to give his master a leg up, Gideon heard him give a miserable sigh. He grinned in the dark, as Tom threw him flying onto the horse's back.

Then he had no time to think about Tom's affairs, for Penny began to kick and prance. The elation that always came with intense activity filled him now, as he tightened his grip on the reins.

"How long since Menzies left?" he asked Tom, who had turned to mount his own horse.

"Since just about dark. We'll have to ride like the dickens, my lord."

Gideon grinned as he leaned forward to pat Penny on the neck. "You hear that, my love? Didn't I promise you an entertaining ride?"

He turned her in the direction of the Kent Road and with a slight loosening of his reins, they were off.

Presumptuous Man! the reason wouldst thou find,
Why formed so weak, so little, and so blind?
First, if thou canst, the harder reason guess,
Why formed no weaker, blinder, and no less?
Ask of thy mother earth, why oaks are made
Taller or stronger than the weeds they shade?
Or ask of yonder argent fields above,
Why JOVE'S Satellites are less than JOVE?

CHAPTER XVII

A moon lit their way, as they twisted down the narrow lanes, separating the neat, little market plots to the north and east of Spring Gardens. Gideon chose this route to avoid the parade of drunken revelers, who would be returning to the boats that had brought them. At this late hour, only wealthy strollers with their servants, thieves, and spies would be awake. Respectable farmers would long have been abed.

Once safely past Vauxhall, he followed Kennington Lane until it ended at a fork. There, he abandoned the road to ride across Lock Fields, not joining the Kent Road until he had skirted the turnpike north of Walworth Common.

As Gideon rode, keeping a watch for any sign of danger, he tried to reckon how far ahead his quarry might be, but soon abandoned the effort as useless. There were too many choices Menzies could have made. If haste was his object, as Gideon believed, he would ride fast and stop often to change his mount. But if concealment played any part in his plan, he would pace his horse, stopping only where he knew he was safe.

This last thought gave him pause, for if Menzies had other places in which to hide, he might turn off the main road anywhere or any time, making his trail easy to lose. Since he had availed himself of two—Lade's inn and Blackwell's printing shop—he could very well have others, which was why Gideon hoped to catch him before he changed his horse.

At least, Menzies had left Blackwell's long enough before that Gideon could be certain he was ahead. Otherwise, they would have had to wait along the road until reasonably certain that the man had passed. But with an hour's lead or more, Menzies would have had plenty of time to walk his horse to the Thames, cross the bridge, and make his way through Southwark, even at a walk.

There were a number of troublesome choices he might have made, but Gideon had placed his bet that Menzies would use the safer turnpiked road rather than risk crippling his horse in the dark.

By the time Gideon had finished this reckoning, the highway had taken a turn south, and Penny had begun to climb the high, chalk hills of the Downs, so he gave himself up to the pleasure of a fast midnight ride. He leaned over her muscular neck and soothed her with his voice and the lightest touch of his hands.

Penny galloped up the first great rise with the strength and exuberance that her famous sire had given her. It was not Gideon's intention either to lame her or deprive her of wind, so he tried to restrain her pace. Even so, her swiftness was such that he rejoiced in the freshness of the air against his face, the smoothness of her stride, and the challenge that staying with her required.

Two hours later, the Downs had begun to give way to the woods and gentler hills just north of the Weald. Coming upon the turnpike gate before Sevenoaks, Gideon stopped to pay the toll, waking the toll-keeper to ask if he had opened his gate for any other lone rider in the previous hour. The grumbling answer was, "Yes," with curses mumbled about gentlemen who didn't have the sense to do their journeying during the day and leave good Christian souls at peace in their beds.

Gideon thanked him for his trouble, reaching into his pocket for an extra coin, which loosened the man's tongue enough for Gideon to learn that he was gaining on Menzies. The quality of his mount was nothing compared to Penny, the toll-keeper told him, adding that Menzies would surely have to change his horse in Sevenoaks.

Penny was tired, but she was far from spent. Gideon hated to push her faster, but the knowledge that Menzies would soon have a fresh mount made it imperative. If he could not catch up with his quarry before the posting-house at Sevenoaks, then his next chance might not be before the Fox and Goose in Pigden—and, then, only if Menzies intended to stop there.

Before spurring Penny on, Gideon trotted her past the next bend in the road. And, there, he stopped to don the blue satin cloak and black half mask that Tom had strapped to his saddle. Then, with a pat on Penny's neck, he urged her to her best.

Fortunately, the toll-keeper erred in his notion of time. Gideon was obliged to ride at a full gallop only a few miles before he was taken up short by the sight of a rider in front of him. He quickly reined in his mare, but he had no sooner crested the hill and caught a glimpse of the man on horseback than the rider heard the hoof beats behind him, and with a hasty glance over his shoulder, took a whip to his horse's rump.

Gideon muttered an oath, before putting his heels to Penny's flanks. He could not be positive that the man was Menzies, but neither could he afford to wait for Tom. Chance was in his favour, so he gave chase with every ounce of Penny's breath. Her breaths were coming harder, but her stride never broke. Gideon prayed that he would recognize the signs before his demands did her harm, but her heart was so steadfast that he knew she might collapse beneath him before she quit.

The rider in front of him was whipping his horse with all the fury of a man who was being pursued by highwayman. But his animal was spent. They had galloped less than a mile, with Penny gaining rapidly, when the horse in front stumbled and fell to its knees. The rider flew over its head to land in a heap in the road.

Gideon pulled hard on the reins, but Penny had already begun to slow, startled by the motion ahead. Gideon could not tend to her, for as soon as they caught up with the other horse, which was struggling to its hooves, and Gideon dismounted, the rider, who had already recovered his feet, pulled a pistol from his waist and aimed it straight at Gideon's heart.

Gideon froze, cursing himself for leaving his pistols with Tom. It was only the greatest good fortune that the man he had chased did not shoot him on sight.

"I have no pistol," Gideon said, showing both of his hands. "I did not come to rob you. Merely to talk."

The gentleman, who had lost his wig in the fall, and stood with his shaved head bared, barked out a laugh between his gasps for air. "Excellent story. I'm sure that a magistrate would be quite entertained to hear it."

"What I said is true—if you are the gentleman I've been chasing. If not, then I beg you to ride on your way—with an apology for any damage to your horse, of course."

Gideon added this last, after a glance out the corner of his eye had revealed that the rider's horse had developed a limp. It did not look severe, but it would require care soon if the horse was not to be lamed.

"And who is this gentleman you are seeking?"

"His name is Menzies."

The man reacted with a jerk. Even in the dark, Gideon could tell that he had hit his mark.

"What do you want with him?" Menzies demanded.

Although Gideon was sure of his quarry now, it would be unwise to let him know why he'd been followed when he had a pistol aimed at Gideon's chest. Especially if he was a murderer.

"I have questions I need to ask. They concern some acquaintances we have in common."

Menzies gave a mocking laugh. "And then, I presume, we should each go our separate ways? I somehow find that hard to believe. It is far more likely that you were sent to kill me."

Gideon opened his mouth to deny it, but Menzies interrupted. "Enough! You will be fortunate, indeed, if I do not shoot you first."

With his gun trained on Gideon, he took a few steps towards his mount, but the exhausted animal saw him coming and shied away. Its lameness was even more pronounced than before.

Menzies swore.

Gideon thought of Penny. He looked behind him at the spot in the road where she had stopped. After that hard ride, she should have been walked until she was cool, and the night was turning chill. If she was not attended to soon, her muscles could cramp.

Menzies must have noticed the direction of Gideon's gaze, for the next time he spoke, his voice held a satisfied sneer. "It appears that I shall have to borrow your horse."

Gideon took an angry step forward, but he was forced to halt when Menzies flourished his pistol.

"I shouldn't do that if I were you," Menzies said, sidling over to Penny and picking up her reins.

If she had not been worn out, she never would have let a stranger approach her so easily. Gideon felt a spasm of fear that he might lose his precious horse.

"A fine animal," Menzies gloated. "I wonder who you stole it from."

With his gun still aimed in Gideon's direction, he placed his left foot in the stirrup and hoisted himself up.

Surprised by the weight of a stranger on her back, Penny tossed her head and her eyes gave a flash. As Menzies worked to calm her, Gideon watched his horse with every muscle in his body tensed. He would have made a grab for Penny's reins if he had been within reach, but Menzies was clearly no novice with a weapon, for his aim never slipped.

Gideon knew that fear for his horse was hardly rational, when the weapon was pointed at him and not at her. Still, he could not bear the thought of losing his mare, and in her exhausted condition, he did not have much hope that she would manage to unseat her rider.

Soon, she permitted Menzies to quiet her. She seemed even docile. Then, as Menzies relaxed, shifting his weight back in the saddle, her tail gave a swish, her ears turned back, and her head bent down.

Gideon's heart made a lunge.

He took a step to the left, in the direction of her tail. "You cannot mean to leave me here! In the road?"

As he hoped, Menzies twisted in the saddle to follow him. With Penny pulling with her head, he could not keep both hands on the reins and still aim his pistol Gideon's way. Then, Penny gave a hop with her hind legs, and Menzies was forced to turn even more.

But his fault was arrogance, and he could not miss an opportunity to sneer, "I daresay the authorities will want to know why you chose to ride out masked at midnight. I shall have to mention your location to the Watch in Sevenoaks."

He was about to say more, when Gideon noted that Penny had raised one of her hind hooves and that both of her ears had gone flat against her head.

He lunged left.

Menzies followed his movement, swiveling quickly to the right, throwing his body awry just as Penny arched her back into a hump and lashed out with her hooves.

She had a cunning angle to her buck, as Gideon knew, as if she could sense the very point of her rider's balance. She had used it on him often enough, until he had learned to ride it. And, though he had cursed her for it a time or two, he couldn't help being proud of her now, as Menzies went flying in one direction, his pistol in the other.

Gideon retrieved the weapon, before approaching his frightened horse. Even with her head jerking in indignation, he could see that she was quivering, and the sweat drying on her coat worried him even more. As he advanced, he cooed gently, telling her what a good girl she was, and soon she stopped tossing her head and came to rest it against his chest. With her soft, warm nose blowing hard in his palm, he finally glanced at the place where Menzies had landed and watched him struggle to his feet. The wariness in his shoulders alerted Gideon to the fact that Menzies was calculating his next move, and that he had not yet ruled out a fight.

It was Gideon who broke the silence between them. "As I was saying," he coolly remarked, "I have a few questions for you to answer."

"I never said I was the man you are seeking. What was his name?"

His evasion made Gideon smile. "His name is Menzies, though he also goes by the name of Blackwell."

Again he could not miss Menzies's reaction, for his body went still.

He said, "I'm afraid you have stopped the wrong man."

"If that is the truth, then I shall apologize, of course. But I believe it is not. If you insist on denying it, however, we have only to wait a short time before my servant Tom will be joining us. He's met you, you know."

Menzies was entirely unprepared for this last bit of news. He did not even bother to conceal his surprise. "Are you the blackguard who's taken over Lade's?" he demanded.

"The very same. And, your recent behaviour to the contrary, I had heard that you wished to meet me."

Gideon's tone, along, perhaps, with the fact that he had not fired the weapon, seemed to give Menzies confidence. He squared his shoulders, which, as hunched as they'd been, must have begun to ache.

Arrogance was in his voice again, when he hissed, "And I still look forward to that meeting."

Gideon involuntarily tightened his grip on the pistol butt, but suppressed the urge to react. "I shall be happy to oblige you on a future date, but for the moment I have a more pressing matter."

"Such as . . . ?"

". . . the murder of Sir Humphrey Cove."

Menzies greeted this statement with silence. Sensing the moment to push, Gideon was about to question him, when he heard approaching hoof beats. Both men turned their heads in time to see Tom ride over the nearest peak in the road.

He spotted them and checked his horse. Then, recognizing his master, he set Beau towards them at a trot.

In spite of Tom's poor timing, Gideon was very relieved to see him.

"I see you caught up with Mr. Menzies, sir."

Gideon ignored the smugness in his groom's voice. "Tom, I need you to walk my horse. She's been ridden very hard."

He had no need to say more. Menzies counted for nothing compared to Tom's charges.

He took one look at Penny and leapt off his horse. "Just you give her to me, my lord." He hurriedly took the reins from Gideon's hands, and examined her legs for any sign of injury. Then, his examination complete, he took the reins to both horses and walked them up and down the narrow road as if he had never taken an interest in this night's work.

"So. It is 'my lord,' is it?"

Until Menzies said this, Gideon had not noticed Tom's slip.

"Then what Lade believes is true? You are for James?"

Gideon had not risked his favourite horse to discuss his part in the Pretender's schemes. So far, Menzies had done everything he could to avoid answering his questions. Perhaps, he would be more helpful if he knew that Gideon was an agent of James's.

"His Majesty *has* entrusted me with a mission. But that is not my reason for following you. I came to ask why you left Sir Humphrey's box on the evening that he was murdered."

Menzies scoffed. "I never murdered that fool! And I cannot believe that his Majesty would waste his time in worrying who did."

His callousness did nothing to recommend him to Gideon. With a sharper edge to his voice, he said, "Nevertheless, I believe he would wish to know if one of his followers was murdered by another. I understood Sir Humphrey to be a faithful adherent of the Stuart cause."

"Faithful, perhaps. But he never did anything for James."

"He never contributed any money?"

Gideon could almost hear Menzies's scowl. "Never as much as he should. But there is nothing unusual in that. None of you English Jacobites are doing what you should for his Majesty."

"Still . . . if he gave money, his loss should count for something. Which makes me wonder why Sir Humphrey was killed, when every gentleman in that box was a Jacobite, except for Lord Hawkhurst, of course."

"What makes you say that?"

"I have my sources." Gideon let those words sink in, before he went on, "Colonel Potter lost his commission because someone told the King that his loyalty was not to be trusted. He tried to obtain a post as secretary to Lord Hawkhurst. His motive was to turn the earl to the cause."

When Menzies made no comment, he went on, "Lord Lovett's part in this is still unclear, though he did introduce the Colonel to Hawkhurst's notice. Somehow, I feel certain that you can tell me what his purpose was."

"Other than bedding the countess?" Menzies sneered. "I don't know that he had another."

Gideon felt a punch of revulsion. This was followed by a spurt of anger so strong that he balled his fists. The strength of his emotions took him aback. He had not believed himself still vulnerable where Isabella was concerned.

He knew that he was no longer in love with her. Nor had he been, since discovering how little he meant to her. Yet, some remnant of his affection for her must remain, for he found himself unwilling to hear insults thrown at her.

Perhaps, he was not ready to face how foolish he had been, he thought. But, then, in a flash, he knew that he simply believed it was unfair for a man to play seductive games when his motive was not love, no matter how willing his victim might be. And, if that was the basis for his reaction, then he had sufficiently recovered from his disappointment to think of Isabella as a victim, too.

All of this flew through his mind in an instant, so he scarcely paused before continuing. "After he won the lady's favour," he said, referring to Lord Lovett, "I presume he intended to use his influence to persuade her and her husband to send money to James?"

"Naturally," Menzies responded. "So you can see that neither of those gentleman had a reason to kill Sir Humphrey."

"I have heard that Sir Humphrey was not always discreet."

"Discreet! He couldn't keep a confidence any longer than it takes to sniff a pinch of snuff. But no one would have been idiotic enough to trust him with anything important."

"You mean that he did not know of Colonel Potter's and Lord Lovett's plans?"

"I doubt that he did. Lovett used him to become acquainted with Lord Hawkhurst and his lady. But Lovett is no fool. He would never have told Sir Humphrey his reasons. He had only to express the desire to be made known to such a lovely lady, and Humphrey would have been satisfied."

"And Sir Humphrey would never have tumbled to their real motive?"

"Never in a thousand years. So if you've been thinking that one of them killed Sir Humphrey Cove in order to keep him from betraying their plan to Lord Hawkhurst, then you've been wasting your time."

Gideon waited, until his pause was long enough to be noticed, before saying, "Then, that leaves us with you."

"I did not murder him, I tell you!"

"But you left the box unexpectedly and did not return. And, since he was killed in the next few minutes, your departure obviously seems suspicious." In a commanding voice, Gideon asked again, "So why *did* you leave the box?"

Menzies answered reluctantly, "I saw someone I recognized from Boulogne. He was standing in the doorway to the pit with Walpole. He could be one of Walpole's spies."

"And, then . . . ?"

"I left the theatre. What else?"

"Did you see anyone else from Sir Humphrey's box? And, if you did, what were they doing and who were they with?"

"I tried to avoid them, but I did catch a glimpse of Potter talking to Lady Hawkhurst's brother." Menzies paused. "And what about Mayfield?" he demanded. "He was sitting in our box, and I know that he attacked Sir Humphrey at Lord Hawkhurst's card party. He is no Jacobite, but if anyone should be suspected of killing Sir Humphrey, it is he. He's the one you should be holding up."

"I am aware of the evidence against Mayfield. You say you saw him?"

"Yes, and from the look on Colonel Potter's face, I gathered that his conversation was not of the most riveting variety."

"Did you see them after they parted?"

"No, but when I passed them, I saw a harlot blow a kiss at Mayfield. She seemed to have captured his attention."

"Anyone else?"

"Only Lovett. He was standing outside the ladies' withdrawing room. Since he escorted Lady Hawkhurst out, I assume he was waiting for her to emerge."

"Is that all?"

Menzies said that it was, so Gideon asked, "How long between the time you saw the whore blow a kiss at Mayfield and your departure?"

"No time at all. I headed straight down the stairs and out the door."

"So you did not see him go down? And you did not glimpse Sir Humphrey at all?"

Menzies emitted an irritated sigh. "I told you, I was trying to avoid being seen. I was keeping a look out for Walpole's spy, and the last thing on my mind was that oaf Mayfield or any of Sir Humphrey's party.

"Now," he said, "I believe I have answered your queries sufficiently. So, it is your turn to answer mine. Who are you, and why are you wearing a mask?"

"If I could answer that, I should have no reason to wear it."

Menzies's frustration was palpable. "How can I be certain that you are not one of Walpole's men?"

"You can't. I can give you my word, but I suspect you will consider that unsatisfactory."

He held the pistol up so Menzies could see it, and peered over his shoulder to see how Penny was doing.

Tom had stopped walking the horses to rub them both down with fistfuls of dry grass.

Out the corner of his eye, Gideon noticed when Menzies took a step. He turned back around, then gestured with the pistol towards Menzies's lame horse.

"You'd better see if that horse can be walked into Sevenoaks."

"I can't. It's too dark."

Gideon was not about to fall for any trick. "Then you can leave it. But you had better start walking if you want to get to Sevenoaks before dawn."

Menzies let loose with a spate of oaths, but he went to capture the injured animal. This time, he was more successful.

Gideon watched him run his hands over the horse's legs and check its hooves.

"He's picked up a stone," Menzies said.

Gideon allowed him to dig in his bag for a hook, though he covered him with the pistol. Before too many seconds had passed, he heard the clack of a stone hitting the road and let Menzies put away his tool.

Menzies walked the horse in a circle, and Gideon noted that its limp was gone.

"You may go," he said. "But if I discover that you lied about Sir Humphrey's death, be forewarned, for I shall find you."

"Then, we shall not be meeting any time soon." Menzies climbed into his saddle and asked, "Shall I carry any message for his Majesty?"

Gideon did not miss the irony in his voice. Menzies's offer, though, recalled the happenings of the past eventful week. "You may tell him that his army is in disarray, that its leadership is undecided, and that the government has launched a broad attack on his adherents."

He heard Menzies hiss. "If I tell him anything of the sort, he'll give up hope."

"As, perhaps, he should." Gideon spoke with regret, but Menzies did not wish to hear it.

He swung his horse around and rode it straight at Gideon. "If you want a message like that delivered, then you can do it yourself!"

Before the horse could ride him down, Gideon leapt out of its way. He landed on his elbow, holding the pistol safely aloft in case it discharged. Ignoring the resulting pain in his arm, his scrambled to his feet, afraid that Menzies would go after Tom, but the sight that greeted him in the moonlight was the rump of Menzies's horse as it galloped towards Sevenoaks.

Tom came running over to see if he was hurt.

"Do you want me to chase him?" he asked, once he saw that Gideon was all right.

"No. But we should leave as soon as possible. I can't be sure that Menzies won't report us to the authorities. Is Penny all right?"

"I think so, my lord. But I wouldn't want to see you ride her too fast."

"I wouldn't think of it. But, since we've got to walk, we'd best leave now."

When they were mounted and had turned their horses towards London, Tom asked, "Did you get what you wanted out of him, my lord?"

"I can't be sure. It wasn't much."

"Then what will you do now?"

"I shall need to speak with Mrs. Kean."

❧

While Gideon was waiting for dark before paying his visit to the Duke of Ormonde, Hester was sitting with her cousin Dudley in the withdrawing room at Hawkhurst House. The Prince of Wales was indisposed, and he had invited Isabella and Harrowby to his bedchamber to play at cards. Since the wagers were sure to be deep and the play to go on for hours, Mrs. Mayfield had insisted on Hester's staying at home to entertain her cousin. Hester could barely contain her frustration.

It was not that she had any desire to watch the Royal couple and their courtiers play until morning, but she had been forced to listen to Dudley's complaints all evening. Even if she could have felt sympathy for him, his attitude would have rid her of all wish to be of service.

His mother had selfishly accepted an invitation of her own, leaving Hester to be Dudley's sole ear. And, in the past two days, Dudley had begun to feel very sorry for himself, indeed.

Whether Sir William had spread the word about Dudley's attack on Sir Humphrey, or other people's suspicions had led them to be indiscreet, Dudley was now being shunned by the members of the Court. Herr Bernstorff himself had paid a visit to Hawkhurst House to tell Harrowby that he should not try the King's grace by bringing his brother-in-law to Court while a shadow of suspicion hung over his head. And even though a direct cut from his Majesty had thus been avoided, it was clear from the behaviour of the peers that Dudley would be excluded from any invitation sent to the Earl and Countess of Hawkhurst.

"I've a good mind to go home," Dudley said, for the third time that evening. As on the other two occasions, he followed this remark with a huff, which seemed to say that it would serve them all right if he did.

Hester bit back an impatient sigh. She had tried to distract him with a game of piquet, but playing cards for no wager with his spinster cousin was not Dudley's idea of fun, and he refused to be amused. He seemed oblivious to the fact that Hester was no more entertained by his company than he was by hers.

Hester was reluctant to dignify his comment with a reaction, but she found herself repeating the advice she had given him before. "If you were to leave, you would give the impression of running away. And I know you wouldn't want that."

"Then what can I do?" he moaned. "The gossips are growing worse.

They act as if I'm a monster."

"You must be patient. Eventually, the real murderer will be caught, and they will realize the error they have made."

"I don't know why you say he'll be caught, when nothing's being done to find him. I thought you said that *we* would discover who did it."

Hester could not truly blame him for this complaint. Although the magistrate had taken statements from everyone present, no testimony had pointed to the killer. There had been no direct witnesses, and without them, even if a motive were found, there would be no way of proving the murderer's guilt.

The magistrate had tried to eliminate Sir Humphrey's guests as suspects by requesting their alibis, but Harrowby was the only one of the gentlemen who had been in someone's company during every moment of the interval. This left the others under doubt, but since Lord Lovett and Colonel Potter had been Sir Humphrey's friends for years and were known at Court, it was not surprising that the bulk of suspicion had fallen first on Dudley, next on the missing Mr. Blackwell, and finally on a stranger in the crowd.

Hester could not wonder that the magistrate had given up. It was unlikely that anyone would ever be brought to trial, which meant that Dudley was safe—if forever being thought of as a murderer could be considered safe. No matter how low her opinion of her cousin was, Hester could not be happy to have any member of her family tarred with such a brush. And besides, it would be a great injustice if Sir Humphrey's murderer went free.

She could not tell Dudley that the Viscount St. Mars was helping her investigate. Nor could she share the information he obtained, when Dudley would naturally wonder how she had come by it. But she did have one idea, if she could only get Dudley to think, too.

Keeping her eyes on the cards, while dealing another hand, she said, "It would help if someone could testify that he or she saw you downstairs after the interval was over."

Although she had tried to make her suggestion sound innocent, Dudley's cheeks still reddened with annoyance.

"I've told you. There's nobody who can do it."

"Not even one of the women selling oranges? Are you certain you did not stop to speak to one of them? If so, she might be able to remember you."

"I didn't—"

But that was as far as Dudley got before the door of the room opened, and Lord Lovett walked in.

He had not been announced, but his visits to Hawkhurst House were so frequent and welcome that the footmen had ceased treating him like a guest.

Hester and Dudley stood to make their obeisances, each with a certain awkwardness. Since the night of Isabella's card party, Hester had found it difficult to meet this gentleman's gaze without feeling flustered, while Dudley's uneasiness stemmed from the way Lord Lovett examined him—as if he searched his face for signs of madness or guilt.

Hester took on the role of hostess to fill the awkward moment. "I know how sorry my lord and Isabella will be to have missed you, Lord Lovett, but they were summoned by the Prince."

"I was aware of their plans this evening, thank you, Mrs. Kean." His piercing black eyes fixed on hers. "I came to see how you were getting on."

He shifted his gaze to include her cousin in this statement, but Dudley was so clearly an afterthought that even he could not fail to grasp this fact.

He tried to overcome his discomfort with a jest. "Oho! I shall have to warn my sister of a rival, shall I, Hester? Lord Lovett will be wishing me to the devil."

Lord Lovett gave him a withering sneer, which made the young man turn red and scowl.

Hester felt embarrassment grip her throat. She did her best to feign ignorance of her cousin's meaning, but when Lord Lovett turned his gaze on hers, it instantly softened. A smile played at his lips, as if to say that he knew how much she detested that sort of raillery and he would not permit her to be annoyed.

Hester wondered how much should be read into a gaze, for there seemed to be even more in his—a confirmation of what Dudley had implied, and not the denial she had expected to see.

To cover her confusion, she offered Lord Lovett refreshments, but this unfortunately drew his attention to Dudley's drinking.

Since the night of the opera, Harrowby had insisted that Dudley only be given watered wine. A carafe with this weakened mixture was standing on the table where they had played piquet. Lord Lovett's gaze traveled to it, and he immediately raised one brow before turning to Hester with a frown.

"I shouldn't have thought that Hawkhurst would leave you alone." He did not seem to care if Dudley was offended by this speech.

Hester gave a quick glance at her cousin and saw that he had grasped Lord Lovett's meaning. His expression changed from crushed to furious.

Before he could speak, she turned back to Lord Lovett, with a measure of reproof. "I am not alone. I have my cousin here to keep me company. We have been enjoying a game of cards."

Her words were not enough to remove the sting of Lord Lovett's, though. Once roused, Dudley's temper was never easy to soothe, and his most sensitive wounds had just been trounced upon.

"I suspect you mean that she is not safe with me," he said, taking a big step towards Lord Lovett with his hands in fists.

Hester hurriedly said, "Now I'm certain that his lordship meant nothing of the kind."

She looked to Lord Lovett for assistance, but he merely stood his ground. His expression said that Dudley might interpret his meaning any way he liked.

She tried again to calm her cousin, speaking firmly. "No matter what anyone says or even thinks, you will never change their minds by becoming upset. What is needed is restraint."

"It's easy for you to talk about restraint!" Dudley turned his fury on her. "You aren't the one being accused of something you didn't do!"

Lord Lovett made as if to step between them, which would not help at all. Hester tried to stop him by raising a hand, but she was obliged to place it on his chest.

This flustered her before she addressed Dudley again. "No, I'm not accused of anything, but since you are, you need all the friends you can get, including your brother-in-law. And I can assure you that he will never forgive you if you start another brawl in his house!"

This warning finally penetrated Dudley's ill-humour. He struggled visibly to overcome his temper, but when he could not, he pushed past Hester, nearly flinging her into Lord Lovett's arms, and stamped for the door. "If anybody cares where I've gone, you can tell them that I've gone out! And I shall stay out until I feel like coming back!"

As soon as the door slammed behind him, Hester realized that Lord Lovett was still holding on to her. One of his arms had gone protectively about her, and the next step seemed that it would be to turn her to face him within his embrace.

Even though her pulse livened at the thought, she would not allow herself to be seduced. She wriggled out of his arms and turned to face him from a safe distance away.

That she had surprised him was evident in the tilt of his brow. Something in the twist of his lips said that she had offended his pride as well. But Hester was not only embarrassed—she was also angry, which, after a long pause, he seemed to realize.

He cast her a rueful glance from under his thick, black brows. "I imagine that you blame me for provoking that outburst?"

His willingness to acknowledge his share of the blame disarmed her. She reminded herself, too, that he was a baron and a guest in her cousin's house, before responding as lightly as she could, "In all fairness to Dudley, I must say that his temper was perfectly even until you made that unwise remark."

Lord Lovett confronted her with an offended laugh. "And if I had not made it?" he asked. "Better still, if I had never come this evening? How long would you have kept your cousin company? Until some little thing you said made him turn his violence on you?"

Hester started to protest, but he cut her off. "And, please, have the goodness to spare me the fiction that Mayfield was keeping you company, instead of the truth, which is that you were set to stand guard over him."

Hester watched him walk a tight, angry circle in the room. She could not deny what he'd said, but she would not allow his implication to stand. "My aunt *did* ask me to entertain Dudley this evening, but not because she fears another outburst from him. It's because he has been asked to stay away from Court, and nobody else will receive him."

He came to a stop behind a chair. "Can you blame them?"

"No, I suppose not. It does not follow, however, that he murdered Sir Humphrey."

He gave her a look that was half-way between frustration and pity. "I understand that you do not wish it to be Mayfield," he said, not without sympathy. "But I have to tell you that it takes every ounce of my restraint not to call him out for Cove's murder."

"You are convinced of his guilt."

He averted his gaze, as if loath to hurt her. Then he nodded. "I cannot imagine anyone else in the role."

"Not even the absent Mr. Blackwell?"

At her question, he quickly raised his eyes. Then, as if needing time to collect his thoughts, he stared down at the chair and ran his fingers back and forth along its back.

"Mrs. Kean," he said, finally lifting his head. "I have trusted you with information that could get me hanged. And the danger for me and my friends has never been more acute. I can only give you my word that Blackwell had no reason to kill Sir Humphrey."

The sincerity in his eyes gave her a chill. He acted as if he could verify Blackwell's innocence, which must mean either that he had seen Blackwell leave the theatre, or that they had been together during the last part of the interval. Naturally, if they had, Lord Lovett would not have been able to give that testimony without alerting the authorities to Blackwell's true identity. But if he was certain of Blackwell's innocence, she could see why he believed that her cousin was guilty.

She did not want to ask him about Colonel Potter, but she had to force herself to believe that he could have been deceived in his friend.

"I have reason to believe that Dudley was engaged in a different pursuit, while Sir Humphrey was being murdered," she ventured.

Lord Lovett furrowed his brow. "What makes you believe that?"

Hester looked down at her clasped fingers. "It has been apparent from the first that he was lying about the reason he went downstairs. He will not tell me what lured him that way. I think he is afraid for his mother to know. But, if the young woman could be persuaded—"

"You think he went downstairs with a harlot?"

His frankness unsettled her, until she realized that honesty was just what she needed.

Still, even grateful as she was, it was not easy to meet his frown. "Go on," he said, as if her revelation had disturbed him.

"I was thinking that the woman, perhaps, might be found. I assume she would be in the theatre on other nights. If someone could help Dudley find her, then perhaps she could be persuaded to swear to his alibi."

But Lord Lovett had begun to shake his head. "When that could land her in Bridewell? Why should any whore do that?"

Hester flushed, but she persisted. "She wouldn't have to say what sort of intercourse they had been engaged in, just that Dudley had been with her during the pertinent time."

Lord Lovett stared quizzically at her. "You realize that someone would have to pay her to testify . . . which means that Mayfield could as easily pay her to lie. Is that what you're suggesting?"

"Of course, not!"

"Then, my dear girl, I'm afraid you will have to think of something better. In the first place, every magistrate is sure to know the harlots working in his neighbourhood. And he also knows that they will swear to anything for the price of their dinner."

Hester felt deflated and chagrined. Hanging her head, she wondered how she could have been so naive. "How stupid of me!" she said, forcing a little laugh. "Of course, you are right. It is just that—"

"Just what?" he said. He had taken a step towards her as if to comfort her, but he halted with another frown. "What else is troubling you?"

She wrinkled up her face with the effort to convey her reasoning. "It just seems so convenient for a murderer," she said. "My cousin is heard to have attacked Sir Humphrey in a drunken fit of temper. Then, Sir Humphrey is murdered when Dudley is a guest in his box. Dudley is distracted by a woman when the murder is being committed, so he arrives back in the box without an alibi. On top of which, someone jostles him in the crowd, so that he spills a glass of spirits on his clothes, which makes him reek as if he's been drinking to excess."

While Hester talked, Lord Lovett's eyes grew narrow. She could almost see the way his thoughts were flying. If, as she suggested, someone had tried to frame Dudley for the murder, then Colonel Potter must surely enter his mind.

He looked distressed. His gestures, which had always been languid, seemed nervous when he said, "You mean that someone caused him to spill his wine on purpose—perhaps even paid the harlot to distract him?"

Until Hester had started speaking, she had not put the two together, although the incidence of the spilled wine had always bothered her. Now, seen as two parts to a plan, they seemed to fit.

"The Colonel said in his testimony that he did not see who jostled Dudley's arm in the crowd, but I have never been convinced that he was telling the truth."

Lord Lovett turned pale. "Promise me that you will not speak of this to anyone else for now. Not until I can question Potter."

Hester tried to hide her quandary from him. She had to share her theory with St. Mars. "I promise," she said, telling a lie.

He looked only slightly relieved. Clearly the fear of his friend's treachery was still uppermost in his mind. But he did not forget to caution her. "If you see Potter, you must never give the impression that you suspect him. There's no telling what he might do, if he thought you did."

"I am not likely to see him. With all the turmoil in the streets, and Dudley to entertain most evenings, I seldom leave the house. And my lord has told the servants that Colonel Potter is no longer to be admitted."

He nodded, and a burden seemed to be lifted from his shoulders, but there were others in his eyes, even more disturbing.

"I cannot tell you how much this distresses me," he finally said. "But for your own safety, you must admit that it is still conjecture. Your cousin may still be the one who is lying. Don't take any chances around him. I will see if the harlot can be found. Then, I'll get what I can from Potter."

Hester apologized for having to defend Dudley by casting suspicion on his friend, but he dismissed her concern.

"It isn't over. Anything could happen. Or nothing. We mustn't let ourselves be overwhelmed yet."

At the door, before taking his leave, he raised her hand to his lips. Then he gave her fingers a squeeze, which Hester found too tight, but knowing how unhappy he was, she concealed this from him.

"When I met you," he said, looking down at the fingers turning white in his hand, "I had no idea that you would overturn my life the way you have." He released her fingers, only to take hold of her chin. And before Hester could blink, he had brought his lips to hers.

The kiss lasted only a moment, but Hester was left with her mouth wide open in a gasp.

Lord Lovett gave her an ironic grin, with one eyebrow cocked, and in the next instant, he had left.

Know then thyself, presume not God to scan;
The proper study of Mankind is Man.
Placed on this isthmus of a middle state,
A Being darkly wise, and rudely great:
With too much knowledge for the Sceptic side,
With too much weakness for the Stoic's pride,
He hangs between; in doubt to act, or rest;
In doubt to deem himself a God, or Beast;
In doubt his Mind or Body to prefer;
Born but to die, and reasoning but to err;
Alike in ignorance, his reason such,
Whether he thinks too little, or too much:
Chaos of Thought and Passion, all confused;
Still by himself abused, or disabused;
Created half to rise, and half to fall;
Great lord of all things, yet a prey to all;
Sole judge of the Truth, in endless Error hurled:
The glory, jest, and riddle of the world!

CHAPTER XVIII

As soon as Gideon returned to London, he sent Katy with a note for Mrs. Kean.

Since Katy had never been into the City of Westminster alone, she was daunted by the challenge of finding her way to Hawkhurst House. So Gideon asked Tom to guide her to Covent Garden to buy strawberries to fill her basket and then to Hawkhurst House. Tom, of course, must not be spotted by the servants with whom he had worked for so many years, so he would have to wait nearby to escort her back to the dock at Westminster Stairs.

Tom's grumblings on receiving this assignment were not as loud as usual. They were so perfunctory, in fact, as to make Gideon grin. He watched them set off from his open window upstairs and almost felt a pang of envy.

It was a beautiful day for a promenade.

Tom and Katy, however, each began the trip with a wealth of misgivings. Tom's were always the same whenever he had to be with the woman he found so attractive.

Katy's were different. She could never be entirely at ease with Thomas Barnes—not when he disapproved of her so strongly—but for once, Tom was not the biggest ogre she had to face.

The very thought of walking up to the gate of an earl's house and speaking to the formidable servant, whose job it would be to keep people out, had her knees shaking before any additional qualms arose. Then others emerged, and together they made a frightening picture.

Even if this "Mistress Kean" did wish to receive Mr. Mavors's message, Katy doubted that any lady living in an earl's house would gladly receive it from the hands of a woman like her. When she had worked in a shop at Tunbridge Wells, she had seen how disdainful the fashionable women could be—and that to Katy's parents, who, unlike her, had always been respectable. Mrs. Kean would not care that Katy had been lured into error by a young crook who had claimed to love her. She would see an unmarried woman who had no business keeping house with two unmarried men.

Deep in the Weald, where everyone about her worked in poverty or crime, she had almost forgotten her shame, but today it had returned with force. How could she face a pious lady?

These were the two fears that had disturbed her sleep the previous night. Now, as she stepped into the boat, with Tom unexpectedly taking her by the elbow to assist her, the worst thought imaginable entered her mind.

With the blood draining from her cheeks, Katy sank onto the wooden seat.

Once, she'd been gulled into doing a favour for a man she had believed loved her. And that favour, so innocently done, had ruined her and landed her in gaol. Now, she was being asked to do something secretive for another man who altered his name.

What if Mrs. Kean was not a lady, but his accomplice, and Mr. Mavors's plan was to rob the earl? Had Katy been chosen to take the blame, when helping them would surely get someone hanged?

She wondered how she could have been such a fool as to take an order like that from Mr. Mavors. If he and Tom were not thieves, why were they hiding? Why couldn't Tom carry the message?

Katy had imagined that Mr. Mavors wanted to send a secret message to his love without alerting a father or a husband, perhaps. He had seemed so kind when he had talked to her about Tom. But kindness could be feigned. She thought she had already learned that bitter truth, but what if she had been fooled again?

Waking to her surroundings, she saw that the current had taken them quickly down river. The waterman was straining at his oars to cross. Soon they would arrive at the opposite bank, and it would be harder to turn back.

Tom sat behind her in the stern. He had never pretended to like her. He had made it clear from the start that he wanted nothing to do with her at all. Yet, twice, he had helped her. Against his own opinion, he had asked his master if she could have the post of caring for his clothes. And he had stopped Mr. Menzies from using her as his wench.

She could not say that Tom was her friend, not when he had no desire to be one. But he might tell her the truth if she asked.

She twisted to face him in the boat. A wary surprise flickered in his eyes. They darted from her face to her lap, then back to her face, and nervously to the other bank.

"Tom," she said, trying to keep her lower lip from trembling, "I can't carry this note for Mr. Mavors until I know what it's about."

She had pitched her voice very low, so the waterman would not hear her over the splashing of his oars, but Tom's brows snapped together in alarm. He threw warning glances over her shoulder, as if to remind her of the rower's presence.

"Are you going to tell me," she persisted, "or shall I tell the waterman to turn around?"

Her boldness annoyed him, but it also seemed to inspire his respect. Seeing this drove her shakiness away.

"I can't talk about the master here," Tom whispered fiercely, casting another glare at the man behind her.

The steady clunks of the oars in their locks nearly covered their words.

"Will you promise to tell me, once we're across?"

A struggle played with his features. "It's not for you to question the master's orders."

"It is, when I'm the one who could get thrown in the clink!"

The shocked look on his face seemed to suggest that her fears were groundless.

He even seemed offended when, reluctantly, he leaned forward to speak softly in her ear. "The master would never ask you to do anything wrong. Why, I can't hardly even get him to ask me! He's always making me stay behind!"

This confused her so much that she drew back to search his face, but she found no guilt—just frustration.

Tom closed his eyes and breathed in deeply. Then he opened them again, as if startled, pulling back so sharply that he lost his balance and nearly fell over the back of the boat.

Katy turned back around and saw that they were about to dock. She twisted to speak to Tom again and saw that he looked miserable.

"Promise me you'll tell me enough to make me feel safe," she said.

These words seemed to strike a reasonable chord inside him. The muscles in his face relaxed, but the only answer he made was a nod.

The boat hit the dock at Hungerford Stairs. Tom paid the waterman, then gestured for her to lead him up the narrow street. When it broadened into an empty market place, Katy stopped and turned around.

Hurrying behind her, Tom nearly tumbled over her in an effort to stop.

Katy grabbed both his arms and forced him to look her in the eyes. "I won't go to prison again," she said. "I won't be sent there for any man."

Tom was gazing down at her. As she expressed her fear, she felt his resistance melting. He put his large, worn palms on her arms, and his touch was wonderfully warm.

"Why does Mr. Mavors want me to carry a message to the lady? He doesn't mean to rob the earl's house, does he?"

Tom, who almost never smiled, broke out into a laugh.

"I don't see what's so funny!" Katy protested, but she did not pull away. She was amazingly comfortable where she was.

"If he did"— Tom was still grinning— "I don't expect there'd be any crime in it."

He was making no sense, and teasing her plainly. But she was the one being asked to behave suspiciously, and she deserved to know why—which she told him then, with a sudden threat of tears.

Tom seemed upset to see the moisture in her eyes. He tightened his grip, bringing her closer to his chest, though there was no one in the nearby stalls to hear him when he said, "You must promise never to betray the master."

Katy promised. She did not bother to remind him that she had already given him her word on this.

"The master is innocent. I should know—I've taken care of him since he was just a little lad. He's never broken any law. But there are them who think he's guilty of murder and would hang him in a minute if they knew where he was."

Katy's mouth fell open, and for a while she forgot about everything but the story Tom told her.

He told her that their master was the Viscount St. Mars, that his father the Earl of Hawkhurst had been murdered, and that his son had been accused. St. Mars had found the man responsible, but he had not got enough proof to take to a magistrate.

The story made Katy shiver, for it recalled her own troubles with the law. She did not want to think about her prison days again, though, so she said, "Then Hawkhurst House is his?"

Tom explained that St. Mars's cousin had been granted the earldom in his stead.

"And who is Mrs. Kean?"

This was harder for Tom to express. What was important, he said, was that Mrs. Kean knew St. Mars was innocent, for she had helped him find his father's murderer. And now, he was returning the favour by helping her investigate the killing of a gentleman by the name of Sir Humphrey Cove.

"I wonder if they love each other," Katy mused.

Tom's hands tightened convulsively on her arms. Then he seemed to recollect himself and released her, taking a step backwards. "Now you see why we didn't tell you?"

She nodded. "You didn't think you could trust me. But now you do?"

His frown told her that their moment of friendship was over.

"You would have asked him yourself sooner or later," Tom grumbled. "And I can't have you thinking the master's a common house thief."

He looked impatiently at her. "Are you ready to go? We'd best be moving or there won't be any strawberries left."

By the time they had walked to the market at Covent Garden, made their purchase, and filled Katy's basket with berries, Tom had reason to feel anxious. He'd seen men congregating in the streets. Shouting matches had erupted, as well as fights like the one he had witnessed in Amen Corner.

He had no interest in politics, but he knew that the former Lord Hawkhurst had often grown heated over party affairs, and that St. Mars had seemed more interested in them of late. Whatever was going on now, it was much worse than usual, which St. Mars would need to know.

He hurried Katy almost into Piccadilly. Then, after assuring himself that she would not run into any rioters, he sent her towards Hawkhurst House, with instructions to tell Mrs. Kean that the streets weren't safe. If she was planning to see his lordship, she had better appoint a safe meeting place.

Then, he fretted while Katy approached the porter's lodge and stopped to speak to the porter, Rufus. Tom felt the hair stand up on the back of his neck when Rufus chucked her under the chin and peered into her basket in an obvious attempt to nuzzle her breast.

"Dirty sot!" Tom growled beneath his breath. "I'll bet you'd keep your hands to yourself, if I was by!"

Katy was smiling at the porter, but even from where he stood, Tom could see that she was nervous. He had watched her enough to know her every thought. Knowing that she wasn't enjoying Rufus's advances made him angry on the one hand, but strangely happy on the other. He didn't want her to enjoy the attentions of other men.

He hadn't felt uneasy at all when he'd told her about St. Mars, which made him feel guilty now. He'd had no right to tell her St. Mars's secrets. But, when he'd seen how scared she was, he hadn't been able to stop himself. And it was true that the master would be safer now that she knew. The more Katy knew, the better she could help him protect St. Mars.

The knowledge that this burden was no longer his alone, but one he could share, somehow made him feel better. And he couldn't have sent Katy into Hawkhurst House, believing that she was doing something wrong. Even if he could, it wouldn't have been right.

Rufus finally let her through the gate, and Tom lost sight of them both. He had to turn his face to the side when Lord Burlington's coachman drove by, and again when he saw a boy from Hawkhurst House running down the street with a letter for the post. Being careful not to be spotted by anyone he knew helped to fill the time, until Katy reappeared outside the courtyard gate.

She waved goodbye to Rufus and came hurrying towards him. He ducked around the corner of a house and waited there, out of sight of his old home.

When she came round from Piccadilly, she looked excited and breathless. Tom did not have to ask if she had delivered St. Mars's message, for she immediately launched into raptures about the beauty of the furniture and the paintings and the servants' livery, about how kind Mrs. Kean had been, and how horrible it must have been for St. Mars to lose his beautiful house.

Tom knew he should quiet her, but he was too entertained, as he shepherded her on their way to the dock.

Without thinking, he had taken her down St. James's Street, where he was more likely to run into people he knew. He had just recalled this when he spotted a familiar face heading in their direction.

"Come on," he said softly to Katy. "There's a fellow up there that I know. Take my arm."

After waiting for a waggon to pass, they crossed half the street, before running the rest of the way to avoid being trampled by a coach and six.

No sooner had they made it onto the footpath, however, than a gang of men burst from between the buildings on the corner of Bennet Street. In their haste they knocked into Katy, who fell onto the pavement with a cry. No one bothered to stop. Instead, they ran, scattering in every direction.

Tom helped her to her feet, just as a troop of militia ran out from the same opening in pursuit of the men. He threw his arms about Katy and shielded her with his body until this second group passed.

As soon as they were gone, he held her away to examine her face. "Did they hurt you? Are you all right?"

She looked shaken, but when she gazed up at him with her soft, brown eyes, she gave a trembling smile. "I'll be all right now, Mr. Barnes."

If Tom had been able to think at that moment, he would have wondered that a woman with her experience could appear so sweet. But all he could manage had more to do with how grateful she seemed, how adoring—how adorable.

He lost all consciousness of where they were, of the people buzzing around them, of the horses in the street, and the need to watch out.

It had been ages since he had kissed a woman, but he had not forgotten how, as he discovered when he found himself kissing Katy. Softly at first, then with an increasing hunger as he succumbed to his weeks of longing.

"What the devil do you think you're doing?"

Tom felt a blow across his shoulders. It jerked him out of his bliss, and he turned to see an outraged pair of fops behind him.

"You had better push along if you don't want to be arrested for a display like that." One of the gentlemen raised his cane, as if to strike Tom again, but he had swept Katy out of the way.

With his ears and cheeks burning, he heard the other man say, "What an impertinence! Why, the fellow's not even a gentleman, by gad! What's he mean by kissing a whore in broad daylight?"

For one terrible moment, Tom felt the shame of what he'd done, but then a sense of anger on Katy's behalf made him stop. He would have turned to confront them, if Katy had not held him back.

"It's all right, Tom. Let them say what they want. They can't hurt me."

But he heard the shame in her voice, and he knew that he was to blame for exposing her like that. They walked on towards the river, but he could hardly bring himself to look at her as they ducked down a side street to circle the Palace.

They were almost to the river when she asked, "Why did you kiss me?"

Tom halted and gave an incredulous laugh. He still could not look at her. "Why do you think?"

Her voice was uncertain when she said, "I don't know. I thought you hated me."

He shook his head in anguish. "I don't. I wanted to, but I can't."

She did not respond, so after a pause they went on. Neither spoke again until they reached the stairs, where four or five boats were tied up.

"Thank you for taking care of me today, Mr. Barnes."

Her subdued tone made him steal a glance. She looked pensive and confused, as well she might, since he did not know what to make of himself.

All he knew was that it was going to be impossible to keep from kissing her from this day forward.

Hester had taken Katy's advice and had named the safest location she could think of to meet St. Mars. Westminster Abbey was not only likely to be empty of rioters, it also had the singular merit of not being a place that was particularly known for romantic assignations.

Isabella had laughed at her request to be permitted to attend more church services during the week, but, after all, Hester's father had been a clergyman. Since many people still went to services every day, her request had not been accounted that strange. Isabella, Harrowby, and Mrs. Mayfield numbered themselves among the more fashionable people who only worshipped on Sunday, except when they wished to be seen at prayers by someone in the royal family.

It had not always been that way. Mrs. Mayfield had often taken Isabella to the Chapel Royal, before she was married, to show her off to the gentlemen of the Court, but this had ceased being profitable when Queen Anne had raised the walls of the pews to put a stop to her ladies' flirting.

On the day following her receipt of St. Mars's message, Hester stepped into the nave of the Abbey church and felt the seep of cool air from the stones beneath her feet. She had to pause to accustom her eyes to the dark, for there were not enough candles in Christendom to illuminate every corner of the vast space. Sunlight filtered through the stained panes of glass high upon the walls, but the shadows thrown by the massive pillars, the choir, and the raised pulpits cast many areas into gloom. Hester began to think that instead of being concerned that St. Mars might be recognized, she ought to have worried over whether she would find him at all.

Visitors touring the Abbey walked about in groups of three and four, conversing in hushed voices. From far away came the high notes of the choirboys at practice.

With the odour of ancient dust tickling her nostrils, Hester headed down the North Aisle towards the back of the nave. She circled a pillar and, from its shelter, peered at the few gentlemen who had chosen to sit this far away from the altar. She thought she spied St. Mars in his fop's outfit, kneeling in prayer on the third row from the back.

She moved to the central aisle before edging closer. She had almost reached the gentleman, whose head was bent devoutly over his hands, when she felt a sharp tug on her skirt. Turning to search for the nail she had snagged it on, she instead saw another gentleman, leaning from the row behind her with one hand gripping her gown.

Hester covered her gasp with a laugh when she recognized St. Mars, whose head was covered in yet a third style of periwig. He had stretched across the back of a pew to grab her before she could speak to the wrong man.

Disturbed by her gasp, the gentleman she had nearly accosted looked up from his prayers and gave her a scowl. She hastily stepped backwards, whispering a string of apologies for having disturbed him.

She would have sat down in the row in front of St. Mars, if he had not beckoned her to sit beside him instead. She moved to the end of her row, where he met her and waited politely for her to be seated before joining her in the pew.

"I thought you said the second row from the back," he teased her, speaking in a low voice, which sent a thrill down her spine. He had leaned closer to speak into her ear, and their elbows touched. As nervous as this made her feel, she realized how much more noticeable they would have been if she had whispered to him over her shoulder.

"I said somewhere near the back. But I'm glad to find you so quickly, my lord."

"And before you joined in that gentleman's prayers. I think he would have been rather astonished if you had."

"Fie! As if I would ever do anything so disreputable!"

"My pardon, Mrs. Kean. I had thought there was nothing you would not undertake in the cause of justice."

"Instead of teasing me, my lord," Hester said, trying hard not to laugh, "perhaps you would be so kind as to tell me what you've discovered."

Their whispers mingled with the other noises in the church, the booming echo of the heavy doors, an occasional cough, and even giggles from some of the tourists visiting the royal tombs.

St. Mars gave an exaggerated sigh. "If you truly insist on being serious, I shall be forced to tell you that I haven't discovered very much. I found George Menzies, or rather Tom did, just before he left for France. We followed him and asked some questions, but he had very little to add that I had not already got from Colonel Potter. However, he did confirm that your cousin Dudley went downstairs in pursuit of a harlot."

"Did he say why he left so suddenly?"

"Yes, he saw someone who is likely one of Walpole's spies in France. He was afraid of being exposed."

"Do you think he was telling the truth?"

This time, St. Mars's sigh was genuine. "I hate to say it, but I believe he was. He insists that Sir Humphrey was completely unaware of the Jacobites' intention to bring Harrowby over to their cause. They used him to gain an introduction to Hawkhurst House, but would never have entrusted him with their plan."

"But what if he uncovered it somehow? Would Colonel Potter have killed him to keep him from telling Harrowby? Once he lost his commission, he seemed almost desperate to secure a post."

"Menzies seems to think that Sir Humphrey was incapable of reasoning anything out for himself. But what do you believe? Do you think he could have done it? And, if he did, would he really have told Harrowby?"

Hester felt frustrated. "I don't know. He was incapable of keeping a secret, that is true. But whether he could have uncovered it himself,

I cannot tell. The one thing that makes me believe he did is what his sister said, that something had been troubling him of late."

They paused, while the gentleman Hester had disturbed rose from his knees and walked past them. He gave them a glance that condemned whatever they were doing. Hester bobbed her head guiltily, but St. Mars seemed not even to notice.

"If Sir Humphrey was a Jacobite, why should he have been troubled by the notion that his dear friend Harrowby might be persuaded to help James?" he asked.

Hester could come up with no reasonable answer, so instead, she told him of her theory, that the murderer had used Dudley's history of violence to implicate him.

While explaining her reasons, she did not tell St. Mars that she had discussed these first with Lord Lovett. The memory of that gentleman's kiss was very fresh in her mind, and she could not think of him without chagrin. She blamed herself for allowing him to know how much she enjoyed his wit, when she knew perfectly well that he was a libertine. She had as much as invited him to take that liberty with her. She had wanted him to find her attractive. The respect that he had shown her had given her a better opinion of her allure, and she had been weak enough to want proof of his admiration.

But his kiss had surprised her. Worse, it had disappointed her. She had always expected to be thrilled by her first real kiss from a gentleman, but no sooner had she dealt with the shock of it, than she realized that surprise was the only emotion he had aroused. She had not felt the thrill she would like to have felt.

She had met only one gentleman who could make her pulses race, and he could do it just by being near.

St. Mars sat very still while she elaborated her theory. Coming to the end, she was conscious of how close they were sitting. His body warmed her side, when the other was chilled. Certain that her voice would begin to waver or even grow hoarse if she did not use it for something very practical, she asked, "Do you think I am being fanciful, my lord?"

"No, I find you as clear-headed as ever, Mrs. Kean. It is highly plausible that the murderer arranged for a harlot to keep your cousin busy so he would return late to the box. And he could have made Mayfield spill his drink quite easily. The only question is, what can we do to prove this theory?"

"I wondered if the woman might not be found. She could tell us who paid her to distract Dudley."

St. Mars did not sound amused when he said, "I hope you are not suggesting yourself for this task."

"No. And I am persuaded that it would be fruitless, for the woman could be paid to lie as well. I had another thought, though."

"You want me to visit every brothel in London, and ask every whore if she engaged in a certain tasteless act with Mr. Dudley Mayfield?"

"Of course not!"

He feigned a sigh. "Well, I am relieved to hear it. I doubt that such a mission could be accomplished in the years that I have left. What is this other idea of yours, then?"

"It would serve you right if I refused to tell you! And I should, if it were not that I cannot handle this myself.

"At the inquest," Hester continued in a dampening tone, "I was almost certain that Colonel Potter was lying when he said that he did not see Dudley spill the wine on his coat. When the Lord Chief Justice asked him about it, he hesitated, as if he had to decide whether or not to tell the truth."

"You think he saw the person who caused the spill and was trying to leave them out of the trouble?"

"Either that or, perhaps, he caused it himself."

"Hmm." He sounded doubtful, but then he sighed. "Well, I suppose the only way to get the answer is to ask him."

"But how can I? I never see him."

"Not you, my dear Mrs. Kean! You cannot think I meant for you to accost him—during his prayers or otherwise. You can leave Colonel Potter to me."

"But how will you get him to tell you?"

"By holding a sword to his throat. It worked remarkably well before."

Hester choked on her shocked gasp of laughter. "I should think it would. You will be sure to be careful, won't you, my lord?"

"I shouldn't dream of allowing myself to be hurt. But—" And here, a note of curiosity entered his voice— "Mrs. Kean, why have you not said anything about Sir Humphrey's other guest, Lord Lovett?"

An unpleasant warmth invaded Hester's neck and face. She had not prepared herself for his question. "I suppose that's because I don't have anything of importance to say."

In the darkness of the abbey, St. Mars leaned forward to peer into her eyes, and Hester was grateful for the poor illumination that hid her blush.

After an uncomfortable pause, he said, "I do not see why Lord Lovett should be exempt from any suspicion."

Again, there was that curious note in his voice, along with another, which was cooler. It made her feel as if a wall had come between them.

"There is no reason," she said, "although I will admit that I find it harder to see Lord Lovett in the role of murderer than the other gentlemen involved."

"Even your cousin?"

Hester gave a start, then reflected before she said, "Yes, I am afraid that is so. Sir Humphrey was a near friend of Lord Lovett's. He was most distressed by Sir Humphrey's death."

"Yet, if Sir Humphrey did become aware of Lovett's and Potter's plans, his knowledge would have been of equal danger to both."

Hester took a deep breath. "Yes, of course."

"Then, what can you tell me about Lord Lovett's movements? Could it be possible that the two men contrived Sir Humphrey's death together?"

Hester drew in a quick breath. "They did return to the box together." Her mind struggled with this distasteful notion. "But that could exonerate them as easily as prove their guilt."

"True. Why don't we go over what we know? Menzies said he saw Lovett, standing outside the curtain of the ladies' withdrawing area. That would have been before Dudley made his way down the stairs."

"He was waiting for Isabella. He escorted her from the box."

"Why did he not return with her?"

Hester tried to remember. "At the inquest, I believe he said something about stepping away to speak to a friend. Both he and Colonel Porter testified that they met up with each other just before returning to the box."

St. Mars leaned back and stretched one arm along the back of the pew. He seemed to study her profile. "Then Lovett would appear to have some time unaccounted for."

"They all do. We only have their statements that they were engaged with something else at the moment of the murder. That is why it is so hard to prove anything."

"Lovett could have waited outside the withdrawing area until your cousin Dudley disappeared down the stairs. Then, he could have found Sir Humphrey and slipped behind the curtain where he was standing, waiting for a chance to stab him through it."

The situation he painted made Hester very uneasy. It was possible. But the thought that she might have been kissed by a murderer was too terrible to contemplate.

"Colonel Potter would have had the same length of time. I still should prefer to believe it was he."

St. Mars was rigidly silent. "Should you?" He hesitated, then asked, "May I inquire why?"

Hester groped for a logical reason she could give. "Lord Lovett behaved very well after the murder. He took care of everything, even though he was quite upset by the loss of his friend. And, since then, he has tried to be helpful, even giving me counsel about Dudley, when I think he truly believes that Dudley is guilty."

"What sort of counsel has he given you?"

She found herself unable to be specific. "I cannot recall any one piece," she said. "But he is the only person who seems to care whether Sir Humphrey's murderer is caught, except Dudley, of course, who only wants to be acquitted. I did mention to his lordship the possibility that Dudley's harlot might be found, but he pointed out how untrustworthy such a witness would be. You would not disagree with that, yourself, I'm persuaded," she added defensively.

"No. But just because Lovett has a good reason for discouraging a particular line of inquiry does not rule out other motives for doing so."

St. Mars was right, Hester had to acknowledge. But if Lord Lovett was the murderer, why would he continue to discuss it with her when it appeared that no proof would ever be found?

She posed this question to St. Mars, but his answer made her even more unhappy. "Perhaps he simply wants an excuse to be with you."

Hester denied it, but her voice lacked conviction enough to convince St. Mars. He seemed almost to retreat from her, but all he said was, "I shall try to corner Colonel Potter again and find out who spilled the wine on Mayfield's clothes. If he can tell us, we'll have a better idea of what to pursue next."

Hester agreed with him, and secretly resolved to be impartial where Lord Lovett was concerned. She might even ask him whom he had spoken to during the critical portion of the interval.

There was no more to discuss at the moment. Before they stood to go, St. Mars asked her if he could send Katy again as a messenger soon without arousing anyone's suspicions.

"I suppose I can tell Rufus to fetch me if she comes again. I can tell him that my aunt was delighted with the quality of her strawberries. That should be reason enough. Since my aunt would never speak with any servant long enough for the subject to arise, she will never have an occasion to deny it."

"Then, as soon as I have anything to tell you, I'll send her again." He paused. "I hope there was nothing about her that offended you?"

"No, not at all! I found her very obliging. A little shy at first, perhaps, but as soon as she got over being afraid of me, she became quite cheerful. Why do you ask?"

St. Mars seemed to ponder this, before replying, "It occurred to me that she was troubled by something last night, and I wanted to be sure it had nothing to do with the errand. But I have the feeling that it has something to do with Tom, who escorted her ." He grimaced. "I shall probably have to speak to him. You would think that an outlaw would be free of domestic problems, wouldn't you? And yet, here I am, with only two servants, and I have to concern myself with their problems. I never had this trouble at Rotherham Abbey."

Hester could not completely stifle her laugh. "You will have to engage a housekeeper to protect you."

"That's what I thought Katy was! Now do I have to hire a duenna for my housekeeper?"

Hester felt better that he could speak of Katy with such detachment. She had tried to tell herself that she had no right to be distressed by how pretty his servant was, but the truth was that it had taken a good bit of her self-respect to hide her jealousy from the woman, though Katy's timidity had helped her overcome such unworthy feelings.

As they stood to part, she remembered the news she had meant to tell him. She put a hand on his sleeve and he turned.

"Pardon me, my lord, I almost forgot—I do not know if you have heard the news, but Lord Oxford was taken to the Tower by the Usher of the Black Rod."

She heard his sharp intake of breath.

St. Mars looked extremely grim. She had scarcely ever seen his features appear so harsh. "If they've taken Oxford," he said, "then Ormonde will be next. I feared it would come to this, but Ormonde did not believe that they would dare. Walpole must have more support than he gave him credit for."

"From what I have heard, that was why he released the report from the Committee of Secrecy yesterday. He had to convince the public that there was good reason for these arrests. Since Mr. Walpole began his accusations, there have been such disturbances outside his house that he has been afraid for his own safety."

As she spoke, St. Mars went as tense as a wire. Hester regretted having to give him such unsettling news.

"I hate to bring you bad tidings, my lord."

"Not at all." His manner was distracted. "I am very much obliged. I might never have heard it, otherwise."

He mused, before saying, "I am afraid this will delay my errand for you, Mrs. Kean. I must make a journey to Richmond."

"Must you, my lord?" Hester did not care if he could hear her fear.

"Yes. I will not abandon our investigation without informing you, though. And if I must, it won't be forever. It may only be delayed."

"That is not my greatest fear, my lord."

"It should be. And I forbid you to have any other." He raised her hand to his lips, gave her a solemn look that spoke goodbye, then left before she could respond.

As Hester watched him vanish into the gloom of the nave—walking with a very un-foplike stride—she prayed that he would not run straight into danger.

Hope humbly then; with trembling pinions soar;
Wait the great teacher Death; and God adore.
What future bliss, he gives not thee to know,
But gives that Hope to be thy blessing now.
Hope springs eternal in the human breast:
Man never Is, but always To be blest:
The soul, uneasy and confined from home,
Rests and expatiates in a life to come.

CHAPTER XIX

Gideon set out for Richmond just before dusk. He rode Looby, since Penny would be too noticeable. He did not bother with an elaborate disguise, but did take Tom along, in case he needed him to approach the house.

They took the Wandsworth Road as far as Putney Heath, then headed across country, keeping an eye open for cover, should they find it necessary to conceal themselves.

Richmond was a sleepy country village on the south side of the Thames. In centuries past, it had been a major centre of court life, but Henry VII's royal palace had been taken down, with little remaining except a lodge, which the Dukes of Ormonde had acquired for a country residence to be near Windsor Castle and the Palace of Hampton Court.

Given Lord Oxford's arrest, not to mention the attacks on his family Ormonde had spoken of, Gideon was afraid that the government might have sent troops to the area to keep the Duke from fleeing. Running into them would pose a risk to him as well, but he reckoned that few common soldiers or even officers would be likely to recognize the Viscount St. Mars. If a King's Messenger had been sent to take the Duke into custody, it was more possible that Gideon might be recognized, which was why he had been forced to wait all day before leaving. And, in case they were stopped, he had asked Katy to dress Tom in a tradesman's jacket and wig, while Gideon wore a smock to pass as his servant.

This was the first time that Tom had been subjected to the discomfort of a wig, and he made his displeasure heard more than once during their hasty ride.

"If you do not stop pulling and tugging at it," Gideon told him, after they had ridden half the distance, "you're going to knock it askew, and then no one will believe you're the master."

"I'll tell 'em I've picked up some lice," Tom growled. "That's what it feels like."

"Well, now I hope that you have an appreciation for the suffering I've been made to endure since my boyhood."

Gideon had been grateful for the distraction of the wig, but as they drew closer to Richmond, he ignored Tom's squirming. His groom grew silent, too, as the dense forest of Richmond Park loomed ahead.

They pulled up their horses to scan the perimeter of the trees for signs of troops, but there were none. "If no one stops us, I shall ride with you to within sight of Richmond Lodge. If all looks safe, I want you to go up to the house. You must tell the porter that you have a message for the Duke, concerning his cousin Jonathan. They should show you in, and once you are alone with Ormonde, tell him that the Viscount St. Mars is waiting in the woods to hear his orders.

"Then, if he wants to see me," Gideon continued, "have the porter wave a candle slowly back and forth from a window that I can see. Have you got all that, Tom?"

"I think so, my lord." Tom made one last adjustment of his wig, but his face was set in a disapproving frown. "But it seems a very havey-cavey way of doing business to me."

"I know. But I haven't been left with much choice. If you run into anyone who might be an officer of the Crown, just pretend to be the Duke's chandler come to collect on a bill. He will send you away, but try to find out what's happened to his Grace before you return to me."

"Aye, my lord."

They circled the park, where darkness had fallen. Gideon had hunted in Richmond Forest more than once, but they were prevented from entering it by the palisade that secured the game. The trees were rustling in the strong summer breeze, so loudly that it was good they had no need to talk. They walked their horses slowly and close to the fence, so as to make no unnecessary noise, and surprised a group of deer grazing near it. When the deer bolted, heads up and tails flying, their small hooves beat a soft tattoo against the compost-covered ground.

No soldiers were yet in evidence, but that did not mean that the Duke was safe. Gideon could imagine that the King would be reluctant to send troops for Ormonde when he was so popular with the men. It would be expected that he would go quietly and legally, though, if the King's Messengers came for him.

Still, when they had ridden to the other side of the park and first saw the Lodge in front of them, he found it oddly quiet. The only light he could see seemed to be coming from the back of the house. He wondered if he might have been too late, for if a Messenger had come for his Grace in the afternoon, Gideon would have had no way of knowing.

He halted in the shelter of a tree. After watching the house for signs of activity, he sent Tom on his errand. He kept a close watch on him until he disappeared behind the gatekeeper's house, then waited for a signal.

Gideon had resigned himself to a possible wait of even hours before the Duke was able to see him. He was worried, then, when Tom reappeared only a few minutes later and came riding straight for him. He gave no sign of alarm, but neither did he beckon, so Gideon waited with mounting unease for Tom to reach his side.

"He's gone," Tom said, drawing Beau up in front of him.

"Gone? Gone where?" Gideon could not believe that Ormonde had started the rebellion, but, still, that was the thought that flew into his mind.

"The porter didn't want to tell me, but I finally convinced him that his master would want you to know. . . .

"He's left for France. The porter said that a letter was brought from London yesterday. His Grace gave orders for his horse to be readied, and he set out right away."

Gideon was stunned. If Ormonde had run, it was because he had no hopes for the rising, and he must have been certain that his own arrest was imminent. "How does the servant know he went to France?"

"The Duke's groom let his daughter know that they'd be riding to Shoreham in Sussex and that he would return alone. Nobody can think of any reason that his Grace would have to go there, unless he was taking passage on a ship."

"Nor can I." Gideon was completely at a loss. If Ormonde had truly gone south, he must not have gone to lead the rebellion in the west. But why had he abandoned the plan? For the past month, supposedly, he had been working towards putting it in motion, but his imminent arrest must have caught him still unprepared. Gideon wondered that Ormonde had not at least ridden west to see how many men he could raise. If the riots and dissent scattered over the kingdom were any indication of James's popularity, then surely the best thing would be to strike before any more Jacobites could be taken into custody. But, in leaving them without a military leader, the Duke would insure their defeat.

James would be devastated to hear the news, which surely he would if Ormonde sought him out. And in that case, there was no longer any need for Gideon to report to him about the readiness of the rebellion. James would hear the truth from Ormonde, himself—if Ormonde went to see him.

Gideon found that he could not simply let the matter rest. He sent Tom back to the Lodge with instructions to find the servant with the greatest authority and ask him if the Duke had left any messages or instructions.

This errand took longer. By the time Tom returned, it was so dark that Gideon didn't see him coming until after he heard Beau's hoof beats.

He scrambled up from the spot where he'd been leaning against the trunk of an oak, and asked, "What news?"

Tom gave a loud sigh. "I found his Grace's man of business. He says there were no messages left, and no letters have gone out either. The porter said it was true. He didn't see anybody ride to nowhere, and before yesterday, he says there was plenty of coming and going to places west."

Gideon didn't know what to make of any of it, but it was still possible that the Duke was simply being careful. He might be planning to send instructions once he arrived at the coast.

Gideon saw nothing for it, but to return to London and see what news he could pick up there.

"Thank you, Tom. I believe you have found out everything that is to be learned tonight."

"I fear so, my lord. Do you want me to help you mount?"

"No, I'll manage." Gideon had gathered up his horse's reins, and now he threw himself into his saddle with one sweeping motion, before turning Looby's head towards home.

"Your lordship did that like a right proper highwayman," Tom said behind him.

Gideon smiled. He knew that Tom was trying to cheer him. But his mind was filled with confusion and disappointment, so all he said was, "As long as I have to play the part, I had better do it right."

The news of Lord Oxford's confinement in the Tower, along with other Jacobites' arrests, still reverberated through the streets of London and Westminster. Visitors to Hawkhurst House all whispered of their fear that a general rising seemed imminent.

Harrowby told his family—very indiscreetly Hester thought—that the Cabinet was almost certain that the army would not stand behind the King if the Duke of Ormonde raised the Pretender's standard in any part of England. They feared it would be impossible to defend his Majesty against the vast numbers that would rally to the Stuart cause.

He revealed this after he and Dudley had joined the ladies in the withdrawing room after dinner, cautioning them all not to be heard speaking ill of the Stuarts, in case the worst should occur.

Harrowby was sitting in a chair by one of the open windows, fanning himself with a delicate fan, on which had been painted a pleasant scene with two swans swimming side by side. Dudley, less morose now that most of the negative attention was directed at James Stuart instead of him, had thrown himself horizontally on a sofa designed for two. Hester, Mrs. Mayfield, and Isabella had been doing little other than trying to stay cool in the abominable July heat, which was so fierce that Isabella had dispensed with the lace tucker at her breast.

"I thought his Majesty had commissioned officers that he can trust," Hester said. She could not help being alarmed by this talk of civil war, though she tried not to let her worries impede her.

For once, not even her aunt took exception to her showing an interest in the Crown's affairs. All eyes turned to Harrowby to see if this comforting notion had any merit.

Their hope was sorely misplaced. Harrowby had not been blessed with the character of a rock in the biblical sense. The best he could do was to say, despondently, "He's certainly made a mincemeat of the army. I've never seen so many changes of officers in so short a time. But how can he be sure that he's routed all the Jacobites? And even if the officers do turn out to be loyal, that doesn't mean that the common soldiers will.

"It's not only the military postings he's changing either. He just dismissed Shrewsbury, too."

This announcement produced a long moment of shock, before Mrs. Mayfield recovered enough to ask eagerly, "Then who's to be Lord Chamberlain?"

Her eagerness made it clear that she had still not relinquished every hope of securing a Court position for her family.

"His Majesty's appointed the Duke of Bolton. But if he suspects Shrewsbury of treachery, then one has to wonder who will be next. I've a good mind to take us all down to Rotherham Abbey and wait for this to blow over. And I *shall*, if Parliament is ever released. But if we were to go now, someone would be sure to say that we were gone to France!"

"Lud, but people can be nasty!" Mrs. Mayfield said. "I shouldn't doubt but that you are right, my lord."

Though she had agreed with him, Hester noticed that the mention of Rotherham Abbey had made her aunt's eyes light up. She could tell that Mrs. Mayfield had begun to muse on the pleasant aspects of a sojourn in the country. She had always found life away from Court very dull, but not only was it miserably hot in London, it was smelly, too. The amusements she found entertaining came at the price of fetid air, reeking with the refuse in the streets, which cooked faster in the summer sun. That, and the necessity of standing at Court, when the heat in the Palace was enough to make anyone faint, must certainly rob the town of its attractions, even for a confirmed town-dweller like her aunt. Yet, not to attend at Court, when their absence might be misconstrued, was a danger that no one could afford in this suspicious climate.

"I am sure that I should be the last to desert his Majesty at a time like this," Mrs. Mayfield said, virtuously. "But I cannot help being concerned about my dear daughter's health."

She gazed worriedly at Isabella, who looked back at her in surprise. "What is there about my health to concern you, Mama?"

Her mother tut-tutted and reached to pat her on the hand. "My dear, you should know better than to think that I cannot read your face like a book. But I shan't say anything more about it, if you want to keep your secret just between you and your hubby."

"What secret?" Harrowby said.

Isabella did not appear to be enlightened on the subject either.

Mrs. Mayfield gave them both coy looks. "Now don't tell me that neither of you has suspected. And the two of you married these past three months!"

Hester was the first to grasp her meaning, and her dismay was so strong that it must have shown on her features. Fortunately, no one was looking at her, so she did her best to compose them. But the only thing she could think of was how hard this news would hit St. Mars—that his cousin should produce an heir to his estates.

Isabella still looked confused. Harrowby seemed not one wit brighter, until Dudley let out with a whoop of laughter.

"So, Isabella's got a bun in her oven! Why didn't you tell us, Bella?"

As both his sister and her husband turned to stare at him, his mother spoke sharply, "Mayfield, I will thank you not to speak in such a vulgar manner! Your sister is a countess, and she will be giving birth to a future earl."

While Isabella's mother settled the sex of their child, the infant's prospective parents began to latch onto the meaning of the conversation encircling them.

"By Jove!" Harrowby cried, with his eyes much wider than their usual proportions. "Zounds! A baby, you say?"

Isabella didn't know whether to be pleased or vexed, but she was clearly frightened. "Are you certain, Mama?"

Hester was amazed by her apparent ignorance, but she understood much better when her aunt began to hedge.

"Well, we cannot be perfectly certain until you start to show. But I know my precious little girl! And I've noticed how peaked you've been looking lately. And you refused the kidney at dinner this afternoon. You said it made you feel queasy, and that is exactly how I felt about kidneys, when I was in an interesting way myself."

So, on these slim pieces of evidence, they were to believe that Isabella and Harrowby had produced the seed of an heir. Hester was relieved that she would not have to inform St. Mars just yet. This was nothing more than a ruse on her aunt's part to get herself away from London. If Isabella proved not to be expecting, Mrs. Mayfield had left her options open.

She had convinced her son-in-law, though, which had been her sole intent, though he still looked astonished. "To think of it!" he said, screwing up his nose in the facial equivalent of scratching his head. "And when I thought . . . ."

He did not finish this interesting phrase, but, becoming aware of listeners, coloured up instead. Then he stammered, "Well—I should say that this calls for a toast. I knew I had made a good business of it when I married you, my dear. Match made in heaven, and all that!"

Isabella had almost decided to be pleased by her maternal prospects before her husband delivered this speech. His cheerfulness made up her mind, and she looked very happy indeed when she flew over to give him a kiss.

But Mrs. Mayfield had not finished with them yet. She crooned to her daughter about how she must take great care of herself, particularly not to become overheated, for everybody knew that there was nothing so dangerous to an unborn child than for its mama to take sunstroke.

With a few more hints of this nature, it did not take her long to prod Harrowby into thinking of a plan, whereby Isabella, Dudley and their mother would go down to Rotherham Abbey as soon as they could comfortably arrange to travel. They could send the carriage back for him, and he would join them as soon as the King adjourned Parliament for the summer.

Or—he remembered—as soon as *somebody* did.

As news of the arrests captured everyone's attention at Court, Sir Humphrey's murder was all but forgotten. Even Harrowby was too absorbed by present dangers to spare more than an occasional thought for the friend he had lost, and this forgetfulness made him stop heaping blame on Dudley for even showing himself in town. Dudley still was not welcome at Court or in their friends' private houses, however. And though this did not seem to matter greatly to him at present, as long as he could avoid direct cuts, Hester knew that having a shadow over the Mayfield name would hurt not only his future prospects, but those of his innocent brothers and sisters as well.

She had almost despaired of clearing his name. If St. Mars could not obtain the answers to their questions about the murder, then she wondered how she ever would. Mrs. Mayfield's plan to remove them to Rotherham Abbey worried her, for, though St. Mars could always visit her there, the move would separate her from all the other people concerned. And without even the chance of speaking to them occasionally, she did not see how she could help St. Mars find the truth.

His methods of detection, for his own safety, must always be clandestine, which certainly would hamper him in some respects. In others, she could only envy him, for she would never be able to dash about the countryside or lurk in darkened streets in pursuit of a suspect. Acutely aware of the limitations that would always be placed upon her by her sex and her dependent state, she hoped to be of use in other ways. It did not suit either her temperament or her character to ask for someone's help, then leave him with every ounce of the bother.

If they moved to Rotherham Abbey, that would be exactly her situation, so as soon as the family dispersed after dinner, she racked her brain to think of something else she could do before being forced to leave. She had more time than usual to do this, because by evening, everyone else in the family had gone out. Harrowby went back to Court, where he could learn of the latest dismissals the King had made. Isabella and Mrs. Mayfield left to call on the Duchess of Bolton to convey their congratulations on her husband's new post. And even Dudley announced plans for the evening.

Hester could only regret the misfortune that had struck so many people, whether deserved or not, but at least the distractions of the trials had removed the burden of entertaining Dudley from her. Dudley announced that he had made a new acquaintance last evening and that he would be meeting him to indulge in some of the activities he had not yet had the pleasure of enjoying. Included in this list was a viewing of the inmates at Bedlam, which he had been assured was a sight not to be missed, to be followed by a cockfight, which had been advertised for this evening at the Cockpit Royal in St. James's Park.

Far from recommending such amusements, Hester still knew that her cousin's choosing them was unlikely to damage his reputation any further. They were the usual fare for gentlemen, and should Dudley erupt in a fit of temper, perhaps his behaviour would be less remarkable in both those places than it would be in a more tasteful setting.

She gladly saw him off, but after musing in her bedchamber for half an hour, she still found herself with no new ideas with which to proceed. She had begun to make a list of all the suspects, not excepting her cousin, when a servant came to tell her that Mrs. Jamison was asking for her below.

Hester went down, surprised by the visit, though she assumed that Sir Humphrey's sister had come to see Isabella and had only asked for her when she found the Countess gone. That was not the case, however, as she discovered after she had greeted Mrs. Jamison, invited her to sit in the smaller of the parlours, and ordered tea to be served.

She tried to keep her visitor from seeing how astonished she was to see her at Hawkhurst House. Mrs. Jamison had never called there alone, and Hester had not expected that she would want to enter a house where Dudley Mayfield lived.

Mrs. Jamison certainly appeared uncomfortable. She kept peering over her shoulder, as if fearing that Dudley might charge into the room. Every distant sound in the house made her jump, until Hester made it clear that none of the family was at home. This eased her visitor somewhat, but it was evident that something still disturbed her.

A servant brought the tea and left them alone. Hester and Mrs. Jamison discussed the extraordinary heat London was having and how remarkable it was that a dish of tea, though hot, could be cooling. They moved on to compare the effects of other beverages, agreeing that citron water was surely the best.

Once Hester had asked about Mrs. Jamison's health and her inquiry had been returned, they seemed to have exhausted all the normal topics. Hester was on the brink of raising the subject of the investigation into Sir Humphrey's murder, when Mrs. Jamison raised it herself.

She lowered her voice and leaned across the table, in spite of the fact that no one else was in the room. "You must be wondering why I have come."

Hester did not bother to deny it, but did her best to look encouraging.

"If Lord Hawkhurst had been at home, I should have asked to see him. But, perhaps, this will be better." Mrs. Jamison gave Hester a nervous smile. "I don't know that I should have had the courage to ask my lord the question I came to ask, but you were so kind when you came with your cousin and her mother to sit with me that I hoped you would do something for me, my dear."

Hester assured her of her willingness to be helpful. Mrs. Jamison looked grateful, though she seemed at a loss as to how to begin.

"I take it that your question has something to do with your brother's death?" Hester said.

"Yes. You see, I remembered that you asked me if I had an idea of anyone who might have wanted to harm him. Then, I answered that I did not, but at the time I couldn't think of anyone but—" and here, she faltered— "that is, I shouldn't have liked to name the gentleman I suspected—not to you or anyone in your particular family, seeing that—and even then, certainly not without proof—"

Since she clearly meant Dudley, but was tying herself in knots to avoid giving offence, Hester tried to help her, even though her heart was ready to sink. "Do you think you have proof now?"

Mrs. Jamison gave a painful sigh. "Not proof, no. But I have been told something which makes me wonder if the person I suspected at first might not have been my brother's actual murderer."

Eagerly, Hester asked her what had changed her mind.

It appeared that a close friend of Sir Humphrey's, one who spent most of his time in the country, had come to see her recently in town to see how she was getting on since the death of her brother. At first she believed that his visit had only been inspired by concern for an old friend's sister, but it soon appeared that a different purpose had brought him.

"This gentleman—I shall not give you his name, for reasons you will soon understand— brought me a copy of a letter that Humphrey wrote to him shortly before he was murdered. I carried it with me." Mrs. Jamison reached inside the pocket of her skirt. She drew out a folded piece of paper, handed it to Hester, and urged her to read it.

If the letter had been the original, written in Sir Humphrey's own hand, Hester might have had serious qualms about reading it. Fortunately, this was a copy, which had been transcribed by the recipient in its entirety, except for the salutation and Sir Humphrey's signature at the end.

The message was very brief, which, on scanning it quickly, she decided must be the result of Sir Humphrey's excited state of mind when he had penned it. Reading it a second time more slowly, she grew excited herself.

"My dear—" the letter said. *"I hope this Letter finds you in excellent Health. I have only a Moment to write, as I am on my Way to the Opera, where I have taken a Box to entertain some Friends. But I do not write to tell you of that, but to alert you to the great Event that is about to come to pass. We have often alluded between us to the Joy we both should feel, should a Righting of a certain great Wrong ever take Place, and I have Reason to believe that that blessed Day will not be long in coming, and that tonight I may play some small Part in bringing the longed for Justice about. I cannot say more. I have been advised to keep my Participation in the strictest Confidence, but you will know the great Event to which I allude, and I could not keep you in the Dark after all the Hope we have*

shared over the past many Years. As soon as I may, I shall write to give you all the Particulars with the Tale of how it all went off. Your devoted Friend—

PS When next I send Robert down to the Country, I shall get him to bring you a Copy of that Verse of Mr. Pope's that all the Scandal has been about. I think you will find it amusing, even if the young Lady's Parents do not."

Hester ignored the postscript, though its triviality confirmed what everyone said about Sir Humphrey's naivety. What had captured her attention was Sir Humphrey's hint that he had been given a task for the Pretender *to be carried out on the evening of the opera.* His attempt at discretion had not been attended with much success. The great event he had spoken of was clearly the restoration of the Stuarts. No one, either knowing him or not, would fail to understand that, which was why the gentleman to whom the letter had been addressed had taken the precaution of omitting both of their names.

The suggestion of sedition was strong enough that she wondered that Mrs. Jamison had been willing to reveal it. Hester looked up with a question in her eyes.

"I don't suppose I have to explain this letter to you?" Mrs. Jamison asked.

"No. Your brother was fairly open about his loyalties. But do you not fear the mere existence of such a letter—with all that is happening?"

Mrs. Jamison shook her head, and tears appeared in her eyes. "I should, if Humphrey were alive. I should fear for his life, but that has already been taken and his estate has gone away from the direct line. Even if the Crown should decide to punish our family, they could not take my small fortune, since it came from my husband's family. They might decide to punish Humphrey's heir, but he is such a distant cousin that I doubt the ministers would agree to it. They would fear that they might then find themselves blamed for their own cousins' loyalties."

Mrs. Jamison's statement contained so much good sense that Hester's opinion of her rose. But she was still puzzled as to why Mrs. Jamison had shown her the letter.

"You seem such a sensible young woman," Mrs. Jamison said, "that I thought I might ask you for advice. As I said before, I had thought of showing it to Lord Hawkhurst, but I doubt that he would have been as observant as you that evening.

"Did you notice if my brother occupied himself with anything other than the performance? Did anything occur to make you wonder what he was doing?"

"No." Hester regretted that she could not be more helpful. "But do you believe that he truly did have a task?"

"What can you mean? He states in his letter that he did."

"I do not doubt that he believed it to be true. But what if the murderer had given him reason to think he had been called to some duty?"

"Why should he have done such a thing?"

"In order to overcome a concern of your brother's, which must have posed a danger to the murderer himself. You said that something had been bothering Sir Humphrey, but that it seemed to have resolved itself by the day of the opera."

Mrs. Jamison mused for a moment. "You could be right. He did seem more than just happy that day. Now that I recollect, it was more that he seemed relieved. Relieved and excited—that was it! It would make sense. But who would have been so cruel as to fool him like that?"

Hester stretched out a hand to cover Mrs. Jamison's. She could sympathize with lady's distress. It was horrible to think of poor Sir Humphrey's being so deceived.

"If it is any comfort," she said, "I doubt that he ever was aware of the betrayal. If he was conscious of being attacked, he must have thought that he had suffered in his king's service."

This notion did provide some consolation for Mrs. Jamison. She pulled a handkerchief out of her sleeve and dabbed her eyes with it. "So you think he might have died believing himself to be a hero?"

"It is highly probable. And, more than that, it is true. He *was* taking a serious risk for his sovereign when he was killed. So, no matter whether his mission was real or not, his heroism was." Hester meant this sincerely, but she could not help feeling pain at the thought that Sir Humphrey's innocence and enthusiasm had been used to lure him to his death. She did not wish to remind his sister of the details of his murder, but instinct told her that the killer had told Sir Humphrey to wait in front of that curtain for something.

More than once she had been confounded by the notion that the murder had hinged so much on chance. If Sir Humphrey had known something dangerous for the murderer, then he would have had to act quickly. And yet, until now, the killer had seemed to rely on luck that he would discover Sir Humphrey in a convenient spot to be killed. Now, this letter made it clear that no such luck had been involved.

Mrs. Jamison thanked her for the comforting notion of her brother's heroism, saying that she would cherish it. "Now, I suppose that I should take this letter to a magistrate, though I doubt that it will do any good. It does not say enough."

"No, but every clue will bring us closer to finding out the truth. Would you rather wait, though, until I ask my lord his opinion of the letter?" She did not really believe that Harrowby would have anything useful to add, but he might say that it would not be advisable to draw the government's attention to Sir Humphrey's politics. For the moment, at least Hester had something real to question her family about. If the letter was more likely to implicate one of other the gentlemen—Mr. Blackwell, for instance, which again seemed probable—then even her aunt might be brought to remember a useful detail.

Mrs. Jamison agreed that she shouldn't approach a magistrate until Lord Hawkhurst had seen the letter. She stood to leave, and Hester promised to send her a letter by the Penny Post as soon as she had spoken to Lord Hawkhurst.

She wanted to discuss it with St. Mars, but she didn't know where he was. She only hoped that he would contact her when he returned from Richmond. She feared more for his safety now than she had since he had escaped from his gaolers, with an almost certain noose about his neck.

No amount of worrying would bring him back to town any faster, though, so she tried to put all thought of his danger out of her head for the night.

This was, as usual, easier said than done.

Heaven's attribute was Universal Care,
And Man's prerogative to rule, but spare.
Ah! how unlike the man of times to come!
Of half that live the butcher and the tomb;
Who, foe to Nature, hears the general groan,
Murders their species, and betrays his own.
But just disease to luxury succeeds,
And every death its own avenger breeds;
The Fury-passions from that blood began,
And turned on Man a fiercer savage, Man.

CHAPTER XX

Gideon returned from Richmond in the wee hours that morning, and had to fret in wait for nightfall again. He could do little but pace like a prisoner during the long daylight hours, but darkness would be essential for him to accost Colonel Potter a second time.

While he paced, he thought constantly about the Duke of Ormonde's disappearance. It still made imperfect sense. If—weeks ago— on being indicted, Ormonde had sent James a message, telling him that his moment had come, James could possibly have arrived by now, even from so far away as Bar. He would not have hesitated for a moment before rounding up his Irish troops on the French coast and taking ship for England. Gideon had been waiting to take this message to James himself, and it still struck him as strange that Ormonde had not taken advantage of his willingness to carry it.

There was only one place he could go for an explanation of this puzzle this side of France, and that was to Lady Oglethorpe's house. With most of her daughters at James's court and deeply involved in the conspiracy, surely she should be one of the first to know what was going on.

He finally decided not to wait until darkness was complete before seeking her. He had visited Westminster twice in the day without being recognized, and he could do it again.

Besides, he would have to wear a different disguise for his meeting with Colonel Potter. The Colonel was not very likely to allow himself to be attacked by the same brigand twice.

The streets should be quieter now that the government had read the Riot Act, making rioting a felony, punishable by death. Habeus Corpus had been suspended, so that anyone his Majesty suspected of conspiring against his person could be held without bail. Parliament had voted a series of measures so extreme that, as the Earl of Anglesea had complained, they would "make the Scepter shake in the King's hands."

Undaunted, the King had moved to strengthen the militia and to raise thousands more Dragoons and Foot-Guards. Artillery had been trundled down from the Tower to Hyde Park, and the Horse-Guards had been purged. A proclamation from King George today had instructed every subject to suppress rebellion, giving them the right to combat it without warrant or the presence of legal authority. Even killing would be considered justifiable, and he charged them to suppress any rebels or traitors with the utmost force.

All Papists and non-jurors had been ordered out of London and Westminster and anywhere within a radius of ten miles. They were to remain confined to their habitations, the reason given that the King had received advice that the Pretender was preparing to invade his kingdom.

Clearly, King George had learned enough about the conspiracy to make him take the threat to his kingdom seriously. Somehow, perhaps through its spies, the ministry had obtained enough information to forestall the rising, even if the notion of James's imminent invasion was wrong. The ministry could not know how thoroughly its attack on Ormonde had crippled the rebellion, and with Bolingbroke and Ormonde together in Paris now, it would fear the worst.

Given the strength of the Crown's vigilance, Gideon reckoned that it would be a mistake to behave even the least suspiciously. Boldness would be required. He would do best to approach both houses as if he had every right to be there. As long as he did not let himself be followed home, he ought to be able to come and go safely, provided he saw no one who knew him well.

By nine o'clock that night, he was ready to take a boat to Westminster Stairs. The day had been overcast and the light of dusk was dim enough that his features would not be that easy to perceive, especially when obscured by his garb.

He wore a long, elaborate peruke of chestnut curls, enough paint to turn his whole face white, a dozen patches (which would have made his former valet, Philippe, very happy to see), and the best of Spanish paper on his cheeks. His *justaucorps* was of a splendid red silk with gold braid. Dressed in a peacock's garb so different from his habitual style, he defied anyone to know him.

With handkerchief and snuffbox in one hand, he made the picture of a fop on his way to Court, but it would not be rare for such a person to call at the house of a lady on his way to St. James's.

His cover was tried the moment he arrived at the opposite bank, for what should be tied up at the stairs but his father's barge. He could not tell whether it had just deposited a passenger, but believed not. Samuel, the bargeman, looked too much at ease. He seemed rather to have poled himself there to chat with some of the other bargemen about the news that would have spread across the river as quickly it had through the streets.

Gideon was tempted to test the worthiness of his disguise by calling out something to Samuel to see if he would recognize him. But his errand was too serious to be risked on a diversion, so Gideon was doubly careful to mince his stride, so that it would not give him away.

Samuel paid him no more mind than he did any other gentleman on the stairs.

Gideon climbed up from the dock, clutching a handkerchief to his nose, as if to filter out the prevailing stench of rotting weeds along the bank, and headed immediately for Lady Oglethorpe's house.

The servant at the door told him that her ladyship was gone to Westbrook Place in Godalming. For a moment, Gideon thought that all his efforts had gone to waste. Then, the man volunteered that Mrs. Anne Oglethorpe was in the house. Gideon asked to see Mrs. Anne, using the same code he had used at Ormonde House.

She received him in her bedchamber, looking pale and eager, and with her skirts rumpled, as if she had just risen from her bed. Gideon no sooner straightened from his bow than she said, in a desperate tone of voice, "Have you come from his Majesty? Is he coming to save my poor Harley?"

Gideon was taken aback, until he realized that she had not seen through his disguise. He revealed himself, and watched the eagerness die in her eyes.

"Then why have you come?" she insisted. "Have you brought us news?"

"No. I had hoped for news myself."

"Well, you will not find it here—unless you have not heard that my poor Robin is like to lose his head." She said this with a bitterness that blamed Gideon along with everyone else.

"I heard, and I am sorry. But you must not give up hope. I doubt that the Whigs will have the courage to kill him, when it's clear how unpopular that would be."

She scoffed, but his sympathy helped to soften her sting. "Would to God that you are right! Perhaps it would help if I told them that if they harm a hair on his head, I shall see them all hanged for the villains they are!"

Gideon could not blame her for these extreme feelings, so he said nothing to contradict them. Instead, he said, "I had hoped to find your mother here. When did she leave London?"

"Last week. She is working for his Majesty in the country. Government spies are always watching this house, but they cannot see every entrance to Westbrook Place. There are some they will never find."

"Did Ormonde send her any instructions?"

She looked startled, before her anxiety built into a frown. "Instructions for what? What is happening?"

Gideon felt his last bit of hope sinking. It plunged as heavily as lead through water. He was stunned by the severity of his disappointment. Until this moment, he had not realized how much he had pinned his hopes on James's cause. He had tried not to let himself be led by promises of things which might never come to pass, and to keep his own goals divorced from his judgment about the rightness of James's cause. But apparently, even agreeing to act for the Pretender in the most minor of ways had drawn him in, in a way that he had never intended. His deepest wants, for lack of any other prospects, had firmly linked themselves to James's hopes.

Anne had been watching the play of these emotions across his face. Now she demanded an answer to her question.

"Ormonde is not at Richmond." Gideon began cautiously in order to spare her a possible shock. "Last night, after I heard about Lord Oxford's arrest, I rode there to see him. But none of the family was at the Lodge. I thought he might have sent word to Lady Oglethorpe or to someone who might have told her where he's gone."

Her face lit with a desperate gleam. "He's gone to Bristol! To lead the rising! That must be the reason that Bolingbroke has gone to Paris. His Majesty is finally coming!"

Then, before Gideon could caution her against this hope, her excitement vanished just as suddenly, as confusion spread across her face. "But if he had, then surely we would have heard. Someone would have told *Maman*, and she would have sent a messenger to me."

Her gaze had moved to the floor as she tried to reason through her perplexity. Now she raised it, as dread set in.

"You do not think he is gone to Bristol," she said, with a brittle edge. "And he is certainly not returned to London, or I should have heard. His servants would tell you nothing?"

Gideon tried to withhold his sigh. "They told my man that Ormonde went to Shoreham in Sussex."

He thought he had prepared himself for her reaction, but nothing could have readied him for this. She stood frozen for many seconds, while his implication sank in. Then, she let out a shriek of anger and grief that would have shaken the windows in their glazings, if its note had only been deeper.

She put both hands in her hair and pulled, so that her physical pain would match her emotions. And as she walked, or rather stumbled about the room, she cursed Ormonde with all her might.

"The coward!" she screamed, with no regard for the servants' ears.

"He's run! And left my poor Robin to die! I shall kill him with my own two hands if anything happens to Harley!"

Gideon wanted to offer her comfort, but there was nothing that he could say to ameliorate the truth. It was true that Oxford was the only one left of the former Tory ministry to have stayed to face trial. First Bolingbroke, and now Ormonde had fled. Lord Oxford's only hope must have been that the rising would save him from the axe.

Gideon urged Anne to sit down in a chair, then went to call her maid. By the time the woman arrived, the worst of Anne's tantrum had played out. Then she cried until drained of all feeling, after which Little Fury, as she was also called, docilely accepted the concoction her maid gave her to drink.

She seemed no longer aware of Gideon's presence, so after making certain that she was in better hands than his, he left, glad only that his disappointment had not been as painful as hers.

He took a chair to Covent Garden. He would rather have walked, but after his confrontation with Anne, he would have found it hard to mince his steps, and disguise was crucial now.

Darkness had finally fallen, but he would need every advantage that surprise could bring to be able to approach Colonel Potter again. And he doubted his ability to maintain the character of a fop for very long. Acting had never been his talent.

Unfortunately, he learned that chairmen, who were often drunk and insolent, were worse than insolent to fops. From the beginning of the ride, these two made no effort to spare him bumps. They staggered and nearly dropped him twice. Then they set him down several streets short of the piazza and tipped him out, before trying to extort a greater fare than they had earned.

Gideon would not agree to be bullied, even to maintain his disguise. When the two drunken brutes tried to frighten the sum out of him, he dropped his affectation and gave them to understand that if they did not give up, he would relieve them of the few miserable teeth remaining in their heads. It cost him a few minutes and a brief scuffle before the change in his demeanour sank in, but once it did, he paid them their due and no more and watched them slink off.

They had deposited him in the Strand at the opening to a dismal alley, where they had obviously expected to find his courage low. The night was dark, and thick clouds obscured the sky.

If not for a need for concealment, Gideon would have been glad for the services of a linkboy. The visibility was so slight, that he could not even be certain what he was treading on as he made his way to the corner of Southampton Street. The light from the cheap tallow candles in the taverns failed to penetrate the corners where harlots and pickpockets lurked. Gideon fended off the lures from the first group and guarded his pockets from the second, as he rounded the corner.

There were more pedestrians here, in groups of two, three and more, keeping together for security's sake. Their linkboys' torches threw beacons of light, which helped him keep to the footpath as far as Colonel Potter's street.

He had decided not to leave their encounter to chance. If Mrs. Anne Oglethorpe had not known him beneath his paint, then Colonel Potter should not either.

Feigning his fop's steps again, he climbed the pair of stairs, leading to the house where Colonel Potter resided, and knocked.

The Colonel's landlady answered. She informed him that the Colonel had gone out to meet a friend. She did not know where.

As she closed the door, Gideon resigned himself to waiting all night if he had to. He was thirsty, though, and thought he might risk a few minutes to go for a mug of beer. He remembered the tavern in Little Russell Street, where he had watched for the Colonel to emerge from Mother Whyburn's house and decided to head there again on the chance that he would find the Colonel in the same place.

He had rounded the corner into Southampton Street again and was heading towards the piazza when a shout for the Watch grabbed his attention.

Up ahead, he saw a group of gentlemen bending over what appeared to be a heap of clothing, but their cries of "Fetch the Watch!" and "Murder!" told him that the mound they had discovered was a body.

Shy of the authorities, he almost turned away, but some pricking instinct drove him forward. He shouldered his way through the crowd that had formed and saw a gentleman lying dead in a pool of blood.

Even before one of the others stooped to turn the figure over and shone a torch on his face, in its deflected beam Gideon had already caught sight of a freckled neck exposed by a part in his periwig.

Turned upon his back, Colonel Potter stared up at the crowd, as if his last living thought had been stunned surprise. His hands still reached for the knife, which must have been used to stab him through the ribs. The weapon had been withdrawn, but Gideon had no doubt that it had been wielded by the same person who had killed Sir Humphrey Cove.

A gentleman in the crowd said that he thought he recognized the corpse. Space was made for him, and he looked closely before pronouncing the Colonel's name, just as Gideon pulled away. Someone else protested the outrage. He said that it could only be attributed to Mohawks or Jacobites. If Mr. Walpole was not even safe from their violence at his house in Arlington Street, then how could any English Christian be safe?

Gideon turned away, distressed by the sight of the Colonel's staring eyes and the blood oozing from his coat. He did not believe that the Colonel's death was the result of random violence, but for the moment he couldn't think.

His mind lingered dumbly on the last words he had heard. Something about the violence in Arlington Street. That must have been the riot into which Tom and Katy had stumbled. Arlington Street had no outlet at its southern end, but Bennet Street, where Tom had reported meeting the rioters, led directly into St. James's from Arlington Street.

Mrs. Kean had mentioned Walpole's fear of the mob before his house, but she had not told him the name of Walpole's street. And Gideon, who had barely heard of Sir Robert Walpole before the appointment of the Committee of Secrecy, had not known where the gentleman lived.

He shook his head in an effort to come out of his daze, annoyed that he should waste his time on these thoughts. Colonel Potter had been murdered and, unless an unbelievable coincidence had occurred, he had been stabbed by the same person who had killed Sir Humphrey.

Which of their suspects was left? Mr. Dudley Mayfield, of course.

He would have to ask Mrs. Kean if Mayfield had been out this evening.

Then, there was John Menzies, alias Mr. Blackwell, but Gideon doubted that Menzies had returned from France.

Finally, there was Lord Lovett, who, as Mrs. Kean believed, did not have the character of a murderer. But why had Potter been killed? Gideon's instincts told him that it was to keep the Colonel from giving information which might have pointed to Sir Humphrey's killer. But why now and not before, when it must appear now that the authorities had given up on the case?

Then he recalled that Mrs. Kean had discussed the murder with Lord Lovett. What if she had told him that she believed Potter had seen the person who had made Mayfield spill wine on his coat? No one knew that Gideon was coming to ask Potter about it, but if Lord Lovett believed that the answer would pose a danger to himself, wouldn't he take steps to silence the Colonel before someone else did? Or might not Colonel Potter have begun to question the significance of the spill himself?

Worry knawed at Gideon's stomach. If Lord Lovett was the murderer and had felt it necessary to kill Colonel Potter, then wouldn't he go after Mrs. Kean?

But why would Lord Lovett kill his friend? The only possible reason was a fear of exposure. Yet he had done almost nothing to hide his Jacobite sentiments.

Then, in a moment Gideon saw it, as the significance of Arlington Street snapped into place.

Lovett *had* feared exposure, but not of the fact that he was a Jacobite. Rather of the truth—that he had betrayed the cause.

With a hitch in his pace, Gideon recalled something Mrs. Kean had said. She had met John Menzies at Lady Oglethorpe's house, where Isabella had taken her in the hope of entertainment. After seeing Isabella and Lord Lovett together at Vauxhall Gardens, Gideon had guessed that Isabella's current notion of entertainment included Lord Lovett. But Lovett had not come to Lady Oglethorpe's, and later Sir Humphrey had mentioned seeing him in Arlington Street that evening. She said that Lovett had looked annoyed to have his whereabouts divulged, but Mrs. Kean and everyone else had assumed that he had gone to visit a different lady in that street.

But what if he had been visiting Walpole's house instead? Sir Humphrey had seen him, and later, he had begun to suspect his friend of treachery. That could have been the worry that had disturbed Sir Humphrey until the night of the opera. And fearing that Sir Humphrey would give him away to the Jacobites, who would certainly seek revenge, Lovett had killed his old friend.

It was only a theory. But Gideon knew that it fit. He would have to warn Mrs. Kean to be on her guard against Lord Lovett.

Then, somehow, he would have to come up with proof.

The next morning, though, when Katy walked to Hawkhurst House with her basket of strawberries and a note for Mrs. Kean, she was told that all the ladies of the house had just stepped out. They had gone to Court to see the Princess and would not return until dinner. Rufus told her that she might leave her strawberries with one of the maids and come back later to be paid.

Katy made up a quick story, saying that she did not dare, for her ladyship might decide that she had no need for strawberries today. Or, as happened all too often to the likes of her, the ladies might keep them until they were bad and then refuse to pay. She told him that she would come back in the afternoon.

Gideon, who had been waiting in Westminster Abbey in the hope of seeing Mrs. Kean, received Katy's news and had to stifle a curse. He had barely slept an hour last night and had risen early to put on his disguise. And now he must wait more hours before he could feel certain that Mrs. Kean would be safe. He saw no solution but to return in the afternoon and send Katy with the message again.

Hester had gone with her cousin and her aunt to take leave of the Princess before they set out for Rotherham Abbey in two days time. Tomorrow was Sunday, so they would wait until Monday to go.

They returned from the Palace just in time for dinner. After the meal, the family dispersed. Harrowby headed for St. James's Coffee House for the latest gossip. Dudley rode into the City in search of a new beaver hat, and Isabella and her mother took the coach to pay their farewell visits. Mrs. Mayfield instructed Hester to supervise the packing of their clothes.

Isabella's maid was perfectly capable of performing the task without supervision, so Hester only watched her make a start, before going to her chamber to begin her own packing. She had far more clothes now than she had when first arriving at Hawkhurst House, so some planning would be required.

She saw no reason to take the dress that had been made for the King's birthday. It should remain here for the next time she went to Court. She had no idea whether her second best gown would be required, but Mrs. Mayfield had hinted that Isabella might entertain guests if they remained at Rotherham Abbey long, and Hester did not doubt that boredom would soon push her aunt to urge the idea.

She took two gowns out of her chest, the one she had worn to see St. Mars at Spring Gardens and the dress she had worn to Mr. Handel's opera. She would not be able to wear either without experiencing powerful memories—happy in one and sad in the other. If she could afford it, she would have given the opera gown away, but she was not in a position to be fastidious about her clothes.

Gazing at the two laid across her bed, she decided that if she had to overcome her revulsion of the one, the sooner she did it, the better. She carefully folded the pink embroidered silk and put it back in the wardrobe. Then, with a determined sigh, she began to fold the pale yellow satin.

She had no sooner taken hold of the bodice than she noticed a stain on its left shoulder. Frowning, she brought it closer to see what it was.

The colour of dried blood made her gasp—with horror when she thought of poor Sir Humphrey—but also with anger, for the laundry maid should have spared her this unpleasant start. Hester examined the hem of the skirt, but the blood that had been on it was gone. Then she recalled that she had only mentioned the blood on her hem to the maid. She had trailed her skirts past Sir Humphrey's corpse as she had handed Isabella from the box.

But that had been her only contact with Sir Humphrey's blood, so where had this other stain come from?

With shaking fingers, she held the bodice up to the window. Immediately she could see an imprint with a shape like the heel of someone's hand. There were two patches, with a space in between that corresponded to a crease in the palm. She lay her own hand on the print and saw that the person's hand was larger than hers.

With a sickening blow to her stomach, she recalled that Lord Lovett had discovered blood on his hand. He said that he had got it when helping to lift Sir Humphrey onto the litter.

But he had not touched her after that. He had wiped the blood off his hand. She remembered his expression when he had discovered it. He had looked shaken. She had seen him shudder, for he had surely felt revulsion, but he had also been afraid that she would guess the truth.

It all came rushing back to her now on a wave of horror and disgust. Lord Lovett had put his hand on her shoulder when he had urged her to remove Isabella and her mother from the opera house. That was before he had touched Sir Humphrey's corpse.

Hester felt so angry that her knees gave way. She sank to the floor and rested her head against the bed. What a fool she had been! She had let Lord Lovett's flattery keep her from seeing the truth. She had been so exalted by his attention that she had refused even to consider him as a suspect. She still did not know why he had killed Sir Humphrey, but this stain was proof enough, even for a magistrate.

Ashamed of her weakness, she marshaled her fury and used it to drag herself to her feet. She threw the gown with its evidence on her bed and thought of what she must do.

She did not dare wait for Isabella and her mother to come home. With Isabella's partiality for Lord Lovett and Mrs. Mayfield's tendency to deny anything Hester said, she could not count on their support. She did not even know if Harrowby would believe her. She would do best to write a letter to the magistrate herself.

She went to use Isabella's escritoire in the parlour behind the withdrawing room. On her way, she passed one of the footmen and told him that she would soon have two messages for him to carry. He promised to be ready when she called. She did not tell him that one would be carried to the nearest Watch-house. The other would have to go into the Post for St. Mars.

She found paper, a quill, and ink on the desk, ready for her use. Sitting down, she wrote first to St. Mars, directing this letter to Mr. Mavors in care of the King's Head at Lambeth. Her hands were still shaking, so writing it took longer than it should have. She wanted to send the footman off before her aunt could return and question her order, but Hester did not fear this greatly since Mrs. Mayfield and Isabella had not been gone very long.

She was dusting sand over her letter when the door opened and Lord Lovett strolled into the room.

Hester gave a start. Conscious of how frightened she must look, she attempted a smile and covered her paper as discreetly as she could.

Her motion did not fool him, as she could tell by his glance at the desk. Lord Lovett closed the door behind him, and a mocking grin curled his mouth, as he crossed to her side.

"Writing a *billet doux*, Mrs. Kean? Dare I hope that it is for me?"

His flattery insulted her in every possible way—as she deserved, she thought, for had she not admired his stinging wit? She had to struggle to bite back a retort.

Unequal to feigning delight, she looked away and answered seriously, "It is nothing that interesting, sir. Merely a letter for my aunt."

"Indeed?" She could not miss his incredulous note. "And you accomplish it without her presence. How very talented of you, I am sure."

There was an unusual hardness beneath his banter. It gave Hester a chill. She met his stare to see if she could put his suspicions to rest.

"I am often employed in such tasks," she said, forcing a smile. "And there is nothing of a personal nature to communicate, so her presence is not required."

He took a sudden step nearer, and reflexively she covered the sheet.

It was the worst thing she could have done.

"If there is nothing personal in it," he drawled, "then I wonder that you should hide it so earnestly. Indeed, I am almost certain that my original suspicion was correct. Either you are penning a love note to me—or to someone else, in which case I insist upon seeing it."

Moving so quickly that she did not see him coming, he snatched the paper from under her hand and held it up over his head. He started to read it as she jumped to her feet.

His irony mocked her, as he said, "I see it is directed to a Mr. Mavors. Is he the gentleman that I shall have to slay for your hand?"

"Give me that letter, sir! You have no right!"

"Have I not? But what of a spurned lover's rights?"

His eyes were cruel in their fury, but Hester would not be fooled by his pose of the rejected lover. He was using it for the same reason he had flattered her before, to conceal his real interest. Her only hope was to convince him that the letter had nothing to do with the murder before he read it, and she tried to distract him by reaching for it on tiptoes and shaming him for looking into her aunt's business.

Her charade was as much as a waste of time as his. He was easily able to fend off her attempts to reach the paper and read it at the same time. "Well, shall we see what you have written to the gentleman? Ah, let's see. You say here, *'You were correct. It was not Colonel Potter. I have Proof that will be good enough for a Magistrate and shall send for one immediately. There is no Need to speak to the Colonel, so if you have not yet, please do not risk it.'"*

Before he came to the end, Hester stopped her undignified protests to gather her strength for the coming confrontation.

Lord Lovett turned his ironic grin on her. It held a mixture of anger and respect. "A very enlightening missive, my dear. Not a love letter precisely. Still I wonder who this Mr. Mavors is whom you have entrusted with your thoughts, when I had hoped to be your only confidant. A pity for him—and you, of course—that he shall never receive this note." He folded it and slipped inside his coat pocket.

Hester said nothing, but eyed him warily. Her fear was that he would look for Mr. Mavors and expose St. Mars.

She glanced at the door in the hope of slipping past him, but Lord Lovett gave her a knowing smile and drew a large dagger from beneath his coat.

She gasped and stared at the blade, which seemed to gleam with an evil intent.

"Now, do not pretend that the sight of this knife astonishes you. I assume from your letter that you have learned that I know how to wield it. I should be very interested to know what the evidence you mentioned consists of. You will tell me, please."

Hester stood frozen. She could not believe that he would murder her in this house, when a servant must have directed him this way. Probably the very footman she had told about the letters he would carry.

She looked for him to appear at the door, but again Lord Lovett read her thoughts.

"You cannot seriously believe that I will permit you to call a servant. No, no, my dear Mrs. Kean, you have caused me more inconvenience than you can imagine. And, now, because of you, I shall have to leave England, when I had expected to live very comfortably here." He took a step closer and pointed his knife at her throat. "Before we discuss how I should repay you, I insist that you tell me about this evidence of yours."

"You would not dare to hurt me here," she said, "not when the servants saw you come in."

"I had rather not, but as I said, I'll be leaving England immediately—today, in fact. In this great big house, I believe I could find a place to hide your body long enough to get away. And," he added, on a threatening note, "if you doubt it, I suggest you refer either to Sir Humphrey Cove or Colonel Potter. Neither of them thought me capable of murder either."

Hester felt a shock on hearing the Colonel's name. She grew faint. She would have fallen back into the chair if Lord Lovett had allowed her, but he caught her around the waist and held the tip of the knife to her breast.

"The evidence, please, Mrs. Kean. What is it?"

She saw no reason to disoblige him. Even if someone else saw it, she doubted they would understand its significance. They would certainly not know who had put the blood stain there.

She told him about the stain and reminded him that he had touched her on the shoulder before he had handled Sir Humphrey's corpse.

"Ah . . . yes. And I thought that the curtain would protect me from any spattering of blood. I was most unhappy to discover I was wrong, but you see, I had to hold Humphrey up for a few moments and his blood ran down the knife. I did not feel it in all the excitement. But you nearly caught me once before, you know, when you saw the blood on my hand. I flattered myself that I had convinced you that it was innocently taken up."

"You had." Hester wished she could struggle out of his arms, but did not dare to tempt his blade. "If you hadn't, do you think I would have received you the way I did?"

He chuckled and pulled her closer. To her horror he kissed her on the neck. "I believe I detect a note of pique. So you were in love with me—I hoped so. But my attentions to you were necessary. For you see, even before I decided to kill poor Humphrey, I discovered that you had a brain, unlike your foolish cousins. And once I decided to kill him, I knew that you would be the only person for me to fear.

"And, sadly, I was right." As he recollected this, he gave her a hug that was far from gentle.

Her ribs ached, and she nearly cried out in protest.

"Tell me about this gown. Have you shown it to anyone else?"

"No, I just discovered it. That's why I was writing the letters."

"Just so. And I doubt that anyone will notice it until long after we have gone—certainly not your cousin or her very unappealing mother."

He moved his knife to her throat and started pushing her towards the door. Hester went. She could not be sure that he would not kill her in front of the servants now, not after hearing how ruthless he was.

He told her that they would walk downstairs together—she, one step in front of him. He would hold the knife in his coat with its blade pointed between her ribs. If she tried to alert anyone, he would first kill her and then the servant.

Hester promised that she would not give him away, and they left the parlour, walking in lock step down the stairs.

The footman at the door could not hide his surprise on seeing Mrs. Kean leave on the arm of one of her ladyship's swains, but Lord Lovett mentioned that Lady Hawkhurst had sent him on an errand to fetch her waiting-woman. Hester had the impression that he purposefully referred to her serving position in order to humiliate her for accepting his advances the way she had. But she was long past that shame. She was much too worried about her survival to waste precious thoughts chastising herself now.

Lord Lovett's coach was standing in the courtyard. One of his own footmen held the door open for her, and she climbed in with Lord Lovett right behind her.

As the coach pulled away from the house, she wondered how long it would be before anyone noticed that she was gone. And even then, there was nothing to say that they would search for her. She would be believed to have run away with Lord Lovett to the Continent, either to be his mistress or—but this was highly unlikely—his wife. In either case, she would be believed to have acted of her own free will, so who would wish to save her? Mrs. Mayfield would rage about her ingratitude and about her daring to think herself fine enough to be the mistress of the baron. Isabella would pout over the loss of her lover and be hurt, perhaps, that Hester had stolen him from her. Dudley would think it all a wonderful joke, and Harrowby would rejoice in having one less mouth to feed.

She had turned her thoughts to St. Mars, when passing through the gate, she saw Katy, waiting just outside it, staring after her in dismay. Hester smothered an involuntary cry. She glanced quickly over her shoulder at Lord Lovett, before curling her fingers over the lowered window and gazing imploringly back. She did not dare call out or even make a sign. But, at least, Katy would tell St. Mars that she had left, and sooner or later he would discover the truth.

Now, all she had to do was stay alive until he found her.

❧

Hester could not know that she had underestimated Katy's resourcefulness. She had been waiting to approach Hawkhurst House again, but had been put off, first by the departure of the ladies and gentlemen of the house, then by the arrival of the black-browed gentleman. Knowing that Mrs. Kean was likely to be the only person there to receive a guest, she had waited for him to leave before speaking to the porter again. She'd been very much surprised to see him put Mrs. Kean inside his coach—and that was exactly how it had seemed, for Mrs. Kean had not looked as if she'd gone very willingly.

The leap of hope in the lady's eyes when she spotted her told Katy that her hunch was right. She knew that her master had sent her here to warn Mrs. Kean about a man by the name of Lord Lovett, so sidling up to Rufus, she asked him who the handsome gentleman was with Mrs. Kean.

Lord Lovett's name was no sooner out of his mouth than she turned and ran after the coach, leaving Rufus with his jaw hanging open. Throwing down her basket so she could hold onto her cap, she ran as fast as her hardworking legs could carry her around the far corner where the coach had disappeared.

There, she ran into a bit of luck. A jam of carriages and a waggon pulled by four teams of horses had slowed the traffic to a stop. While the drivers untangled the mess, she was able to catch up with Lord Lovett's coach, though she realized that she must not seem to be chasing it. If she did not take care, the footmen clinging to the back would be sure to notice her. She ran on until she passed it, before slowing to a walk. Then she moved on down the street, glancing occasionally over her shoulder to make sure that it was following.

Unfortunately, she reached the bottom of the street before the carriage did, so she had to wait to see which way it would turn. Just before reaching the corner, she noticed a magnificent edifice, which gave her something to pretend to gawk at, while Lord Lovett's vehicle turned to the left. As soon as it did, she hitched up her skirts and ran again.

They passed a landmark she knew, Charing Cross, which gave her some hope that she would find her way back. The master was waiting in Westminster Abbey, but she was certain that he would want her to see where Mrs. Kean was taken before fetching him.

By the time the coach drew up in front of an elegant, new house, Katy was hot, dirty, and gasping for breath. She collapsed against a lamppost on the corner, trying not to be seen, as Lord Lovett took Mrs. Kean firmly by the arm and marched her out of his carriage and into the house.

In Parts superior what advantage lies?
Tell (for You can) what is it to be wise?
'Tis but to know how little can be known;
To see all others' faults, and feel our own.

Why has not Man a microscopic eye?
For this plain reason, Man is not a Fly.

CHAPTER XXI

Gideon waited impatiently for a reply to his message. Sitting in the cool dark of the nave, he had nothing with which to entertain himself but his thoughts. Over most of the day, these had been divided between the failure of James's cause and the danger in which Mrs. Kean had embroiled herself.

Both made him angry. Not at James or at Mrs. Kean, but at others who played their dangerous games around them, and at the selfishness and greed that could cause such unhappiness.

What had possessed Ormonde to offer himself as general of James's troops, if he was not committed enough to organize the rising?

And why did people like Lord Lovett believe that their self-interest was more precious than other men's lives?

He was still fuming when Katy came hurrying around the stone pillar in the aisle. Her cap was loose, her cheeks were flushed and shining with heat, and she could hardly speak through her gasps.

Gideon leapt to his feet to meet her, then pressed her into a pew. "Get your breath first, then tell me what has happened."

"He's got her, sir," she gasped out. "I saw him enter your house, but I didn't know who he was—till I saw 'em both get into a coach. Then I asked, and your porter, he told me—it was Lord Lovett. I could tell she didn't want to go with him, sir. So I ran after 'em. Ran the whole way! But I can take you. They'll still be there."

Gideon heard her out, first with fear, then with a fury that threatened to explode. He cursed himself for taking the time to ride to Richmond Lodge, when that one day's delay had put Mrs. Kean in danger. He would not waste his anger here, but he would guard it to fuel himself for a fight.

As much as he wanted to rush, he could see that Katy was spent.

"You won't have to take me," he said, "if you can tell me where they are."

She looked up anxiously. "But I don't know the names of the streets."

He tried not to be impatient. "Can you tell me the way? Is it far?"

She shook her head to this last, and her look turned eager. "It's in a street full of pretty, new houses. They've all got roofs over the steps—like little crowns—and steep, pitched roofs."

Gideon was about to ask her where it was relative to the park, when she tapped herself angrily on the forehead.

"I'm that worn out, I almost forgot. There's a low wall with an iron railing at the bottom of the street and a statue of the Queen, too. I'm that stupid, I should have thought of the statue first."

Only one street in Westminster fit that description, and it was very near by. "I know it," he said. "You have done extremely well. Now, as soon as you can walk, I have one more favour before you can rest."

Exhausted as she was from all her running, Katy made no protest. She was a strong woman, however, and she rose soon enough even to satisfy Gideon's impatience to be gone. As he led her into the Palace Yard, he told her to find Tom and send him to Queen Square just south of Birdcage Walk. "Tell him to bring Looby saddled, and my weapons, in case I should need them."

Katy would have run off directly, but he put her into a hackney coach and handed her money for the driver and the waterman. Then he told the coachman to drive her to Parliament Stairs to take a boat.

If Gideon had not been so eager to rescue Mrs. Kean, he would have been amused to see Katy's round eyes, but he wasted no more time before covering the short distance to Queen Square.

As he arrived in the street, which was lined with new houses, he noticed a commotion in front of one of the doors. A crested coach stood in front of it, and servants were hurrying in and out, packing it with chests and boxes for a journey. Gideon asked a passing groom if he knew behind which of the doors Lord Lovett lived, and he was pointed to the house where the bustle was going on. Not surprisingly, the curtains were drawn and there was no visible sign of Mrs. Kean.

Gideon found himself in an intolerable quandary. He would be smarter to wait for Tom, in case he needed reinforcements. Expecting to meet Mrs. Kean in Westminster Abbey, he had not brought his sword. It had suited his foppish disguise to carry a cane instead, and he would never be able to subdue a trained swordsman and his servants with no better weapon than a cane.

But against these prudent thoughts, he could not bear the thought of what Lord Lovett might be doing to Hester. He could tell himself that Lovett would be frantically getting ready to flee, now that he had been seen taking Hester from Hawkhurst House. But Gideon could not forget the look of stunned surprise that he had seen on Colonel Potter's face.

While he stewed briefly over his course of action, a post-chaise clattered around the corner and pulled to a stop behind the coach. The groom who had been sent to fetch it stepped down, and instructing the postillions to wait, ran up to the house.

It seemed that now would be the only chance Gideon would have, unless he could stop them on the road. And not knowing how long it would take Tom to find him, he simply could not take that risk.

He pulled the handkerchief and snuffbox out of his pocket and posed them elegantly in his left hand. In his right he carried the cane, as he sauntered up to Lovett's door.

"Here, you scoundrel!" he said, in his most affected voice to the footman he met on the steps. "I insist upon seeing your master on a matter of urgent business."

Before the servant, who was toting a heavy box to the coach, could think to block his path, Gideon dodged him and headed up the stairs. He moved quickly, ignoring the protests that floated up behind him. Then, at the top, he hesitated only a moment before trying the first closed door he came across.

His guess regarding the location of the withdrawing room was correct. Inside, Lord Lovett halted abruptly on his way to the door. He had a wicked grip on Mrs. Kean's right arm, and it appeared that he had been dragging her across the room.

Both looked up when Gideon burst through the door. Mrs. Kean's face lit with a mixture of hope and fright. She did not seem to have been harmed, but the relief in her eyes told him that he had not been wrong in believing her in danger.

Annoyed and impatient, Lord Lovett had paused in the centre of the room, but now he raked Gideon's figure with scornful amusement, taking in the extreme fashion of his garb.

Gideon believed his only chance would be to disarm him with a lie.

"Ye gods!" he exclaimed, taking a few swaying steps into the room, while throwing the door closed behind him. "I thought that I saw you coming in here, Mrs. Kean, but I could not credit my wits! This will not do, ma'am, y' know! I beg you will reconsider. Think of the scandal for your poor family!"

Lord Lovett did not even blink. "This gentleman is a friend of yours, my dear?" he asked, drawing Mrs. Kean close. "Curious, isn't it, that we have never met?"

Gideon did not trust his smoothness, nor did he care for the flash of fear in Mrs. Kean's eyes.

"I was a friend of Mrs. Kean's father, sir, in Yorkshire. I hope you do not mean to deny it, ma'am?"

He had been almost certain that Lord Lovett had seen through his pretence, but his indignation had planted a doubt. It was not beyond the bounds of reason that Mrs. Kean would have acquaintances from her former life in Yorkshire whom Lovett would not know.

"I see," Lord Lovett said, changing his tactics. "Then, I can assure you, sir, that you have nothing to fear on Mrs. Kean's account. We are on our way to be married, so there is nothing for her family to be upset about."

"Married! By gads! Well, why did you not say so, my dear! I'm certain your old father would have been pleased. May I be the first to shake your hand, my lord?"

With that, Gideon started to mince his way towards them, the cane gripped tightly in his fist.

He had meant to raise it and bring it down hard on Lord Lovett's head, but something gave him away—either the white of his knuckles or more likely the intention of violence in his eyes—for before he could lift the cane half-way, Lord Lovett took a sudden step backwards, pulled out a dagger, and slipped it in front of Hester's throat.

She gave a strangled cry.

Gideon froze. He gaze flew to hers, but all he could read in it was an apology for getting him into this danger.

Lord Lovett had moved without a word, but now he courteously remarked, "May I assume that this is the Mr. Mavors in your letter, my dear? You will pardon me, I hope, if I express a touch of disappointment. I had expected you to have better taste.

"Now," he said, "if your friend will excuse us, we have a carriage waiting." He began to edge with Hester to the door, keeping a watch on Gideon's eyes, as they turned with him.

Gideon knew that he was confronting an experienced swordsman. Only a swordsman would have known to read his opponent's intention in his eyes. He dared not try any tricks, for the blade was already pressing into Mrs. Kean's throat so hard that she could barely swallow.

He was finding it difficult to swallow, himself, out of fear of what Lord Lovett might do to her.

They passed close to the chimney, where Lord Lovett paused. He told Gideon that if he did not wish to see Mrs. Kean's throat slit right there, then he should turn to face the wall.

Gideon did as he was told.

He heard a clank of iron, heard Mrs. Kean shriek, "No!" and in the next painful instant, all around him went black.

Hester was so shocked by the sound—between a crack and a thud—of the poker hitting St. Mars's skull, that she went completely stiff. This made it easier for Lord Lovett to half-carry, half-drag her to the chaise.

She did not fight him. Even in her dazed state, she sensed that the best thing for St. Mars—if he was still alive—would be for his assailant to be miles away. She had no doubt that Lord Lovett would kill him with no compunction if he proved to be more trouble.

The fear that he might already be dead, made her stomach roil so violently that she could barely separate this sensation from the rolling of the vehicle. She could not imagine a world without St. Mars.

She had not realized that he was unarmed until she had seen him lying on the floor with no sword at his hip. She had always known him for a courageous man, but that he should attempt to free her with no weapon at his command stunned her with the selflessness of his daring.

She stayed in this trance for many minutes. Before she became aware that any time had passed, they were rumbling across London Bridge. She might not even have wakened then, but for the shouts of the vendors on the bridge. Then, she started and looked about her, jerked to the danger of her situation by the sight of Lord Lovett, lounging against the opposite wall and staring at her with an intrigued expression.

"I trust you have recovered from that unpleasant incident?" he said, as if she had just witnessed a family spat.

Hester decided that she would no longer play his game of politeness. "It amazes me that you can speak of murdering a fellow creature as if a human life were nothing more than an inconvenience." She heard a quiver in her voice, but it was from fury, not fear. Her only concern at this moment was for St. Mars.

She was astonished to see Lord Lovett flush. She had thought him beyond desiring anyone's good opinion but his own. He would not oblige her with further proof of his conscience, however, but made his expression neutral and gave a negligent shrug.

"What may seem heartless to you was a matter of necessity to me. No one has been injured who could have been spared."

"But, why?" she said in anguish. "Why, when Sir Humphrey was your friend?"

He gave a surprised laugh, which unsettled her as much as, apparently, her question had him. "You still do not know? And I thought you had discovered everything."

She shook her head, and said, through tightened lips, "A blood stain can tell me who committed a murder, but certainly not why."

He stared at her, his smile tinged with self-mockery. "Do you know? I do not believe that I shall tell you. Who knows but what—" He did not finish, but she could see that he was forming some new plan in his head.

She straightened her spine and stared him in the eye. "It does not matter why. I presume you did it to save your own skin, which makes you cowardly and despicable, no matter what the reason."

She could tell by the way he blinked that she had injured him again. His lip curled derisively, but he was not proud to own the truth. Then, she remembered that he had murdered two of his friends and realized what a fool she had been to provoke such a dangerous man. She had much better be silent and accommodating and with luck he would let her go once they were safely at the coast. If he left her earlier, he would be able to travel the rest of the way by horse, which would be much faster, if she could only persuade him to let her live.

She put an end to their conversation by pretending to gaze out the window. She had traveled in a post-chaise only once before, and their speed relative to a private coach was remarkable. She had not given much thought to their destination, but she wondered about it now. While locked in Lord Lovett's drawing room, afraid that he meant to kill her, she had heard him giving orders to his servants, so she understood that they were going to France.

Now, looking at the passing scenery, she realized that she had traveled this way before. It was the route to Hawkhurst and Rotherham Abbey.

Her heart gave a leap of hope. She could not think of this road without remembering a magical night only a few months ago when St. Mars had swept her up onto his saddle and changed her life. Then, before an instant could pass, she recalled that St. Mars would not be coming. If Lord Lovett's servants had called for a constable, he might have been taken up and thrown into Newgate, where he would face trial for murder and treason. Even worse—he might still be lying on the floor where Lord Lovett had left him, bleeding to death.

She wondered if Katy knew what he had done and if she would manage to tell Tom in time. Wouldn't Tom, as attached as he was to his master, do something to save him?

She couldn't know how much initiative St. Mars's servants would show. But it was so much more comforting to think of their helping him than to worry about how desperately injured he might be, that she turned her thoughts in that direction and prayed with all her might.

They traveled in this uneasy silence for more than an hour, before Lord Lovett broke it. "What a remarkable creature you are, Mrs. Kean! Here you have been abducted, and you have not once inquired what I intend to do with you."

"It makes no difference, for wherever you leave me, Isabella will send her husband or her brother to fetch me."

"Now, we both know that is false, when I left them with the particular impression that you and I were running away together. Your cousin Isabella will be jealous because you have stolen her lover. Your aunt will rant that you were always an ungrateful chit. Dudley Mayfield will not give tuppence what becomes of you, and his lordship will make some excuse so that he won't have to call me out. Given that, I am surprised at your lack of interest in your fate."

"I suppose you will tell me when you are ready."

"Such compliance, though! When I was beginning to think you had lost your affection for me. It is most gratifying."

She turned to face him. "You can mock me all you like. But I have nothing of which to be ashamed, unless it was shameful to imagine that a person of your capacity was too intelligent to be a murderer."

"Touché!" If Hester had hoped to wound him, she had missed her mark. He seemed to be enjoying himself now. "That is much more like you. Has anyone ever told you how attractive indignation on the face of an intelligent woman can be?"

An angry flush rose into her cheeks. "I have no wish to be credited with *your* sort of intelligence, my lord."

"But there was a time—not so very many days ago—when you did. You cannot pretend that you did not flatter yourself that you were the only person in your household who understood my wit. I had not known you above a week before I perceived that you despised your empty-headed cousin and her husband and her mother for their stupidity. And you were grateful for any relief from their insipidity, which I provided. Now, confess it, Mrs. Kean."

His words were painfully true, and she regretted that she had valued his cleverness higher than Isabella's goodwill. But Hester would not let him crush her with blame. She knew she would suffer enough remorse for her stupidity, but her failures were as nothing compared to his sins.

"I was sorely mistaken in your character, sir. If I must confess something, let it be that I saw how you used my cousin, yet I did not see any reason that you would have to use me."

"That is because you underrate your abilities. I feared them, you see, from the moment that you first started asking questions. I feared that you would find me out. And you did, so you see that I was correct."

"That was why you pretended an interest in me. I am well aware of that, my lord."

"Certainly, that was my principal reason, but I have enjoyed our battle of wits, Mrs. Kean—so much, in fact, that I have a proposal to make."

She could not imagine what he was about to say, but his expression held a dare.

"I shall be taking you with me to France," he said. "I have a notion that you will do exceedingly well at a French court."

Hester felt as if the bottom had fallen out of her stomach. Her incredulity and her outrage were such that she could not immediately speak.

He gave her one of his mocking grins. "I see that my proposal has taken you by surprise, but I advise you to consider it. The alternatives could not be very palatable. I'm afraid I cannot permit you to return to your cousins, for you would be sure to report my crimes to a magistrate, and I should prefer that no one know them for certain. Besides, you cannot really wish to live with those idiots. Then, of course, I could kill you, too, but I find the prospect rather distasteful. So, you see, it would be better for you to come with me to France. I was not jesting about your cleverness, and the French have always appreciated intelligent women."

"So much that they will maintain them at their expense?" Hester didn't know why she bothered to reply. He had certainly gone quite mad, for his notion was preposterous.

His grin turned into a genuine look of amusement, and there was a curious pleasure in his smile, when he said. "I find that your wits are a bit slower than usual this evening, my love, but perhaps the journey has tired you. It is I who shall maintain you, of course."

Her first thought was that he was offering her a bribe. An independence in exchange for her silence. Then, she understood the significance of his smile, and a shudder passed through her.

Now, she did feel shame—that he would entertain for even a moment the possibility of her consent.

"And forget the blood that is on your hands? Is that it?"

"It would be wise for you to do so."

"You cannot truly believe that I would!"

He shrugged, as if her refusal would be of no great matter. "I fail to see why not. It would be smarter, as I have said, and as we are agreed that you are a sensible woman, I expect you to make the sensible choice. We have got along in the past, so it is reasonable to assume that we shall in future."

Cringing, Hester turned her face to the window to hide her distress at his notion of her. "May God grant me death before I ever become as reasonable as you, my lord."

He did not respond. And Hester refused to face him again, even if by doing so, she could prevent him from stabbing her in the back. She could not bear to be reminded of his wickedness—or of his *flattering* proposal, as he appeared to think it. It had made her feel as if she would never be clean again.

She wrapped her arms about her body and leaned her forehead against the glass to get as far away from him as she could. The carriage bumped and lurched, even over the best part of the road, but she hardly noticed the knocks. Despite the heat of the July afternoon, she felt cold.

Gideon woke to find two footmen standing over him. One was the same servant he had slipped by at the door. He could not be surprised, therefore, when he received little sympathy. And it was only when he had dragged himself up from the floor that he was able to persuade the other to bring him some wine for his head, and only then because of the quantity of blood he had spilled on their master's carpet.

He discovered that he had been unconscious for over an hour before anyone had checked the room, which meant that Lovett already had an hour's start, at least.

Gideon took his long wig off and felt for the split in his head. The bleeding had nearly stopped because swelling had shut it off. Lovett had struck him hard, and Gideon had his thick peruke to thank that he was still alive. His head hurt dreadfully, though, and when he stood, nausea almost overcame him.

Moving into a chair, he asked the servant for a basin of water and told him that he would make it worth his while. He was bathing the blood from the back of his head, when a loud knocking came downstairs at the door.

A moment later, he heard Tom's voice raised in outrage. Gideon pushed himself to his feet with a groan and made his way to the head of the stairs.

"Here I am, Tom," he called, over the pain in his head. He picked his way down, while Tom stared up at him in horror.

"Lord, what's happened to you, sir! Are you all right?"

"He got away," Gideon said, ignoring his question. "He took Mrs. Kean. They left an hour ago."

"There's blood all down your coat!"

"Yes, but you know how head wounds can bleed. He would have killed me if he could have, but my wig defied him. Have you brought Looby?"

He had reached the open door by now and, peering out, saw that a boy was walking their horses in front of the house.

"I came as quick as I could, sir. And when you wasn't where Katy said you'd be, I waited, but after a while I got worried."

"That's quite all right. I'm sure the sleep must have done me good. Is everything on my saddle?"

"Yessir. But are you sure you can ride?"

"I shall have to, I'm afraid. I can't let him take Mrs. Kean. And we've got to find them as soon as we can—before he decides that he doesn't need her anymore."

As concerned as he was for his master's head, Tom did not think of protesting, when of all the friends who might have helped his master, only Mrs. Kean had.

He gave St. Mars a leg up into his saddle and climbed into his own, before throwing the boy a coin.

When St. Mars headed down to the horse ferry, Tom grew worried because the ferryman had seen his master so many times that he might see through his disguise. But every minute would count, and it would take much longer to go round by London Bridge.

"They're traveling by post-chaise," St. Mars said. "I assume his lordship's coach will follow them later. He will want to move fast."

"Then he'll be sure to take the Dover road."

"If he doesn't, we'll find out soon enough. I'm afraid that you will have to ask for news of them. I hate to say it, but I shall be doing well just to arrive."

Tom had not seen how white his master was beneath his paint, but as he turned, startled by St. Mars's admission, he noted the thinness and pallor of his lips.

"Are you sure you can do this, my lord? If you want me to, I'll go after them."

"No. I can't send you after a man like Lovett alone. He's been trained with weapons and will be quick to use them."

They had reached the horse ferry now, and said no more. The ferryman did not look twice at the gentleman in the bright scarlet coat and long chestnut wig, not even at the blood still on his coat. He should have recognized Tom, at least. But except for directing a narrow squint at Tom's horse, as if wondering where he might have seen it before, he took no more notice of Tom than he did of St. Mars.

St. Mars said very little, but what he did was spoken in a nasal voice, with expressions Tom had never heard him use before. Fretting with impatience, but in no more than the usual time, they reached the opposite bank, where they led the horses up the ramp and turned their backs on Westminster.

As soon as they left the inns and market gardens of Lambeth behind,

St. Mars stopped his horse on the edge of St. George Field. He removed his peruke, vest, and coat, and, leaving only his white shirt and yellow breeches, made a bundle of his garments and stuffed them in his pack with his ruby-heeled shoes.

"It's good that our friend the ferryman has such poor eyesight," St. Mars said, as he pulled on the tall boots that Tom handed him from out of his own bag.

"Ay, my lord. I was sure that he would know you."

"Apparently, I make quite a different figure in those clothes. It was you I was worried about, but as you have not been charged, you can always say that you have entered someone else's service."

St. Mars had managed to relieve his face of some of its patches, and a handkerchief wiped off most of the paint. He seemed relieved to be free of these and his heavy clothes, which Tom could understand now that he had felt the weight of a wig only half that length. But he did not like the look of his master's colourless lips or the dark, swollen patch on the crown of his head.

"My lord, why don't you wait for me at the house. If he's making for the coast, he could take any one of a dozen roads. You could rest until I find their trail."

St. Mars hesitated—which told Tom more than anything could how much his head must be bothering him. But he declined. "If I'm not much mistaken, we'll hear of them soon enough. It's still light, so the turnpikes will be open. Someone will have seen them."

"But how do you know that he won't head into Sussex like his Grace of Ormonde?"

"I don't. But if we don't pick up their trail on either of the first two routes, then we shall have to split up to find them. I will not let him take Mrs. Kean."

A deadly purpose was in his voice.

Tom would rather have seen him agree to rest, but he could not argue with his feelings. Or with his logic, for the roads in Sussex were a notorious maze. Anyone would have to have a particular reason to choose one of them, even over the deep, narrow roads of Kent.

With no further discussion, they turned their horses towards Deptford to the junction of the two turnpiked roads.

Cease then, nor ORDER *Imperfection name:*
Our proper bliss depends on what we blame.
Know thy own point: This kind, this due degree
Of blindness, weakness, Heaven bestows on thee.
Submit.—In this, or any other sphere,
Secure to be as blest as thou canst bear:
Safe in the hand of one disposing Power,
Or in the natal, or the mortal hour.
All Nature is but Art, unknown to thee;
All Chance, Direction, which thou canst not see;
All Discord, Harmony not understood;
All partial Evil, universal Good:
And, spite of Pride, in erring Reason's spite,
One truth is clear, WHATEVER IS, IS RIGHT.

CHAPTER XXII

The post-chaise had not been seen on the road to Rochester, which meant that he was probably not taking her to Dover or Deal.

When Tom asked if a post chaise and six, driven by two postillions and carrying a lady and a gentleman, had been noticed passing through the turnpike on the road to Deptford, it took the better part of an hour to establish that someone had seen it. The keeper at the gate had only recently stepped away, and his youngest son had taken over the duty of collecting tolls. While St. Mars waited, growing restless—for there was nothing to be done until they either confirmed or ruled out the Kent Road—Tom was forced to ride back towards London to look for the man.

He finally found him in the Bull Inn, close by the one-mile stone, after inquiring at every establishment on the way. It took every ounce of Tom's restraint not to box the man's ears, and he roundly cursed him for leaving his post before dark. But knowing how anxious his master would be, he stopped himself far short of a proper satisfaction to carry the welcome news that Lord Lovett's chaise had been spotted when the postillion had paid the toll.

Gideon used the time to bathe his head in the local trough. The cool water revived him. Then he sat with his face cradled in his hands to rest. The jarring movement of his horse had seemed intolerable already, and if he did not want to flag, he knew he was going to have to moderate his gait.

Tom's news acted on him like a tonic, however, and they quickly paid their tolls before pressing onto Deptford, where the turnpiked highway split. They tried the Dover Road first, because it was the more frequently used, since it passed through flatter country on its way to the coast and ended closer to France.

But no one they asked on the highway to Chalk had seen a vehicle of the kind they described since much too early in the day for it to be Lord Lovett's, so they retraced their steps again to Deptford and started down the familiar road to Bromley.

Here, despite its familiarity, they had to be most careful, for both were very well known on this road. Tom had to choose places that had never been honoured with Lord Hawkhurst's patronage, while Gideon waited astride Looby with the brim of his hat pulled low. He did not even dare to show his face to the children, playing chase in the dust in front of the inn where Tom had stopped to inquire, for, before he was arrested, their parents might have pointed out the Viscount St. Mars to them. And with a price of three hundred pounds on his head, Gideon made no doubt that they would be quick to know him again.

His head felt a little better, but far from clear, and his greatest fear—even more than the fear of being recognized—was that he would lose consciousness along the way. This was why he had decided to take Tom along. He had not exaggerated the danger of challenging Lord Lovett. A man who had killed twice would not be slow to kill again. Yet, if Gideon *were* to lose consciousness, Tom would have to go on in his stead, for he could not bear the thought of leaving Mrs. Kean in a murderer's hands.

Obviously, she had discovered Lord Lovett's guilt, and he had learned of her discovery. Gideon could think of no other reason for Lovett to have taken her. Perhaps, she had heard about Colonel Potter's murder that morning, and turning her suspicions towards the only suspect left besides her cousin, she had thought of something she had previously ignored. She might even have guessed about his visit to Walpole in the same way Gideon had, by putting together Lovett's stop in Arlington

Street with a motive for killing his Jacobite friends.

But that would all be there to discuss when Mrs. Kean was safe. Gideon prayed for the chance to save her. He also prayed for the strength not only to find her, but to tear her clean away from the murderer's arms.

At least—and this piece of luck was by no means slight—it appeared that Lord Lovett had not gone through Surrey into Sussex, where he might have lost his pursuers in the tangled web of that county's roads. He had chosen a smoother route, for after the blow he had dealt Gideon, he must have felt no reason to fear pursuit. True, a man on horseback would have no difficulty catching a coach, even a post-chaise and six, but who besides Gideon would have bothered to save Mrs. Kean?

Lord Lovett had taken her from right under the noses of the Hawkhurst servants. Gideon doubted that anyone in either his or her family would have the brains to suspect the truth or go to the trouble of retrieving her, if they did.

This thought made him furious, and his head began to pound anew, so he tried to calm himself and gather his resources. It was bad enough that he was growing anxious over the delay, while Tom made his inquiries. But they did not dare ride all the way to Sevenoaks unless they could confirm that the post-chaise had traveled this way. The gatekeeper might have mistaken another chaise for the one they were chasing, or he might equally have lied, though Gideon supposed that a fairly honest man had been chosen for that important post. Still, people made mistakes, and it would be a waste of precious time to ride in any direction unless they were certain that it was the correct one.

Meanwhile, the shadows were growing longer. Lord Lovett's lead was growing longer, too. Gideon, who hadn't had a bite to eat since breakfast and didn't dare spare a moment to eat now—and who had a throbbing knot on the back of his head—could only pray that Mrs. Kean was all right.

Tom came out of the inn yard, hurrying towards him, and Gideon's heart gave a leap at his servant's eager expression.

"This is the way, my lord. They were seen passing through here at about five o'clock this evening."

"You're sure?" While Tom repeated the details he had heard, Gideon took out his watch and studied it. "That was about three hours ago. That should be right." Pulling in his reins then, he said, "Let's go. He must be taking her to Rye, and they will have changed horses in Sevenoaks by now."

He did not wait for Tom to mount, but, doubting his own ability to keep up for once, set a measured pace for Bromley.

Earlier, Gideon had wondered if Lovett might not leave her when he reached the end of the turnpiked road, but now he realized how unlikely that was. If he left her alive, she would certainly set a magistrate upon him and a posse would be raised in time. If he killed her before sailing away, the crime would quickly be discovered with the same result.

As hard as it was even to speculate in such fearful terms, this logic gave Gideon hope. With his head in such a miserable condition, he would not be able to ride very fast. But, after reaching the end of the turnpiked portion of the highway in the town of Tunbridge, Lord Lovett would have to go on in a coach with a hostage, instead of making better time on horseback. As long as Gideon could stay in the saddle, he and Tom would catch them before they got to Rye.

The boost of energy he had got from being in his own country did not last. Before many miles had been covered, Gideon found his head splitting with pain, and his eyes began to play tricks.

The next thing he knew, it was dark, and a man was lowering him to the ground. He struggled to sit up, but Tom's voice came to him. "Just you take it easy, Master Gideon! You'll never catch up with the young lady this way! Not if you can't ride without falling into a fainting fit."

Gideon acknowledged his sense. Frustration with his weakness made him angry, but relieved to find himself in Tom's care, he allowed himself to be lowered onto the grass by the side of the road. He lay beneath a hedge until his head was clearer, then asked, "How long since I swooned?"

"I'm not really sure, my lord. Likely, a ways back. I didn't notice you were in a faint until you were halfway to the ground."

"What a hellish juggle this is!" Gideon tried not to clench his teeth. "If I do it again, you must leave me, take both pistols, and stop them yourself."

"Yes, my lord."

"I don't want you hurt, but you will know what to do. Just do not underestimate Lord Lovett. He's capable of anything."

"If needs be, my lord. But, mayhap, you'll do better if we don't ride quite so fast. Even if we walk the horses some, we ought to catch them before Rye, what with all the stops and the changes they'll have to make. We're nearly at Tunbridge now, so they'll soon be moving at a snail's pace. And the horses will last a mite longer if we go easier, too."

Gideon struggled to think. It was true that, after Tunbridge, the road was so deeply rutted that a carriage could only crawl. Even taking more care with their horses, he and Tom should easily gain on the chaise.

"I'm sure you're right," he eventually said, "but my head is too cloudy to reckon the time. We must have gained an hour on them already, mustn't we, Tom?"

"I'm almost sure of it, my lord."

Gideon pushed himself up in a sitting position. When he'd sat until his head had stopped spinning, he stood carefully with Tom's help.

"We'll try it your way then." He reached for Looby's reins. "I want you to tie me to the saddle. Then, if I lose consciousness again, you can keep us moving towards Rye."

Their pace was slower after that. With his hands secured to his horse's neck, Gideon was jerked awake more than once as he slipped to the side, but he allowed himself to doze as Tom pulled his horse through the night. Eventually, as the night air cooled, the pain in his head grew less, and his wakefulness improved. They stopped a couple of times to rest the horses, and Gideon ventured to drink. The water revived him, so that by the time they reached Lamberhurst he could take charge of his reins and abandon all thought of Tom's going on alone.

As they neared the village of Hawkhurst and Rotherham Abbey, however, they did not dare to ask for news about Lord Lovett's coach, for they both were too well-known in these parts. They could only persevere in the assumption that Lord Lovett would be heading for the nearest port.

When another hour passed, and they had not caught up with the post-chaise, Gideon's sense of urgency pushed him faster, for soon they would pass into Sussex and then only a few miles remained before Rye. He could do nothing but hope that he had not mistaken Lord Lovett's intentions.

They had just crested a hill, with the pale sky of the short summer night revealing the village of Newenden below, when he saw a post-chaise with only one postillion threading its way down the road. He signaled for Tom to stop.

"There they go." As Tom pulled up beside him, he pointed. "We'll have to follow until we find a safer place to stop the carriage. We dare not use a pistol near the village or we'll have men from both counties chasing us."

"Are you sure you can manage this, my lord?"

Gideon gave a brief nod, then scouted the landscape ahead. Now that the prey was in sight, excitement and relief had infused him with strength.

"We should ford the river. I don't want to run into the Watch in Newenden, and the fewer people who see us, the better. Someone in the village will likely be stirring soon."

"I misdoubt Beau won't like that ditch."

"That can't be helped. We'll have to surprise them at just the right moment. There are only about six miles between Newenden and Rye with little open land between."

He dug into his pack and drew out his mask and his blue silk cape. "Get ready to cover your face."

Tom obeyed, pulling a knotted kerchief over the bridge of his nose. "If anybody sees us dressed like this, they're sure to start a hue and cry."

"That well may be. But if we're going to succeed, we need to frighten the postillion. Come on, let's go."

ꝭ

Long past midnight, when the chaise had bumped its way into Hawkhurst and continued through without even a pause, Hester had given up her last hope of escape. She was already more than a little sick from the incessant swinging and lurching of the carriage over the rutted roads. The spring rains had dug grooves so deep that, without six horses to pull them, the vehicle would often have been stuck.

She had not thought it possible to sleep in such uncomfortable circumstances, but exhausted by emotion, she occasionally dozed off. Each time, she soon started awake and found Lord Lovett keeping a close watch over her.

At the end of every posting-stage they descended to change the carriage and horses. At the first one, she had hoped to convey the desperation of her situation to someone at the posting-house. But soon she had learned that Lord Lovett had no plans to leave her alone, except for the minute it took her to relieve herself, and even then, he remained in the parlour with her until the chamber pot was brought, and stood guard outside the room so that she dared not call out.

Hester had never known how oppressive such a confinement could be. Never to be out of hearing or out of sight of a murderer. Her disgust with him had increased throughout the night, so that sleep had become her only deliverance.

But now they were entering a part of Kent that was foreign to her. And, foolish as it was, she realized that as long as she had recognized the villages and towns they passed, she had nursed a glimmer of hope that someone she knew would stop them before they reached the coast. She was not sure of the distance remaining, but she knew enough to guess that no one would be able to stop them now.

Several miles, and more than an hour later, they crossed a river, which she supposed was the Rother. That meant that they had come into Sussex, and not knowing anything of that country, she wondered who she would find to help her, even if Lord Lovett could be persuaded to let her go.

She had not quite given up the thought that he might leave her behind in England, in which case she would still be lost. Without either money or acquaintances, she did not know how she would make her way back to Rotherham Abbey. But, at least, if she were abandoned in Rye, she would be able to ask for help of the rector or vicar. If she could persuade the cleric to send a letter to the Abbey, the steward would send money and a servant to fetch her, surely.

But being abandoned in France would be entirely a different story. She doubted she would find her schoolroom French sufficient to the task of explaining her predicament. Suspicious of a foreigner, people would assume the worst, and she should be ruined, if she did not starve. She did not even know if the Catholic Church would extend charity to Protestants.

One thing she had decided, though, was that no matter how desperate her situation might be, she would never accept Lord Lovett's proposal. She would rather die than submit to a man who might have murdered St. Mars.

Her belief in his recovery had taken a negative turn. She could not help feeling that if he were still alive, he would have found her by now. Fear of his death brought a painful ache to her throat.

Lord Lovett spoke. "When we arrive in Rye, I shall have to negotiate our passage."

"I have no passport. And I doubt that the French authorities will permit me to enter without one."

"That would be a reasonable assumption if we were sailing on the packet, but we shall be taking a different boat. There are always ways of crossing into France without alerting the authorities. But do not concern yourself over the arrangements. I shall see to everything. Sadly, however, that will mean tying you up at the inn until I've found us a means of conveyance."

Hester tried again to convince him to leave her by the side of the road, but he said, wryly, "And suppose that bad weather prevents me from sailing today? No, my dear Mrs. Hester, I shall not take that risk, particularly when I look forward to your eventual cooperation."

She was on the point of retorting that he should never have it, when he moved closer to her on the seat. She could not see his face clearly in the dark, but a sudden change in his breathing made her pulse flutter with a strange kind of fear.

"I did not enjoy killing Humphrey," he said hoarsely. "I only did it because it was either his life or mine. Just think what a superior life we could lead at St. Germain, you and I!"

He faltered for a moment, before going on in a voice of entreaty, "You could not prefer to be left friendless and penniless in Calais—when you might live at the height of elegance—all for a few foolish scruples."

"Foolish scruples? Like honour? How paltry a thing honour is, to be sure, when compared to elegance! I can certainly see your point. Strangely, though, I should rather starve to death in a French port than live with you in the manner you describe."

He slowly leaned back against the side of the chaise. "And I had thought you an intelligent woman." His tone was hard. "Well, my dear, perhaps you shall have your way."

Hester had turned her back to him again, when a shot rang out. The postillion gave a frightened cry, as the horses started to weave and plunge.

Hastily lowering his window, Lord Lovett called out, "What is it?"

"Highwaymen, my lord!"

A pulse that was beating in Hester's stomach leapt into her heart. She had never heard a more beautiful phrase.

"Impossible!" Turning to peer out, Lord Lovett drew a pistol from inside his coat. "What highwayman would be this far from London?"

The sight of his gun banished the joy from Hester's breast. She could not bear to see St. Mars shot. She would ten times rather struggle with Lord Lovett alone.

"Stand and deliver!"

Regardless of her fears, those words, issued in the familiar voice, sent a thrill down her spine.

"Stay here!" Lord Lovett commanded. "I shall not keep you waiting above a few minutes."

Hester did not like his confident note. She saw him tuck the pistol in his waist and cover it with his coat.

With her heart in her throat, she watched him open the door and step down. He turned to face the front of the chaise, then reached into his coat as if to draw out his purse.

Before he could finish, she threw herself through the door. As she tumbled out, landing near Lord Lovett, she glanced to her right and saw St. Mars, dressed as Blue Satan in a black mask and blue satin cloak, sitting astride a horse, with a pistol aimed at Lord Lovett's heart.

Hester cried out, "Beware! He has a pistol hidden!"

Then, several things happened at once.

St. Mars gave a spur to his horse, urging it towards her. Tom, who was waiting out of sight, came crashing out of the undergrowth to intercept his master. Surprised by her cry, Lord Lovett recovered in time to grasp her by the waist and pull her in front of him.

Hester felt the cold steel of his pistol pressed into her cheek.

St. Mars reined his horse, stopping as if on the head of a pin, and called out to Tom, "Stop!"

Tom pulled hard on his reins, too, spinning his mount in a circle before bringing it to a halt.

For a moment, no one spoke. Over the pulse in her ears, Hester could hear Lord Lovett's laboured breathing.

St. Mars sat frozen on his horse. In the pale summer night, she could see how tensely he held himself. His gaze was mostly fixed on Lord Lovett, but occasionally he darted a glance her way, as if he could not prevent himself from checking to see that she was alive.

He wore no hat. His long fair hair was tied in a queue down his back. The top of his shirt was damp and open, revealing the lean muscles of his neck. He looked nothing like the fop who had burst into Lord Lovett's withdrawing room yesterday afternoon.

Lord Lovett was the first to speak, and he did it with a vicious hug of her waist. "Now, this is more like, my love! And still you've surprised me. I should never have guessed that you would take a common highwayman for a lover."

Frightened by the jealousy in his voice, Hester said, "You are mistaken. I do not know these men." She was afraid that he would shoot St. Mars.

"Truly?" he asked. "Then, how strange that they appear to know you! If they did not, then I doubt that they would have lowered their weapons." He gestured briefly at the ground with his pistol. "Throw them down. Then dismount."

"You wouldn't dare shoot," St. Mars said. "If you did, then we should be on you in an instant."

Lord Lovett pressed the barrel against Hester's throat so hard that she gave an involuntary cry. "That may be true. But somehow I doubt that you will test me."

Hester could see St. Mars clenching his jaw, but he gave a signal to Tom, and they both obeyed, keeping a wary watch on her captor.

"Now, drop your reins, and move away. I am weary of traveling in this manner, and besides, the boy seems to have fled. Either of these horses should suit us. Wouldn't you agree, my dear? And I doubt that your friends will follow us into Rye, not after we inform the constable that the infamous Blue Satan is working this road."

St. Mars had tightened his hands into fists. He looked pale, and Hester thought she could see confirmation in his eyes. He could not risk riding into town without a disguise, for Lord Lovett would be sure to describe him well.

But she mistook his thoughts, for he said, "I believe the authorities will be much more interested in you, Lord Lovett, when they hear not only that you have murdered two gentlemen, but that you are a spy."

Hester felt a convulsive jerk from the arm around her waist.

"It appears that you are more informed than I thought. What a pity! Still, I suppose it was foolish of me to think that my sins would go undetected. That means that France will be our home from now on, my love."

It would have made Hester furious that he kept referring to her as a willing partner, if she had not been aware of his own anger underneath. Apparently he had convinced himself that he was going to be able to return to England someday with no one the wiser. Now that this portion of his plan had been ruined, he was eager to punish the person who had done it. Better her than St. Mars or Tom.

He would not shoot them, for he would never be able to reload before the other attacked. This knowledge gave her courage, even though the thought of remaining his prisoner repulsed her. If only there were some way to strike the pistol from his hand!

But she couldn't. Not with it pressed against her throat.

He gave her a shove with his chest, and walked behind her to St.

Mars's horse. Then, pointing the pistol at her back, he told her to mount.

Hester was not an experienced horsewoman. Her family had been too poor to keep a horse, and neither Mrs. Mayfield nor Isabella had seen fit to provide her with a mount. Her fumbling with the reins and stirrup was genuine, but Lord Lovett suspected her of trying to trick him. So, he put her aside, and keeping his aim straight at her breast, put his foot in the stirrup and hauled himself up.

He was reaching down to pull her up behind him, when the pistol slipped in his hand.

St. Mars took two running steps and lunged.

Catching her by the waist on his way down, he rolled her clear of the horse. As they tumbled, Hester saw Tom take a step towards his gun, but Lord Lovett stopped him by pointing his weapon his way, and calling out, "Stop right there or I'll fire!"

St. Mars had landed on top of her. For a long moment, Hester felt the full burden of his weight. Then, he seemed to rouse himself, and, lifting his head, as if in pain, he started to his feet.

Lord Lovett shifted his pistol to aim it at St. Mars.

This time, he cocked it.

"No! Don't shoot!"

As St. Mars struggled to stand, he wavered, appeared to lose consciousness, and collapsed, just as Hester threw herself in front of him.

She expected to hear the explosion of gunpowder in the fraction of a second before the bullet tore into her flesh, but Lord Lovett's gun stayed silent. She opened her eyes to find him staring her with an expression that revealed something between pain and relief.

It was a moment before he spoke, and when he did, his voice was unsteady. "You should know that my being up on a horse changes the rules of the game. I can shoot your friend and no one is likely to catch me. If you do not wish for that to happen, I suggest you give me your hand."

He reached towards her, as if to help her mount.

In the road behind her, St. Mars stirred.

"If you shoot him, you will have to shoot me first," Hester said.

Lord Lovett kept looking down at her. For a moment, his mocking look was gone. Then it returned, and his lips gave a bitter twist.

"It would appear that your highwayman has spoiled more than one of my plans. When he wakes, pray make him my compliments. Goodbye, my dear." And with that, he turned on St. Mars's horse and galloped away.

Neither Hester nor Tom wasted a moment before hurrying to St. Mars's side.

"It's his head, ma'am," Tom said. "He took a nasty blow."

"I know." The memory of that sound made Hester shiver again. "I saw him hit with the poker. How did he ever make it this far?"

Tom hesitated. "I don't know, but he was powerful determined. We'll have to get him out of here before that blackguard raises a hue and cry."

Before Hester could ask how they would manage with only one horse, St. Mars's opened his eyes. Seeing Hester, he started quickly up, then gripped the back of his head. "Lord Lovett?" he asked, looking about him with squinting eyes.

"He left. And he took Looby with him. Do you want me to chase after him, my lord?" Tom asked anxiously, almost afraid to hear the answer.

"No, let him go. We've got what we wanted. And I'll know where to find him later." He turned to Hester and subjected her to a close scrutiny.

"Did he hurt you, Mrs. Kean? If he did, rest assured that I shall not sleep until he pays." Then he winced, as if from a shooting pain. His mouth twisted in a self-deprecating grimace. "That is, once I can be sure of staying awake. I can hardly recommend my services at the moment."

"I am not at all hurt, my lord, just very glad to see you both. But we must get you to a place where you can rest."

She looked to Tom for an idea, but he seemed as much at a loss as she. "We've got the post-chaise," he said. "They'll be searching for it before long, but we could get him nearer to Pigden in that. We'll have to abandon it before they come after it, though."

Then St. Mars took the decision out of their hands. He told Tom to unharness one of the post-horses and ride it, saying that he and Mrs. Kean would ride Beau.

"But where to, my lord?"

"Why, we escort Mrs. Kean to the Abbey, of course."

He rallied long enough to stand to make it easier for Tom to boost him up behind Mrs. Kean. Then he told her, "You will have to take the reins, I'm afraid. I am likely to faint again. And you must pardon me, if I lean on your back when I do."

With his arms bound about her, Hester guided Beau after Tom, who rode the post-horse using the postillion's saddle. She would not have wanted to manage such a big horse alone, but after coming such a long way, the big gelding behaved like a gentleman.

It was nearly dawn by the time they caught a glimpse of Hawkhurst House through the trees by the side of the road. St. Mars had managed to stay awake through most of their ride, but the caution they had been forced to take had made the journey slow. Daylight would be here soon, and people would be moving about.

"We'll have to hide out here in the abbey ruins," Tom said, when they stopped to let Hester down on the road to the gate. "If we don't, I'm sure we'll be spotted."

She took one good look at the pallor in St. Mars's cheek and made up her mind. "Your master will never make it unless he can rest, and I doubt that sleeping on the stone of those ruins will help him overmuch."

She could see the frustrated protest forming on Tom's lips, so she quickly added, "I shall have to go in and wait for the fuss over my sudden appearance to die down. While I tell my story and see that a messenger is sent up to London, please take my lord through the secret passageway to the house. He told me that you know the way, but perhaps you do not know that it opens into my chamber. I shall see that he rests and gets a meal. Then, you can take him home after dark."

It was a moment before Tom saw the sense in her plan, but in the end, he agreed. The only change he made in it was to suggest that she take the post-horse with her. He would keep Beau, and just after dark, he would bring his master another horse to ride.

They parted. Hester clucked to the weary horse and Tom gave it a slap on the rump to make it walk. Then, he led Beau, with a barely conscious St. Mars, to a place in the hedge where he knew of a passage and, under the cover of a wooded hill, brought him to the ruins which had given Rotherham Abbey its name.

St. Mars came to his senses again, as Tom helped him out of the saddle. He looked about him, and asked, "Mrs. Kean?"

"Mrs. Kean has gone into the Abbey, my lord." Tom told him about the plan they had devised, half-hoping that his master would refuse the young lady's offer. Tom could not bear the thought of walking through that tight, dark tunnel, not even for St. Mars. He had always hated small places, and he could think of no greater nightmare than an underground passageway.

It was built by one of St. Mars's ancestors in the last century, as an escape route for his family when the Roundheads were terrorizing the countryside. St. Mar's father, the last Lord Hawkhurst, had entrusted him with its secret. Now, Tom and Mrs. Kean were privy to it, too.

But St. Mars made no complaint. Tom lent him his arm down into the undercroft where the entrance was hidden behind a pile of stones. He was not even aware that he had started to breathe in constricted gasps until St. Mars pulled away to examine his face in the pale morning light.

"I don't think that I'll need you in there, Tom." St. Mars casually made this remark, as if he had not noticed Tom's perspiring face.

But Tom was not fooled, and he flushed. The first time he had begged not to be taken into the passageway, it had been dark, and St. Mars had thought he was afraid of ghosts. Now it was day, and the unnamed source of his fears still had the strength to make him shake.

"I can't let you go in there alone. What if you fall into another fit?"

"I won't. The cool air will revive me. And the prospect of a bed at the end should be enough incentive to keep me awake."

Tom would have argued longer, if St. Mars had not admonished him to take care of Beau. The horse would need water, and must be hidden, though it would need to graze.

Tom glanced to make sure that Beau had not wandered within sight of the house, and when he turned back, St. Mars was gone.

Self-love, the spring of motion, acts the soul;
Reason's comparing balance rules the whole.
Man, but for that, no action could attend,
And but for this, were active to no end:
Fixed like a plant on his peculiar spot,
To draw nutrition, propagate, and rot;
Or, meteor-like, flame lawless through the void,
Destroying others, by himself destroyed.

CHAPTER XXIII

Hester was greeted at the door by Lord Hawkhurst's servants with open astonishment. The footman ran immediately to fetch the steward, Robert Shaw. After telling Mr. Shaw enough about her abduction to convince him that a message should be sent to Hawkhurst House at once, Hester begged to be served some breakfast in her chamber and to be left alone to sleep until she recovered from her ordeal. She begged them not to send for Mr. Henry until she asked.

She made certain that St. Mars was not in her room before she allowed the footman to enter to fill her ewer and basin with water. Then she waited nervously for the food and chocolate to arrive, locked the door after the servant who brought them, and hastened to look behind the secret door.

Earlier that year, St. Mars had shown her how to find the mechanism, a particular piece of carving in the elaborate paneling, which operated a spring in the wall. She turned the piece, which resembled a pineapple from the Indies, and the door in the wall sprang open.

St. Mars looked up from where he was sitting on the top step, but not before Hester caught a glimpse of the angry spot on the back of his head. The sight of his injury chased every self-conscious thought from her mind.

She rushed to help him. "Oh, your poor head! You must permit me to wash off the blood, so I can see how serious it is underneath."

In the ensuing bustle, while she washed the tender knot, examined his cut, helped him off with his shirt and boots, and tucked him into her bed, she had no leisure to think of the impropriety of his being in her chamber or to wonder what he thought of it himself. She suspected that he thought nothing of it at all, for it was clear that St. Mars needed rest. His head still hurt, though she was hopeful that he would mend enough to ride that night, and that a week or so would render him as good as new.

He was so exhausted that he never spoke. She wondered if he was even aware that it was she who ministered to him. She would have sent for Philippe, but he was in London with Harrowby, his new master.

Then, when she moved near the bolster to draw the bed curtains, St. Mars surprised her by taking hold of her hand. With his eyes closed, and still not saying a word, he drew her fingers to his lips and pressed them with a kiss, before yielding to the swoon that he had fought all night.

When Hester woke from a deep sleep in the window seat, she found St. Mars sitting on the edge of her bed, dressed to go, with his blue cloak thrown over his shoulders. He sat facing her with his boots propped on the bed frame, his arms resting across his knees. The soft glow of twilight shining from the window told her that the sun had recently set.

St. Mars smiled teasingly, and the intimacies they had shared that morning rushed back to warm her cheeks.

"I would have wakened you and offered to give up your bed, if you had not been sleeping so peacefully," he said.

Righting herself, and wondering just how long he'd been observing her in her disordered state—and how *bad* it was—Hester replied, as calmly as she could, "I was perfectly comfortable, my lord." Making an effort to tidy her hair, she asked him how his head was feeling, and he assured her that it would do for now.

"I still don't know what prompted Lord Lovett to abduct you." His tone was serious. "I assume you discovered some kind of proof and confronted him with it."

Hester grimaced. "I did not confront him on purpose, my lord."

She explained about finding the bloodstain on her gown, and told how Lord Lovett had walked in upon her when she was writing a letter to Mr. Mavors.

This last piece of information seemed to shake him. Looking grim, he said, "We can be thankful that he did not decide to kill you right then, what with the danger you posed. Especially when he had already disposed of two of his friends. I suppose he wanted to be certain of his escape from England before giving up his hostage. But he must have done it sometime, for you would be equally dangerous to him in France."

"How so, my lord?" Hester did not want to tell him about Lord Lovett's proposition, for it might have been a lie. Somehow she believed that he had been speaking the truth for once—at least as it had appeared to him, then. But she would never be certain, and she could not think of any reason why St. Mars should believe it.

"I still cannot comprehend why he killed Sir Humphrey," she continued. "And he refused to tell me."

St. Mars looked abashed. "Forgive me, Mrs. Kean. If I had not been in such a miserable condition last night, I should have told you immediately. I discovered it quite by accident when I came across Colonel Potter's body. I knew, then, that Lord Lovett must have killed both men, but I could not believe that he would have murdered Sir Humphrey simply for being indiscreet. Not when he always had been, and no one would confide anything incriminating to him.

"No, the secret Lord Lovett wanted to hide had to be something of a much more dangerous nature. I was musing over what that might be, when someone in the street made a remark about the mob that had menaced Mr. Walpole at his house in Arlington Street. Then, I recalled that Sir Humphrey had mentioned seeing Lord Lovett in Arlington Street on the evening that your cousin expected to meet him at Lady Oglethorpe's house. And that his excuse for not coming there had been very different."

"Yes!" Hester said, excitedly. "He told Sir Humphrey that he would be on a relative's business in Kensington. I remember that he was not very happy to have Sir Humphrey blurt it out, but at the time, I thought that he had been visiting a paramour. That was the impression he gave us."

Hester recalled how he had noticed her watching him, immediately after Sir Humphrey's revelation. She could not doubt that it was at that very moment that Lord Lovett had decided that his friend must be killed, and that he had spotted her as the one person present who might stumble upon the true significance of Arlington Street. That night, too, had marked the first instance of his using flattery to win her trust.

She related most of this to St. Mars, leaving out the personal details. She did not think she would ever get over the shame of her willingness to receive Lord Lovett's compliments.

"Since I woke a while ago," St. Mars said, "I have been thinking more about his motives. If we are correct, and he did offer information about the Jacobites to Mr. Walpole and the Committee of Secrecy, he must have done it after Walpole's announcement that arrests would follow their report. He must have believed that the Pretender's cause was lost, and that, if he wanted to advance himself, he would have to change to the other side."

"I suspect, you are correct, my lord. Before the announcement, he had become almost dangerously outspoken against King George, so the change was very sudden. Mr. Walpole's speech certainly sent many people into a fright—perfectly innocent people, like your cousin Harrowby, for instance. *His* reaction would not have been precisely the same as Lord Lovett's, but I can see how the threats and the secrecy, the locking of the doors to the White Chamber, and the announcement that some Jacobites had already been taken might have persuaded Lord Lovett to change sides before it was too late."

"Especially if he had been involved with the cause very long," St. Mars said wryly. "He must have known how poorly organized it is—or was. And, being clever, he would have been aware of its lack of leadership."

"Oh, Lord Lovett is *very* clever." Hester could not stop herself from uttering this bitter outburst. "He is very proud of his intelligence. He values it above everything, even other people's lives."

She saw that St. Mars was regarding her with a mixture of concern and another unpleasant emotion. She could not tell, but it seemed almost like anger.

An uncomfortable silence fell between them. Hester wished that she had bit her tongue before allowing her sense of injury to show. She could only imagine what St. Mars must be thinking, especially since earlier in their investigation she had refused even to consider Lord Lovett as a suspect. And, since St. Mars's thoughts were likely to be worse than the truth, and she knew that his courtesy would never permit him to ask, she decided to offer a partial explanation.

"When Lord Lovett abducted me," she said, at last, "he told me that he had always feared I should be the one to discover the truth. And, because of this, he took great pains to gain my friendship by flattering my intellect. I am only annoyed with myself for letting vanity—for I *was* very flattered—for letting my vanity deceive me."

She could see from his doubting expression that St. Mars was only partly reassured by her statement. He did not press her, though, but looking at his watch, said that he ought to be going or else Tom would be in a fret.

As he got up to leave, Hester hurried to stand, too. She saw that St. Mars had recovered his balance and should be ready to ride.

She stopped him as he moved to open the secret door. "But what will happen to Lord Lovett, my lord? Regardless of how he deceived me, I cannot bear the thought that Sir Humphrey's murderer will go unpunished."

He turned to face her and grinned. "You can rest assured that Lord Lovett will soon be regretting those murders, Mrs. Kean. I have a solution that should satisfy us both."

"You mean to follow him to France?"

"Yes, but don't worry. The punishment I've planned for him will not cost me the least bit of trouble. I have failed to catch him two times already and will not leave the third to chance."

He clearly did not wish to tell her exactly what he had in mind, and she was willing to let the subject drop in favour of one that was far more important to her.

"And then what, my lord? Will you stay in France or do you mean to return?"

The last time she had asked him this question, he had not been able to reply with anything definite, and her question had obviously disturbed him.

This time, he answered her cheerfully enough, "I have a few journeys to make, but I expect to be back before the end of the summer. I shall count on seeing you then."

He made her a sweeping bow and stepped through the door. As he started down, he seemed to recall something and turned back to lean one hand on the door frame above his head.

"I have not thanked you for the use of your bed," he said. "The next time you invite me into it, I shall hope to be a more entertaining guest. Goodbye, Mrs. Kean."

It took Hester more than a few seconds to digest these words, and by the time she had—and had gasped—St. Mars was gone. Her mind spun, trying to discern another meaning for them, but she could only think of one.

"He could not have meant that," she told herself, as she closed and locked the secret door. It was impossible, especially since he must have seen her sleeping with her mouth gaping open. For all she knew, she might even have snored! He must have meant something else entirely.

But, turn the phrases over in her mind, as she did the rest of that night and for many weeks thereafter, she could not for the life of her think of what it was.

In the Palace of St. Germain-en-Laye, high above Paris, the court of James Stuart carried on without his presence. This was the home that had been given to his father, James II of England and James VI of Scotland, when the English had driven him out. King Louis XIV, himself, had welcomed his Catholic cousin on the terrace of St. Germain and, greeting him with the embrace of a brother, had given him the country palace which had served the French kings before the construction of Versailles.

More than twenty years later, the French had been forced to expel his son, the Pretender, in their peace with England, but he could not afford to house his courtiers in Bar. So they remained here, living off a pension that belonged to James's mother, Mary of Modena, the former Queen of England. With nothing much to do, they intrigued, while waiting to hear that the English were ready for their true sovereign to return.

Lord Lovett arrived at St. Germain only days after the news that the Duke of Ormonde had escaped arrest in England and taken refuge in Paris with his patron, Lord Bolingbroke. The failure of the rising had cast a pall over the court, particularly the Queen, but it provided Lord Lovett with a perfect excuse for his flight. Everyone immediately assumed that he had fled the threat of his own arrest, so he was warmly welcomed by the Queen, who promised to do what she could to maintain him.

The court proved not to be very much to his liking, however, since the Queen's strict devotion to her religion put a serious damper on amusements. The poverty of the court was distressing enough, but its pious tone was scarcely tolerable. Lord Lovett decided that he would remain just as long as required to secure an income, before seeking greater pleasure at Versailles. The Earl of Stair, the English ambassador, would be there, and he might be willing to arrange an exchange of money for secrets.

A fortnight later, in the middle of August, he was standing up from a game of cards, in which he had neatly increased his wealth, when he found Eleanor de Mézières at his elbow.

He bowed to hide his sudden nervousness. This was the first he had seen the marquise since coming to St. Germain, and, of late, he had wondered about the danger she might pose. Mrs. Kean might have told Lady Oglethorpe that he had murdered her friends. Whether Lady Fury would believe her or not, he did not know. Standing before her daughter now, however, he thanked his sense of caution, which had prevented him from divulging his reason for murdering Sir Humphrey to Mrs. Kean. Without that piece of the puzzle, it would be only her word against his, and no matter how clever she was, he defied her to out-connive him.

After the first exchange of pleasantries, she said, "I have a friend who wishes to be made known to you, my lord. May I present the *Vicomte de St. Mars?"*

She turned, and a young gentleman stepped forward.

As they completed their bows, Lord Lovett had a faint sensation that he had met this gentleman before. He studied the young man's aquiline features, his fair colouring and athletic grace, and the impression grew stronger, though he could not recall where they had met.

"I understand that you are recently come from England," the *vicomte* said, and his voice, too, seemed familiar.

Lord Lovett was mildly surprised to discover from the young man's accent that he was English, but he said, "That is correct. I'm afraid that our country has grown too dangerous for the likes of us, *monsieur.* But only for the present, I hope.

"What brings your lordship here?" he inquired in return.

Before replying, Lord St. Mars asked if he would like to take a stroll on the terrace.

Madame de Mézières seemed to have abandoned them, so, relieved to have come through that particular meeting unscathed, Lord Lovett fell into a leisurely pace beside him. Together they left the salon and its courtiers behind.

"You do not appear to know my history," the *vicomte* said. "My father was killed in his Majesty's service."

"Indeed? You will have to forgive me, *monsieur,* but I am not familiar with all the French titles. Was your father the former *Vicomte de St. Mars?"*

"No."

They had walked through the door onto the terrace, where the late evening sun was casting long shadows. In front of him on the drive, Lord Lovett spotted a French *prêvot* with his lieutenant and a troop of archers, standing by a coach. The door of the coach was open.

He halted, and glanced instinctively at his companion's face.

St. Mars turned to meet his gaze. "My father was the Earl of Hawkhurst. He was murdered."

"I am very sorry to hear that, *monsieur."*

The name could not be a coincidence—and, suddenly, Lord Lovett knew where he had met this young man before.

The mask and the darkness had softened his hawk-like features.

And then, he recollected another stranger. A fop, with a face covered in so much paint that all he had noted at the time was the number of patches the fop wore.

Cursing inwardly, Lord Lovett inclined his head and bestowed an angry smile on the gentleman who had beaten him.

Lord St. Mars made a gesture to beckon King Louis's men. They came and took Lord Lovett by the arms.

"Do you know where they are taking me?" he asked.

"I believe that his Majesty King Louis was heard to mention the citadel of Pignerol. You should be pleased with the company there, though I hear that the mountain air can be very cold.

"Your servant, my lord." With a sweeping hand, the *vicomte* reminded him that his carriage was waiting.

Lord Lovett felt a tug on each of his arms. As he turned and walked numbly towards the vehicle, only one clear thought emerged.

Begging leave of his captors, he turned again to face St. Mars, who had remained on the terrace to watch his departure.

Lord Lovett said, "I must beg you to convey my regards to Mrs. Kean."

Then the last he saw of the Viscount St. Mars was a constrained bow, before the archers turned him and forced him into the coach.

THE END

AUTHOR'S NOTE

I have tried to be as fair as possible to the historical figures portrayed in this book, but the job has been complicated by the bias of survivors and the lack of references. In the case of King George I, the English formed such strong prejudices against him that I worked very hard to get a truer picture of his character. After reading his biography by Ragnhild Hatton (by all accounts the most balanced since the author was the only one to use German references), I was almost persuaded to give him more benefit of the doubt. But, at the end of the day, it is very hard to like a man who imprisons his wife and forbids her ever to see her children again, and later tries to do the same thing to his son.

There is one error about George perpetuated in this novel, however. There is no foundation for the belief that he committed incest with Madame von Kielmansegg. It appears that she was his illegitimate half-sister, but she was not his mistress as the English believed. Since neither George nor his father publicly acknowledged their bastards, however well they treated them otherwise, their relationship was never explained. Madame von Kielmansegg accompanied her brother to England because she had run up extensive debts in Hanover and wanted to escape them. Since she arrived with his real mistress, Madame von Schulenberg, the English assumed that she was one, also. This rumor was actively promoted by the Jacobites to give the English a disgust of their German king. The falsehood was so firmly entrenched that I found it repeated in reference after reference, and only learned the truth when reading the Hatton biography.

George never did learn English, and few of his courtiers spoke either German or French, so the contemporary accounts of him by his English subjects are very rare and biased. Lady Mary Wortley Montagu called him an amiable dolt. Mary Lady Cowper, lady-in-waiting to the Princess of Wales, described him as everything charming and amiable until he banished her mistress from Court, at which point she grew very silent on the subject of the King.

The only quote ascribed to him in the *Oxford Book of Quotations* is, "I hate all boets and bainters." In some references, this is attributed to George II, his son, but it may have been one of the few opinions they shared. The proof seems to be in the pudding, for unlike the Stuart years, the period of both Georges' reigns is fairly bereft of art and poetry, except what was produced under other people's patronage.

The English greatly resented George's German servants. He brought about seventy-five with him initially, but few remained. The incident I relate involving Madame Schulenberg and the mob did take place, and her response, "I have only come for your goots!" is one of the most famous stories of George's reign. Both she and Madame Kielmansegg grew wealthy, selling their influence to help the English obtain Court positions.

The "niece" Madame Schulenberg wanted to bring over as a companion was one of her daughters by George I. George spent most of his evenings with his mistress and daughters, and by all accounts it was a happy family circle. I can understand that he might not love his wife by an arranged marriage, and his having a mistress. It was his cruelty to his wife and legitimate children that is harder to forgive.

Alexander Pope's *Essay on Man,* whose verses I have used, were dedicated to Henry St. John, Viscount Bolingbroke, mentioned only peripherally in this novel since he had already fled to France, but whose actions as minister and Jacobite were instrumental in the creation of the events I have chronicled. As a Catholic, Pope had Tory sympathies and numbered the Tory ministers among his friends, as well as the Earl of Peterborough, also mentioned. This essay was written years after the events in this novel, but to me, it seems to be peppered with references to them. It certainly shows a wisdom that none of the participants seem to have had.

The fictional characters in this novel were suggested to me by a number of actual Jacobites, particularly the character of Sir Humphrey Cove. He is taken from accounts of Sir Thomas Cave, who apparently did write his friends from time to time to ask them how the conspiracy was coming along. Lord Lovett was loosely based on one Cameron, Lord Lovat. There was also a Colonel Porter among the Jacobites, but I know nothing about him. I just used a similar name.

The Oglethorpes and their escapades, of course, were real. In later years Lady Oglethorpe's son, James, founded the Georgia Colony. He was the only member of the family not to become involved in the Stuart cause. One of his friends died as a result of the horrible conditions in an English prison, and he dedicated most of his energy to the founding of a penal colony as a humanitarian measure to give debtors a second chance. My portrayal of Lady Oglethorpe is not very flattering, but she must have been nicknamed "Lady Fury" for some reason.

John Menzies was truly a Jacobite agent with the job I have given him. Unfortunately for James, he was abrasive and arrogant. He alienated many of James's supporters in England by making excessive demands upon them. My research told me that his contact in England was a printer by the name of Blackwell, but I was not able to discover the location of Blackwell's shop. It is a safe bet that it was near Stationers' Hall, since most printers were located nearby. When apart, Blackwell and Menzies corresponded by letter in a code as from doctor to patient.

The details of how Jacobites entered and left the country, transported messages, and referred to James were taken from reference works.

The eclipse, which I referred to in my first Blue Satan novel, apparently did take place. I could not find any report of it in the London newspapers, except for the notice a month later that a child had been born with the sign of the eclipse on her forehead. So I must contradict my note in the first edition of *The Birth of Blue Satan.* The eclipse that was predicted by Mr. Halley did, in fact, occur.

SWAIN.

VIEW OF ST. JAMES'S PALACE, TIM